and that knowledge makes her work shine."

—*Chicago Tribune*

"This sequal to AN EYE FOR MURDER has it all – action, excitement, increasing tension – with the usual family complications . . . Recommended." *Library Journal*

"Hellman owes a debt to fellow Chicagoans Sara Paretsky and Barbara D'Amato, but she's the brash young thing making this formula new again. I can't wait for her next book." —*Aunt Agatha's Book Store*

"An exciting new adventure . . . better written than the first . . . will keep you up late at night . . . highly recommended!" —*Mystery Time*

"Hellman has surpassed herself. Well-crafted, intense and exciting, right up to the last page . . . a must read!"

—*Midwest Book Review*

"Hellman once again has made it convincing that this amateur would ne involved in the investigation of a crime . . . A PICTURE OF GUILT is a page-turner of a novel, with an ending even Ellie herself didn't see coming."

—*Reviewing the Evidence*

Titles by Libby Fischer Hellmann

AN EYE FOR MURDER
A PICTURE OF GUILT
AN IMAGE OF DEATH

AN IMAGE OF DEATH

LIBBY FISCHER HELLMANN

BERKLEY PRIME CRIME, NEW YORK

This is a work of fiction. Names, characters, places, and incidents either are the product of the author's imagination or are used fictitiously, and any resemblance to actual persons, living or dead, business establishments, events, or locales is entirely coincidental.

AN IMAGE OF DEATH

A Berkley Prime Crime Book / published by arrangement with the author

PRINTING HISTORY
Berkley edition / February 2004

Cover design by George Cornell.
Interior text design by Julie Rogers.

For information address: The Berkley Publishing Group, a division of Penguin Group (USA) Inc.,
375 Hudson Street, New York, New York 10014.

ISBN: 0-425-19504-X

Berkley Prime Crime Books are published by The Berkley Publishing Group, a division of Penguin Group (USA) Inc.,
375 Hudson Street, New York, New York 10014.
The name BERKLEY PRIME CRIME and the BERKLEY PRIME CRIME design are trademarks belonging to Penguin Group (USA) Inc.

PRINTED IN THE UNITED STATES OF AMERICA

10 9 8 7 6 5 4 3 2 1

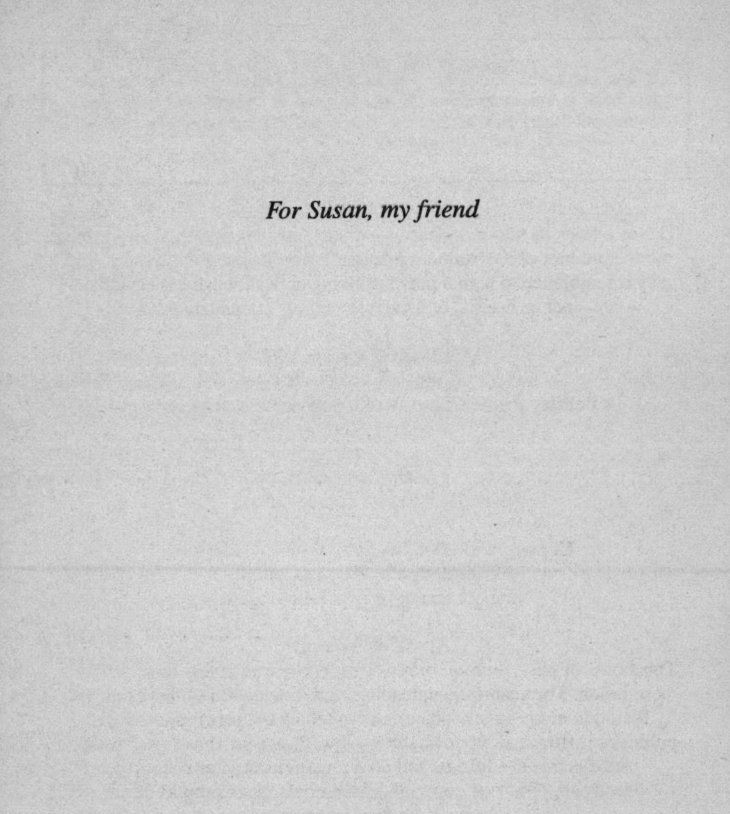

For Susan, my friend

ACKNOWLEDGMENTS

Many people gave up their time and expertise to make sure I got it right this time. I'm grateful to Lisa and Sarkis Markarian; Dave Heppner, Chicago Police Department; Mike Nystrand, Northfield Fire Chief; Deputy Chief Mike Green, Northbrook Police; Bill Lustig, Northfield's Chief of Police; Chris Bell, Northfield Police officer; Paul Mosele; Don Whiteman (how is it you show up in every book?); Trudi Ellis; Ann Hill; Beth Chensoff; and Janusz Olechny. Any errors are entirely the fault of the author. Also, special thanks to Cindy Kuo, webmystress from heaven, and Laurie Clayton.

I'm grateful, also, to Deborah Donnelly and Roberta Isleib, "Sex" and "Lies." I could not have finished this book without your wisdom, inspiration, and humor. I'll try to follow the advice on the road sign.

To Jacky Sach, agent extraordinaire, and to editors Samantha Mandor, Barbara Peters, and especially Nora Cavin, heartfelt thanks for helping shape the manuscript—and my career.

And . . . as always, I appreciate the insight and suggestions of the Red Herrings, the best writing group east of the Mississippi. You keep me honest.

And there is not greater disaster than greed.

LAO-TZU (604 BC–531 BC), *THE WAY OF LAO-TZU*

PROLOGUE

THE PAIN ROLLED *over her in waves, especially when air whistled through her mouth. She'd never lost a tooth before; her mouth felt curiously empty. Where had it fallen out? Had they found it? Could they use it to track her? She wouldn't have thought so, but pain was fogging her mind. She shook her head as if to banish the thought, but the movement touched off more throbbing. She tried to breathe through her nose.*

She brushed her fingers along her jaw. The last time she'd looked in a mirror, she hadn't recognized herself. She was glad she didn't have one now. Hopefully, the makeup covered most of the damage.

She walked up to the front door. A house. Not an office or clinic, but a house. Two stories. Brick. Surrounded by others just like it up and down the street. All of them identical except for the color of the paint and which side the garage sat on.

She took off her dark glasses and rang the bell. They'd told her to be there at fourteen hundred, but it was well past that now. A curtain of dusk was descending, and the air was heavy with the metallic smell that precedes snow. She shivered, unfamiliar clothes scratching her skin. Her coat was too flimsy for this bitter cold, but it was all she'd been able to get. She rang the bell again.

She shoved her hands into her pockets and fingered her money. Cash only, they'd said. Dollars. Where were they? Maybe she should look. But as she started around to the back, a sudden movement startled her. Fear knifed through her.

It was just a bare branch swaying in the wind. She let out a slow breath and watched the branch rise and fall, eerily silent in the fading light. Where was the sound? Back home the wind made noise. Whether a whispering breeze or the shriek of a gale, it didn't sneak up on you. This quiet was unnerving.

She cornered the house. A chain-link fence marked the edge of the property. Beyond it was a field with spindly clumps of grass poking through gritty snow. A tire lay on its side. The field was so flat, civilization seemed to stop at the fence line. This part of the world was like that, she recalled. Something to do with a glacier. Perhaps she would fall off the edge of the world.

She found a second door on the side of the house. She pressed her face against the glass but a window shade blocked her view. She shifted her feet. In the thin, flat shoes she was wearing, her toes were already numb. She looked around. No movement. No sound. Nothing to indicate a human presence. She grabbed the doorknob and turned. The door opened easily, and a gust of warm air blew over her. She slipped inside, squeezing her eyes shut in pleasure. She might never have felt anything this good before.

It was a plain but clean room. Wood paneling on three walls, a white linoleum floor flecked with brown. Two chairs sat beside a low table. She took off her glasses and sank into a chair, kneading her fingers. She glanced down at her wrist to check the time, momentarily forgetting she'd lost her watch. Without the thick leather band, her tattoo was plainly visible.

Looking up, she saw that the fourth wall, the one that wasn't paneled, was marred by a thick crack that snaked from floor to ceiling. It reminded her of the winding creek near her grandparents' home. The one window in the room was covered with the same flimsy material as the door, but a thin strip of light seeped around its edges. Enough to make out a light switch on the opposite wall. She went to it and flipped it on. Shading her eyes against the glare, she saw a door cut into the wall with the crack—she hadn't seen it before. She tried the knob; it was locked.

On the ceiling rows of square, spongy tiles looked soft enough to punch her fist through. She tracked the squares to a corner where the ceiling and the wall met. A small black box was anchored to the wall. A camera? Here? She had heard the stories about Chicago. Al Capone. Gangs. Crime-ridden streets. Maybe there was some truth to them.

Her stomach growled. She hadn't eaten a decent meal in two days. But even if she'd had the time, how could she chew with this pain? A muffled sound escaped her throat. Where were they? They had to be expecting her. Why else leave the door unlocked?

"Halloa," *she called out.*

No response. If no one came soon, she would have to leave. But where would she go? The two days she'd been on the run felt like two years. She didn't have much time; she knew they were looking for her. The woman in the airport bathroom said a man had been asking about her outside the door. He claimed to be her brother, the woman said. But Arin didn't have a brother. She told the woman it was her husband, that she was running away from his abuse. The woman clucked sympathetically and let Arin buy her scarf to use as a disguise. Arin snuck down to the gate, her head covered, praying she wasn't seen.

Now she threw her coat on a chair and sat in her cotton T-shirt and jeans. She should be home with Tomas. Cooking his supper. Helping him with his studies. She should never have left home. But it hadn't been her idea to take a vacation. And she'd never been to that part of the world

A few days in the hot sun seemed like a gift. How could she have known he *would be there? That he was behind it, all of it? She held her head in her hands. She should have figured it out. But she hadn't. Years of uneventful transactions had dulled her instincts.*

A noise from outside startled her. Thumps. Footsteps. Then a whisper. Finally. They had come. She felt almost weak with relief. As the door started to open, the scalloped edge of the grimy window shade trembled in the incoming draft. A sudden image of delicate cotton doilies sprang into her mind. With embroidery around the edges. Part of her grandmother's hope chest, she'd coveted them as a little girl. Her grandmother promised they would be hers one day.

She turned eagerly toward the door.

ONE

Ricki Feldman is the type of woman best admired from a distance—if you get too close, you might find some of your body parts missing. But here I was sitting next to her at La Maison, one of the toniest restaurants on Chicago's North Shore.

We were seated in a private dining room with dark wood beams, stucco walls, and terra-cotta floor tiles. Huge arrangements of fresh flowers—a significant feat in the middle of January—surrounded us. The occasion was a ladies' luncheon in Ricki's honor. The directors of WISH, Women for Interim Subsidized Housing, had organized it to thank her for a twenty-thousand-dollar donation, dollars that would help support low-cost housing for kids who'd been in foster care but couldn't afford to live on their own.

Charity. *Tzedakah.* A simple act of philanthropy. Except with the Feldmans, nothing was ever simple. The daughter of a hugely successful real estate developer, Ricki had taken over the company several years ago at her father's death, and was proving to be just as ambitious and shrewd. In fact, you got the sense that good deeds, money, even people, were just commodities to the Feldmans. Bargaining chips for some future quid pro quo. Which was why it was wise to make sure you left with everything you came in with when you dealt with them.

Two waiters hovered over her now, refilling her water glass and whisking imaginary crumbs off the white tablecloth. With silky dark hair, magnetic brown eyes, and a willowy build, Ricki was the kind of woman it was hard to look away from. Even so, her expression was always calculating, measuring, taking stock. I kept my hands in my lap and my knees pressed together.

The eight other women at the luncheon were decked out in designer finery. I spotted a Missoni label on one woman, another with a Fendi bag. Silver flashed at their necks and ears, and it was hard to find a wrinkle on any face. I felt like the hired help in my Garfield & Marks slacks. In fact, when Ricki introduced me around as the woman who produced the video about "The Glen," I repressed the urge to pay fealty.

You see, Ricki and I weren't friends. And I wasn't a contributor to WISH. A few months ago Feldman Development had built a luxury housing project on the old naval base in Glenview, and Ricki hired me to produce a video about it. I'd had misgivings—environmentalists were trying, unsuccessfully, it turned out, to preserve the land as prairie. But she threw a lot of money at me, money I needed to make ends meet. So I took it, produced the show, and tried not to dwell on what the shortage of grasslands would do to global warming.

"The Glen" eventually became one of Feldman's most successful properties, and when Ricki invited me to lunch, I thought it might be a belated thank-you, so I accepted. You might disapprove of their methods, you might not like their style, but the Feldmans were tireless. They got things done. Plus, it's not often I get the chance to hobnob with women of wealth and privilege.

Now, though, as chatter about exotic vacations, haute couture, and the latest Hollywood scandal drifted over the table, I silently shoveled salad into my mouth, feeling just a bit overwhelmed.

The waiters cleared our plates, then brought out brandy snifters filled with sorbet. As I smiled up my thanks, I caught the waiter staring at my chest. I looked down. A dark oily stain was spreading across my blouse. Salad dressing. And I hadn't worn a jacket. The waiter sniffed and moved on. I propped an elbow on the table, in an effort to hide the offending spot. Resting my chin on my hand, I tried to appear thoughtful.

It was a short-lived attempt.

"You don't like sorbet, Ellie?" Ricki asked.

"Oh, I like it." I smiled weakly and reached for my spoon. As my elbow moved, Ricki's gaze dropped to my chest.

"Oh, dear. I'm sorry."

Suddenly eight pairs of eyes were on me.

I dipped my napkin in my water glass and dabbed at the spot, but, of course, that only made it worse. My heart's not enough—I have to wear my lunch on my sleeve, too. I dabbed some more, but it was hopeless. There was only one solution, especially with this crowd. I tossed my head, put my hands in my lap, and affected a je ne sais quoi nonchalance. Next time I'd wear a haz mat suit.

A blond woman with skin so tight it looked like stretched canvas rose and tapped a knife against her water glass. "Now, ladies." She looked around the table, a brilliant, pasted-on smile encompassing us all. "In honor of Ricki Feldman's generous donation to WISH, I thought we'd play a little game."

I knew these games. A variation of a roast, someone asks silly questions about the individual being honored, and the person with the most correct answers wins a prize. I gazed around the table. During the course of producing the Glen video, I'd learned a lot about Ricki. Where she went to school, her cat's name, her favorite movie. I stood a good chance of winning. I wondered what the prize was. I wouldn't waste my time over perfume or candy, but a day at a spa, or a gift certificate for some trendy store could be worth it. I dug out a memo pad and pen from my bag.

The game was momentarily delayed when the maitre d' rolled the pastry cart up to the table. Leave it to a man to tease us with the foods we crave but shouldn't eat. They're still trying to get even for that Eve and the apple thing. One woman ordered flourless chocolate cake, and another chose a flaky apple tart. I summoned up my willpower and tried to pretend they were laced with cyanide. Or botulism.

The lady with the face-lift stood up again. "Ready now, ladies? Oh. I almost forgot." She looked around and grinned. "Whoever wins gets a massage and facial at North Shore spa." She seemed to rest her eyes on me.

Not bad, I thought, and smiled back, eagerly anticipating questions about siblings, birthdays, best friends in kindergarten.

The blond cleared her throat. "All right. First question. Who's wearing a brand-new diamond today?"

Diamonds? The women tittered, and two hands shot into the air. Ricki fingered a diamond solitaire at her throat.

"No, no, ladies." The blond woman waggled a finger at us. "You're supposed to *write down* how many ladies you think are wearing diamonds today. And they have to be *new*."

More giggles and surreptitious glances. I squirmed. Diamonds? What kind of game was this? Maybe I'd made a mistake coming. I could be at home, surfing the Net or planning the important, hard-hitting documentary I would produce one day. I snuck a glance at Ricki. A confirmed workaholic, she could be making deals, building shopping centers, collecting rents. But she was smiling benevolently, as if she had nothing more pressing to do than decide between a two- or three-carat prong set ring.

It suddenly occurred to me I might not win this game.

The blond woman waited until the rest of the group had finished writing and licked her lips. "Okay . . . second question." She flicked an imaginary speck off her Thierry

Mugler jacket. "How many ladies are wearing a new outfit today?"

My smile felt glued to my face. These women may not have gone to Harvard, but the way they scrutinized one another, working their way up from shoes to earrings, was just as intimidating. I imagined a classroom filled with women clutching number-two pencils, filling in designer names on their SATs.

"Ready to move on?" the woman chirped.

I took a sip of water.

"Now for our third and final question." She paused dramatically, then slid her eyes toward me. "Who knows what Ellie Foreman does for a living?"

I slumped, trying to ignore the knowing looks cast my way. Now I knew why I was there. They wanted me to produce a video for WISH. Ricki must have told them all about me. Hell, she probably promised to deliver me on a platter. I was the lamb led to slaughter. The dog to the pound. And Ricki Feldman was holding the leash.

"Waiter!" I shot my hand in the air, no longer caring about the stain on my blouse. If I was going to pay for this lunch, the least I could do was order dessert.

TWO

As I climbed into the car a half hour later, I counted my fingers and toes one more time. Ricki hadn't approached me about a video, but she had worn a complacent smile for the rest of the luncheon, and the other ladies were entirely too solicitous.

I pulled out of La Maison and headed home. I'd probably get a call next week. They'd want a modest, ten-minute kind of thing. Interviews with the founder of WISH, the young people they'd helped, maybe even—they'd pause self-effacingly—the board of directors. And oh, they'd add, since they were a charitable organization, could I do it pro bono? WISH was undoubtedly not-for-profit, which, over the years, I've learned is code for I shouldn't make one, either. If I objected, they'd argue that it couldn't be that hard. Their kids could probably produce the piece with the digital gear they'd bought them for Christmas. Frankly, they'd say in a low but earnest voice, they were doing *me* a favor. All the positive publicity would reflect well on my reputation.

I turned up the heat. A weak flow of air filtered out of

the vents. My Volvo was getting old and cantankerous. Don't get me wrong—I'm not a tightfisted person. Or a misanthrope. But my ex-husband's child support payments are negligible, and producing videos is how I support my fourteen-year-old and myself. Playing Lady Bountiful, as noble as it may be, doesn't put food on my table.

It was barely four when I drove past the forest preserve, but daylight was already fading. It had snowed again last night, and the tree branches were bowed out with a ribbon of white. The coating was so thick that the skinny dark edges of the branches underneath looked like a drop shadow. Still, there was something soothing—almost elemental—about the combination of brown branch, white mantle, and pale sky.

By the time I turned onto our street, the heater finally kicked in, and I made it to the house in relative comfort. I live in a small three-bedroom colonial that I struggled to hang on to after the divorce. It's not new or plush, but they'll have to carry me out feetfirst. I pulled into the garage and went inside.

"Rachel?"

No reply. I ran upstairs and changed into a pair of sweats, then went into the bathroom. The mascara I'd put on this morning was still there; gray eyes fringed with clumpy black lashes stared back at me in the mirror. I ran a brush through my hair, which used to be black but is increasingly streaked with gray. I sighed. I'd never be as well preserved as the Women Who Lunch. They could afford plastic surgeons and exotic beauty treatments. The best I could do was a fresh application of concealer. Still, I hang on to the fact that a guy once told me I could pass for Grace Slick. Never mind that it was thirty years ago, and we'd been in a dark room smoking weed.

I was downstairs chopping tomatoes for a batch of chili—this was turning out to be a day of continuous meals—when the kitchen door flew open.

"Hi, Mom." Rachel bounded in, accompanied by a gust of frigid air. "What's for dinner? I'm starved!"

I shivered.

"Oh. Sorry." Rachel slammed the door and sniffed her way to the stove. Her cheeks were flushed, and despite the weather, her blond curls were damp.

"Were you running?"

She nodded. She'd been trying to stay in shape for her newly discovered passion, field hockey. Soccer with a stick, she called it. Even though it was a fall sport, she was thinking ahead to next season—a significant feat for a fourteen-year-old. Not only was she jogging regularly, but she was also exercising with a huge rubber ball.

I wouldn't admit it, but I was thrilled. Her keen interest in the sporting life—regardless of how long it lasted—was a sign that our troubles of last fall had abated. That, for the moment, she was navigating the *Sturm und Drang* of adolescence smoothly. The best part was the occasional flash of maturity that hinted at the magnificent adult she would become. I kissed the top of her head, not an easy task, since she's only two inches shorter than me.

"It's chili."

"No kidding. It took almost a mile to warm up."

When I gestured to the package of chili seasoning, she shot me one of those exasperated teenage expressions that says for all her adult ways, she still has a few years to go.

"And bread and salad. But it's going to be a while."

"No prob." She headed out of the kitchen. "I'll do some rotation exercises." She'd made me buy her one of those huge rubber balls for Hanukkah and was doing all sorts of twists, contortions, and stretching. To increase flexibility, she claimed.

We didn't eat until 7:00, and we were finished by 7:10. I was stacking plates in the dishwasher when the doorbell rang.

"I'll get it," Rachel said.

The front door groaned as she opened it. The car wasn't the only thing feeling its age.

"No one's here." Then, "Oh." The whine of a vehicle pulling away floated through the door. "It's a package."

I wiped my hands on a towel. I couldn't remember ordering anything that would bring UPS to the house. Especially after the holidays, when I'm at my most parsimonious. Rachel came into the kitchen carrying a lumpy manila envelope. She flipped it over, shrugged, then handed it to me. There was no label on the package, and my name, the *E* in *Foreman* missing, was scrawled in formal cursive. The handwriting, filled with swirls and curlicues, leaned left, not right.

There was nothing else on the envelope. No markings. No UPC code. I chewed on a nail. The anthrax scare might be over, but once my confidence in public institutions has been shaken, it never rebounds to the same level. And I have a history of mistrust toward institutions. "I'm guessing it wasn't UPS."

Rachel shook her head. "Some kind of van dropped it off."

"A minivan?"

"No. Bigger. Well, boxier, I think. I only saw it from the back."

I studied the envelope. Except for the lump, it looked innocuous. I didn't hear any ticking or smell anything unusual. It crossed my mind to call the police, but village detective Dan O'Malley has had enough of me for a lifetime. What would I say, anyway? A package came, and I'm afraid to open it?

Still.

I looked up at Rachel, then headed toward the steps.

"Where are you going?" she asked.

"I'm taking it down to the garage."

"Mom, it's just an envelope."

"I realize that. I want to check it out."

"You're being really paranoid, you know." She took a step forward as if to snatch it from me.

"Young lady, don't you dare."

She stopped and shook her head. "You're nuts."

I hesitated. She had a point. If something untoward was going to happen, it probably would have occurred by now.

I went to the cleaning supply cabinet and took out a pair of yellow rubber gloves.

"Now what are you doing?"

I slipped the gloves over my hands. "You have my permission to go upstairs anytime you want."

She raised her chin. A defiant silence caromed around the room.

I backtracked to a drawer and took out my Cutco knife. A neighbor's son sold it to me two summers ago, and it's the sharpest knife I own. Brandishing it in one hand, I edged up to the table, bent over, and slit the envelope at one end.

THREE

Nothing blew up. No cloud of toxic poison dispersed above our heads. I looked over at Rachel. She didn't say anything, but her eyebrows shot up, just like my father's when he's about to say *"Nu?"*

I grabbed it and peered inside. The bulge turned out to be a VHS cassette. I took it out. It was a workhorse brand of videotape, the kind that's sold in supermarkets and drugstores. There were no markings on it, and no label on the top or the spine. I turned the envelope upside down, thinking a note might fall out. Nothing did.

"I wonder what it is."

"Try videotape," Rachel said.

"Thanks for your astute observations. But who would send me a tape? And why?"

"Hello . . . you are a video producer."

I produce industrials: product introductions, training films, and corporate videos, but I didn't have anything in production at the moment, and I couldn't think of any former clients with a reason to send me a tape. "No one drops off tapes in the middle of the night. Why didn't they come in?"

Rachel shrugged. "What are we waiting for? Let's look at it."

I tightened my grip on the tape. My gut told me not to let her see it. What if it was some porno hotshot with a stable of girls? Or some kind of booby trap that would blow up when I pushed Play? I couldn't think of anyone who would actually go to the trouble to do that—my enemies are more the gossipy, backbiting kind—but I *had* been involved in some scary things recently.

"Muhhtherrr . . ." A sulky look spread across my daughter's face.

I was probably overreacting, ratcheting up my protective instincts to compensate for the lack of a male presence at home. Rachel was right. It was probably nothing. I loosened my hold. "Okay. Go turn it on."

Rachel skipped into the family room and flipped on the VCR. I followed, slipped the tape into the deck, and hit Play.

A burst of snow zipped across the screen. Then it cut to black. We waited. More black, but no picture. We watched for a full minute. The TV screen stayed dark. Rachel zapped the remote and fast-forwarded another few minutes. Still no picture.

She frowned. "Nothing's on it."

"Maybe it's a prank."

We let the tape advance even more. No snow. No picture. Nothing.

Relinquishing the remote, Rachel got up. "I'm out of here. Call me if something happens." She headed for the stairs.

I settled back on the couch. The tape was still rolling. I watched indifferently, wondering why someone had sent me a blank tape. I'd just about convinced myself to eject it when an image materialized on the screen.

It was a black-and-white picture, but the focus was soft, and there was hardly any contrast. I paused the tape and fiddled with the settings on the TV, but when I restarted the tape, the quality was only marginally improved. I was looking down at a wide angle of a room. From the wall panels and floor tiles, I thought it was someone's basement, but when I saw the window with light seeping in around the edges, I realized it couldn't be belowground. A room addition, maybe. Except the only furniture in the room was two chairs and a coffee table. Not your average family room.

A figure huddled in one of the chairs, but I couldn't tell whether it was male or female. After a moment, the figure rose and raced across the room. When it reached the other side, it fumbled with something on the wall. Light filled the frame, and I saw the figure was female. But her movements were rapid-fire and jerky, like an old Charlie Chaplin movie where he waddles across the screen at warp speed.

I was about to pause the tape for a closer look, when the woman darted from the light switch to a door on the opposite wall, the only wall without paneling. She grabbed the doorknob and twisted, but the door stayed closed. Her shoulders sagged.

I frowned. From the angle of the shot, the camera must have been mounted on the ceiling, or near it. It was as if someone had installed a surveillance camera in the house. Some parents did that these days to monitor their babysitter while they were at work. I looked for a baby toy or a blanket wadded up in a corner, but found no evidence of a nanny or her young charge. So why was a camera recording what was happening in the room?

The woman's gaze swept up to the ceiling. Thick chin-length hair framed her face, but I couldn't make out any features. She lurched back to the chair and stripped off her coat. A slim woman, she was wearing a T-shirt and jeans. She put her head in her hands. Then she abruptly raised her head. The outside door opened and two figures hurried in. The woman stood up.

I gasped when I saw what happened next. Was this some kind of trick? A hoax? You could do all sorts of things with video these days. I rewound the tape and put the VCR on slow advance, which, as a video producer, was one of the extra features I allowed myself when I bought the machine. As the tape rolled, I noticed that the black portion looked uneven and bumpy, as if the tape had been repeatedly erased or recorded over.

The action slowed, but the image was still jerky. Still, when the woman gazed at the camera, I could see bruises on her face. The droop in her shoulders, moreover, said she was exhausted. The expression in her eyes, too. Maybe this wasn't a joke.

When the figures first burst in, the woman leaped out of her chair as if she'd been waiting for them, but when they closed in, she staggered back against the wall. Their faces were hidden by ski masks, but their bulk and the way they moved indicated they were men. As they bore down on her, she twisted around and threw an arm over her head. A puff of smoke exploded beside her, and she crumpled to the floor. Something dark began to creep across her chest.

The two men hurriedly escaped through the door they'd come in. One of the men favored his right leg. The woman lay on the floor alone. The only movement was the stain on her T-shirt, silently expanding like the petals of a dark flower. The picture went black.

I STOPPED THE tape and took deep breaths to center myself. A woman had been alive. Now she was dead. It didn't look—or feel—like a hoax. For one thing, if someone was going to alter reality, the quality of the image would have been better. People who play around with video have sophisticated software and equipment. Chances are they wouldn't create a scene with a grainy, wide-angle, static shot. This was chillingly real.

I looked toward the stairs. Thank God Rachel hadn't seen it. She'd seen murders on TV, but stripped of the Hollywood trappings, this was the unequivocal cold-blooded taking of a human life. What do you say to a child who witnesses something like that?

When my breathing returned to normal, I raised the shade on the window. A sharp, clear night, the lights on my neighbor's house winked in the breeze, and the snow cover produced a flat, eerie light that eliminated shadows. Without the scrim of leafy trees and bushes, it's hard to sneak up on people. I'd been feeling safer than I had in months.

Still, as I peered down the block, an uneasy feeling crept up my back. Was the tape some kind of warning? A signal that I should beware? But why? And of what? I'd promised David and my father I wouldn't get involved in any more risky activities. I'd be the consummate suburban mom. Take care of my family. Stay close to home. This didn't augur well for it. I lowered the shade.

I took the tape out of the deck and popped the tab to prevent it from being recorded over. Then I started into the kitchen to call the police. The phone rang before I got there.

With a teenager in the house, you don't worry about answering the phone. It's never for you. So I was surprised when Rachel yelled down the steps.

"Mom. It's David."

I still don't know quite what to call David Linden. He's too old for "boyfriend," but too young for "companion." Too conservative for "lover," and not PC enough for "significant other." But David is the man I love—and almost lost. I'm not very good at intimacy—just ask my ex-husband. David and I have experienced a few problems in that area, too, but we're trying. Still, I sometimes sense a distance between us, as if he's not sure whether to trust me completely. I can't blame him. I'm not, either. I took the call in the kitchen.

"Ellie, how are you?"

I looked down at the tape in my hand. I wanted to tell him about it, but I knew he wouldn't be pleased. "Fine," I lied.

He didn't pick up on the falseness in my voice. "Something pretty amazing happened today," he said

Though he's well into his fifties, David can sound like an enthusiastic boy at times. It's one of his most endearing qualities. I glanced at the photo of him that sits beside the coffeepot, the one where he's running a hand through his prematurely white hair. His blue eyes were bright. "What?"

"I got a letter from a woman who lives in the village my mother came from."

"In the Black Forest?"

"Outside Freiburg."

David's mother had come to the States as a teenager in the thirties, the only member of her family to survive the Holocaust. She met David's father here, but he died at the end of the war. Seven years later, she died, too, in a car accident, and David spent most of his youth in foster care. As an adult, he'd become passionate about tracing his roots. That's how we'd first met, in a roundabout, tangled way.

"She says she might have information about my uncle."

"Lisle's brother?"

"Yes. I can't believe it, Ellie, but she thinks he could be alive!"

I sank back onto the couch. "But I thought—"

"The last letter my mother ever got from him, he said he was going to try to pass. Actually, your father told me about it. I guess she showed it to him."

My father had befriended David's mother soon after she arrived in this country—that's part of the tangled history we share. In fact, they'd been more than friends at one point, and I'm convinced their link was one of the reasons David became so attached to us. In his eyes, we were *mishpocha*. Family.

"Anyway, this woman, Mrs. Freidrich, said another man in the village got an anonymous letter, asking questions that made them think whoever sent it lived there once upon a time."

"Anonymous?"

"Yes. But here's the thing: The writer asked what happened to the Gottliebs, and specifically, the girl who went to America."

"Oh, David." I felt goose bumps on my arms.

"I know." He paused. "It's the middle of the night in Europe, but first thing tomorrow, I'm calling Mrs. Freidrich."

"She speaks English?"

"Someone from the bank will translate what I don't understand."

"Tell me again . . . how did you meet this woman?"

"When I first went over there years ago to trace my mother's family, she was very helpful. She told me things about my mother and her family I never knew. I gave her my card. You know, just in case she thought of something else."

"But the letter wasn't sent to her?"

"No. It went to one of her neighbors. I'm going ask them to fax me a copy."

"Hold on a minute." I switched the phone to my other ear. "Something doesn't make sense."

"What?"

"You said the letter was anonymous?"

"That's right."

"Why would someone ask questions—specific questions about the Gottliebs—but not include their name or address for a reply?"

"I'm not sure that's the case. There may not be a signature, but there could be an address or post office box. That's why I need to talk to the man who received it."

"I guess." I started to pace around the kitchen. "But why the anonymity? Particularly if it is someone who used to live there?"

"I don't know, Ellie." His voice sounded raspy. "But do you realize what this could mean? I . . . I might have family of my own. Alive. After all this time!"

I was about to tell him not to jump to conclusions. It was just a letter, anonymous at that. It could be from anyone. Indeed, the possibility that it was written by his uncle —or any other relative —was remote. But the emotion in his voice told me how much he wanted it to be true. I kept my mouth shut.

"Look," he went on. "I could be making assumptions here. I understand that. But what if I'm not? What if it's true? Ellie, this could be the most important thing that's ever happened to me."

I waited for him to say *Except for meeting you.*

He didn't.

"So, what have you been doing?" He asked after a pause.

I nattered on about the luncheon. He followed up with a question or two, but I could tell he wasn't really interested.

"I think they may ask me to produce a video for them."

"The women you went out to lunch with?"

"They call themselves WISH," I explained.

"Subsidized housing for foster children?"

"Apparently it started out in California. Now it's expanding east."

"I could have used help like that."

"You did fine on your own."

"It wasn't easy." He was quiet. "You know, I wonder if it's a sign."

"A sign?"

"You know, you help out some foster kids, and I find a long-lost uncle. *Mitzvah goreret mitzvah.*" Good deeds beget good deeds.

Given what he'd been through in life, David's faith always surprises me. It isn't a blind adherence to dogma. He's even studied Talmud to better understand his heritage. And while Judaism does sanction the nonbeliever, in fact, encourages us to act "as if," his bedrock convictions make my doubts about God seem petty.

He said he'd call tomorrow once he knew more. After we hung up, I wandered back into the family room. I was glad I hadn't told him about the tape; I was looking forward to a quiet winter of cocooning and staying warm. No danger. Or trouble. Or fear. In fact, I should call the police right now. Let them deal with this.

Halfway to the phone, I stopped. What if the tape *was* a hoax? Doubtful . . . but not impossible. If I handed it over to the cops, I'd look like the biggest fool east of the Mississippi. And if it wasn't a hoax, there was clearly a reason the tape had been sent to me. If I gave the tape to the police, I might never know what that reason was.

Except that the idea someone sent me a tape of a woman being killed didn't do much for my security. Living on the North Shore confers a sense of safety, of protection that I've come to expect. Any violation of that security—even if it's just an image on tape—punctures a tiny hole in my bubble of well-being. Common sense said I shouldn't get anywhere near this. I headed back into the kitchen to call the police.

I stopped at the refrigerator. It wasn't as if a dead body was lying on my floor. I had an image on videotape, an image that might or might not be real. There was no telling when the tape was shot or when the woman on it had been killed. It could have been recorded months, even years ago. Which meant the perpetrators were long gone. Why was I hurrying to hand it over?

Someone wanted me to have the tape. Didn't that bestow on me just a slight sense of duty, of responsibility, to follow it up? I'm no lawyer, but I know there's no statute of limitations on murder. The smart thing might be to make a backup of the tape. I could make a quick copy at Mac's in the morning, *then* hand it over to the cops. That would allow me to puzzle out who sent the tape and why on my own terms. Regardless of what the police might do.

If I wanted to.

Which, of course, I wasn't at all sure I did.

Then again, curiosity has always been the spur of my Achilles' heel.

I dropped the tape into my bag.

FOUR

WHEN RACHEL ASKED me about the tape at breakfast, I said there was nothing on it. "Someone's idea of a practical joke."

"Weird," she said between bites of toast.

"Don't talk with your mouth full."

"You like see food?" Her jaw dropped open, revealing a mouth full of half-chewed bread.

"Hello, world. I'd like to introduce you to my stunningly mature, well-bred daughter."

She wrinkled her nose.

I emptied my coffee mug in the sink. "You didn't happen to see a license plate on that van, did you?" I asked casually.

She shook her head.

"Color of the plates?"

"Nope."

"Okay. Well, we'd better get a move on. You don't want to be late."

After I dropped Rachel at school, I drove over to Mac's. Kendall Productions occupies several suites in a small industrial complex in Northbrook. MacArthur J. Kendall III and I have been working together for years. Mac's an excellent director, and he puts up with my antics. I put up with his WASP name and background. Things between us did become strained a few months ago, but, on the whole, it's worked out better than most of my relationships with men.

Hank Chenowsky might have something to do with that. A youth spent in front of the tube has, in his case, made for a qualitative contribution to mankind. He's the best video editor I've ever seen. And he's only been at it for five years.

I stuffed my gloves into my pocket and pushed through the door. A buzzer sounded. That was different. I took in the new furniture, carpeting, and paint job. Mac had just finished remodeling his studio. Apparently he'd added a few security measures too. I helped myself to coffee from a shiny new Starbucks machine. Things must be going well.

A shuffling noise sounded. I turned to see Hank sauntering down the hall toward me. "Ellie, hey. How are you?"

Thin and gangly, with light blue eyes and long pale hair, Hank's coloring is almost albino, although when I teased him about it once, he hotly denied it. I learned later that a lack of skin, eye, and hair color can be associated with mental retardation. Hank is as sharp as the light on a crisp autumn day, but his outburst made me wonder if someone else in his family wasn't.

"I'm good." I gave him a hug. "How were your holidays?"

"Cool." A contented smile spread across his face. "Sandy took me home to meet her parents."

"Already?" They'd only been going together a couple of months.

He nodded, blushed, and shrugged, all the while managing to look quite pleased with himself.

I patted his arm. Then I peered down the hall. "Is Mac here?"

He shook his head. "Debbie's down with the flu, and one of the kids has an ear infection."

"Too bad." I hoped my voice didn't sound too insincere. It was better Mac wasn't here; he wouldn't approve of my plan. "Hank," I said in my sweetest voice, "you think you could do me a little favor?"

"Depends what it is."

I headed into the master editing suite. A bank of monitors was built into the wall above a flat table. Another set of screens was attached to the back edge of the table. A keyboard plus two other instrument panels sat on top. Hank followed me in. A photo of a freckled, flame-haired young woman hung on the wall. Behind her was a view of the lake. She was smiling broadly.

I dug out the tape from my bag. "Think you could dub this for me?"

He pulled his hair into a ponytail with both hands. "What is it?"

"Someone dropped this off at the house. I thought it would be a good idea to copy it before I hand it over to the police."

"Police?" From the way his hands dropped to his sides, you'd think the tape was contaminated with Ebola. "Ellie, I don't know. Mac said—well, you know how he gets."

Mac was cautious. Always played by the rules. "I understand." I nodded. "I don't want to put you in an awkward position. How about I call him?"

Hank frowned. "I told him I wouldn't bother him unless it was an emergency."

I shrugged. "It's VHS. And it's only about ten minutes."

He shifted. "What's on it?"

"I'd . . . I'd rather not say."

He cocked his head. "Ellie . . ."

"By the way," I barreled on, "do you think maybe you could dub it onto DVCAM? The picture is pretty lousy, and I'd like to play with it at some point. Not now, of course. And not here. But you know . . ."

"Ellie, before I digitize this, I need to know what's on it."

I hesitated. "There's no way to do it without looking?"

* * *

While Hank was dubbing the tape, I dialed the police nonemergency number. "Dan O'Malley, please," I said to the dispatcher.

"Not here. He has the late shift this week. You want his voice mail?"

"Sure." I started. "No. Wait. Is . . . is Georgia Davis there?"

"I think she just came in. Hold on."

Davis was the youth officer on the police force. I'd met her last fall when Rachel—and I—were having problems.

I heard silence on the line, a few clicks, then a female voice. "Davis."

"Officer Davis, it's Ellie Foreman, Rachel's mother."

"Oh, sure. Hi. How's Rachel doing? Nothing wrong, I hope?"

"She's running four miles a day and exercising like crazy. Field hockey."

She laughed. "There's worse things."

"Tell me about it."

A pause followed, which I knew I was supposed to fill.

"Officer Davis, er—an unusual package was delivered to my house last night."

"Oh?"

"It was a videotape. VHS. Black and white."

"Yes?"

"There was no label on it. No return address, either. Just my name." I hesitated. "I took it inside and screened it."

"Uh-huh?"

"I think it shows a woman being murdered."

When Hank handed me the copy of the tape, his eyes were burning. "I don't want to know anything about this," he said grimly. "In fact, I never want to see it again. I'm erasing it from the decks."

I nodded.

"And that's the last time I ever do you a favor, Ellie."

"I understand."

His voice softened. "Let the police deal with it. Stay away."

"That's where I'm headed."

"Then why . . . why did you make a—" He cut himself off. "What are you going to do with this?"

"Nothing."

He looked me up and down.

"Really."

"Get out of here. And don't you ever tell Mac what we did."

GEORGIA DAVIS MET me in the lobby of the police station. She was in uniform, and her shoulder-length blond hair was tied back in a ponytail. With large brown eyes, a creamy complexion, and an hourglass figure, she made the boxy blue uniform look like designer fashion. Only a crooked nose kept her from being a beauty.

I motioned toward her clothes. "You're not a youth officer anymore?" When I'd met her last fall, she was in civvies.

"Been back on patrol since New Year's."

I couldn't tell from her tone whether that was good or bad. "You like it?"

"Sure. More action."

I wondered what kind of action that might be. We live in a small bedroom community twenty miles north of Chicago where policing tends toward stolen bikes and drunk drivers, and the most exciting event of the past three years was a drive-by shooting on Happ Road. No one was hurt.

She ushered me into a windowless room. A conference table and chairs took up most of the space. A VCR and monitor stood at one end. Three of the walls were cinderblock, and if it hadn't been for the large mirror covering the fourth, we might have been in any suburban office.

"Have a seat." She went to a phone on the wall and

punched in three numbers. "She's here," she said into the phone.

A minute later a big man in uniform with a fringe of gray hair and weathered skin sailed into the room.

"Morning," he said brightly. "Deputy Chief Brad Olson." He offered me a meaty hand. A gold eagle was pinned to his collar.

I shook his hand. "Nice to meet you."

"Likewise. Detective O'Malley has kept us up to date about your . . . you." His smile was so elliptical, I couldn't tell if he was being tongue in cheek. Still, I was struck by his cheery manner. He'd probably been a cop forever. Where was the hard-bitten cynic? The "I've seen it all" disdain?

He waved a hand. "Please, sit down." He sat at the end of thc table and folded his hands. The top of his head gleamed in the fluorescent light. "Officer Davis says you have a show for us."

I took a seat on the side of the table. "I guess you'll be the judge of that, sir." *Sir?* Was this former all-cops-are-pigs-activist really calling a police office "sir"?

His smile deepened, as if he had read my thoughts.

Davis sat down across from me, tore off a blank form from a pad, and attached it to her clipboard. "Tell us what happened," she said.

I explained.

"You say Rachel brought it in." She tapped a pen against the table. "Did she see the color or make of the vehicle? Or the plate?"

"No. And she doesn't know what's on the tape." I told them about the long lead-in at the head end and how she'd gone upstairs without seeing anything. "I told her it was blank. A practical joke. Are you going to have to talk to her?"

Davis and Olson exchanged glances. "Why don't we come back to that," Olson said.

"What about the people on the tape?" Davis asked. "Thc gunmen. Did they look familiar?"

"Do you mean, do I know them?"

She nodded.

I stiffened. "Of course not."

"Never saw them before?"

"Never." I fidgeted in my seat. It never occurred to me the police would think I knew the killers. "But they were wearing ski masks."

"What about the woman? You ever see her?"

"No."

"Are you sure? Not even casually—in the store, the dry cleaner's, someplace like that?"

"I've never seen her," I said firmly.

"And there was no note, or explanation why you were receiving the tape?" Olson interjected.

"Nothing."

Davis made a note on her report, then slid the tape out of the cardboard sleeve. She put the tape in the deck and hit Play.

I cut in. "What you're about to see was recorded in time-lapse. To conserve tape. Which means everything will be speeded up. Like an old-time movie. You may not be able to catch it all. I had to screen it twice."

"We're familiar with surveillance tapes," Olson said.

I felt heat on my cheeks. Of course they were.

Both officers focused on the screen. When the woman crumpled to the floor, Olson's expression didn't change, but Davis grimaced. She rewound the tape and screened it again.

Neither spoke after the second run-through. Davis got up, ejected the tape, and slipped it into a plastic bag with the word *EVIDENCE* repeated around the edges in navy blue letters.

"Other than you, has anyone else touched this tape?"

I thought for a moment. "Rachel brought it inside."

"Anyone else?"

Hank had handled it when he dubbed it. His prints were probably all over it. Which they were bound to find if they checked. But I couldn't tell her that without admitting I'd made a copy. Which didn't seem like a prudent idea. I kept my mouth shut. "Well, if we find any prints, we may ask you and Rachel to provide us with a set for elimination purposes, okay?"

I shifted my weight. A potential problem was looming. I should probably fess up. "So—so, what happens from here?"

"We'll send it to the crime lab," Olson said. "Then, who knows? Depending what they find, it could end up leaving our jurisdiction."

"Because you don't know where the crime was committed?"

"If there even was a crime."

"You don't think that was real? How can—"

"We're not paid to make opinions, Ms. Foreman. Our job is to assemble the evidence. It looks real, I'll grant you. But you're a video producer. You know how images can be manipulated."

"You can't possibly think I had anything to do with this?"

Olson raised his eyebrows. Davis watched me carefully.

"I never saw this tape before last night."

"Okay," Olson said. "Let's go over this one more time, shall we?"

I went over the chronology again, trying to reassure myself this was normal. Like he said, they weren't getting paid for their opinions. They had to suspect everyone. As I talked, Davis took notes.

"What about the room?" Olson asked. "Have you ever seen that room before? Or been in one like it?"

I shook my head. "At first, I though it was somebody's basement, but then I realized it couldn't be."

"Why was that?"

"Light was seeping around the edge of the blind or curtain or whatever was covering the window. So it had to be aboveground. During daylight."

"Do you have any idea why someone sent you the tape?"

Maybe he did believe me. "I don't know. I can't figure out whether it's a threat or—"

"Why do you think it may be a threat?"

"Because of the events I was involved with last fall. And before that. But I have no idea why I would be a target now. That's why I say I don't know if it's a threat or . . ."

"Or what?"

I paused. "A plea for help."

"A plea for help?"

"Maybe someone wanted me to look into the matter. Even bring you the tape."

"For what reason?"

I shrugged. "I don't know."

He and Davis exchanged another glance. Then he said, "Well, you're right about one thing."

"What's that?"

"It's impossible to see what's going on." He turned to Davis. "Let's get someone to take a closer look."

"At least there's only one camera," Davis said.

"We got lucky."

"What do you mean?" I asked.

"With most surveillance systems, there's usually more than one camera," Davis answered. "In a large office building, for example, there could be eight or ten security locations with a camera at each. But only one tape."

"Are you saying that images from multiple cameras are recorded on one tape?"

She nodded.

"Why?"

"Cost. Otherwise, you'd have to buy a separate recording device for each camera. Which I'm sure some companies do, but most—well, they just do the minimum."

"I didn't know that." I studied the cinderblock cracks on the wall. A tape that's constantly flipping between cameras would be a meaningless jumble of frames and scenes. And if it was recorded in time-lapse, it would be virtually impossible to make any sense out of it.

"I did try to slow it down on my VCR. It helped." I thought about the woman's tired expression, the burst of smoke when the gun went off, the blood seeping across her chest.

"Thank you, Ms. Foreman." Olson leaned back. "You've been most cooperative. We'll take it from here."

"You don't think I had anything to do with this, do you?"

He smiled but didn't answer.

"Could—could you have Detective O'Malley keep me informed?"

"O'Malley?" Olson looked over at Davis. "Officer Davis will be working the case. I'll make the necessary changes in the schedule. Give you a couple of weeks to look into it. You'll work directly with me."

"Yes, sir." She looked down at her clipboard. A smile tugged at the corners of her mouth.

"There is one more thing," Olson said. "We will have to talk to your daughter."

I bit my lip. "Will she have to view the tape? I don't want her to see it."

"I don't think that will be necessary," Olson said after a beat.

"I have an idea," Davis said. "What if I pop over tonight, just to say hi?" She turned to Olson. "I know the girl." She turned back to me. "We can talk to her together."

"Wonderful." It would be easier with someone she knew and trusted. "But . . . do you think . . . I—we—Rachel and I are in any danger?"

"There are all kinds of ways to send a message," Olson said, not answering the question. What we need to ask is why someone would go to all the trouble of taping a gruesome crime like this and then send it, anonymously, to a video producer."

"I don't know."

"Neither do we. But it's clear the people who sent this to you don't want to be identified. They went to a lot of trouble to stay hidden."

Olson let that sink in and then stood up. Davis and I followed suit. She stacked the tape on her clipboard.

"Ms. Foreman?" she said as we exited the room.

"Oh, please. It's Ellie."

"I just have one more question."

"Sure." I trotted cheerfully down the hall. They didn't think I was involved. I was just a good Samaritan, performing a distasteful but necessary service. And she would be coming over to help explain it to Rachel.

"You got the tape last night, correct?"

"That's right."

"Was there any particular reason you waited until morning to call it in?"

FIVE

My father lives in an assisted-living apartment building in Skokie. With a card room, a gym, and a snack bar, the place looks more like a college dorm than a home for seniors. Females outnumber males two to one, so it also makes for some interesting social situations. Which Dad addressed soon after he moved in.

Banding together with three other men, he commandeered the card room every afternoon for a game of gin rummy or poker, during which it was made clear no interference from the ladies would be tolerated. The strategy worked, primarily because of their secret weapon: Dad made sure the men all smoked cigars. Lots of them. It was a brilliant tactic. How many women—even those fueled by Viagra-induced fantasies—would pursue their quarry through a cloud of reeking cigar smoke?

But I wasn't thinking about my father's sex appeal as I headed down the expressway to pick him up. I was thinking about how I had lied to Georgia Davis. When she asked why I'd waited until morning to call it in, I'd said I thought whoever dropped off the tape might realize they'd made a mistake and come back for it last night.

It was a lame excuse, and we both knew it. I should have admitted making a copy. It wasn't illegal. She might have even understood the sense of responsibility I was feeling. And curiosity. But the truth is I've been uneasy around cops for years. Which makes it hard to be forthcoming.

About five years ago I was caught shoplifting in a department store. When the cops came, they hustled me into the back of a squad car and took me down to the station. They shuffled me into a cinderblock room with handcuff bars on the wall. No one talked to me while we waited for my husband to bail me out, but I saw their contempt and scorn.

The humiliation of that experience is burned into my psyche. Even now, the thought of being too close to a cop makes me nervous. Part of it is the fear that they'll uncover some new sin and haul me in all over again. The other part is a fear that they'll always look at me with jaundiced eyes. They'll never trust me. And since they won't trust me, I won't trust them. Which, in an irrational, roundabout way, makes us even.

I exited the Edens at Old Orchard. A thick gray overcast pressed down. I threaded my way through Skokie, passing a lawn still decorated with Christmas regalia. But we were well into the third week of January now, and the reindeer looked tawdry, the icicles and lights garish. The homeowners ought to be fined for defacing their property. At the next light I pulled out my cell and checked my messages. Ricki Feldman had called. I dropped the cell back into my bag.

I parked in the fire lane at Dad's place next to a mound of snow that had hardened into dirty brown ice. I knew I was risking a ticket, but I felt reckless. Dad was in the card room playing three-handed gin with Frank and Al. The fourth seat was empty. His friend Marv had passed away right after Thanksgiving. Another man at the home wanted to take his place, but, for now, the guys were keeping the spot vacant as a memorial.

I snuck up from behind and kissed the top of his mostly bald head.

He didn't turn around. "Her Royal Highness has arrived."

He's been calling me that since I was little. He insists I was named for Eleanor of Aquitaine, but I'm certain my mother didn't have the medieval queen in mind when I was born. Eleanor Roosevelt was more her style.

"Thank God you're here to take him away." Frank rolled his eyes at me. "You know what happens when he goes to your house, don't you?"

"You finally get a shot at the pot?"

"He does it to you, too?" Frank grinned. "Make sure you check his sleeve. Might find a few extra cards in there."

Pulling himself out of the chair, Dad swatted Frank on the shoulder. "No fresh bagels for you tomorrow." We usually stop at the kosher bakery on the way back.

He picked up his cane, put on his coat, and shuffled outside. He'd been using the cane more often these days, I noticed. He groaned as he climbed into the car.

"Are you all right?" I asked.

"How could I be? My body is eighty-three years old, but my brain still thinks I'm forty."

I suppressed a smile.

"You just wait." He settled himself in the seat. "You'll see. Marv says—used to say—we're all on Timex time anyway."

"Timex time?"

"You take a licking, but you keep on ticking."

I closed the passenger door and went around to the other side. No ticket. Things were looking up. But Dad gazed straight ahead.

"You miss him, don't you?"

"He was a lousy poker player," he said gruffly. "Couldn't bluff worth a damn." I heard the catch in his voice.

I waited. "How's Sylvia?"

Dad had made one exception to his politics of social nonengagement. Sylvia Weiner, he claimed, made brisket almost as well as Barney Teitelman's mother. Barney was his best friend as a teenager, but Dad hadn't been near

Mrs. T.'s brisket in over sixty years. I knew it was just a cover for the fact that he really liked Sylvia.

"Not so good," he said. "You know all those jokes about Half-heimer's? Well, they aren't so funny anymore."

"But she seemed so—so with it over Thanksgiving."

"About a month ago she went for a walk and didn't come back. Six hours later the police got a call from a motel near Libertyville."

"That's twenty miles away."

He nodded. "Somehow she hitched a ride and walked into a room. She was sitting on the bed looking for her dog Heidi." He paused. "The dog died twenty years ago."

"I'm sorry, Dad. What's going to happen to her?"

Dad shrugged. "We'll have to wait and see."

I saw the pain in his eyes. When you get to be his age, "wait and see's" don't usually augur a happy ending. Turning onto the expressway, I cast around for something cheerful to say and launched into my encounter with Ricki Feldman. As I explained, he rubbed the head of his cane, an elegant silver crown, the kind of metalwork you don't see much anymore.

"Ricki Feldman," he said. "Is that Stuart's daughter?"

"That's her. But, I can't figure out why she's so involved. Granted, she'll generate some goodwill for making those housing units available, but she donated over twenty grand to them. That's a lot of goodwill."

"I know why."

"Tzedakah?"

Dad grunted. "If you say so."

"What does that mean?"

"Come on. You remember what happened to Stuart Feldman. About eight or nine years ago."

Eight or nine years ago, my marriage was falling apart, but I was still pretending everything was fine. I was also raising a five-year-old, keeping my career afloat, and dealing with my mother's cancer. I wasn't keeping tabs on real estate moguls. I shook my head.

"Don't you remember when those kids came down with cancer in that housing development near Joliet?"

"Joliet?" I squinted as fragments of memory surfaced. "Wasn't there a lawsuit about it?"

"Exactly. They claimed Feldman knew he was building on toxic land but put up the homes anyway."

"For the money."

"They called him a murderer. A monster. Accused him of child abuse. And that was the nice stuff."

"I guess I do have a vague recollection of it. But I don't remember how it ended."

"They settled the case. It damn near ruined him. He had a stroke. He was never the same afterward."

"That must be when Ricki took control," I said.

Dad nodded.

"Do you think she knew about it?"

"How could she? She had to be pretty young when it first happened."

"But not when she was cleaning it up." I went quiet for a moment. "You know, I made a video for her last year. She's sharp."

"Sharp?"

"She seems like the type to cut corners."

"Cutting corners is a far cry from what her father did."

"Granted." I exited the expressway at Willow. "So now she's spreading around bundles of cash and mitzvahs."

"She's doing *chuvah*. Penance."

"And rebuilding her reputation at the same time."

"A mitzvah is still a mitzvah, *mein lieben*." We turned the corner onto my block. "So, how's David?"

"He called last night. He was pretty excited." I told him about the letter.

"His uncle? *Emes?*" He rubbed his hand over the top of his cane. "It should turn out well for him. After all the suffering, he deserves some *naches*."

We pulled into the garage. "I don't know, Dad. What if it's a scam? Like those Nigerian e-mails?"

"What?"

I always forget Dad doesn't own a computer. In fact, he'd been almost contemptuous when they first came out. "They won't amount to anything," he grumbled. "All they are is a fast pencil." He still considers Bill Gates a college dropout—never mind that it was Harvard.

"There are these get-rich-quick schemes on the Internet that purport to be from a wealthy Nigerian who needs to shelter his money in America. All you have to do is send him your bank account number, and he'll pay you a huge commission."

Dad sniffed. "David's not stupid. If it is a con, he'll deal with it." He looked over. "And don't forget. Miracles can happen."

I kept my mouth shut.

He started to unfold himself from the front seat. "So, what's for dinner?"

"Ratatouille."

"Stew?" he asked without enthusiasm.

"And homemade apple pie."

He brightened.

We were finishing dessert when Officer Georgia Davis showed up. She shook snow off her jacket as she came inside.

"I didn't realize it had started again," I said.

"It's just a dusting."

I motioned to the family room. "Make yourself at home. I'll get Rachel."

It only took a minute for Davis to explain what was on the tape. She made sure to emphasize that the reason I hadn't told Rachel myself was my concern about her reaction. "In fact, it was smart for your mom to bring us the tape as soon as she did."

I looked at the floor.

"So I don't want to hear any complaining about why she said what she said, okay?"

"No prob." Rachel shrugged, as if the tape was the least important thing in her life. "Is that it?"

Davis and I exchanged glances. She turned back to Rachel. "No. I need to ask you some questions about the van that delivered the tape." Davis asked her to describe the van as best she could: shape, color, make.

Rachel bit her lip. "It was dark. I couldn't tell. It was just—well, it was a van."

"Light-colored or dark?"

"I don't know."

"Any distinguishing features?"

"Like what?"

"A name on the side of the van, any dents on the body, rust stains?"

"No."

Davis nodded. "What about the driver? Did you catch a glimpse of him?"

She shook her head. "By the time I opened the door, he was driving away. I didn't see anything except taillights."

"Did you happen to see the license plate?"

A troubled expression slipped over her face. "No. I'm really sorry, Georgia. I guess I wasn't paying attention." She folded her arms and slouched on the couch.

Davis touched her arm. "Don't worry about it. You did fine."

"Really?"

Davis smiled. "Yup."

"Cool." Rachel's face smoothed out. She got up. "I hope you find the jerks who did it." She came over to me and gave me a hug. "Actually, Mom, I'm glad I didn't see it, you know?"

I nodded and hugged her back, astonished. She bounded back into the kitchen to help Dad load the dishwasher. Davis stood up and pulled on her jacket.

"That was easy," I said. "You clearly have the touch."

"She's a great kid. So . . ." She zipped up the coat. "Any problems today?"

"Nothing. All quiet."

"Good." Her gaze rested on me. It might have been my imagination, but I thought she looked almost expectant, as if she were waiting for me to go on.

I opened my mouth. It was time to tell her about the copy of the tape. "You . . . you'll keep me up to speed, won't you?"

She cut her eyes to the door. "I will."

I watched her walk to her car through a veil of snowflakes. As she pulled away, I quietly closed the door. I'd had the chance to set everything straight. But Georgia Davis was a tough read. She'd had on her game face. She hadn't given out anything. I didn't know how she'd react to my lying. As far as I could tell, the only thing I had going for me was that I was Rachel's mother. Maybe it was intentional. Some people can sense innocence in others and let down their guard. Apparently, I didn't qualify.

SIX

I CALLED RICKI Feldman the next morning. Her secretary's voice, which I'd learned ranged between obsequious and haughty, depending on who was on Ricki's A-list for the day, radiated an irritating self-importance when I told her my name. I figured I wouldn't get through, so I was surprised when I heard Ricki's voice.

"Good morning, Ellie," Ricki said cheerfully. "Glad you could get back to me so fast."

Who was she kidding? I'd waited almost twenty-four hours. "No problem, Ricki. What's up?"

She laughed. "I think you know."

"Is this about a videotape for WISH?"

"You got it." On reflection I decided her laugh sounded practiced. "I figured you needed a night to sleep on it."

"You know me too well."

"I try. So, what's the verdict?"

She was wrong about one thing. Bouncing between bouts of Dostoevskian guilt and paranoia over the tape, I'd hardly slept at all. But I had given some thought to WISH. No question I'd taken a visceral dislike to the Women

Who Lunch, although to be fair, that might have had something to do with my former lifestyle. Had I stayed married to Barry, I might have been one of them, too, tapping into untold spigots of money. At least before he lost it in the market.

I'd also debated whether I wanted to put myself in such close proximity to Ricki again. I wasn't enthusiastic. In the end, though, it was David's experience that persuaded me. He grew up in foster care, alone, with no mentors and few friends. He'd managed to overcome his past, but he is a remarkable person. If the video called attention to the plight of kids like him, if it eased their journey toward self-sufficiency, it would be worthwhile. Despite the personalities and lifestyles of the people involved.

"What about the budget?"

"My donation should get you going, and we'll raise whatever else you need. I'm not concerned. We know you'll do the job without fleecing us."

I gripped the cordless, unsure whether that was a compliment or an insult. "I'll do it."

Her voice lifted. "Wonderful! You'll be glad you made that decision." Before I could ask what she meant, she went on. "It's going to be a substantive film, Ellie. Not PR fluff. Important people are backing these efforts. There may even be federal funding involved." She cleared her throat. "I know you think WISH is a group of frivolous ladies with too much money and time on their hands. But once you meet the guy who's driving the effort here in Chicago, I think you'll change your mind."

"You mean, the women aren't—"

"Ellie, the women you met are very good at one thing. They know how to separate people from their money."

"I noticed."

"I'm talking about raising money. For charity. The women you had lunch with are consummate fund-raisers. As a group, they've raised millions of dollars."

I started to pace. It's no secret that benefits, auctions, and galas seem to grow more lavish—and lucrative—each year. And the North Shore is full of ladies who raise fortunes for their pet causes in between their manicures, tennis, and shopping. I'd even joked with Susan Siler, my closest friend, about what could happen if you unleashed them on the federal deficit. But I hadn't realized the Women Who Lunch were part of that species.

"In any event, you won't be dealing with them. And I won't be involved much, either. I just wanted to make sure we had the right team in place."

"You'd make a good drill sergeant."

I heard a rustling in the background, as if she was shuffling papers. "Sorry, what was that?"

"Nothing." No need to get churlish. She was handing me a nice piece of business. I took the phone into the family room and raised the shade. An inch of snow had fallen last night, but the streets were clear, and bands of sunlight slanted across the ceiling.

"I hope you don't think I'm being pushy," she went on. "But I set up a meeting for you in Evanston with the man who's the mover and shaker behind the program. Just you and him. His name's Jordan Bennett."

"When is it?"

"This afternoon. At one."

I paused just long enough, then said cheerfully, "Sorry. No can do."

"You—you can't?" She seemed taken aback.

"I have another appointment. But I could manage it tomorrow."

"Well . . ." Her voice turned suddenly chilly. "Here's his number. Why don't you call him yourself?"

"Good idea, Ricki. Thanks."

After hanging up, I allowed myself the tiniest smile, then wondered what to do for the rest of the day. I was about to go upstairs and shower, when a movement through the window caught my eye. A white van with large windows on the side pulled up to my neighbor's house. Five or six women huddled inside. A moment later a woman in a drab olive wool coat climbed out. I saw a flash of pale face and tired eyes. She had no hat or boots, and her shoes disappeared in the snow. She shook it off, one foot at a time, and headed up the driveway. A cleaning lady.

Fifteen years ago, the cleaning ladies up here came mostly from Poland, grateful to escape a repressive government and make a few dollars to send home. They'd come to my house when I could afford them, and Rachel still remembered a few words: *Dziekuje . . . Dobry . . . Prosze.*

After the Soviet Union collapsed, though, the Poles were replaced by an influx of women from far-flung spots like Moldovia, Belarus, and remote parts of Russia. These women weren't escaping repressive regimes: They were fleeing a world where highway robbery, enforced prostitution, and rampant killing were daily events. Life had turned cheap in that part of the world. Or maybe it always was, but it took the collapse of an empire to expose it. Still, the women in the van were the lucky ones. They'd escaped.

The driver, who'd accompanied her to the front door to translate what my neighbor wanted her to do, headed back to the van. Short and squat, he wore a brown coat and one of those large, fur-lined Russian hats they wore in *Dr. Zhivago.* He looked like a small bear. Before climbing back into the van he reached into his pocket and took out a pack of cigarettes. As he dug out a book of matches, he turned toward my house, and I got a look at his face. Long and angular, it was the face of a tall man. I had the impression that it had somehow been attached to the wrong body.

Expelling a mouthful of smoke, he gazed expectantly in my direction as if he were waiting for something to happen. An uneasy feeling slid around in me. Why was he looking my way?

I started to lower the shade, which proved to be the wrong thing to do. The man hadn't realized anyone was at the window, but when he saw the shade move, he started. Flicking his cigarette to the ground, he threw himself into the van and quickly backed out of my neighbor's driveway.

I tried to catch the license plate as he sped away. I saw the familiar Lincoln profile and a lot of red, white, and blue, but the numbers were obscured by a layer of muddy ice. I stared at the retreating vehicle. Did he have something to do with the tape? Rachel thought the tape had been dropped off by someone in a van. Was he the man? If so, what was his connection to it? If only there had been a note or a letter.

As I slowly lowered the shade the rest of the way, I realized there was another problem. Even without a note, whoever dropped off the tape knew where I lived. What if the killers found out, too? What if they learned they'd been caught on videotape and decided to eliminate anyone or anything that connected them to the crime? Couldn't that eventually lead them to me?

Maybe I should have confronted the driver. No. Whoever dropped off the tape clearly didn't want any direct contact with me. If this man *was* the messenger, I'd already scared him off. And scared people do foolish things.

I went up to the bathroom and ran hot water until the windows steamed up. Should I call Georgia Davis? No. This was just a maid's service, for God's sake. And a man smoking a cigarette. She'd probably tell me I was imagining things. And, to be fair, who's to say I wasn't? Maybe the man was daydreaming and just happened to be gazing at my house, his mind a thousand miles away. Maybe the movement of the shade jerked him back to reality, and he jumped into the van, realizing his schedule would be thrown off if he dawdled any further.

The real issue was the identity of the woman on the tape. Why had her life ended in a shadowy room with wall paneling and linoleum tiles? Figuring that out was a wiser use of my time than worrying about a man on my neighbor's driveway. Assuming I wanted to worry about any of it at all.

I stepped into the shower, trying to imagine what she'd done to warrant such a vicious, cold-blooded death. I couldn't come up with anything, but my experience with murder is limited. Unlike the men on the tape. They'd seemed comfortable with their task. Practiced. Ski masks to hide their faces. No hesitation before they attacked. As far as I could tell, they hadn't even talked to each other while they were killing her. And there were two of them. Someone wanted her dead badly enough to use two men for the job.

I stood under the hot water, rinsing off soap. If only the quality of the tape were better. A sharper image might have revealed the woman's face, or at least some distinguishing feature. Something in the room might have told me where it was.

The police said they were sending the tape to the crime lab. But they didn't say how long it would take. The lab serves all of northern Illinois's law enforcement agencies, including Chicago's. There could be dozens of videotapes waiting for forensic analysis. It might take weeks, even months, to get anything back. What if the man driving the van wasn't the innocent I was trying to convince myself he was? Did I want to wait a month or more to find out?

I toweled off, got dressed, and went into my office. A tiny purple ceramic shoe sits on top of my computer monitor, a birthday present from Susan. She'd attached a card to it that said: "No one will ever fill yours." I sat down, booted up, and went online.

A few minutes later, I found an article about video forensics written by someone in the Chicago area who started out as a videographer but was later "certified"—whatever that meant—as a forensic analyst by the Cook County Sheriff's Department. When I looked him up, he turned out to be in Park Ridge, a village about twenty minutes away. I punched in his number.

A gravelly voice answered. "Mike Dolan."

I put on my most charming voice. "Good morning, Mr. Dolan. My name is Ellie Foreman, and I have a digital tape that needs some work. I was hoping you might be able to help me."

"What law enforcement agency are you with?"

"I—I'm not."

"You with the press?"

"No." I hesitated. "I'm a video producer."

He cleared his throat, and when he spoke again, his voice was even more scratchy. Years of smoking, probably. "If you have evidence that a crime has been committed, you should be talking to the police."

"I did," I blurted out.

"And?" His voice sounded stern.

"I—I was just wondering, if I wanted to have it looked at privately, how much are we talking about?"

"Four hundred an hour," he said, not missing a beat. "And another five for setup."

"Are you kidding? Nine hundred just to walk in the door?"

"You're a video producer, you say?"

"That's right."

"You've got a client, right? It's not coming out of your pocket."

"But I—I don't have—my budget doesn't have that kind of flexibility. I can't afford nine hundred dollars."

"Sorry." He sounded almost cheerful.

"I can tell." I disconnected and tossed the phone onto the chair.

SEVEN

I THOUGHT I'd stepped back in time when I walked through the door in Evanston the next day. Tucked away in an alley off Sherman Avenue, the building looked like an old carriage house that had been renovated once before but needed another go-round. The entry hall had high ceilings, crown moldings, and a massive door, but the moldings were chipped, the walls needed paint, and the carpeting looked like it had been there since the Vietnam War.

It wasn't just the architecture that evoked an earlier era. The walls were papered with colored flyers advertising everything from adoption counseling to yoga for couples. As I squeezed past a couch so battered even the Salvation Army would reject it, I imagined a Movement office next to the Organic Food Coop, which would be next to Benefits for Returning Vets.

A sign on one of two offices down the hall identified the occupant as Jordan Bennett, PhD, MASC. Underneath his credentials was the word *Transitions*. The door was partially open, so I pushed through, anticipating a guy with a beard in scruffy jeans and Birkenstocks.

The only thing I got right were the jeans, but they weren't scruffy. Sitting behind a desk was a leaner, lankier version of Denzel Washington. A blue crewneck sweater set off his skin, and when he smiled, which he was doing now, he was definitely "hot," as Rachel would say.

"Thanks for rescheduling the meeting." I pushed a lock of hair behind my ear. I was glad I'd worn the new sweater she'd given me for Hanukkah.

"Ricki said you were a busy person." He gave my hand a businesslike squeeze, almost as if he knew what his effect on women was and didn't want it to interfere with his agenda. He motioned to one of two chairs facing the desk. "Please, sit down."

I sat and checked out the office. Despite the high ceilings, the room had a musty smell intensified by an excess of steam heat spewing out of the radiator. Stacks of folders lay on the floor, and cartons were pushed into corners. A framed poster leaned against the radiator. Nails protruded from the walls, with rectangular discolorations around them, which made me think the previous occupant's artwork had hung on the wall until recently.

"You just move in?"

He glanced around. "Not exactly. As a matter of fact, up until a week ago, I thought I was moving out."

"Oh?"

"I came east from California about a year ago to set up the Chicago office of Transitions. We got up to speed pretty fast, but then—"

"Transitions? I thought it was called WISH."

He looked puzzled.

"WISH," I repeated. "Women for Interim Subsidized Housing."

He paused, then leaned back. "Is that what the women are calling themselves?"

I frowned. "Am I missing something?"

"The organization's name is Transitions. But we're new and relatively obscure, as nonprofits go. One of our strategies is to build networks and partnerships. Ally ourselves with other groups."

"The women."

He nodded.

"I thought they were your fund-raising arm."

"Frankly, I'm not sure how they're set up. Or why they call themselves WISH. I'm just grateful they're around."

I grinned. "Transitions, huh?" The women probably didn't want their mission to be misconstrued as a menopause support group.

"What's so funny?" he asked.

"Nothing." I wiped off my smile. "How . . . how did you hook up with them?"

"Through Ricki Feldman." He gestured to the mess on the floor. "It's her fault the office looks the way it does."

"Now you've lost me."

"This was the cheapest space I could find. I signed a two-year lease, but then last month I get a letter saying the owner wanted to buy out my lease and tear down the building. I met Ricki when I went to her office to persuade her not to."

"Feldman Development owns this building?"

"That's right." The radiator clanged and hissed.

"I get it." It was my turn to pause. "But you're still here."

Bennett pushed up his sleeves to his elbows. "We struck a deal. She said she'd wait until we had the money to move."

"Which she's now helping you to find."

He grinned. "You *do* get it."

"She's something else."

"Yes, she is." His smile deepened.

It occurred to me Bennett hadn't said anything about a family moving east with him. It also occurred to me that Ricki Feldman wasn't the type of person to let any opportunity pass her by. And with his intelligence, charm, and killer looks, Jordan Bennett had opportunity written all over him.

"But we're grateful for support from any quarter. Including video producers."

"You've been checking me out."

"You passed." He rocked back in his chair.

"So, tell me about Transitions. Or WISH. Or whatever it's called. And how you got involved with them."

He squared a piece of paper on his desk. "I grew up in foster care."

"I thought you said the organization was relatively new."

"That's right."

"Then how did you—I mean . . ." I waved a hand.

"A woman in Marin County took me in. Taught me how to dress, how to talk, how to eat with a knife and fork. She had connections. It was through her I got a scholarship to UCLA." He paused. "I was lucky. Some kids aren't." He paused again. "Did you know almost twenty percent of the homeless were in foster care at some point?"

A door opened and closed down the hall. I shook my head.

"Most people don't. Once a kid is eighteen, he's supposed to be out of the foster care system. But a lot of them have been bounced from home to home, or they've been depending on lawyers and social workers to solve their problems. They don't have a clue how to rent an apartment, how to buy groceries, how to open a bank account. It's all too much for them. When they go out on their own, they give up."

"Give up?"

"Some get pregnant and go on welfare. Others get involved with gangs or end up on the street."

"You didn't."

"Like I said, I was lucky. I'll never forget the thrill the first time I bought my own groceries. Or put the clothes I bought myself in my own dresser. It's a high, you know? I decided other kids should experience it."

"I thought this was just about subsidized housing."

"We also want to teach them how to live on their own. At least to know what's expected of them."

"And you want the video to raise awareness of their plight?"

He nodded. "We want opinion leaders and legislators to see it. We're lobbying for changes in the housing codes. Of course, with this administration, it's like spitting in the wind."

"How come?"

"There's an undersecretary at HUD—a holdover from the Clinton years. But he's fighting an uphill battle, and I'm afraid if we interview him, he'll lose his job. We need every friend we can muster in that town. Happily, there's also a congressman who'll say that a few well-placed grants will save money in the Section Eight programs. And he's from southern Illinois."

"You want to interview him."

He nodded and launched into an explanation of federally funded housing programs and how they were geared toward families, not singles. My mind wandered. David had grown up in foster homes all over Pennsylvania. Had he felt the same way as Jordan Bennett? David had the proper social graces, but I never thought to ask how he'd learned them. In fact, it occurred to me I didn't know very much about his life before we met. A brown leaf, somehow left over from fall, drifted past the window.

"My . . . a close friend of mind grew up in foster care."

He looked at me with new interest. "No wonder Ricki wanted you in on this."

I was about to tell him Ricki couldn't possibly have known about David's background. Then again. . . . I kept my mouth shut.

"You said you could run an eight-minute mile," Rachel called out as she sprinted past me on Voltz Road.

"I could, once upon a time." I picked up my pace, but it was hopeless.

"You're slipping, Mom," she yelled over her shoulder.

I laughed and let her widen her lead. Rachel's always

been built for speed. I remembered her at six, streaking across the front lawn one Sunday morning chasing a rabbit. It was spring, and she was wearing her *Beauty and the Beast* nightgown—the one she refused to take off for about a year. She thought we'd bought her a bunny for Easter. We had to let her down easily. Not only did we not buy it, but we didn't celebrate Easter.

Now though, watching her pass me on the bike path, her cheeks flushed, eyes bright, I felt unaccountably grateful. She was a child of divorce, and she hadn't been raised with the extras that others consider their birthright, but she hadn't been shunted around to strangers. She had loving parents and family, good friends, and was even starting to think about her future. I blinked. Maybe there really was a God.

Rachel turned around, jogging in place. "Oh, I almost forgot. Is it okay if I spend the weekend with Sara? Her parents invited me to go to their house in Galena."

Galena, a small town on the Mississippi at the western edge of the state, has become a trendy vacation spot. With skiing in the winter and boating in the summer, it's an all-purpose, inexpensive resort, assuming you can bear its refurbished nineteenth-century charm. "The whole weekend?"

She nodded. "We'll leave after school on Friday. Be back Sunday night."

David was coming out Friday. We'd have the house to ourselves. For two days. And nights. Yes, there really was a God.

EIGHT

My dear Herr Meyer,

In the hope that this letter finds you healthy and well, I beg your indulgence for this intrusion. I have been reluctant to pose these questions heretofore—perhaps I did not want to know the answers. However, life has led me to a juncture in which it is necessary that I make the effort.

Sixty years ago the Gottlieb family lived a few buildings down from the synagogue in the central part of the village. Herr Gottlieb was a tailor; he and Frau Gottlieb had four children. The family was assumed to have perished during the war—with the possible exception of the eldest daughter, Lisle. It was thought that her parents arranged passage by steamship to a relative in Chicago, Illinois, USA, in 1938.

Herr Meyer, I would be most grateful for any

information about Lilie and her progeny—from any quarter. Indeed, it is most urgent that this occur. Please direct any persons with information to reply to the following address.

P.O. Box 58 (Antwerp 11)
B-2013 Antwerp
Belgium

I handed the letter back to David. He folded it and put it into his pocket.

"What do you think?" he asked.

We were eating dinner at a village restaurant that seems to reinvent itself every five years. A French bistro in its current incarnation, it has art deco walls, white floor tiles, and plenty of attitude. But neither of us was paying much attention to the milieu.

"Tell me again how you got it."

"Meyer read it over the phone to a woman at the bank. She translated it for me."

"Meyer?"

"Mrs. Freidrich and Mr. Meyer are neighbors. He got the letter. She called me."

"So he told her about it?"

"I assume so," he said impatiently. "But that's not important. What do you think?" he asked again.

"About what?"

"Do you think it could be from my uncle?"

"I'm not sure I can answer that. I have no way to tell. Why would he be in Antwerp?"

Our waiter, who'd been hovering a few discreet feet away, asked if we wanted another drink. When I nodded, he whisked our glasses away.

"Antwerp is the second largest city in Belgium," David said. "It's the home of the painter Rubens. An international center for diamonds." He paused. "And there's a large Jewish population. At least compared to other European cities. Maybe he settled there after the war."

"It's possible."

"You don't sound convinced," he said worriedly.

"It's not that. It's just—what part of the letter makes you think your uncle wrote it?"

The words were hardly out of my mouth. "First off," he cut in, "the writer knew exactly where the Gottliebs lived. There—"

"Anyone who was familiar with the village might have known that."

"That's true," he conceded. "But it's obvious the letter was written by someone of a certain age. Someone who was alive during the war."

"Or someone whose elderly relatives told him what the village was like."

The waiter returned with fresh wine, chardonnay for me, merlot for him. David tugged at his shirt collar, as if it were too tight. "Maybe. But how many people would call her 'Lilie' ?"

"Lilie?"

"It means lily in German. That's what her little sister called her. She couldn't pronounce Lisle, so she called her 'Li-li.' "

"How do you know that?"

"My mother told me." His chin jutted out. "That's not something just anyone could know."

I didn't answer.

"Ellie, why do I get the feeling you don't believe me?"

"It's not that."

The hollow patch at the base of his neck throbbed. "Then what is it?"

I rubbed my temples. It was clear David wanted the letter to be from his uncle so much, he was trying to persuade me into agreeing. I couldn't blame him. Still. "I . . . I just don't want you to be disappointed if it's not what you think."

He was silent. Then his mouth tightened. "Typical."

"Excuse me?"

"Any time something comes up in my life, especially

when it concerns my family, you're always quick to dismiss it or disparage it or tell me it's not what I think."

Where was this coming from? "I—I didn't—"

"You couch it in these 'oh, I don't want you to be disappointed' terms, but the truth is, Ellie, I wonder if you want me to find out anything about my family. Like the Iversons. I think you're afraid you'll lose something if I strike out on my own."

I struggled to hold on to my temper. "I'll lose something? Like what?"

"Control, maybe? The upper hand? I don't know. I'm not a shrink. But I do know it's always about you."

I blinked. I do have issues of control. Money, airplanes, shoplifting—it's an ongoing struggle. But I wasn't convinced that was the case now. David was upset—that much was clear. But had I done something to provoke him, or was I just the nearest target? I chose my words carefully. "David, there were good reasons to be cautious about pursuing your family connections in the past."

He shot me a dubious look.

"I didn't want you in the middle of my problems. They turned out to be dangerous, if you recall."

"That was then."

"Yes, but it was a letter from a stranger that triggered the chain of events then, too."

He didn't answer.

"Look. I know how important this is to you. I'll help in any way I can. And . . . it wasn't all bad. Back then." I reached for his hand. "If I'd never gotten that letter," I said softly, "you and I would never have met . . ."

He sank back in his chair, his anger dissipating like the tail end of a storm. "You're right. I'm sorry. I just . . . I'm so keyed up."

I squeezed his hand. "It's okay. And you're right about one thing. Whoever sent the letter knows something about the village. And the Gottliebs."

It wasn't a smile, but the lines on his forehead smoothed out. "The problem is we—I—don't have much time. There was that phrase about being at a juncture that required him to write."

"You think whoever wrote the letter is ill?"

"Don't you?"

I opened the menu, a sheet of parchment inside a faux leather binder. "I don't know." I scanned the stiff mottled paper. "But tell me. Why is Mrs. Freidrich so eager to help you?"

"Her cousin was my mother's best friend when they were children. I think she feels some . . . some responsibility."

"She's not Jewish."

"No. And she claims she didn't know anything about the Holocaust until years afterward."

"Oh, sure."

David shrugged. "She says there were no textbooks in German schools for years after the war. And no one ever talked about it, either—it was as if someone took a scalpel and surgically excised the Hitler era from German history."

"What did she think happened to the Jews? They all packed up and went on vacation?"

"Ellie." He scowled at me. "She was only a child."

"She had parents."

"They weren't party members. They owned a grocery store."

"You're telling me they didn't know what was happening?"

"She says the only thing her mother ever said—and this was years later—was that Germany got what they deserved."

"Why?"

He paused. "Because, she said, they raised a hand against God's chosen people."

I didn't have a comeback.

"Mrs. Freidrich said they were even talking about renovating the synagogue a few years ago." He made a small sound in the back of his throat. " 'Course it'll never happen."

"Why not?"

"There aren't enough Jews in the village for a *minyan*."

The waiter came and took our order, then took it over

to the chef, who was hunched over a huge wood-fired grill in the middle of the room. Orange flames erupted into plumes, then obediently subsided, like children who'd been roundly disciplined. I was staring at the flames, thinking about David, his mother, and a village near the Black Forest, when a movement near the grill skipped across my peripheral vision. Three people were heading in our direction. When I recognized one of them, I slouched in my seat.

"What is it?" David asked.

"Don't look, but Ricki Feldman's got us in her sights, and she's zeroing in."

"Who?"

I explained.

"The woman who recruited you for the video?"

"Yes, but—"

David turned around. "She's a knockout."

I inched a finger up the stem of my wineglass. Gee, thanks.

"Good evening, Ellie."

"Hello, Ricki." I pasted on a smile as Ricki, accompanied by two men, came over. Her hair was down tonight. That, combined with the silky dark brown outfit she was wearing, intensified her eyes. Which were wholly focused on David.

"My, my, who is this?"

I grudgingly introduced her to David.

"You're the one who got Ellie involved in Transitions," he said.

"That's right." She flashed him a dazzling smile before withdrawing her hand. Slowly.

"Ellie's been telling me about it. It sounds like a wonderful program. I—I was a foster child myself."

"Really." She flicked her gaze back to me. "Doing research, were we?"

"Actually, David and I met last year. He's . . . he and I—"

"Have a lot in common," David cut in.

"I see." Again, a dazzling smile.

For some reason, I thought back to a comment Jordan

Bennett made during our meeting. Something like: "No wonder Ricki wanted you on the project." Could it be she already knew about David? But how? That would mean . . . Before I could dwell on it, one of the men with Ricki cleared his throat.

"Oh, dear." Ricki turned to her companions. "Where are my manners?"

I nodded politely as she made introductions. I recognized Stanley Lawrence's name from the green-and-white signs that dot most of the construction sites around the North Shore, but I didn't know her other companion, a short, rotund man with thinning gray hair and eyes that bugged out so much they seemed to eat up his face.

"This is Max Gordon, an old friend of my father's. He started Gold Coast Trust."

He came around the table, and we shook hands. He couldn't have been much taller than five four, but he sported a large diamond ring, a Cartier watch, and a suit that had to have been custom-tailored. Though he looked prosperous and respectable, something about him made me think of a wizened Pillsbury Doughboy.

David extended his hand. "We've heard great things about Gold Coast Trust."

Gordon moved over to shake David's hand. "Are you in the business?"

"I'm the Director of Foreign Currency Trading at Franklin National Bank in Philadelphia."

"Is that so?" A flicker of interest swept across Gordon's face. "We specialize in international markets."

"Max is just about to build the first major skyscraper in downtown Chicago in twenty years," Ricki said importantly.

"Congratulations," David said.

Gordon smiled and rocked back on his heels. Why is it small men always build big buildings?

"Well now, Ellie." Ricki returned her attention to me. "Are you going to interview David for the video? I'll bet he'd have some fascinating input."

I felt my face flame. David's turned crimson, too, except

his was from pleasure—mine was pique. Only Ricki Feldman would have the chutzpah to tell me how to produce a video. I should have expected it. Last year when I was shooting the Glen video, Ricki would pop in with suggestions to include or exclude certain people or places, all of which sounded reasonable and innocuous at first glance. Ultimately, though, those suggestions always portrayed her as a smart, savvy businesswoman with a heart of gold. Of course, she was paying the bills then, and I didn't have a choice. I took a sip of wine. She was paying the bills now, too.

Still. "I usually don't put people I know in my films, Ricki. It can strain the credibility of the piece, especially if the audience knows there's a connection. And there's always the risk of getting too close to your subject. You lose objectivity."

Ricki's gaze, suddenly disinterested, wandered off mine. "I'm sure you're right, Ellie. You did talk it through with Jordan, didn't you?"

Was she showing off, or was it just her nature? I bit back a reply. "Jordan Bennett runs Transitions here in Chicago," I explained to David.

"He grew up in foster care, too." As Ricki recounted how he moved here from California, I waited for a proprietary smile or an excessively casual shrug, something that would reveal the nature of their relationship. But she gave no hint of her feelings. "You and Jordan should meet, she concluded."

"I'd like that," David said.

I gritted my teeth.

Our meals came, and Ricki made her good-byes. The men fawned over her as they helped her on with her coat, and as she exited the restaurant, the maitre d' kissed her hand.

"She was nice," David said between bites. "Not at all what I expected."

I sawed through my steak. Men could be so obtuse. "She's probably trying to finance a new venture."

"I don't think so."

"How do you know?"

"You don't know who Max Gordon is."

"Should I?"

"Gordon owns one of the most aggressive, fastest-growing banks in the country. Maybe the world. Gold Coast's asset base has practically tripled over the past few years. *Fortune* did an article on him not long ago. He's definitely a comer."

"Must be nice." I dug into my potatoes.

"He's been actively involved in rebuilding the economies of Eastern European countries. His investments have done well. They say he has the 'touch.'"

I polished off the potatoes, not much interested in bankers, *Fortune,* or Eastern Europe. "I hope you're not upset by what I said about interviewing you."

David shrugged.

He was.

"But we've . . . you've never really talked about it. Foster care, that is."

"You never asked."

"I figured if you wanted to tell me, you would."

"Maybe you figured wrong."

"Okay." I put down my knife and fork. "I'm asking now."

The silence that followed was so long, I thought he'd changed his mind. He looked down at his plate. Then he looked up. "You know how at Halloween kids bob for apples in a tub of water?"

I nodded.

"Imagine you're one of those apples. You never know who'll take a bite out of you. If you'll be snagged. Where you'll end up. What the people will be like. You might still be licking your wounds from the last place, but you're worried sick about the next."

"But you survived it."

He shook his head. "Survival isn't the issue."

I shifted. "What is?"

"Terror. The sheer terror of having absolutely no control

over what happens to you." He waved a hand in the air. "You take all of this . . . for granted."

I looked around. "All of what?"

"The security. The safety. You have support systems. Family. People who back you up. Christ, Ellie, I had nothing. And I was a little kid. When I . . ." His face was impenetrable.

"What?"

Another shake of the head.

I leaned forward. "David, did . . . did something happen to you when you were in foster care?"

Shades of pain passed across his face. He took a breath. "I'm fine."

"I know you are." I reached for his hand. "I understand. That wasn't my question."

"Ellie, stop with the third degree, okay? I don't want to be interviewed. You're right. I did survive." He pulled his hand away. "And I made a promise to myself never to be in that situation again. And I haven't. But don't tell me you understand, because you don't. This guy Bennett probably can. And you remember Dory; she could, too. But not you."

I felt like I'd been slapped.

"Your life is easy. You do what you please, go where you want. You take it for granted people are there for you. And they are. But that's not how it is for most of us. You just don't know."

"No," I said, my voice tight. "I guess I don't."

OUR LOVEMAKING THAT night was passionate and angry. He dug his fingers into me and pounded me with hard, bruising thrusts. He cried out when he came, then pulled out and turned away. I lay awake afterward, spent and sore, listening to him fall into a restless sleep.

NINE

I WOKE UP with the sheet knotted around my legs. Drowsy, snug, and warm in my own private Idaho, I wondered what had jarred me awake. When the doorbell rang again, I thought about the frigid winter air stinging my skin and decided Rachel could get it. Then I remembered she wasn't home. Grumbling, I threw off the quilt, wrapped myself in a robe, and headed downstairs.

Georgia Davis was at the door. Her face and voice were as cold as the ice rimming the windowsill. "You want to tell me why you called Mike Dolan about working on one of your tapes?"

My stomach clutched. "You'd—you'd better come in."

But she just stood there, arms folded across her chest. "What are you trying to pull here, lady?"

"I—I'm sorry . . . this is all a huge misunderstanding."

"I'm listening."

David called down from upstairs, his voice stuffy with sleep. "Is everything all right?"

"Fine," I said. "Go back to bed."

An irritated silence followed. Did he sense I'd gotten

involved in a "situation" again—after I promised I wouldn't? Or was it something else? Nothing like having the whole world ticked off at you. It was only nine in the morning, but I had a craving for chocolate.

I turned back to Davis. "I—I made a copy of the tape. Before I brought it to you."

"Why?"

"I thought . . . I didn't know you would be handling the case. I thought I'd better have my own copy in case you—I mean the police—decided not to pursue it, or it got lost or something."

"Or something?"

"I was also thinking I should have a record of it—in case—well—in case—"

"In case something happened to you?"

"Right."

"So you made your own copy."

"I was—I was going to tell you."

"When? After it showed up on the ten o'clock news?"

"I wouldn't do that."

She eyed me suspiciously. But then, why should she believe me? I was a video producer, and I used to work in television.

"I'd never go to the media. And I tried to tell you about it the other night." The door was still open, and I started to shiver. "Please come in."

After a moment, she did. I closed the door and motioned her into the kitchen. She didn't move.

"No more bullshit. You wanted the tape so you could start playing around with it yourself, didn't you?"

I didn't answer.

"I want it," she said. "And any other copies that exist. And just so you hear me loud and clear, I've already talked to the states attorney. I can get a court order in about an hour."

I nodded. As I went into the family room to pull it out of my bag, I heard David shuffling around upstairs. How much had he overheard? I backtracked to the hall and handed it over.

She slipped it inside an evidence bag. "You're skirting right up to the edge, you know. You can't be out there free-lancing. You could be jeopardizing my investigation. The last thing I need are problems with chain of custody."

"I'm sorry."

She shook her head. "O'Malley warned me about you."

I felt like a kid who's been sent to the principal's office.

"Look. Just let me do my job. Believe me, I want to get to the bottom of this as much as you." She bit her lip, as if she'd unwittingly revealed something she wanted to keep private.

I took that as an opening. "I'm making coffee. You want some?"

She didn't answer, but she made no move to leave. Deciding that meant yes, I went into the kitchen and busied myself with the coffeepot. She followed me in and leaned against a counter. As coffee slowly dripped into the pot, I caught her studying the pictures that were taped to the fridge. In one of the shots, Rachel's arm was looped around her friend Katie. In another her face was in extreme close-up, and she wore a maniacal grin. A third showed the two of us parking our bikes at the botanic gardens. David took it last summer. The coffee-maker beeped. I filled a mug and handed it to her. "Sugar's on the table." I poured a second mug for myself.

She set down the coffee, unzipped her jacket, then lifted the mug with both hands. "Listen. We realize there's got to be a reason the tape was sent to you. And, down the road, once we know what we're dealing with, I might need more information from you. But you can't be interfering right now."

I nodded. We sipped our coffee in silence.

After a moment, she sighed. "But I know you're concerned." She glanced at the pictures of Rachel. "So I'm willing to make a deal with you. For her sake."

I looked at her sideways.

"You stay out of my investigation, and I'll tell you what I can."

I thought about it. "It's a fair deal."

"It's the only one you're gonna get."

I smiled. I could have sworn she cracked one, too, but she covered it with sips of coffee. In between, she swirled the liquid in the mug. I got the sense she was mulling something over, debating with herself. Finally, she looked up. "You know anything about video forensics?"

"Not much. We use some of the same filters when we edit. To vary contrast and brightness or sharpen the image. But the equipment in forensic systems is much more powerful." I shrugged. "At least, that's what I hear. I've never seen one in action. I'd like to."

She arched her eyebrows. "How'd you find Dolan?"

"The Internet."

"Uh-huh."

"How about you?"

Her eyebrows arched higher, as if she was surprised I had the nerve to ask. "Dolan has a longtime relationship with law enforcement," she said after a pause.

I thought about the article he'd authored on the Web. "He's not a cop."

"Doesn't have to be."

"I'm sure he knows what he's doing." I tried for an offhand tone.

She shot me a look.

"I don't physically operate any editing equipment, but I can tell whether a tape is first, second, maybe even fifth generation. I can also tell whether any effects have been laid on. Sometimes what they were. That could be helpful . . . in the event it turns out to be a hoax."

"You're in no position—"

I laced my fingers around my mug. "You know, it may be the tape was sent to me because of my knowledge of video."

Davis canted her head.

"Maybe whoever sent it wondered if it was a hoax, too. Maybe they wanted me to figure out if it was."

"It didn't look like a hoax to me."

"Me neither, but it could be the sender doesn't know."

She crossed her arms. Hey, I'd try anything.

"Well . . ." I said. "One thing's for sure."

"What's that?"

"The quality of the image is going to look much better on a monitor at Dolan's studio than it did on the VHS at the station. You lose detail every time you make a dub. I'm sure Dolan will be able to figure it out."

We finished our coffee, eyeing everything in the room except each other. The trill of the phone broke our silence. I reached for it, temporarily giving Davis my back. It was Katie, wondering when Rachel would be home from Galena. I told her she'd call tomorrow. As I hung up and turned around, Davis was slipping something into her pocket. She put her mug down and zipped up her jacket.

"Well, I'll be going now. Thanks for the coffee."

"You're leaving?" I was flustered. "But what about—I mean—"

"Ellie, I'll do my job. You do yours, okay?"

My shoulders sagged.

She made her way to the door. "I appreciate you handing over the tape." She hunched her shoulders against the cold and started out toward her Saturn.

"You know where to find me," I called out. "If you need me."

She lifted her hand in a wave.

I closed the door and went back into the kitchen. As I was gathering up the mugs, there was a knock on the door. When I opened it, Davis silently handed me a business card, then headed back to her car. I scanned the card. Emblazoned on the left was a six-pointed star, the logo of our village police. On the right the card read: "Officer Georgia Davis." I turned it over. Scrawled in pen were the words: "Dolan. Monday. Ten A.M."

TEN

Park Ridge has always been a schizophrenic suburb. Fourteen miles northwest of downtown chicago, it's unsure whether it wants to be the home to *Little House on the Prairie* or the Mall of America. You'll be driving past neat frame bungalows, garden plots, and tall, graceful trees, when the street abruptly turns into a commercial venue crowded with strip malls, car dealers, and gas stations. But what can you expect from a town that originally went by the name of Pennyville?

I turned off Northwest Highway and headed south. Davis's Saturn was parked off Touhy in the driveway of a tiny brick Cape Cod. Two dormer windows jutted through a steep, gabled roof. Bushes flanked the porch—junipers, I guessed, their boughs bent with the weight of the snow. A crooked path the width of a snow shovel led to the front steps.

A round of fierce barking greeted me as I reached the porch. "Good dog," I chirped carefully. "You're a good doggie, aren't you?"

The barks changed to snuffles and whines, and nails

scratched the other side of the door. I felt braver and rang the bell. Unfortunately, that prompted a fresh round of woofs, which were promptly silenced by a deep shout. "Raus!"

The barks stopped instantly.

The door was opened by a man whose upper body was so buff he could have passed for Arnold Schwarzenegger before he became a politician. I couldn't tell much about his lower body because he was in a wheelchair, but he had bristly gray hair, a matching mustache, and deep-set eyes that were so blue they reminded me of the chroma key screen we use for effects. Or would have, had they not been narrowed in a deep scowl. Meanwhile, the dog, a long, slim creature that looked like a cross between a setter and collie, sat on tensed haunches, as if waiting for the command to attack. This was not the picture of gracious suburban living.

"Yeah?"

I recognized the gravelly voice from the phone. "Mike Dolan?"

"Who wants him?"

"I—I . . . My name is Ellie Foreman."

His eyes tracked me up and down. "So?"

I sucked in a breath. I'm not a timid person. I operate in bold colors and seek out similar types. But I try not to dispense with common courtesy—it was something my mother drilled into me. I cloaked myself in an icy formality. "By any chance is Georgia Davis here?"

He didn't answer.

I hoisted my bag farther up on my shoulder. This guy was either one of those bitter types who assume they can flout convention because they're disabled, or he was just a jerk. Either way, I didn't want to waste any more time finding out. Though I knew I was kissing off my chance to witness video forensics in action, I gathered up what was left of my dignity and turned to leave. I'd just made it off the porch when Davis appeared at the door.

She placed a hand on Dolan's shoulder. "It's okay, Mike. I told her to come."

"She's a civilian."

So are you, I wanted to say.

"She's the one who brought us the tape. And she knows something about video."

He sniffed, then rolled his wheelchair back from the door. The dog followed him. "Well, if you don't give a shit . . ."

She nodded at him, then at me. She was dressed in jeans and a beige fisherman's knit sweater. Her hair was pulled up with a barrette, but several strands had come loose. It gave her a softer, feminine look.

"Thanks," I said.

She gave me a brief nod. I followed them across a comfortable living room with a blue sofa, working fireplace, and glossy hardwood floors into what should have been the dining room. Apart from the same hardwood floors, though you'd never think it was part of the same house.

The two windows were covered with thick, dark material. In front of them a bank of equipment stretched from one wall to another. Monitors, speakers, A/V boards, and at least eight different video playback decks were stacked in a tower from floor to ceiling. I spotted a one-inch deck, a Beta SP, several half-inch VCRs, even an old three-quarter-inch pneumatic player. Nearby was a DVD player. A color video printer sat on a monitor stand.

A series of bays filled with what looked like purple mail slots lay at floor level. Green lights glowed above them. That had to be the Avid. Bisecting the stacks of equipment at chair level was a wide shelf with a phone, keyboard, and mouse. A small audio mixer was there, too. A warren's nest of cables hung over everything.

The dog followed us in and, after sniffing my pants legs, laid his head on Dolan's lap. Dolan scratched his ears. The dog retreated to a braided rug in the corner, circled it a couple of times, and flopped down, head on his paws. When Dolan smiled at the animal, his entire expression mellowed, and he looked almost human. Dolan, that is.

"What kind of dog is he?"

"A red-and-white setter."

"Never heard of them."

"About a hundred years ago they bred the white out to make Irish setters. But Jericho's the real thing."

At the sound of his name the dog pricked up his ears, but Dolan turned away and wheeled himself up to the shelf. Sighing mournfully, Jericho lowered his head.

I could relate.

"So, Davis," he said, "let's see what you got."

Davis dug out both thc original VHS and the digital cassette I'd made, and handed them over. He took the VHS, examined it, and laid it on the counter. Then he looked at the digital cassette. "Where'd you get this?"

Davis yanked her thumb in my direction.

He threw me a skeptical look. "You?"

I nodded.

"You're that producer, aren't you? The one who called the other day."

"Nine hundred just to walk in the door."

He looked from me to Davis, then back. I shoved my hands into my pockets, expecting to be told to get the hell off his property. Instead, he said, "Well, you get points for persistence."

I relaxed.

"Since you're here, Foreman, make yourself useful. Hit the power switches on the monitors."

I did.

He picked up the VHS tape. "You do a field analysis on this, Davis?"

"We couldn't. We have no idea where it was shot."

"Which means you don't know when it was recorded?"

"No."

"Or how?"

"What do you mean how?"

"I mean how often the tape was recorded over."

"How could I, Dolan?" Her voice spiked. "You know how we got it."

"Yeah, yeah. Okay." He examined the tape, then leaned

over and slid it into a deck. Seconds later, the image of the woman in the room appeared on a monitor above our heads. Unlike normal TVs, the monitors in an editing suite have more lines and pixels, and render a sharper image. Though he hadn't done anything to the tape, the image looked better already.

We watched the scene play out. I'd seen it several times, but I was drawn in again. The woman's fatigue, the way she cased the room, the eagerness with which she greeted her killers—at least initially—was so familiar I could predict what she would do and when. It was discomfiting, as if I knew her in some visceral, fundamental way. I stole a look at Davis, but her face was impassive. Dolan was quiet, too, making occasional notes on a yellow pad, until we got to the scene where the gun went off.

"Who screened this tape?" he barked.

"I did," I said.

"So did I," Davis added. "And Deputy Chief Olson."

"How many times?"

Davis and I exchanged glances. "Twice, maybe three times."

"Who put it on pause?"

She frowned. "We all did. Why?"

He glared at me. "You, too?"

I nodded.

"*You* should have known better."

"What are you talking about?"

"See where it gets blurry?"

I squinted. Just as the gun was visible in the shot, the image *did* become slightly blurred. But you could only see it if you were looking for it. Dolan looked at me expectantly, shades of challenge on his face.

I stared at the screen, wondering what the hell he was talking about. Then I got it. "Shit . . . You're right."

Davis looked worried. "About what?"

I ran a hand through my hair. "When you put a tape on pause, the tape stops running, but the heads of the machine don't. They keep revolving. That causes friction on the tape where it's paused and can make the tape degrade. I should have remembered that when we were screening it."

Dolan dipped his head in acknowledgment.

Davis jumped in. "But we had to pause it. We were trying to identify the weapon."

Dolan pointed to the image on the monitor. "You should have waited until you brought it to me. Avoid any risk of damage."

Davis's mouth tightened. "I didn't know."

"Next time you will," Dolan said imperiously. He rewound the VHS and clicked on a few icons.

Davis and I exchanged another glance. I shrugged. "When do you start the enhancement?"

"After it's digitized." Two buttons on the monitor glowed red. "But we don't use that word *enhance*. We say *clarify*. Goes down better in court."

Ten minutes later, the digitizing was done. Dolan double-clicked on an icon, and the image, now in a digital format that could be manipulated more easily, popped up in a new window on the right. A second window popped up beside it. Underneath both windows was a bar with an icon that looked like a hamburger in the center. When he clicked on it, a new set of menus appeared on the left.

"What now?" I pushed my chair closer.

"Now we convert from time-lapse to real time." He explained that the machine would calculate the rate at which the tape had been recorded and automatically convert it to real-time motion. He typed in a couple of numbers, then clicked on the words *create and render*. When a new icon appeared on the left monitor, he hit Play.

Suddenly the Chaplinesque jerkiness was gone, and the woman on the tape was moving in real time. She entered the room naturally, sat on the chair, got up smoothly and switched on the light.

"That's unbelievable!" I blurted out.

"You're incredible." Davis leaned forward, her eyes locked on the monitor.

Dolan grinned. "That's what they all say the first time."

"I don't get it," I said, ignoring his crack. Video normally records and plays back at thirty frames per second. The tape of the murder had been recorded at a much slower rate—maybe five frames per second. But it was playing as if it had been recorded at normal speed. "Where did the extra frames come from?"

Dolan looked amused. "There aren't any. Essentially, the system figured out what rate it was recorded at and changed the playback speed."

I nodded. The image wasn't that much sharper, but because it was playing at normal speed, we were able to take in more. For example, I could tell the woman's T-shirt had some kind of logo on the front. The room seemed to be better defined, as well. As Dolan advanced through the video, I noticed something black and blurry streaking up one of the walls. "What's that?" I asked.

Dolan paused and played with more menus. The image came into focus. "It's a crack."

Davis peered over my shoulder. "A big one." Zigzagging from floor to ceiling, it looked like a bolt of lightning that had somehow been captured and imprisoned.

"Happens in houses with weak foundations." Dolan rubbed his hands together and looked my way. "You see that anywhere?"

"Sorry. No."

"Okay. Let's take a look at that shirt. Clothes are one of the biggest identifiers we have." He stopped the tape, and played with more menus.

"What are you doing now?" Davis asked.

"Making a freeze frame of the scene. Actually ten seconds of a freeze frame. Then I'll put it on the time line and magnify it."

A moment later we were looking at a still image of the woman, much larger than the original. Though her face was turned away from the camera, her T-shirt was visible. But the logo was still murky; it looked like a smudge of dirt.

"Hold on." Dolan traced an electronic square around the

smudge and dragged it to the other window. "This is a target box." He clicked on the left-hand monitor, where yet another series of menus appeared. "The effects pallet," he explained. "With filters you're not gonna believe."

He pulled down several menus with words like *sinc* and *catrom*. As each filter was applied to the target box, gradually the smudge condensed and gathered together. The image became brighter and sharper until finally, the mark on the shirt was visible. An arrow. No, more like a check.

"A Nike logo!" I breathed.

Davis couldn't take her eyes off the monitor. "You pulled that image out of nowhere!"

"Yup." He flipped to the before and after shots. A smudge. Then the logo. The difference was dramatic. He laced his hands behind his head and gave us a smug smile.

"There's only one problem," I said.

"What's that?" Dolan asked.

"There's about a hundred million people on earth with the same shirt."

"So let's keep going," Davis challenged. "Find something else."

"Pushy broad." Dolan grinned, it wasn't as smug. "First lemme make you a photo of the shirt. You want a Polaroid or CD?"

She paused. "A Polaroid. For now."

He pushed a few buttons. The color printer on the monitor stand whined and slowly spat out a still.

"What about when the woman looks up at the camera?" I asked. "Can we get an enhanced—I mean clarified—shot of her face?"

Dolan advanced to the scene in which the woman looked up at the camera. Again he created a freeze frame, magnified it, then dragged a target box over her face. After a few minutes with the effects palette, we saw her face more clearly. She looked young. About Davis's age. Huge dark eyes, even darker circles rimming them, pale skin where it wasn't bruised or swollen. Dark, wavy hair framed her face. I wondered if she was foreign. Hispanic maybe.

I felt Davis watching me. "You're sure you've never seen her before?" she asked.

"I'm sure. I would have remembered." I touched my forehead. "The eyes."

"What about the location? Anything familiar about the room?"

"Nothing." I studied the shot of the woman again. Something was marring her face. Something subtle around her mouth, which was slightly open. What was it? I leaned forward. "She's missing a tooth!"

Dolan leaned forward, too. "Damn!"

"Let's see." Davis squinted at the monitor. "Hey, you're right. What's the name of those ones in front?"

"Incisors," I said.

She nodded, made a note, then said to Dolan, "Gimme a shot of that." Dolan ran off a print and handed it to her. She motioned with her free hand. "Let's check out the intruders."

Dolan selected a shot of the men, but after working on it for over an hour, we came up empty. The killers' clothes were nondescript—no Cubs hat or other identifiers, and the ski masks hid their faces. The big man's mask had dark circles around the eye and mouth holes, but Dolan said there could be thousands of masks like that. It could be red, he said, with blue markings. Or maybe the reverse. The other man's mask was solid—black, probably—and his hair was long and stringy.

"What about the limp?" I asked. "The big guy's?

"What about it?" Dolan snapped.

His wheelchair suddenly seemed to fill the room. "I—I—can you tell anything about it? Where he might be injured, for example?"

"Other than his right leg, no. Could be his knee. Or hip. Who knows?"

Dolan concentrated on the gun. Although he couldn't get a make on it, he was sure it was an automatic. "You can see the slide." He pointed to an area inside the target box. "Could be a Sig."

As the tape ended, Davis slumped and stared at the screen, her earlier enthusiasm gone. I felt drained, too.

"What do you think she was doing there?" Dolan asked after an uncharacteristically thoughtful silence. I wondered if it had gotten to him, too.

"Waiting," Davis answered.

"For what?" he scoffed. "The bus?"

She shook her head. "Whatever it was sure as hell wasn't what she got."

A sour taste rose in my mouth. No one should get what she did. I started to turn away from the monitors, when Dolan let out a sharp cry. "Look!"

Jericho raised his head. His dog tags jangled.

I spun around. We were at the end of the tape, and the woman was splayed across the floor, one arm above her head. Blood was seeping across her shirt. The scene looked the same as before.

Dolan pointed. "There! On her wrist."

I squinted. This time I could make out a dark area on the inside of her wrist. It looked more like a shadow than anything concrete. If Dolan hadn't pointed it out, I would have never noticed it.

"I'm gonna check this out."

Again, he froze, magnified, and sharpened the image, but there seemed to be an urgency to it this time. Even Jericho lumbered over to see what was up. Ten minutes later, a new image popped up in a window.

Davis and I crowded in to look.

"It's a tattoo!" I said. Dolan nodded. Davis seemed to be holding her breath.

"What is it?" I asked.

"Looks like a torch," Dolan said. "With some stars around it." He traced the image with the arrow from the mouse: a long, conical base with wavy lines rising up from the top. It looked a little like the torch on the Statue of Liberty without the disk in the middle. Just above the flames were two five-pointed stars. It was a small tattoo, probably no bigger than two inches, but the design had been carefully inked.

"Is that some kind of gang symbol?" I asked.

Davis hiked her shoulders. Dolan shook his head.

"You'd think the Latin Kings would have a crown," I said.

"What are you talking about, Latin Kings?" Dolan growled.

I looked over. "I don't know. I kind of—well, I thought she might be Hispanic."

"Hispanic . . . Italian . . . South American . . . Foreman, there are more gangs in Chicago than rats in New York City." Dolan sniffed. "And that doesn't include the imports." He rubbed a finger across his mustache. "But I'll bet you one thing."

"What's that?"

"If it is gang-related, Davis here'll figure it out."

ELEVEN

IT DIDN'T HURT *the night they got the tattoos. Of course, the liberal amounts of vodka they'd anesthetized themselves with might have helped. They hadn't planned it in advance; Arin had no intention of leaving the base with Mika. It was just another lonely evening, their husbands off on maneuvers. The men were always off doing something. The life of an up-and-coming Soviet army officer was busy.*

Arin couldn't complain. She was living a life of luxury: perfume from France, music from America, shoes from Italy. She drew a silk scarf across her face. The soft material kissed her cheek. Her husband was a lieutenant at the Vaziani base in the republic of Georgia, and her father-in-law was the major general. She could have anything she wanted.

But trinkets and privileges didn't make up for Sacha's absence. How many times had she reached for him at night, only to feel empty air instead? How many days had she spent weighted down with an ache in her heart? If she'd known how much time they'd be apart, perhaps she wouldn't have been so quick to leave Armenia.

Mika poured out the last of the vodka. Arin tossed it down. Funny, she never thought she could be friends with a real Russian, much less marry one. Her parents had taught her to be wary: Russians were uneducated, uncultured, and violent. Godless, too. Then again, everyone was godless to Arin's mother. She still said her prayers every morning.

But Sacha wasn't like other Russians. Neither was Mika. She and Arin had much in common: both plucked from their homes by their men—Mika from Moscow, she from Yerevan; both young and pretty, Arin dark and lithe, Mika a sturdy blond. Mika's eyes were slightly crossed, and she had a small scar on her lip that she covered with cosmetics. Arin never found out how she got it.

Then there was Vladik, Mika's husband. Like Sacha, he was a lieutenant. Were it not for the pale eyes that sharply contrasted with his skin and dark hair, Arin might have thought him a black Russian. Her mother used to sniff that the royal house of Georgia was descended from Africans; why not Russians, too? But Vlad never talked much about his family, and Arin didn't know what part of Russia he was from.

Tonight Mika and Arin were restless. Her father-in-law, who expected Arin to dine with him when Sacha was gone, was off at some conference, and her mother-in-law was visiting family back in Russia. Major General Dimitri Yudin was an important man, often attending meetings in Geneva and Brussels, especially now that Gorbachev was pushing for arms control. So Arin and Mika had dinner together and shared stories of how they'd met their husbands.

Arin had met Sacha after the 1988 earthquake. Her aunt, a doctor, asked her to volunteer at the hospital after the quake struck the northern part of the country and claimed 25,000 lives. The Soviet army rushed troops in for disaster relief, but poor food and lack of field sanitation had caused mass illnesses among the men. The rescuers had to be rescued.

The first time she saw Sacha, she knew he was the one.

He was pale and weak and nearly delirious with fever, but she couldn't look away. With his blond hair and fair skin, so different from her dark, Gypsy looks, she thought at first he might be a fallen angel. It was only when she felt hot and cold at the same time and her insides grew wet and slippery that she realized, angel or Russian, she wanted him.

She spent all her time at the hospital, sponging him with cool cloths when he was sweating. Covering him with blankets when he shivered. Forcing him to drink the water they'd shipped in from Turkey. When he tossed and turned, occasionally groaning or murmuring words she didn't understand, she sat on the edge of his bed and soothed him.

Finally, the fever broke, and he opened his eyes. Arin had never seen such deep pools of blue. She continued to visit every day, bringing oranges and cakes from home, once in a while a piece of chocolate. She chattered about school, her friends, her family. Eventually, he was strong enough to go for walks. She took him down the tree-lined boulevards of Yerevan, pointing out the volcanic tufa that made the buildings pink. Showing him Mount Ararat, which you could see from almost any spot in the city.

It was during their walks that Sacha started to talk. He didn't want a career in the military. He was a musician, and he wanted to play in a rock band. To become as famous as the Stones. Arin grinned. She loved Mick Jagger. She had a bootleg cassette of Tattoo You. *It was one of her most prized possessions.*

As Sacha got stronger, they ventured farther, sometimes taking the bus to the parkland on the city's eastern edge. Each day they sat closer together, and one day, his hand casually grazed hers. The next day, he pinned her behind one of the monuments and kissed her, long and deep. When she could breathe again, she kissed him back. The next day she took him into an abandoned church not far from the hospital. They were married four months later.

Now, caught up in the memory, Arin smiled and started humming "Start Me Up," the first track on Tattoo You.

"I know that song," Mika said thickly. She was stretched out, half drunk, on the floor.

Arin explained. It was their song, hers and Sacha's. She would sing or hum it whenever she wanted Sacha to touch her. To "start her up," she'd sing in broken English. Usually he would comply.

"Tatuirovka? *Tattoo?" Mika asked.*

"Da."

Mika rolled over and pushed up to her elbows. "Now that is an excellent idea."

Arin tilted her head. "What?"

Laughing, Mika rose unsteadily to her feet. "Put on your shoes and come with me." Her eyes shone. "Do not worry. The men will love it."

A few minutes later, she and Mika were en route to Tbilisi, forty kilometers away. Their ride dropped them off at the top of a cobblestone street in the old city. Tottering in flimsy shoes, Arin clutched Mika's arm as they stumbled down the rise. Sacha said the old city was supposed to look like Paris—whatever that looked like. Here, though, someone's laundry was strung across a porch. You wouldn't see that in Paris, she was sure. "Where are we going?"

"A place that Vlad knows."

Arin frowned. Vlad was a charmer, but there was something wild and dangerous about him. Sometimes she caught him staring at her with those pale blue eyes. But just as she would begin to say something, he would break into a crooked smile and make some wonderfully funny comment or joke. He was a born leader, Sacha said, a soldier who knew how to dangle the carrot as well as the stick. He could be ruthless, particularly when it came to dyedovschina, *the fierce hazing of new recruits. But the men in his unit were devoted to him, and Mika said he would rule the world one day. She was only half joking.*

As they passed narrow buildings separated by even narrower streets, Arin's head felt light and spongy. She hoped they didn't have far to go. Thankfully, Mika turned into an alley and stopped at a dimly lit shop. Arin could just make out pictures, cartoons really, tacked to the shop's window. Across the alley was a video parlor, featuring the latest titles from Japan. Next to it was a seedy-looking souvenir shop. A radio somewhere was playing sad music.

The man who opened the door eyed them suspiciously, but after Mika explained, he grunted and swung the door wide. Arin was troubled by the gritty, dingy look of the place, but Mika seemed at ease, and Arin was too drunk to pick a fight. After negotiating the price—Mika could talk anyone into anything—she lay down on the table and unbuttoned her blouse.

She and Arin had decided on the design on the ride into town. The tattoo would include two stars on either side of a flaming torch. Arin remembered seeing the same design on some of the soldiers' arms. When she asked Sacha about it, he said Vlad had come up with it. The two stars represented the stars on a lieutenant's shoulder board. The torch symbolized fire. Fire was a powerful, masculine energy, Sacha had said. Uncontrolled, it was destructive and unpredictable, but when it was used properly, it could vanquish anything. Just like the soldiers in their divisions. But she wasn't expected to understand, Sacha added. She was just a woman.

But Arin did understand one thing. A tattoo would mark her as his. Forever. And that was what she wanted. When it was her turn, she rolled up her sleeve and lay on the table. Squeezing her eyes shut, she ignored the sting of the needle, imagining instead how she would reveal the tattoo to Sacha. She would wear a long-sleeved sweater until bedtime. Then she'd slowly draw it over her head and flick her wrist toward him. She'd ask him to kiss it, maybe salute it, too. Then they'd make love. Fiery, passionate love.

She smiled to herself. If he liked it—and she was sure he would—maybe she'd get another. On her left breast next time. Just above her heart.

TWELVE

By the time Dolan made Polaroids of the tattoo, it was after two. I shrugged on my parka while Davis gathered up the tape and photos and slipped them into evidence bags. She and Dolan made their way across the living room, chatting about invoices and next steps. As we reached the front door, Dolan nodded in my direction.

"You're okay, Foreman."

I tried not to let on how pleased I was. "How long have you been doing this?"

"About three years."

"Only three? You seem to know—"

"I was a cameraman in Nam. Back when we still shot film. Shot the siege at Khe Sahn with an Arri-16."

"By yourself?"

"I had a sound man, but one morning he walked across an open stretch of ground to take a leak and got hit in the face by a sniper round."

I wondered whether that was why he was in a wheelchair.

As if he was reading my mind, he went on. "I made it back to the world and started shooting local news." Jericho came up to his chair. Dolan fondled the dog's ears. "But life's a bitch, you know? I make it through the Tet offensive, come home in one piece, and then get my leg blown off in a goddamm gas main explosion in Harvey." He shook his head, as if he were still puzzled about the whole thing.

I gave him my hand. "I'll think of you the next time I have a nine-hundred entrance fee."

He grinned as we shook. "Gotta keep out the riffraff."

I waited for Davis outside. The temperature seemed to have risen a few degrees, and the faint scent of wood smoke hung in the air. "You want to grab some lunch?" I asked when she joined me. "I saw a place around the corner on Touhy. Greek Isles."

She hesitated a fraction too long. "Sorry. I—I don't have time."

"No problem." I shoved my hands into my pockets. "Listen, thank you for letting me come. I know what you can do with video, but that system really takes it to the next generation."

She nodded.

"So what happens now? We have a Nike T-shirt, a woman missing a tooth, and a tattoo of a torch and stars. Do you think we—"

She cut me off. "*We* aren't going to do anything."

"I—I didn't mean—"

"Look, Ellie, this ends. Right now. I wanted you here because you do know something about video, and I thought, with a better image, there was a chance you'd recognize the woman. Or the location. But you've got to leave it alone now. Let me do my job."

I had a vision of myself as somebody's maiden aunt, an interfering, pesky busybody you tolerate, but just barely. Was that how Davis saw me? We walked to her car. "But you do think the tattoo is significant, don't you?"

She opened the Saturn's door, deposited her briefcase, and slid into the driver's seat. "Ellie, I'm going now."

I leaned into the space between her seat and the door,

reluctant to let go. Part of it was the camaraderie. Once Dolan got over his attitude, the three of us had worked well together. I didn't want it to end. But there was something else, too. A nagging feeling, perhaps a piece of information that I knew and needed to share with Davis. The problem was I couldn't dig it out of my memory.

"Ellie." She grasped the door handle. "I have to go."

I straightened up. Whatever it was would come. "Okay. But, listen—if you need anything . . ."

"I know where to find you."

The car door slammed shut, and the engine turned over. I trudged back to my car. Narrow rivulets of water from melting snow trickled down Dolan's driveway. I wondered who did his shoveling. A neighborhood kid? Or one of the landscaping services that turn into snowplow businesses during the winter months? Fouad, my Syrian friend and sometime gardener, says he makes better money in winter, just by hooking a snowplow to his truck. The secret, he claims, is the cost of labor. The Mexicans he hires each summer go back home from November through April, so he pockets pretty much all of his revenue.

I got to the Volvo and fished out my keys. Mexican gardeners, Greek restaurants, Russian cleaning ladies—the North Shore was becoming an international crossroads these days. I pictured Peter Lorre and Sidney Greenstreet slinking around the backstreets and alleys of Winnetka. I smiled It would never work. The fez would be a dead giveaway.

I opened my car door, thinking about hats, white suits, and foreign intrigue. Then I stopped. A man in a Russian-looking hat had been staring at my house the other day. Driving the cleaning ladies' van. When he realized I'd seen him, he fled. And Rachel had said a van was involved in the delivery of the tape. I spun around.

Davis was pulling away from the house. I ran after her, waving my arms. "Wait!" I cried. "Hold on!"

Her brakes squealed, and the Saturn lurched to a stop. She rolled down her window.

"Officer Davis . . ." I panted as I caught up to the car. "Remember what Dolan said about imports? You know, gangs from other parts of the world?"

She blinked. "Yeah?"

"Well, that would—I mean—that could include Russian gangs, couldn't it?"

"Anything's possible."

"I think you should follow me home. There's someone I want you to meet."

WHEN I WALKED into Lillian Armstrong's kitchen, it was clear why she needed a cleaning lady. A tower of dirty dishes balanced beside the sink. Torn HoHos wrappers littered the floor. Open cartons of Chinese take-out, their contents congealed and gummy, lay on the counter. A dirty ashtray sat on the table, the butts smeared with lipstick. The sharp odor of ammonia cut through the residue of stale cigarette smoke. Two cats streaked out of the room as we entered.

I wanted to take a blowtorch to the place. Instead, I crossed to the window. "Would it be okay if I opened this?"

Lillian shrugged resignedly, as if I were an irritation she was obliged to endure. She and I didn't have what you'd call a "neighborly" relationship. In fact, in the five years she'd lived next door, this was the first time I'd been inside her house. The day she'd moved in, she made sure to tell me how she wouldn't be around much, since she spent summers at her cottage in Michigan and winters in her Florida condo. Glancing around now, I was glad she'd been true to her word.

A heavy woman with thinning blue hair, she wore a quilted red robe and matching slippers. Despite some tautness around her cheekbones, the result of at least one face-lift, pockets of flesh sagged under her eyes, and a wattle seemed to be growing under her chin.

She took a drag off her cigarette. "You're lucky you

caught me." She addressed herself to Davis, who stood at the kitchen threshold as if taking another step would land her in a DMZ. "I had to fly up for a doctor's appointment. Then I got the flu."

Given the organisms that were likely proliferating in her house, I was surprised it wasn't plague.

"I won't keep you too long, ma'am," Davis said. "I just have a couple of questions. Do you engage a cleaning service, Mrs. Armstrong?"

Lillian gazed around, as if noticing the detritus for the first time, and nodded. "They do a lousy job, don't they?" She sighed. "But then, what can you expect?"

Davis didn't reply.

"Not one of them speaks a word of English," she went on. "And they don't know the first thing about cleaning. How could they? They were milking cows or picking potatoes two weeks before I got them. And the turnover. I get a different one every week. I just get 'em broken in, and there's a new one." She rolled her eyes. "I've been thinking of changing services."

"I'd like the name of that service, ma'am. And the number."

"Is there a problem?"

"No, ma'am. Just a routine check."

Lillian stubbed out her cigarette in the ashtray. A curl of smoke hovered over the kitchen table. "If they're illegal, I don't know a thing about it, see? All I do is hire them. I don't ask for their green cards."

"We realize that, ma'am."

Lillian arched her eyebrows, as if she expected Davis to tell her exactly what she did know, but Davis had her game face on. "When does the service come?"

"As a matter of fact, they'll be here tomorrow."

None too soon, I thought.

THIRTEEN

When I looked outside the next morning, Davis's red Saturn was parked at the curb. She was huddled in the front seat, holding a cup with the familiar green logo on it. I'd assumed she would call DM Maids yesterday, after we left Lillian's, but she shook her head when I brought it up.

"I call now, I warn them we're looking for something. They'll circle the wagons, and I get nothing. I'll meet the van tomorrow morning." She added, "By myself."

Now I made a pot of vanilla coffee and poured myself a cup. Coffee is one of the few domestic things I do well. I thought about offering to freshen hers, but, recalling her admonishment not to get involved, I refrained. I did test the waters with a wave as I took Rachel to school, just to see what would happen.

Not much, it turned out, though Rachel merited a smile.

"What's Officer Davis doing here, Mom?" Rachel asked.

"It has to do with that tape that was dropped off the other day."

"The one I don't want to know about?"

"That's the one."

"Oh. By the way, the U.S. Field Hockey Association is coming through Chicago this weekend, and they're having a demo at Soccer City. Can I go?"

"I don't see why not." I turned onto Sunset Ridge Road. It had sleeted overnight, and a thin layer of ice coated the street. I drove carefully. "How'd you find out about it?"

"I was surfing the Net. And guess what."

I flicked on the windshield wipers. "What?"

"They're having this camp over Presidents' Day weekend, and I sort of asked—well, I e-mailed someone and they wrote back, and said if I—"

"Whoa," I cut in. "What did you do?"

"They're gonna let me scrimmage with some of the players at the demo on Saturday, and if they think I'm good enough, they might let me into the camp."

"Oh, they might, might they?"

"Yeah." She shot me a look. "So, what do you think, Mom?"

A truck thundered by in the opposite direction, spewing clumps of wet snow across the Volvo's windshield. I turned the wipers on high. "Assuming you get in, who's going to pay for this camp? And, by the way, where is it?"

"Virginia Beach."

"The East Coast?"

She flashed me a hopeful smile.

With her blond curls and blue eyes, my daughter doesn't look that much like me, but our personalities were becoming uncannily similar. She was already finagling, manipulating, trying to order the universe to her liking. And it probably rankled her—as much as it did me at her age—that she still needed an adult to supply things like money and permission and plane reservations.

On the other hand, field hockey was an activity any parent should want to encourage. A teenage girl running around a field outside for hours—what could be wrong with that? It was healthy, it kept her out of trouble, and the pride she'd feel if she did make the camp was one of those affirmations the Character Ed people at her school say every kid deserves. I pulled into the school's parking lot.

"Tell you what. If you get in, I'll call your father. Maybe we can work something out. An early birthday present or something."

"Thanks, Mom!" She beamed as she got out of the car.

I blew her a kiss. If that's what it took to make her happy, I'd call my ex five times a day.

I was nursing a second cup of coffee back home when a white van rolled up Lillian's driveway. The side door slid open, and a woman climbed out. I recognized the frayed coat and tired walk. It was the same woman as last time. Apparently, there was no turnover this week.

The driver's door swung open, but the man who jumped out wasn't short or squat. Nor was he wearing a fur hat. Bundled up in a hooded green parka, this man was tall and beefy. I put down my coffee. I should tell Davis it wasn't the same man. She shouldn't waste her time. But before I could throw on my coat, she was out of her car.

She waited until the driver had escorted the woman inside Lillian's house before intercepting him. As he headed back to the van, she flashed her ID at him. The man froze, then slid one hand into his pocket. Panic spilled over me. What did he have in his pocket? I lunged for the phone.

Davis stood her ground and shifted, but kept her hands near her sides. The man's hand came out of his pocket with what looked like a driver's license.

I put the phone back on the base.

Davis took the license, pulled out a notepad with her other hand, and started scribbling. I could see her lips move, but the man's responses were limited to an occasional nod or shake of his head. Not much of a conversation. A few minutes later, the driver hurried back to the van, hoisted himself up, and pulled away. Davis shoved the pad back into her pocket and started toward her car. I went outside and caught her just as she opened her door.

"It wasn't the same man," I said.

"I gathered that," she said dryly. "He said he's new on the job."

"Did he say what happened to the other guy?"

She shook her head. Then, as if suddenly realizing I wasn't a cop or anyone worth sharing information with, she gave me a brisk nod and lowered herself into her car. "Have a nice day Ellie. And no, I don't need any help."

Driving down to Cabrini Green that afternoon, I automatically locked the Volvo's doors before realizing I didn't have to anymore. For nearly thirty years, Cabrini, one of Chicago's public housing developments, was synonymous with gangs, drugs, and violence. People driving into the city avoided Division, the street where Cabrini was located, and it wasn't a stop on any sightseeing tour.

In the mid-nineties, though, the cluster of buildings known as the "reds," the "whites," and the "rowhouses" were slated to be torn down. Quickly. Most of them were. One day there was urban blight; the next day it was gone. No one needed to ask why. North of the Loop and west of the Gold Coast, Cabrini was prime Chicago real estate. With the right kind of development, the land would generate major bucks. So the residents moved out, Starbucks moved in, and acres of luxury housing rose from Cabrini's ashes.

There was one exception. A smattering of low-income housing was figured into the plan, no doubt to relieve the city's guilt at relocating thousands of people. Twenty-four low-rise units were put out for bid, and Feldman Development snagged the job. Ricki Feldman proceeded to build four small apartment buildings on a narrow street near Division and Sedgwick. Construction was nearly complete when she announced that one of the buildings would be donated to Transitions for foster-care graduates. In a few weeks' time, some lucky young people would be living practically rent-free in a sparkling new Chicago apartment.

I slowed as I turned onto the street. Just when I thought it was safe to dislike Ricki Feldman, she did something, well, almost noble.

Jordan Bennett, his shoulders hunched against the cold,

waited as I parked the car. He rubbed his hands together, as if the leather gloves he was wearing weren't doing much good. He probably got them in L.A. I wound my scarf around my neck and crossed the street. He grunted and led me inside.

Mac and the crew were already setting up. We'd decided to shoot B-roll inside the empty apartment and do an interview with Jordan. Then we'd come back in a few weeks to film the young people moving in. That would allow us to create a nice before-and-after sequence—from scenes of an empty apartment to the same shots of the apartment full of people, furniture and hope.

Mac Kendall is the black sheep of his family. His relatives come from places like Winnetka, Barrington, and Lake Forest, but he lives in a small house in Northbrook. Even more appalling, at least to his family, is the fact that he actually works for a living. He began by shooting weddings, graduations, and Bar Mitzvahs, but has since built up a thriving corporate business. We met when we were both working for local TV and were assigned to cover a story about graft in the restaurant business. We've been working together ever since.

He was setting up lights when I walked in. Lean and rumpled, with shaggy brown hair, he'd been growing a neat Van Dyke beard. Much to his chagrin, though, it was coming in equally gray as brown. A wicked-looking scar on his left cheek deters most people from messing with him. It also hides the fact that he's one of the most gentle, sensitive men I've ever known.

"Hey, Mac, how goes it?"

He grunted, too. Must be the weather. Chicago winters have a way of making you conserve your strength. He finished bouncing a light off the ceiling, then pulled out his exposure meter. Fifteen years ago you needed a crew member just to light a set, today most people shoot with available light. Except Mac. He uses lighting to create a specific mood. It takes time to set up, but the results are worth it.

I wasn't sure what he was going after today: a bright, cheerful eight o'clock morning? Muted afternoon light? Or maybe a limbo-type scene with faces appearing out of a dark, undefined background? Over the years, it's become a game: I try to figure out his intention from the angle of the lights, the scrims, and filters. When we've discussed it in advance, it's a no-brainer, but other times, like today, he keeps me guessing.

"Okay," I said. "We're going for a bright, hopeful look. Ten o'clock in the morning. Springtime. Right?"

Mac pushed his hair off his forehead. "Close." He favored me with a smile. "First day of kindergarten. Cheerful. Clean. Nothing but possibilities."

"I like it."

Once he was satisfied with the lights, we laid down a variety of shots: establishing shots, pans, moves, a few passes on a dolly. Then we reset the lights in the hallway for the interview with Jordan. I ran him through the questions, and he answered smoothly, basically repeating our conversation in his office. When we were done, Mac shot cutaways.

It was after three by the tune we finished. We still had a few minutes before the light began to fade—winter afternoons in Chicago merge into dusk without warning—so Mac shot some exteriors, including few tracking shots of Jordan walking into and out of the building. I watched as Mac directed, telling Jordan where to start, stop, and which side of the door to enter. It occurred to me, as I watched the child of privilege working for the child from foster care, that the universe has a way of balancing the scales.

"Okay." Mac looked up from the viewfinder. "That's a wrap."

As Mac and the crew broke down the equipment, Jordan crossed the street. He looked like a kid who's been given everything he wanted for Christmas. "This is really gonna happen, isn't it?"

"What do you mean?"

He slipped his hands into his pockets and grinned. "I've

been working on this for a long time, Ellie. We came close once or twice, but something always fell through. Now, though—well, we're really doing it, aren't we?" He glanced toward the building, his breath rising in the air like little clouds of hope.

I grinned back. "Yes, Jordan, we are."

"Thank you."

"It wasn't me. Thank Ricki."

"But you're helping. You know, sometimes I feel like this is all a dream."

"Well, then, let me be the first to pinch you."

He laughed. "Careful what you do to this dude, sister."

Mac said he'd strike window dubs with time code tomorrow, so I started home. Traffic was already stop-and-go on the expressway. I inched forward behind a moving van that emitted a gassy smell. My mind was still full of the video.

It should enlighten and teach, but it should also settle uncomfortably in the gut. Viewers should see these kids teetering on the rim between success and failure; they should feel the precarious tightrope they walked. After watching the video, people should hug their own kids, grateful not to have to grapple with the same issues. Yet they should be motivated to do something—even a token act. A donation, a phone call, a letter would mean we'd succeeded.

A gauzy filter of dusk descended over the highway, and headlights flashed on. The kids should tell their own stories. The camera should look into their souls, capture their hopes, frustrations, and dreams. Minimal narration. No voice-over, either, except maybe Jordan's, for perspective. Lots of close-ups, warm lighting, quiet music. Maybe some jazz that could sound cheerful or mournful by turn.

I checked the time. Thirty minutes had passed, and I was still two miles from the junction. I turned on the radio, realized I didn't want to hear any noise, and snapped it off. I glanced at my cell, lodged in a small compartment under the dash. I hadn't heard from David since last weekend. Ironically, I'd learned that Transitions got its start after one of the founders saw a documentary about a similar program in Germany. Too bad the budget wouldn't support a trip overseas to check it out. David and I could have gone together, he to check out the letter, me to do research. I'd have flown eight hours—in turbulence—for the chance to put the sense back into our relationship.

It was after five in Philadelphia, but he usually works late. I punched in his number. His secretary picked up. "Mr. Linden's office."

"Hi, Gloria. It's Ellie."

"Oh, hello, Ellie."

"Is David there?"

"Er . . . no, he isn't." She sounded surprised.

"Oh, do you know when he'll be back?"

"He didn't say. But I'm sure it'll be at least a week or ten days."

"A week or ten days?"

"Don't you think so?"

"Gloria, where is he?"

She hesitated. "You don't—he didn't—" Usually Gloria likes to chatter. She's always asking about Rachel and my father and when I'm bringing them east to meet her. Today she sounded cautious.

"No."

"Ellie, David's gone to Europe. He caught a flight yesterday." My stomach twisted. "He flew over to Frankfurt." She sounded uncomfortable. "Then he's going to Antwerp. But I was sure he'd—"

I clutched the cell. "Gloria, do you have his itinerary?"

"Ellie, I'm sorry. I don't. He wasn't sure where he'd be when. But I'll certainly let him know you called."

FOURTEEN

THERE ARE TWO types of people in the world: those who eat when they're upset, and those who don't. I'm one of the former, and Susan Siler, my closest friend, is one of the latter. Fortunately, she was feeling pretty chipper the next morning, which made for a fortuitous confluence of circumstances. We met at Walker Brothers on Waukegan Road, where I packed away half of the richest, sweetest, most calorie-dense apple pancake east of the Mississippi.

"You know what the worst part is?" I stirred my coffee. A wood-paneled eatery with surprisingly soft lighting, the placed radiated a patina of elegance, unusual for a pancake house.

"Other than his leaving the country without telling you?"

A tall, slim redhead, Susan seems to lead a flawless life. She's married to a stockbroker who's also active in village politics, and she has two kids, neither of whom are juvenile delinquents. She works part-time in an art gallery, and has such an innate sense of style, she could wear a hospital gown and look chic. The most embarrassing thing I know about her—aside from the fact that she accidentally broke her daughter's collarbone—was that she threw up a spaghetti dinner on a church altar when she was twelve. Thirty-some years later, she still doesn't eat tomato sauce. Now, she finished her sliver of pancake, pushed her plate away, and delicately wiped a napkin across her mouth.

"The worst part was his secretary," I said. "She didn't know David didn't tell me. The poor woman was embarrassed as hell."

Susan eyed me, then sipped her coffee. "You realize that David still has a lot of work to do, since he found out who he was."

"You mean who his father was."

She nodded. "It wasn't that long ago."

"I know, but—"

"The calendar doesn't specify deadlines for dealing with grief or anger or acceptance. And family issues cut right to the core."

"I thought I was helping cushion it for him. Helping him get through all the . . . the confusion."

"He's got to do it himself. You know that."

"But what if . . . after he gets through it . . ." I fumbled, suddenly finding it hard to breathe. "What if he decides—"

"What if he decides he doesn't want you to be a part of his life, whatever that life turns out to be?"

A waitress scurried by, balancing a tray of eggs, waffles, and pancakes. I nodded, not trusting my voice.

Susan chose her words carefully. "It's true you were the catalyst for his discovery. Without you, he would never have known who he was. He could have some residual feelings."

"Are you talking about a 'blame the messenger' thing?"

"It's possible."

"Susan, I couldn't bear to lose him. He's welded to my soul. The connection's so powerful, there are times I can sense when he's thinking about me." I looked out the window. A heavy, gray cloud cover stripped the color out of everything. "If that connection were severed, I would live in a perpetual winter."

"He's got to work it out for himself," Susan repeated softly.

I went quiet. Then, "at least it's not another woman."

Susan didn't answer.

"Well, that's something, isn't it?" When she still didn't answer, I said, "Hey, good friend. This is the place where you're supposed to say don't worry about it, Ellie. It will work out. Love conquers all."

"I hope it works out, Ellie. You know I do."

The waitress came over and asked if I was through. I looked longingly at the rest of the pancake and sighed. "I'm done."

"You want a doggie bag?"

When I hesitated, Susan arched an eyebrow.

"I—I guess not."

The waitress took our plates and promised to come back with the check. I leaned my elbows on the table. "Susan, something happened the other night that made me wonder if there were other things involved. Besides family issues."

"What other things?"

"I don't know. It wasn't anything he said. More like what he didn't say. As if he was going to tell me something, then changed his mind. It occurred to me that there might be some unresolved things from his foster care days."

"Such as?"

"I'm not sure. Maybe some kind of abuse. Physical, sexual, mental—I don't know."

"If there are, it would explain why he's so anxious to trace his roots." She dipped her head. "You know. To disown what happened. Convince himself it was an aberration. Not something 'real family' would do to each other."

"Do you think the video I'm doing on foster kids might be acting as a prod? You know, motivating him to step up his search?"

"I thought the letter from Germany triggered it."

"Yeah, you're right. I guess. I'm just trying to find reasons. I folded my hands. "I wish there was something I could do."

"And you have to do *something,* don't you?" She tapped a finger against her chin. "I suppose you could talk to someone who has some insight into foster kids."

"A shrink?"

"I would think there are similar patterns of behavior among people who have unresolved issues about their parentage."

"You sound like Genna." Genna Creger, a friend of ours, is a social worker.

"She may know someone."

"I'll take it under advisement."

The waitress brought us our check. Susan shifted. "So, what else has been going on?"

I told her about the tape that was dropped off at my house.

"How awful!" She gave me a sympathetic frown. "What did you do with it?"

I told her how I'd given it to Davis, how we'd looked at the tape at Dolan's.

"But you still don't know who the woman was?"

I shook my head.

"Or where it took place?"

"No. And I'm a little nervous about it."

"Why?"

"Because. You know. I don't want Rachel to be in any kind of jeopardy."

"Why do you think she might be?"

"The tape wasn't what you'd call family entertainment. And whoever dropped it off knows where we live."

She rolled her eyes. "What is it with all these X-rated scandals on videotape?"

"What are you talking about?"

"It just seems there's a lot of it floating around these days."

"Huh?"

"It's not as grim as what you've been dealing with, but it is kind of—well, telling."

"What is?"

"The Wooddale tape."

"The what?"

She leaned forward. "Wooddale. The neighborhood in Glenview no?" When I shrugged, she added, "You haven't heard?"

"I never hear anything—except from you."

Susan explained that last summer a middle-aged couple left their Wooddale home for an extended vacation. While they were gone, a group of teenagers broke into their house and trashed the place. When the couple returned, they quickly discovered who was responsible and filed a suit claiming invasion of privacy. Once the lawsuit was filed, however, a videotape mysteriously surfaced and was circulated around the North Shore. The tape showed the wife, dolled up in a cheerleader outfit, performing certain acts on her husband.

"No!" I squealed. "You lie!"

Two people in the next booth turned around.

"God's honest truth. Apparently the kids who broke into their house found it, stole it, and made dozens of copies." She settled into her seat. "The couple dropped the suit a few days later."

"You're kidding. They dropped the suit?"

She nodded.

"They shouldn't have done that!"

"The kids? That goes without saying—"

"No. The couple. Why did they drop the suit?"

"Clearly, they were mortified. Humiliated. They even put their house up for sale."

"But they would have won! It's the worst kind of voyeurism. What judge would rule against them?" I scooped up the check. "Did you know the average American is captured on videotape at least six times a day? At the mall, the bank, the ATM . . . No one respects privacy anymore. And yet it's supposed to be a constitutional right, even if it's a woman dying alone, or a couple cavorting in their own house. Someone's got to take a stand."

Susan's face got that distant look it often does when I rant.

"We've finally succeeded in living vicariously. Trading reality for illusion. Sex. Murder. Violence. Watch it on TV. Rent it at the video store. Copy it for your friends."

"If you feel that strongly, maybe you should find another way to make a living."

I grunted, paid the check, and headed out to my car, pondering the relationship between videotape, privacy, and cheerleading outfits.

FIFTEEN

A BROODING SKY blanketed the forest preserve as I jogged across Voltz Road that afternoon. I told myself I was atoning for this morning's pancake, but I knew I was trying to outrun my anxiety. David *always* tells me when he'll be traveling, even when he isn't going overseas. The fact that he hadn't this time made me a little queasy.

Back home I showered, thoughts of him still overwhelming me. I remembered taking a shower one day last fall. I'd been lathering up facing the spray and didn't hear David step in. His arms had circled my waist from behind. I turned around and drew soapy circles on his chest. He pulled me close, and we made love, the water cascading around us, slippery white bubbles gliding off our skin.

Now, I yanked off the water, dressed, and headed downstairs. Maybe I'd run over to Mac's and pick up the window dubs. But as I headed out, Davis's red Saturn pulled up to the house.

"You remember the driver you described the other day?" she said when I intercepted her. No greeting or preamble.

"The guy who was checking out my house?"

She nodded. She was wearing jeans, a turtleneck, and thick black boots.

"Yeah."

"You think you'd recognize him if you saw him again?"

I thought about it. A bearish man whose face looked too big for his build. Worried expression. Brown coat and a fur-lined hat. I nodded.

"You busy for the next couple of hours?"

Twenty minutes later we pulled into an apartment complex in Mount Prospect. The farther away from the lake you go, the flatter everything gets, as if the architecture has been forced to mimic the land it sits on. The Loop has Sears Tower and its Mies van der Rohe skyscrapers, the near suburbs their Frank Lloyd Wright homes. But farther and the roads are west, structures seem to squat close to the ground, and the roads are dotted with stubby boxes that look like they've been squashed by giant lids.

The development we turned into consisted of a large parking lot ringed by seven identical one-story buildings, differentiated only by white numbers on their facades. Walkways led up to each one. Davis pulled into a space in front of number five. I assumed we were going inside, but she made no move to climb out of the car.

"What are we doing?" I asked.

"We're waiting."

"For what?"

She pointed to the building on our left. "DM Maids is over there. I paid them a visit yesterday. Or should I say her." She flashed me a look. "A woman named Halina Grigorev owns it. She's originally from Russia. Been here twenty years."

Another Russian.

"She pretty much stonewalled me about the driver. His name's Milos Petrovsky. She said he blew out of town. Disappeared. The 'here today, gone tomorrow' type, she claimed."

I wasn't sure how to reply. Davis had never been this forthcoming. "You don't buy it?"

"It's bullshit. I've been keeping an eye on the place, and a guy fitting the description you gave us has been in and out twice. I need you to confirm it's the same guy."

"How long are we going to sit here?"

"Why? You have plans?"

"No."

"Good." She lapsed into silence, and we waited. Thick dark clouds overspread the sky, and pellets of sleet and snow spit down. The inside of the car windows steamed up. Every so often, Davis turned on the wipers and cranked up the heat. Then she would lean back and close her eyes, only to snap them open at the whine of a car engine. Meanwhile the asphalt beneath us disappeared under a coating of snow, and a muffled quiet descended.

An hour later as dusk was falling a white van pulled in and parked in front. The van door opened and closed with a thud. Davis came instantly alert. "Look alive, Ellie. Is that the guy?"

I wiped my sleeve across the inside of the windshield. The man who had climbed down from the van was short. He was wearing a brown coat and a large fur-lined hat. "That's him."

"You're sure?"

"I'm sure."

I waited for Davis to get out of the car and confront him, but she didn't move. In fact, for the first time since I'd known her, she looked uncertain. While she deliberated, Petrovsky disappeared inside.

"You're not going to question him?"

"I am. But not here."

"Why not? He's probably bringing in the day's receipts. They'll have to settle up. You have time."

"I—this isn't the right . . . setting."

"What do you mean?"

She blew out a breath. "Look, I don't want to screw this up. The truth is I have no reason to approach him. He hasn't done anything. He's just finishing up work, for Christ's sake. If I show up, and he's got any brains at all, he won't tell me a goddamned thing, and I'll have to let him go." She shook her head. "Then I end up with nothing."

"So what's the plan?"

She didn't answer at first. Then, "I'd like to—well, it'd be nice to get Mr. Petrovsky into a situation where he'd be more—cooperative."

"What kind of situation?"

She didn't say. A few minutes later, Petrovsky came out, pulling his hat low across his brow. But instead of going back to the van, he fished out some keys from his pocket and unlocked the door of a black Buick two cars away. Davis wiped the inside of the Saturn's windshield and jotted down the plate number, then switched on the ignition.

"What's he doing?" I asked.

"I don't know. He's never switched cars before."

"What are you going to do?"

Davis hesitated. "Follow him. Maybe he'll get into trouble. Or something that looks like trouble." She threw me an appraising glance. "Except . . ."

"What?"

She stared through the windshield at the swirling snow. Then she sighed. "Nothing. It can't be helped." She seemed to be talking to herself more than me.

Petrovsky started the Buick and pulled out of the lot. Davis backed out and swung the wheel left. The car went into a skid. "Fuck." She muttered under her breath.

I belted myself in.

SIXTEEN

Following a car in the middle of a snowstorm at twilight is not an easy task. A blustery wind tossed the snow around in bursts. Traffic was slow, and the streets were already clogged with fender benders. An occasional red-and-blue Mars light pierced the gloom. Still, Petrovsky was pushing it five miles above the limit. Must be all those Russian winters.

Rand Road runs generally south and east, except for a few sharp angles. Petrovsky plowed down for a few miles, then turned off, ending up on Northwest Highway—the same one that runs through Park Ridge. The snow intensified, and eddies of white, illuminated by the Saturn's headlights, almost obscured our view. Even Petrovsky slowed to a crawl.

While Davis concentrated on her driving, I dug out my cell and called home. Rachel was making soup.

"Katie's coming over to do homework," she said.

"Her mother's bringing her over in this?"

"Her feet work just fine. And she's got boots."

Her one-liners were starting to remind me of Dad.

"They're out of hot chocolate, and I told her she could take some of ours. Oh, by the way, Dad called." It took me a second to realize she meant Barry. "He was returning your call. He said he was sorry he didn't get back to you sooner."

My ex-husband and I got divorced, at least in part, because I didn't like the people we were becoming: defensive, mean-spirited, and petty. But we'd been on unusually good terms recently. I wasn't sure why; I hoped we were finally achieving a degree of rationality. Even maturity. "I'll call him when I get home. But it won't be for a while." I looked over at Davis.

"No prob. I'm cool. See ya later, Ma."

As I dropped the cell back into my bag, Petrovsky braked hard and turned right into a parking lot.

Davis braked, too. The Saturn fishtailed, then skidded to a stop. "Roll down your window," she ordered.

A blast of icy air swept through the car. She craned her neck and looked past me through the window. A green-and-blue neon sign on the side of a small frame building read: "Celestial Bodies—A Gentleman's Club." The letters *D, I,* and *E* in *bodies* sputtered. The Buick nosed into a space directly underneath the sign. Petrovsky climbed out.

Davis drove a few yards past the lot, then made a U-turn, provoking a chorus of angry horns. She U'ed again, swerving in back of a snowplow that was spewing out streams of salt. She snapped on her turn signal, but by the time there was a break in traffic, Petrovsky had disappeared. She pulled into the lot, parked five spaces away from the Buick, and cut the engine.

"I want you to stay in the car." She looked over. "I'll leave the keys so you have heat."

I peered at the neon sign, the seedy building, the blinding snowstorm. "I don't know where we are or what we're doing. All I know is that I'm outside some strip joint in a strange place in the middle of a blizzard. If you think I'm gonna stay in a car by myself, you're nuts."

She looked like she wanted to argue the point. Then she squinted through the windshield. Someone was coming around the back of the building. It wasn't Petrovsky—this man was big and husky, although the heavy parka he wore might have added to his bulk. Still, he wasn't the kind of man I'd want to meet in a dark alley. Or parking lot. He flicked a lit cigarette into the snow and headed over to a Blazer parked near the Buick.

Davis watched him open the door and slide inside. The wipers snapped on. When the Blazer's windshield and rear window were clear of snow, he backed out.

"You think he saw us?" I asked.

"I don't think so."

"Who is he?"

"I'd lay odds he's the bouncer."

"How do you know?"

"You see the size of him?" Her eyes slanted sideways. Then she sighed. "Okay, you can come. But stay close to me. And don't say one fucking word. You hear?"

We climbed out of the car. A surge of raw, biting air stung my face and snatched my breath away. The Hawk was out tonight. I followed Davis to the front of the building. She shoved her shoulder against a thick metal door. It gave an inch, but she had to push again before it opened.

We entered a large shadowy room, illuminated by disco balls on the ceiling. About twenty tables were grouped around a makeshift stage, but no one was sitting at them. A brass railing curled around the edge of the stage. To the left was a bar, a portable affair that looked like it had been hastily added. I wondered what Celestial Bodies had been in an earlier incarnation. A furniture showroom? A hair salon?

Speakers hung from the walls on either side of the stage, but the faint instrumental music filtering out wasn't coming from them. It seemed to be coming from the back. It sounded like something from *Zorba the Greek.*

Two women, one blond and one with long hair so black it couldn't be natural, sat on the stage, their legs dangling over the edge. Dressed in bathrobes, they smoked cigarettes and chattered in a guttural language that might have been Russian. Their faces looked green in the light.

My eyes were still adjusting to the gloom when the blond stood up and ground out her cigarette on the stage. When she spotted us, Davis started forward, navigating the narrow space between tables. Davis's jeans were tight, and her hair was down. The blond ran her tongue around her lips.

"We close now," she said in a thick accent, but her interested expression hinted that something could be arranged.

Davis cleared her throat. "I just want to talk."

The woman pouted.

I took a step forward. The blond was older than I first thought, in her late thirties, maybe even forty. The one with the black hair was younger but had a glazed, vacant look. I wondered what she was on.

Davis brushed snow off her jacket. "I'm looking for the man who just came in."

The women exchanged blank glances. Was it possible they hadn't seen him?

Davis must have been thinking the same thing. "Short. Big hat. Brown coat?"

The blond shrugged. "Many men in and out. But not now. We take break."

Davis kept her gaze level. "He came in, not five minutes ago." When the woman still didn't reply, she said, "Well, then, would it be okay if I took a look myself?" Bracing her arms on the stage, she ducked under the railing and swung herself up.

The blond blocked her path. "You no go."

Davis pulled out her badge and flashed it at the woman. "Ma'am, I'm a police officer."

The blond gulped down air. Taking a cue from her companion, Blackie scrambled to her feet.

"Where are you going?" Davis said. Blackie froze. Davis eyed her. "If you were thinking you might yell out a warning or something like that, well, that probably wouldn't be a good idea."

The two women exchanged looks. The blond looked in my direction.

Davis followed her gaze. "She's with me." She looked back at the women. "Like I said, I hope you don't mind if we take a look backstage." The blond didn't answer. "It would be even nicer if you 'escorted' us," Davis added.

The blond hesitated, then started tentatively across the stage. Blackie followed. Davis brought up the rear. Halfway across, she looked at me over her shoulder.

I hung back, not at all sure I wanted to explore the bowels of an unfamiliar building with strangers. But Davis was a cop. She must know what she was doing. I swung myself up under the railing and fell in behind.

Backstage reminded me of one of those seedy Vaudeville theaters you sometimes see in movies. I caught a glimpse of a birdcage, a feathered boa, manacles, and something that might have been a trapeze. We passed through a door on the right, which led to a hallway. The women, padding in white socks, stopped halfway down at a closed door. The music was louder here.

Davis proceeded to the end of the hall and looked around. "Back door," she muttered. Was that for my benefit, or was she checking it out for herself? She came back down the hall. "What's in there?" She pointed to the closed door.

The blond shrugged and knocked.

A high-pitched female voice replied in a stream of incomprehensible language. We didn't need a translator to hear her peevish tone.

Davis answered in English. "Police, ma'am. Open the door."

The music stopped, and it suddenly grew very quiet. Davis's hands slipped to her sides. Then the door slowly opened, and a woman stuck out her head. Another blond, her hair was piled high in a twist. Heavy makeup surrounded blue eyes. She wore a flowered Oriental robe sashed at the waist. Large, fuzzy pink slippers covered her feet.

"Da?" Like the others, she had an accent.

Davis flipped open her badge.

I could have sworn the woman flinched, but it was subtle,

and I could have been wrong. In any event, she recovered quickly, and her lips parted in a smile. Gold flashed in her teeth.

"I'm looking for a man who just came into this—this building." Davis described him.

"No men. You see?" She swung the door open, then leaned against it, sliding her sash through her fingers. "Just us girls." Her smile broadened as she caught sight of me. "You pretty girl. You want come in and see Sofiya?"

Davis answered, "She's with me."

The woman cocked her hip. "That's okay. I very sexy. They give movie contract me almost."

A rush of heat streaked up my spine, but Davis seemed unperturbed. "Ma'am, you do realize you're speaking to a police officer, don't you?"

Sofiya's smile dimmed. She gestured for us all to enter. The women from the stage, whose trepidation seemed to have melted away once they realized Davis wasn't out to bust them, flocked to a sofa, eyeing us with curious glances. I hung back near the door.

The room had been cobbled together into a crude dressing space. Two bathroom mirrors hung on a wall. Someone had thrown up a strip of theater lights on top. Underneath was a makeshift vanity covered with hairbrushes, lipsticks, and other cosmetics. Clothes were piled everywhere—on the couch, on chairs, spilling onto the floor. In one corner was a rack of skimpy costumes with lots of sequins, spangles, and rhinestones. A dozen pairs of glittery high heels lay on a rack below. Most of the costumes were shabby and threadbare, and a musky female scent permeated the rack.

"What's your full name?" Davis asked Sofiya.

"I Sofiya Cakars." She cranked up the wattage on her smile. If it grew any wider—or more brittle—her face would crack. "What this man do?"

Davis shook her head. "I just want to talk to him." She glanced at the other women. "Ask them if they've seen him."

She said something in what I assumed was Russian. The

women shrugged. "They no see." Sofiya faced us. "They know nothing. I here four years," she said proudly. She looked over at me. "You see sign? It say 'Sofiya and the Angels.' "

I hadn't, but I nodded.

She nodded back, apparently satisfied. Then she turned the radio back on. Slow, mournful music spewed out. Her voice dropped to a stage whisper. "They good girls. They do nothing bad. Just dance." She nodded vigorously, as if that might convince us to agree with her. "But no people come tonight again." She looked out a small barred window. "Too many snow."

"You're here alone?" Davis asked.

"Manager get dinner."

"Look," Davis said. "I'm not here to give you any trouble with immigration. And I don't give a shit what you're snorting or smoking or shooting. I just need information."

As Sofiya translated, the remaining tension in the room dissipated, and the women on the couch relaxed. Sofiya's mood changed, too. Her smile faded, and a calculating look came into her eyes. I sensed that beneath her affectations was a hard-nosed businesswoman.

Davis pulled out a Polaroid of the woman on the tape and handed it to Sofiya. "Do you recognize this woman?"

Sofiya's mouth tightened as she studied the photo. Then she looked at Davis with what I took as genuine distress—witnessing death tends to sober you, even if it's just a snapshot after the fact. She shook her head, and passed it to the others. The blond winced and uttered a soft exclamation, but Blackie, the one who was stoned, looked at it dispiritedly and passed it back without comment.

Sofiya said something sharp to her in Russian, making me think the girl might be a problem in other ways besides drugs. As Blackie launched into what must have been, from her tone, a defense of some kind, a fourth woman appeared at the door. She wasn't more than a few feet away, but she didn't appear to notice me. Probably because I was wedged up against the wall.

Another blond with short, spiky hair—someone probably told them American men preferred blonds—she was wearing faded jeans and a denim shirt, mostly unbuttoned. Gold tassels hung from her nipples. She was painfully thin, and her eyes were slightly crossed. She looked like she might have been pretty once, but time had flattened her features. The women in the room, while not acknowledging her presence, didn't seem concerned by it, either.

"There's something else I'd like you to see," Davis said. Standing at an angle to the door, she didn't see the new arrival and pulled out another photo. I recognized the tattoo on the dead woman's wrist.

Sofiya took a look at it, then passed it on. This time, no one spoke. Or looked up. When Sofiya finally did, she looked at Davis, then me, then the wall. Everywhere—it seemed—except the woman in the doorway.

"Well?" Davis asked.

Sofiya shook her head.

"What about the others?"

The women shook their heads, but one of them threw a furtive glance at the woman with the tassels. Davis didn't catch it.

"What about the design? You ever see these stars and flame before? Maybe not on a tattoo, but something else? A paper, a coin, a piece of clothing?"

As Sofiya translated, the woman at the door started to fidget. Her eyes darted around the room, and the rapid rise and fall of her chest made her tassels swish. When her gaze landed on me, she froze for an instant, her eyes wide. Then she edged away from the door, turned around, and hurried down the hall.

A buzz skimmed all the nerves of my body.

Davis was distributing business cards, her back still to the door. "Something comes to you, anything at all, you call me. The girl in this picture was young, you know? Someone should pay for her death."

She still hadn't seen the woman in the doorway. I shifted. I wasn't supposed to get involved; Davis specifically ordered me not to. But this woman appeared to know who I was. Shouldn't I find out how? What if she had something to do with the tape? A tide of conflicting urges swept through me. Davis didn't want me to interfere, but if I didn't follow the woman, we might miss a huge opportunity. I stole another glance at Davis. Her back was to me. I peered down the hall. I slipped out the door.

The woman was working her way to the backstage door.

"Hey, you," I called. "Wait!"

She whipped around. Panic shot across her face.

"Don't go!" I raised my hand in the air. "I—I need to talk to you!" She paused and turned around for a moment, like a bird hovering in mid-flight. It occurred to me I had no idea if she spoke English. I thrust my hand into my bag, which was slung over my shoulder. "Look . . ."

She recoiled, turned around, and sprinted through the door. Damn. She thought I had a gun. "Wait! It's my card. My business card!"

But she didn't stop. I started after her, but she'd already ducked out of sight. I hurried through the backstage door after her, trying to figure out which direction she'd taken. I guessed left and tentatively started across the stage.

Another door slammed somewhere in back, and a man's voice cut through the air. Then a woman's—it had to be hers—in low, urgent tones. A second man's voice followed. Petrovsky? Had he been here the whole time? Before I could think it through, the door slammed again. Moments later the whine of a car engine floated through the air.

I stopped. I should go back to the dressing room. Tell Davis what happened. She'd want to know about the woman—and the men whose voices I'd heard. I started to creep back across the stage, trying to stay in the shadows, hoping no one would see me.

Halfway across, the footlights slammed on, and a deep, male voice bellowed out. "Stop!"

I stopped.

"On your knees!"

I dropped. I tried to make out who was there, but the glare of the lights blinded me. A large beefy man hurled himself onto the stage. The man who'd taken off in the Blazer. Except this time he wasn't leaving. He was heading straight toward me, and he was pointing a gun at my head.

SEVENTEEN

The wind moaned fitfully as it whipped through the walls. I didn't move. I hardly breathed. But my heart was pounding so loud, I was sure he could hear it above the wind.

The man jammed the gun against my forehead. "Don't move!"

He had the same accent as Sofiya. I tried to focus on his tone and inflection, thinking I might gauge his mood, but a woman's voice overrode him. High-pitched. Jittery. I snuck a look. The woman with the tassels stood at the edge of the stage. Our eyes met. She looked away. The man with the gun wedged it farther into my flesh.

"Please. Could I explain—"

"Shut up! Look at floor!"

I bent my head. The man snarled something, all the while keeping up a steady pressure on the gun. The woman closed in and helped herself to my bag. She pawed through it, and made a triumphant exclamation, as she pulled out my wallet. More conversation as she flipped through the plastic sleeves. She stopped at one and squinted. In broken English, she recited, "Eleanor Foreman. Two, four, nine . . ." Then she lapsed back into Russian. I recognized the first three digits of my social security number. She was reading my driver's license.

The man with the gun barked out a command. The woman looked doubtfully at me at first, as if she wanted to argue, but then reconsidered. Stuffing the wallet back into my bag, she tossed it on the floor and retreated. A door slammed. It was quiet again.

My heart kicked in my chest. Where was Davis?

"Now stand," he ordered.

I struggled to my feet, still unable to see my assailant. But I felt him. A rough hand patted me down, fumbling with my sweater, jeans, even my boots. Apparently satisfied I didn't have a weapon, he grabbed my arm and shoved me forward. "Move! But keep head down."

I couldn't tell for sure, but I thought we were heading back across the stage. The important thing was I wasn't dead, and that fueled me with hope. Then his fingers dug into my arm. I stopped and looked up. A huge face, too close to register features, leaned into mine. A greasy, almost chalky odor came out of his mouth. Almost as if he'd been eating fries. From McDonald's.

"Talk now," he growled. "What you doing here?"

I felt the gun prodding my temple. "We were looking for the man who just—"

He cut me off. "We?"

Shit. Me and my big mouth. I'd just tipped him about Davis. His grip tightened, and the gun inched closer to my skull.

"Who is 'we'?"

Sweat dripped from my neck. I squeezed my eyes shut, fully expecting a white light to explode any second.

Suddenly, the sounds of a scuffle broke through behind us. Footsteps raced across the stage, and several voices shouted at once. Then a clear female voice rang out. "Police. Drop the gun. Now!"

The gun remained wedged against my temple, but I thought I felt a slight release in pressure. I saw a pair of boots, police issue, on the floor in the middle of the stage. Behind them was a pair of fuzzy pink slippers. Two pairs of socks appeared behind them.

"I said, drop it. Now!" Davis shouted. "And keep your hands where I can see them."

Nothing happened. The gun was still against my forehead. His other hand still clutched my arm. No one moved or spoke. Even the wind was silent. It crossed my mind that the last face I'd ever see might not be Rachel's or Dad's or even David's, but the face of a man with french-fry breath in a strip joint in Des Plaines.

Then the man took in a breath, and blew it out slowly. He grunted, and the gun clattered to the floor.

I sucked in a ragged breath. Davis was crouched in a shooter's stance, both hands gripping her automatic, which was leveled at my attacker. Sofiya and the other two women huddled behind her. I hurried over. The women opened up a space and let me into their midst. The man's hands shot up in the air.

"That was a smart decision," Davis said to him. "Now move away from the gun."

The man glowered but did what she said. Davis inched forward, and keeping her gun on him, picked his up, and stuffed it into her waistband.

"Well, now, it looks like we're all gonna live another day." She edged to the back of the stage, where the women formed a tight knot around me. "Let's go. We're done here." Keeping the gun trained on the man, she lifted her chin. "You. Don't move until we're gone."

The man tilted his head, a quizzical expression passing over his face. But whether that was because he didn't understand English, or because he expected more trouble, an arrest maybe, or a trip to the station, I didn't know. Frankly, I didn't care.

Davis motioned for me to move. I crept across the stage,

dropped to the floor, and headed for the front door. Davis followed, slowly backing away. When she reached the door, she lowered her gun.

"I'll be sure to note how cooperative you were in my report."

EIGHTEEN

If it wasn't on the North Shore, Solyst's, our village watering hole, would be a seedy place. But up here, nothing is "seedy"—it's "casual." Solyst's is further redeemed by a stone chimney and fireplace which, tonight, was blazing cheerfully. Because of the storm we had our pick of tables. Within minutes we were well into a pitcher of beer.

Davis took a long swig. "The asshole's got to be wondering why I didn't run him in."

"Why didn't you?" I wolfed down a fried mushroom. They were greasy and not at all filling, but I was hungrier than I'd ever been in my life.

She stared into her beer as if the answer to my question was in the hops and foam. "Because I screwed up."

"How?"

"I shouldn't have been there."

"What are you talking about?"

"It wasn't my turf. I barged in like a frigging rookie. No backup. No heads-up to the locals. And with a civilian, for

Christ's sake." She hunched her shoulders. Worry lines pinched her brow.

"Why didn't you call for help?"

"I didn't think we would need it. I mean, hell. There was a blizzard outside. Who's gonna be out in that? And then, well, things happened so fast . . ." She shook her head.

"You're forgetting one thing. You saved my life. That was no screwup."

She poured more beer into her glass. "I know you're trying to make me feel better, but that's not the way it works."

I tilted my glass toward her. She refilled it. "How does it work?"

"If it gets out, Olson might not let me out on patrol. Hell, I'll probably be bounced back to the desk."

"But don't you have to write some kind of report?"

She nodded. "I have to send his gun in to property, too."

"Huh?"

"Every gun we recover gets checked to see if it's been used in other crimes." She sighed. "The problem is explaining how I got it. Once I lay it out, they'll—"

"Do you have to—lay it out for them?"

"What do you mean?"

"I mean, do you have to tell them exactly what happened out there?"

"What are you suggesting?"

"I was the one who forced you into the situation. I should never have followed the girl in the first place. I should have told you about her. Let you handle it."

"Yeah. But I should never have had you with me in the first place."

"Well, then," I said, "I guess we both screwed up."

She eyed me curiously. "You have every right to tell Olson what happened, you know. Even if I get suspended."

"I'll remember that. But I think I lost his number."

She shot me another look, then went to the bar. I wondered what she was going to say on her report. I decided not to ask.

"I gotta hand it to you." She came back with another pitcher. "You were pretty cool in there."

I laughed, grateful that I could. "It was an act."

"Yeah?"

"I was paralyzed. I couldn't have moved if I'd wanted to." I picked the crust off another mushroom and pushed the plate toward her. She took a bite of one, then screwed up her face. I pushed them away. "But I am concerned about one thing."

"What's that?"

"The woman with the tassels took the license out of my wallet. She knows where I live."

She frowned. Then, "They don't have any reason to come after you."

"How do you know?"

"There's no guarantee, but don't forget, we know where to find them. They know that. They'd be crazy to try anything."

"I wish I were as confident." I paused. "So, what is your take on Natasha and Boris and the others?"

"Natasha and . . . ?" Her face clouded for a moment, then cleared. "Oh." She shrugged. "What I'd like to know is what happened to Petrovsky."

"I heard a door slam and a car start right before it all happened," I said. "I was thinking he might have been making a break for it."

Davis shrugged again.

"They could have been protecting him."

"Who?"

"The women. Or some of them. The Buick was gone when we left."

"Why would they need to protect him?"

"I—I don't know."

"Because he dropped off the tape at your house?"

It was my turn to shrug. It did seem flimsy. I changed the subject. "Does that mean you think Petrovsky did drop it off?"

"Hard to say."

"Rachel said it was a van. And he was staring at my house a few days later, like he was wondering who I was and what had happened to the tape. And then, when we followed him—well . . ."

"Logic isn't evidence."

"Not even circumstantial?"

"Not even close."

I studied my glass. "I'd sure like to know who Tassel Woman is. The way she looked at me—it was as if she knew me."

Davis grimaced. "The shit they're on, some of those women wouldn't recognize themselves in the mirror."

"She was straight. I could tell."

Davis didn't say anything.

"So what happens now?"

"I'll file my report. Talk to Olson. With any luck, he'll send me back out there with another cop. Or maybe he'll have the Des Plaines cops check it out. Or maybe he'll tell me to call it a day."

"Take you off the case?"

"You gotta admit it's looking thin. All we have is a weird look from a guy driving a van. And another weird look from a woman in a strip joint."

"And the tattoo. And the location."

"Neither of which we know a damn thing about."

I scooted my chair closer to the table. "What about the tattoo? You making any headway on that?"

"I talked to our guys who do gang work, and they told me to call downtown. I have a call in to them. I called the Bureau, too. A guy over there's looking into it."

"The FBI?"

"Yeah."

I recalled my dealings with an FBI agent last fall. I poured more beer into my glass.

"The guy doesn't know when he can get to it, though. Other priorities."

"Do you think anyone at Celestial Bodies knew the woman on the tape?"

"No way to tell without more canvassing."

"So we're basically back where we started?"

She sipped her beer.

"Which means I nearly got my head blown off for nothing."

She looked down.

"You know, there's something I don't get. If everything is so vague, if we really don't have any solid information, why did the guy pull a gun on me?"

"You really are from a different world, aren't you?"

"What's that supposed to mean?"

She stared into her glass.

"What are you saying?" I repeated. "That they're Russian mafia or something?"

"I don't know why people dignify them with a name. It's like giving them an—an honor, a respect they don't deserve. They're scumbags."

"I don't know. From what I read, the Russians make the Italians look like nursery school kids."

"They're all assholes," she said. "But the—the Eastern Europeans, the Russians, have an edge. They'd sooner waste you than reason with you. You look at them wrong, it's over."

I shivered, thinking how close I'd come to being one of the wasted.

"We were lucky." Davis nodded, as if she knew what I was thinking. "Why do you think the women didn't tell us shit? They knew what would happen to them if they did."

I recalled Sofiya's smile, toothy but empty. "All those stories about white slavery, women being forced into prostitution. Is that what we saw tonight?"

"It's what they do. They lure girls out of villages and spin all sorts of stories about the life they're gonna have in the West. They tell 'em they'll start out as maids or nannies, but then, who knows? Models, movie stars, rich husbands. The girls, all dirt poor and naive, eat it up. They can't wait. Then they get here, or Germany, or wherever they're going, and find they've been turned into whores."

She sniffed. "They weed out the pretty ones and send them to the strip joint."

I thought back to the women who cleaned my neighbor's house. Their lined faces and rounded shoulders. None of them were young. Or pretty. "So why don't you bust them—the girls, I mean? Wouldn't that get them away from these creeps?"

"As soon as they're out, they'd go back. Most of 'em are on drugs, anyway. And the ones who aren't don't have any money. Or clothes. The pimps even take their passports." Davis shook her head. "These are men who throw women out of third-story windows. With other people watching."

"Oh, come on."

"True story." She swilled down more beer. "Guess it does make the Outfit look warm and fuzzy, huh?"

"So why don't the police go after the pimps? Or are they too busy going to Dunkin'—" I stopped short. I'd almost forgotten who I was talking to.

"As a matter of fact," she said, ignoring my crack, "the pimps'd like nothing better. They love our jails. They get fed, they get clothes, they even get a fucking lawyer. Compared to their country, it's heaven."

I reached for another mushroom, took a bite, and folded what was left into my napkin. "Do you think the woman on the tape was one of them? A prostitute?"

"And got killed because she said something to the wrong people?"

I nodded.

"Beats me."

Two men with red cheeks came into the tavern, shaking snow off their jackets and boots. They gave us a once-over, then sat at the bar. Their conversation, louder than it had to be, was filled with bravado about four-wheel drives and antilock brakes.

Davis drained her glass. She was throwing them down pretty fast. I wondered if she was as looped as I was. Then she set her glass down, leaned back, and squinted at me, as if she'd just noticed I was there. "You don't like cops much, do you?"

I thumped my glass on the table.

"I bet you were one of those protestor types, weren't you? The ones who called cops pigs. What . . . did someone beat up on you during a protest march?"

I shook my head.

Her eyebrows shot up.

It was cold and late, and I was too drunk to prevaricate. "I was caught shoplifting once." I launched into the story. Even though it was five years ago, the disgrace, the humiliation, rolled over me like it was yesterday.

She listened. Then, "Scared straight, huh?"

"I guess." I looked at the floor. You could see how uneven it was. How it sloped down from the middle of the room.

"Man, I wish there were more like you. The streets would be a whole lot safer."

I looked up. She was grinning. I swirled the last of the beer in my glass. "Yeah. That's me. Citizen of the year."

She laughed.

"What about you? Why'd you become a cop?"

Her smile faded. After a long moment, she said, "You ever see the movie *Monster's Ball*?"

"The one where Halle Berry has an affair with Billy Bob Thornton?" I paused. "I saw it. But he's a prison guard, not a cop."

"Not that." She waved her hand. "There's this one scene, in a bar, I think, or maybe a really small grocery store, and there's this sign in the window that says: 'Georgia is peachy.' You remember that?"

"Maybe."

"Yeah? Well, I always thought that's where I came from."

"I don't understand. You thought you were from Georgia?"

"When I was a baby, my mom always used to sing that Ray Charles song, you know, 'Georgia on My Mind'?

Then afterward, after she split, I thought I'd . . . well, maybe she went back there, and I'd try to . . ." Her voice trailed off. "Hell, what did I know?" She lapsed into silence. Her eyes had a haunted look.

I kept my mouth shut. She hadn't answered the question. Then again, maybe she had.

NINETEEN

They knew it *was coming. There was plenty of warning; the Berlin wall in '89, the Velvet Revolution in Czechoslovakia, a more violent one in Romania. Still, no one thought it would spread to the republics. They were intrinsic parts of the whole, not appendages that could be lopped off at will.*

But when the Baltic States started to make noise about independence, a subtle tension came over everything. Arin could feel it on the streets of Tbilisi. Perhaps not a tension, she corrected herself, but a stirring. A subdued energy. She saw it on faces; no longer listless and stoic, but expectant. Even hopeful. As if they were about to cast off a burden.

At the Vaziani base, though, soldiers still went out on maneuvers, officers ran through drills. Her father-in-law, the major general, kept going to international conferences, bringing back words of reform, not revolution. Everything would settle down, he claimed, when the economy improved. And there were many, he said, Westerners included, who wanted to help with that improvement.

Arin wasn't reassured. She heard the hushed talk over

bottles of vodka late at night. Saw the uncertainty during the day. She felt as if they were all dangling over a cliff, like those American cartoons where you saw someone's legs spinning in the air before they fell.

Then, after a turbulent year during which the Soviet flag was lowered from the Kremlin for the last time, there was no more denial. The unthinkable had happened: The Soviet Union had collapsed.

That first winter, the streets were full of passion and hope and infinite promise. By spring, that sense of possibility spread to the base, when it was announced the Russian army would replace the Soviets. For the Russian officers already in the military, it was an emotional moment. The Red Army, once a proud symbol of Russia's might, would once again assume its rightful place among the great militaries of the world. What's more, the new president of Georgia had close ties to Russia, and the two countries had signed a treaty allowing Russia to maintain its bases in Georgia. The future looked bright.

For Arin life went on in much the same way. She spent her days largely unconcerned about geopolitics and world events. She was still the wife of an important young army officer, with all the attendant privileges. Indeed, she had other matters to occupy her mind. She'd skipped her period twice now, and she was beginning to have nausea in the mornings. A trip to the midwife with Mika confirmed it. Arin was pregnant.

Deliriously happy when she broke the news to Sacha, only later did she realize he didn't seem quite as thrilled. Oh, he kissed her and held her and touched her, but, in retrospect, she realized his response was muted. She didn't dwell on it, though, and threw herself into ordering furniture from Turkey, linens from Armenia, baby clothes from the west.

As time passed, though, money began to be a problem. The rubles that flowed in from Moscow to support the troops slowed to a trickled, then stopped. Her father-in-law said it was temporary; once the transition was complete, all would be well. But as months passed with no money for salaries, equipment, or supplies, conditions on the base deteriorated. Soldiers, many of whom had not been paid in months, grew desperate. Some scrambled for odd jobs to support their families. Others left the base.

By July there wasn't enough money to pay the rent on their apartment, and Arin and Sacha moved in with his parents. Arin was bitterly disappointed. She and Sacha and the baby would share a cramped room; plans for the nursery would have to wait. Still, she tried to keep her spirits high. She was six months pregnant, glowingly healthy, and the baby kicked all the time. This was only a temporary setback. Once the money rolled in from Moscow—and hadn't the major general said it would?—life would return to the way it was.

But the money never came, and the number of soldiers abandoning the army swelled. The day that Vlad left, with Mika tearfully following him, was one of the worst in Arin's life. They were moving into town, Vlad said. They needed money to survive. Arin made Mika promise to stay in touch, but as days, and then weeks, passed without a word, Arin worried. Was Mika all right? Or was she angry at her, jealous, perhaps, that Arin was still on the base?

It wasn't long afterward that the stories surfaced: stories about supplies and materials disappearing from the base. In the beginning it was mostly uniforms and equipment, goods that could be quickly fenced. Soon, though, the rumors included small arms, grenades, and other munitions.

Everyone knew former soldiers were ransacking the armory, but the major general said it was an insignificant problem. A little of that was to be expected in any military organization. Though unfortunate, it was something that had been condoned for ages. Especially in hard times.

So Arin didn't dwell on it—until Sacha started spending long periods of time off base, not coming home until late at night. When she asked where he'd been, he'd say he was visiting Vlad. But he never seemed to have any news about Mika, and he never told Arin what Vlad was doing.

As his absences grew more frequent, Arin tried to convince herself Sacha wasn't involved in the thefts. He was an officer, the son of the major general. He never wanted an army career in the first place. He wanted to be a musician. Perhaps that was what he was doing off base. Trying to find work in a band. Musicians kept late hours, didn't they? Arin buoyed herself with the thought that any day now he would surprise her by becoming lead guitar in a band.

When Sacha began staying out until dawn, though, Arin knew something was terribly wrong. His sour breath and bloodshot eyes were bad enough. But now, for the first time since their marriage, he turned away from her in bed. Arin knew some men were afraid to make love to a pregnant woman, but Sacha had never seemed uncomfortable before.

She wondered if there was another woman—he was exhibiting the classic signs—but she was afraid to confront him. In the meantime, she vowed to get her figure back after the baby was born. She would not let herself wear the shapeless dresses and babushkas her mother-in-law did. Arin would stay young and beautiful and vital. Sacha would not need other women.

Tomas was born during a gentle morning rain the last week of October. Sacha wasn't home for Arin's labor and didn't see his son until a day later. Arin's mother-in-law attended the birth, all the while telling her about the pain she'd endured in childbirth.

But Tomas was robust and healthy, and he took to the breast right away. Her mother-in-law claimed babies didn't smile until they were six weeks old, but Arin knew better. Tomas smiled at eight days and stole Arin's heart. Over the next few weeks, as she regained her strength, Tomas became her only focus. Feeding him, bathing, rocking, walking. And if Sacha didn't seem very interested in his son—or her—Arin didn't mind. Tomas depended on her completely.

It was during their walks in a borrowed stroller that Arin noticed how ragged the base had become. Part of it was the frigid winter, but there was something else, too. No one was trying to keep up pretenses anymore. Even her father-in-law, a fastidious man with a crisply pressed uniform and well-shined medals, was looking disheveled.

A snowstorm swept in the night Sacha didn't come home, and they couldn't search for him until the next afternoon. When they did, they found his body at the end of an alley in Old Town. No one knew how he died, or if they did, they weren't saying. He'd been beaten, the police admitted, but they couldn't determine if that had caused his death. One of the officers tried to shift the blame back to the army, claiming Sacha died from dyedovschina, *the fierce hazing of new recruits. But Sacha had been an officer for years. Another officer tried to say it was suicide—a growing problem in the military—until he was apprised of Sacha's bruises and blows.*

Arin knew it was all a cover. She'd heard the rumors, whispered on the wind, about soldiers forced to borrow money from "commercial interests." When they were unable to pay it back, it was said, these commercial interests thought nothing of taking the soldier's life in exchange. In the wake of the government's collapse and the ensuing chaos, they had become powerful forces.

Curiously, the major general didn't pursue the investigation into Sacha's death. He skulked around the base, tight-lipped and morose, but he didn't intervene with the police. Nor did he assign any military investigators to the case. Arin assumed it was because of his grief. Sacha was his only child. Nothing could bring him back, he said. Why prolong the agony?

So Sacha's death was officially ruled a mugging. At first Arin thought it was better that way. Her memories would remain unsullied and pure. When they buried him, Arin placed her cassette of Tattoo You *in the coffin.*

She was surprised when Vlad came to the house after the funeral. She was more surprised when he and the general went behind closed doors. Then she recalled a conversation with the major general at dinner months before. He had said what a good officer Vladik was: strong, decisive, and smart. She'd had the feeling her father-in-law wanted Sacha to be more like Vlad.

Vlad looked relieved when he emerged an hour later. He even flashed her his crooked smile. Arin asked about Mika. Vlad said she was fine.

"She hasn't seen the baby yet," Arin said. "Please tell her to visit."

Vlad said he would pass along the message, and when he showed up again a few weeks later, Arin expected Mika to be with him. But Vlad was alone. After he spent another hour closeted with the major general, she walked him to the door. He seemed reluctant to leave.

"How are you, Arin?" His pale eyes bored into her. "You're looking well, you know."

She shrugged.

"I understand." He hesitated. "If you ever need anything, anything at all . . . all you need do is ask. You know that, don't you?"

She nodded, but as he gazed at her, a sense of disquiet washed over her. She felt like he could see her naked. She opened the door, eager for him to be gone.

As time passed, Vlad's visits became more frequent. Arin grew puzzled. What business did he have with her father-in-law? Why hadn't he come around when Sacha was alive? Something wasn't right.

She was strolling Tomas around the base one sunny day, a day that made her think the worst of winter was over, when she heard someone softly call her name. She spun around. Mika emerged from behind a tree.

Arin barely recognized her friend. Mika's clothes were dirty and tattered; dark circles ringed her eyes. Her blond hair was stringy, and Arin saw grime under her fingernails.

"I heard about Sacha." Mika embraced her. "I am so sorry."

Fighting back tears, Arin hugged her back. They stood with their hands on each other's shoulders. "What has happened, Mika?"

Mika shook her head but said nothing. Arin thought she might burst into tears. But then she bent over the stroller, and a smile broke over her face. "He's beautiful!" she cooed.

Arin dragged Mika back to the house. Her in-laws were gone for the afternoon and, after putting Tomas down for a nap, she made lunch for her friend. Mika wolfed it down, and as her stomach filled, her tongue loosened. Things were not well, she confessed. She and Vlad had separated.

Arin's hand flew to her mouth. "Why?"

"It doesn't matter," Mika muttered, but her face was shadowed with pain. "I—I have not seen him since . . . since before Sacha . . ." Her voice trailed off.

"Then you don't know he's been coming here."

"Vlad here? To the base?"

"He's been meeting with the general."

Mika's lips tightened.

"Why? What is it? What do you know?"

Mika bowed her head and told her. Arin felt as if an earthquake had suddenly torn open a hole in the ground, and she was teetering on its edge. But it was a quiet cataclysm. No one proclaimed the world had shifted. Still, as she struggled to take it all in, she knew her worst fears had been realized.

"Vlad made me swear not to tell," Mika said. "He said he would hurt me if you found out."

"He threatened you?"

"More than that." Mika looked down.

Arin shivered and put her arms around her friend. "What are you going to do?"

"I—I have been thinking I will go to America."

"America?" Arin's stomach clenched. "But it is so far away."

"I have a cousin there. She will help me."

Arin nodded. Money. Jobs. America was the land of opportunity. And Mika couldn't stay here. Vlad would destroy her. As he had Sacha. Arin laid her hand on Mika's arm. "Please. Do not go without saying good-bye."

Mika just looked at Arin.

Arin's eyes filled as she realized what her friend's silence meant. "Oh, Mika. I will miss you."

After Mika left, Arin dried her tears and started to clean the kitchen. Before Sacha died, when things were first coming apart, she'd suggested they move back to Armenia. It wasn't far away, there would be job opportunities for Sacha, and with the baby coming, she could use her mother's help. Sacha had refused. But that was then. This was no place to live, to raise a child. She could even smell the decay.

When Vlad showed up a few days later, Arin waited for him in the kitchen. He ambled in, wearing American jeans and cowboy boots, his jeans so tight, Arin couldn't help but think he wanted her to notice.

"You are looking beautiful, Arin." He shot her one of his smiles.

That was one of his weapons, she realized. That charming, crooked smile. She rose from the table. "You killed him!"

His smile faded. "Killed who?"

"Sacha. Maybe you didn't do it yourself, but you let it happen."

A steely look came into his eyes.

"You betrayed him. Pushed him into a deal, and when it went bad, he was the one who paid."

"I do not know what you are talking about."

"What was it, weapons? Did you have him stealing weapons for you? Selling them, too?"

He shifted. "Does it matter?"

"It all matters. He was your best friend."

He gazed at her with those pale eyes. "It did not need to happen, Arin. He panicked. Fell apart at the wrong time."

A swell of fury swept over her. "You should never have put him in that position. He was your friend. He trusted you."

"He made the contacts. With the wrong men. I tried to warn him."

She felt her eyes narrow as she weighed whether to believe him.

"He wanted to break away from his father—from all this. He thought this was the way. He said you wanted him to."

She couldn't disagree. They had talked. But she had never insisted. Never demanded. "Not like this."

"If I said I was sorry, would you believe me?"

She didn't answer, but Vlad must have misinterpreted it. He moved in close and brushed his fingers across her cheek. "You never belonged with him, you know."

Her stomach knotted.

"He did not have the same passion, the same ambition as you, Arin. Everyone knew. Even his father." He paused. "We are the same, you and me. We are a good match."

"You have a wife."

He blew out his breath, as if it was just a trifling problem. "She was a whore when I met her, and she is today."

A spit of fury shot through her. "If she is, you forced her into it."

His eyes grew cold. "You saw her."

Arin bit her lip. She'd hadn't meant to say that. She'd promised Mika. She tried to twist away, but Vlad grabbed her shoulders and spun her around. "You belong with me, Arin."

He pulled her close and buried his mouth on hers. She struggled, pushing hard on his chest. When she broke away, she drew back her hand and slapped him. He tried to block it with his arm, but the blow landed on the side of his cheek.

"Monster!" Arin cried. "It will never happen!"

Patches of red flared on his cheek, and a bright anger suffused his face. Arin sensed he was waging a fierce internal struggle to control himself. Then, without warning, the anger retreated. Almost as if he'd flipped a switch. The old crooked smile reappeared. "Never is a long time," he said lazily.

Her hands clenched into fists. "You will pay." She seethed. "Perhaps not today, or tomorrow, or the day after. But you will. I will make sure of it."

She ran from the kitchen. When she reached her own room, she slammed the door. She could still hear Vlad laugh through the walls.

In bed that *night, Arin stared at a spider crawling across the ceiling. She'd assumed she would live as an officer's wife, then the wife of a musician. She had been wrong. She pulled the scratchy covers over Tomas, curled up peacefully beside her. Brushing the tips of her fingers across his downy hair, she glanced at the tattoo on her wrist. She traced the outline of the stars and the torch. Sacha was dead; she was alive. But what kind of life was ahead for her? She was a mother, a widow, and she was not yet twenty years old.*

TWENTY

THE STORM DUMPED five new inches of snow on the ground, but the streets were clear by ten. So was my driveway, thanks to Fouad, who must have plowed before dawn. I was grateful. I was nursing a wicked hangover; I doubted I could have picked up a shovel. Turning onto Happ Road, I had to shade my eyes. Winter on the North Shore can look like one of those Currier & Ives scenes you see on cookie tin lids. Today, though, the sun shot bursts of light through the trees like artillery fire. Everything was too bright, too intense, too loud.

I headed down to Skokie to pick up Dad. He'd been having heart palpitations again, and I was taking him to a different battlefield, the managed-care clinic.

One of the reasons Dad had moved into an assisted living situation was the availability of a comprehensive health plan. I'd encouraged him; at the time, it seemed like the solution to a host of problems. But after three years of endless waits, frustrated doctors, harried nurses, and anger from all sides, I lost my enthusiasm for managed-care. Still, you don't mess around with your heart.

I dropped him at the door to the clinic, then parked a

block away. My boots crunched on packed snow as I rounded the corner. They plow the streets right away in Chicago—mayoral elections depend on it—but shoveling the sidewalks is another matter. As I pushed through the door, I caught my reflection in the glass: bundled up and bowed against the cold.

Inside, I took a number and tried to steel myself for the experience. Dad took out his pocket chess set and arched his eyebrow at me.

"Do you really feel the need to humiliate me?" I asked. He knows I can't play chess.

He shrugged. "A win is a win."

"You can't wait for Rachel?" She can give my father a real game.

"Not today." A subtle look, part grimace, part fear, passed across his face. That's when I realized he was as worried as I was.

"Okay." I yielded. "Rack 'em up."

"Rack 'em up?"

I shrugged.

Dad shook his head and fiddled with the board, slotting tiny pegs into the appropriate spaces. It was only mid-morning, but the waiting room was full. Most of the patients were young children with runny noses and phlegmy coughs. Some had red cheeks, fever, perhaps, or worse. I did see two seniors: a man who didn't seem to know where he was, and a woman with a tired expression next to him.

I smiled at an infant in a stroller across from us. His eyes had tracked mine as I signed in and walked across the room. The strings from a red woolen cap were tied in a bow under his chin. He didn't smile back, but continued to stare at me with that wise, knowing look infants are born with. I wondered what was going through his young mind. Probably just flashes, impulses, a disjointed stream of consciousness. I kept smiling. Maybe he'd think the world was a friendly place.

* * *

THREE HOURS LATER, Dad and I were digging into soup and sandwiches at Karl's, a deli in Skokie.

"That wasn't so bad."

"If you don't mind waiting for Godot." I pointed to his chin. "You missed a spot."

He ran the napkin over his chin. "I thought Godot never came."

"Neither did the doctor." I paused. "Almost." I took a bite of my turkey sandwich. "When we're done here, I'll run you home and get the prescription filled."

He nodded. "This one ought to do the trick."

"Last fall the doctor said there were at least nine different medications we could try. What number are we on?"

"Three, I think, but who's counting?" He sipped his seltzer, which he still calls two cents plain. "What is it you kids used to say? Better living through chemistry?"

I grinned. "By the way, I may go to Philadelphia next weekend."

"Will David be back by then?"

I nodded.

"What's the news?"

"I haven't heard from him."

"But he'll be back next weekend?"

"That's what he said."

"What about Rachel?" Dad asked.

"She'll be staying with Barry."

"How nice."

My ex-husband was still being cooperative. In fact, he'd offered to take Rachel without my having to ask. After years of wearing a flak jacket when I dealt with him, I wasn't sure whether to trust it. But my father rubbed his palms together, the way he does when he's pleased.

"This is good news. You two are getting along better?"

"It would appear so."

"*Shalom bayit.* Peace in the house. That's the ticket."

I didn't remind him that Barry hadn't lived in the house for years.

"What happened to that hockey camp Rachel was so excited about?"

"She tried out last weekend, but they told her she needed a little more 'seasoning.' "

Dad winced. "Was she upset?"

"For about an hour. Then a guy she likes from school called and asked her to go to the movies. She made a remarkable recovery."

"Ah, youth."

"It's hormones, Dad," I grumbled. "Thick as jam."

As the waitress warmed up our coffee, a woman and a teenage boy commandeered the next booth. The boy, wearing a sweatshirt and jeans, had that sullen expression that said he was made for better things than a restaurant meal with an adult. Slouching down in the vinyl seat, he slipped his headphones, which had been draped around his neck like a necklace, onto his ears. Even from a distance, I could hear the bass. His mother—I could tell by her tired air of resignation—didn't seem at all disconcerted by his behavior and gazed serenely at the menu.

"Amazing what they get away with these days." Dad shook his head.

I kept my mouth shut, knowing, as all mothers do, there would inevitably be circumstances somewhere, sometime, under which I'd allow Rachel to do the same thing.

Dad wagged a finger at me. "Did I tell you about Al's grandson?"

Al was one of his buddies in Skokie. "No."

"The kid was a Bar Mitzvah last month. His parents, Al's daughter, did it up right. Hundreds of people. Big service. Bigger party. The whole nine yards. They even invited all the kid's friends from camp."

That was big.

"So, one of the camp friends was this nice little girl from Ohio. The kid's girlfriend, Al said. Blond hair, blue eyes, cute little turned up nose. *Verschtay?*"

"She was Gentile."

"Right. So, there they are at the service. The kid's just

finished his haftarah and his speech. The candy's all been thrown. The rabbi's given his blessing. They're just about to start *Musaf,* and you know what happens?"

"What?"

"The kid gets up, goes to the back of the sanctuary, gets the girl, sits her down in the first row, and puts his arm around her. Right in front of everyone."

"No!"

"Yes. Al says it's like they were in a movie theater about to start necking."

"Come on. You're making this up!"

"*Emes!* You shoulda heard Al. 'Holy shit,' he says to me, 'the kid's got his arm around a shiksa at his own Bar Mitzvah!' He almost had a heart attack."

I glanced at the kid in the next booth, who was bobbing his head to some unheard beat. It probably wasn't the right time to tell Dad the boy who asked Rachel out to the movies was the son of the Episcopal priest.

Dad speared an olive on his plate with a toothpick. "So how's the new job?"

"It's going to be a nice video. It'll be finished by spring."

"Good, good. You hear anything more about that tape they dropped off at your house?"

Talk about heart attacks. If I told Dad about Celestial Bodies, we'd be back at the clinic in record time. "N—not really. The police are handling it. I'm out of it."

He rubbed his palms together again. "Well now, this is a good day. You've got a nice job, you're getting along with your daughter, *and* you're getting along with your ex. You sound almost normal."

I gave him a thin smile.

DAVID CALLED AS I was getting ready for bed. "Hello, Ellie."

I'd forgotten how the sound of his voice made me melt. I felt shy. "Hi."

Silence. Then we both spoke at the same time.

"I'm sorry I haven't—"

"How's it been going?"

"Sorry."

"My fault," I said. "I cut you off." I wondered if I should say anything about his going to Europe without telling me. I didn't have the chance.

"It's him, Ellie."

I blew out air. "You're sure?"

"It's my uncle. Wilhelm Gottlieb. He showed me pictures of him and my mother and their sister as kids. And he's got a watch that belonged to my grandfather. With his initials. LDG."

"Leopold Gottlieb," I breathed.

"Leopold Dieter Gottlieb."

A prickle ran up my spine. For years David had been combing through dusty attics, museums, and village records searching for his relatives. Now, apparently, he'd connected. Part of me wanted to rejoice and celebrate with him—I knew how much he wanted this—yet, it raised important questions. Why hadn't his uncle been in touch before? Why didn't anyone else know he was alive? What had he been doing for the past sixty years? I remembered part of the letter: something about circumstances that now required him to write. What circumstances? What did he want from David?

Thoughts raced through my brain like a freight train until it occurred to me that if I had all these questions, what must David be thinking? Suddenly, only one question seemed important. "How are you holding up?"

He paused, as if this was the first time he'd really thought or spoken about it. "I'm not really sure. It feels like I'm sleepwalking. That I'm going to wake up, and none of this will have happened, and I'll be alone. Again."

"Never alone," I whispered.

He didn't answer. I felt like I was walking on glass.

Then he said, "He's been living in Antwerp for the past fifty years. He's a diamond dealer."

"A diamond dealer?"

"During the war, he passed. He was blond and blue-eyed, like my mother. It wasn't hard, he said, if you kept moving. He went from town to town. Always on the run. Afterward, he fell into the diamond trade. Turns out a number of Holocaust survivors did."

"How come?"

"Some Jews found it hard to put down roots afterward. They never felt secure. They made sure they could travel light if they had to—to make a speedy exit. Diamonds, rubies, whatever—dump them in your pocket, sew them in the lining of your clothes. You're always ready to run."

"But he did settle."

"I guess, eventually, he got tired. Or else decided it was safe to stay in one place. He moved to Antwerp and opened a small shop in the Jewish quarter. On the *Hovenierstraat.* He took in a partner, another German survivor. The partner died four years ago. That's why I've been so busy. The partner's daughter inherited half of the business, and we're trying to figure out what to do."

"What do you mean 'figuring out what to do'?"

"My uncle never married."

"Why not?"

"I don't know." David hesitated again. "But he's sick, Ellie. Advanced kidney disease."

I bit my lip. "Is he on dialysis?"

"Not yet, but it's not out of the question." He sighed. "That's why he wrote Mrs. Freidrich. He didn't know whether my mother survived, whether she ever got married, or had any children. But he wanted to find out before . . . well, you know . . ." His voice cracked. "He wants to leave me half the business."

"You're kidding."

"So we've been trying to figure out an equitable arrangement. It's complicated."

"Complicated, how?"

"He's a small dealer, but he has an excellent reputation. De Beers has a standing offer to buy him out."

"Really."

"He's not sure what he wants to do. And, of course, the daughter of his partner wants him to sell. We've been talking to lawyers all week."

"You don't want it, do you? The business, I mean?"

I heard the churn of emotion in his silence. Then, "I don't know what I want right now. But I did manage to convince him to come home with me."

"To the States?"

"I want him to get checked out at Penn. I told him I'd take care of him. Even help him get a transplant, if it comes to that." He paused. "He said he'd come."

"David, that's wonderful."

"Yes."

His response was subdued. Not what I'd expect from someone who just located his only living relative. I pushed the thought away. "How did you track him down? You had no idea where he lived."

"I located the post office where he rented a box and kept an eye on it until his partner's daughter collected his mail. Then I followed her."

"You'd make a good detective."

A noise came out of his throat, but I couldn't tell if it was a laugh or a sneer.

"So, when are you coming home?"

"We should be there by Wednesday."

I felt a flush of excitement. "I could fly in for the weekend. I'd love to see you. And meet your uncle."

David cleared his throat. "Well . . ."

I nattered on about airline schedules and tickets. We hung up a few moments later, with me saying I'd take an afternoon flight on Friday. It wasn't until later, as I was getting ready for bed, that I realized I'd invited myself.

TWENTY-ONE

THE SAME WOMAN has cut my hair for ten years. During that time she changed her name from Ann to Jasmine, started lifting weights, and now competes in bodybuilding contests. Over the same period, I haven't varied my hairstyle. Which probably says something about our respective abilities to embrace change. Still, I wouldn't think of switching. How many people get their hair done by a flower child who can bench-press a Cadillac?

As Jasmine draped a black plastic sheet over me, I watched in the mirror, thinking how much I looked like a turtle whose head just emerged from a shiny black shell. She picked up a lock of hair with more salt than pepper. "When are we going to do something about this?"

"Soon."

"You've been saying that for years."

I hunched my shoulders. I haven't colored my hair, not because of any aversion to vanity or chemicals. Or even resistance to change. I just can't sit still for the length of time it requires. But Jasmine keeps trying.

A woman sailed through the door, waving her nails in

the air. "Hello, Jasmine, dear. I know I don't have an appointment, but you wouldn't mind doing a comb-out, would you? I forgot I'm going to a fund-raiser tonight. Can you believe it?" Ignoring me, she flashed Jasmine one of those "oh how embarrassing" looks.

Judging from her carefully applied makeup, I found it hard to believe she forgot why she was putting it on. Jasmine raised her eyebrows at me in the mirror. I checked my watch.

"I don't know, Melody . . ." Jasmine began.

"It's all right." I climbed out of the chair. "I have a few minutes."

Jasmine mouthed her thanks.

Melody smiled broadly and sat down, still avoiding eye contact with me. "Well, you know, Jasmine, it's just been the busiest time. We only just got back from Arizona, and we're supposed to go to Florida next week, and—"

"Ellie, there's a TV in the other room," Jasmine cut in. She operates out of the back of a rather large nail salon. She pointed her comb toward the main room.

I nodded.

Melody finally looked my way as if she'd just noticed another human being was occupying the same time and space as she. She blinked like a sleepy owl.

I wandered into the big room, which was divided into twelve stations, a manicurist at each. The smell of nail polish permeated the air. I eavesdropped on a woman talking about fire-eating and how empowering an experience it was, then drifted over to the TV.

The early news had started, the blow-dried, perfectly accessorized male anchor reporting that six children were hospitalized following the evacuation of an inner city school. After the obligatory sound bites from the hospital spokesman and father of one of the kids, the anchor looked camera left with a perfectly timed sigh. "Jill, I hope you have some happier news."

The coanchor, his female mirror image, frowned slightly. "Sorry, Jack, I don't." She turned toward the camera, her chin tilting down. "A double homicide in the northwest suburbs last night has Des Plaines police puzzled."

I edged closer. A reporter was doing a stand-up in front of a modest brick house. "Police are investigating the deaths of a brother and sister, both Russian immigrants, in this quiet suburb. The couple ran an illegal dentistry office out of their house, and this wasn't their first brush with the law."

Several pairs of eyes looked up from the manicurists' stations. The reporter went on to say that the victims had been dentists in the USSR but never obtained the proper American licenses. Police raided the place last summer and closed it down, but, apparently, they'd reopened. Not surprising. If most of their clientele were Russian immigrants who couldn't afford or didn't want to be treated by American dentists, there probably was a healthy demand for their services.

The report cut to file footage from last summer's raid, a pan of the waiting room where the murdered couple was found. Three of four walls were paneled and there was a white linoleum floor. With the exception of two chairs and a table, there wasn't much furniture in the room. I started to feel queasy. Then the camera panned across the wall that wasn't paneled. In the center of the wall was a huge, unmistakable crack that zigzagged from floor to ceiling.

Davis answered on the first ring.

"It's Ellie. Did you see the news?"

"I'm on it."

"Is it the same place?"

"Look, I can't talk. Olson fixed it so I could be there when the techs processed the scene. I need to keep this line free."

"They said on the news it was past Wolf Road. Near Elk Grove Village."

"Don't even think about it, Ellie. You wouldn't be able to get near the place, anyway. It's a crime scene, for God's sake. You show up there, my ass'll be in a sling."

"Why?"

"Because—because they'll probably think I've been talking."

"Davis, don't be paranoid. It was on the news."

"Don't do this to me, Ellie. It's my case."

I thought about it for a while. "Okay. But you owe me."

She didn't answer.

"The least you can do is tell me what's going on. I know you have a gut feeling. Is it the same place?"

She grew quiet. Then, "We're waiting for blood sample results."

"Blood samples?"

"Luminol raised a shitload of blood smears, and the techs got enough to type some of them. They'll compare them to the victims' blood type, and if a third type shows up, we're in business."

I remembered the dark spot oozing across the woman's chest on the video.

"Look, I gotta go," she said brusquely. "I've got a lot to do."

"Like what?"

"Checking mud sheets. Ownership records. Des Plaines is doing some of it already, but they said they'd work with us."

"Okay. Just one more question. Davis, was there a camera mounted on the wall of the room?"

"Ellie, I already told you more than I should. I could—"

"Davis . . ."

She paused for a long moment. "Yes."

I breathed out. This was a big break.

"Des Plaines is saying it could be a vendetta," she said. "A revenge killing."

"For what?"

"Who knows? The victims—well, it's not as if their clients are high society. The people who got their teeth fixed at the place are the kind who generally keep a low profile. But there's no sign of a break-in, and nothing appears to be missing. The victims were shot once through the head. With a small-caliber automatic. That's the way they do it."

"Davis, do you think the brother and sister were involved in her murder?"

She hesitated. "I'm trying not to think until I have some evidence. And I'd advise you not to, either. In fact, if I find out you talked about this with anyone, I might have to break both your legs."

I laughed. Sort of.

TWENTY-TWO

PHILADELPHIA IS A city that evokes strong emotions. My friend Genna, who lived there for two years, thinks you could drop it off the New Jersey turnpike and no one would miss it. Susan, who has relatives in Doylestown, loves the historical section and drags her kids to the Liberty Bell every time she visits. I haven't made up my mind, but I wonder about a city whose streets are narrower than a Chicago alley, whose accent has spawned dozens of linguistics textbooks, and whose cheesesteaks, hoagies, and soft pretzels have created the junk food capital of the world.

I was able to book a flight, which turned out to be so smooth and pleasant I decided it was an omen for the weekend. I grabbed a cab at the airport and gave the driver David's address. He lives on Society Hill, a trendy area of rehabbed townhouses, exotic restaurants, and shops near the river. Genna assured me it was the place to live if you were forced to live in town. First though, we skirted the southeast edge of the city, where the emissions from a working oil refinery choked the air with a noxious, gassy odor. I was began to see her point.

But then we passed Penn's Landing, a recently developed park with concerts in the summer, ice skating in the winter, and a series of permanently moored ships to tour. As we turned toward Society Hill, I twisted around in my seat. Late-afternoon sun slanted down on the Ben Franklin Bridge, splashing molten light across its steel cables. David and I could take a walk down here over the weekend. A bit of quiet time, by ourselves, without any pressure, might soothe the raw spots in our relationship.

The cab pulled up in front of a four-story Federal townhouse near Second and Pine. I'd been here before, but each time I visit I like it more. It's a straightforward, proud house with redbrick facade, white trim, and sand-colored shutters. It suits him. My favorite spot is his backyard, a walled garden with two flowering cherry trees. I hadn't seen them in bloom yet, but I planned to visit when the delicate pink flowers blossomed this spring.

When David answered the door in rolled-up shirt sleeves and jeans, a ping shot through me, and all thoughts about trees and flowers melted away. It was all I could do not to climb all over him. He leaned in and gave me a kiss. I rested my hands on his arms. He looked tired.

"How are you?"

"It's been a long couple of weeks."

I stepped into a narrow entrance hall that was decorated with arches and chair-rail moldings. "How was the trip back?"

"Both flights were delayed. Otherwise uneventful."

"How did your uncle bear up?"

"Willie did fine."

"Willie." I smiled. "Where is he?"

"Up in the den." Despite a spacious living room on the first floor, David spends most of his time upstairs, where the kitchen, den, and dining room are located. He started up, carrying my suitcase. "His English is passable. He speaks Dutch, French, and a little Russian, but, of course, he's most comfortable in German."

I followed him up the stairs, letting my hand trail up the

banister. I'd decided I wouldn't say anything about his leaving for Europe so precipitously until we'd had a chance to unwind. He had a lot on his mind. I didn't want to add any stress. Then I heard myself saying, "I guess you were pretty rushed when you left."

He stopped. "What do you mean?"

"You never called or e-mailed to tell me you were leaving. Not that you had to, of course . . ."

He paused briefly, almost imperceptibly. "Right. I'm sorry. I just—well, things did get hectic."

That wasn't what I was hoping to hear. But what did I expect? That he'd fall all over himself apologizing? Sweep me into his arms and swear not to neglect me again? I was probably making too much of it. Finding his uncle was one of the most important events in David's life. It was *my* need for security and reassurance that was exacerbating the situation. I resolved to push away my anxiety.

At the top of the stairs he set down the suitcase, crossed the hall, and opened a partially closed door. *"Willie, die Ellie ist da."*

I peered into the room. A man rose from David's couch. He was tall and gaunt, with hollow cheeks and a lined face. Iron gray hair, and lots of it, was combed to the side. But his eyebrows arched so high they seemed tethered in a perpetually surprised expression, and the blue eyes beneath them reminded me of a summer sky. I thought I saw a resemblance between him and David, something around the mouth, perhaps, though when you're looking for a similarity, you're apt to find one, whether it's there or not.

He was wearing a white shirt, tie, and dark pants. He rolled his shirt sleeves down, grabbed a suit jacket from the back of a chair, and shrugged into it. "It is my pleasure, Miss Foreman."

You could see he was in poor health, but there was something very appealing about him. He struck me as a gentleman, a kind man, a man for all times. We shook hands. "Please. Call me Ellie."

* * *

THAT NIGHT WE cabbed over to Bookbinders in Center City for dinner. The original restaurant had been around the corner from David's, but it was closed. The décor of the Fifteenth Street place was disappointing: dark wooden floors, draped nets, and predictable pictures of fish on the walls.

Once we were seated, Willie slipped on a pair of small, round glasses with metal frames. I've always found glasses attractive; they gentle a person, especially a man. He inspected the menu, peppering David with questions in a combination of pidgin English, French, and German.

Our appetizers came right away.

"There's so many questions I want to ask, Willie," I said, after a few bites of crab cake. "Do you mind?"

"*Nein*. You ask." He gave me a courtly smile.

"Tell me how you survived the war."

His story, accompanied by lots of enthusiastic hand motions to bridge the language barrier, started on a sunny afternoon in the summer of '39 when the SS came to the Gottliebs' house in Freiburg. Willie's father, David's grandfather, knew right away what was happening and tried to resist. He was killed. Willie, who happened to be down the block at a neighbor's, heard the shots. A few minutes later, his mother and younger sister were taken away in a truck. He never saw them again. That night, he stole back to his house, packed a bag, and ran. He spent the rest of the war bouncing from one town to the next, hiding out in the woods, never staying in one place more than a day or two. He never admitted he was Jewish. Just a boy who'd been orphaned by the war.

Over time he hiked north, cutting over to Belgium and the Netherlands, where the atmosphere was slightly more tolerable. Some people helped him; others didn't. When he couldn't borrow or steal eggs and fruit, he foraged in the woods, learning by experience which berries and plants were edible. He had the stomach problems to prove it.

David asked if he remembered the one letter he'd managed to send his mother.

Willie nodded vigorously. "*C'etait un fermier*—a farmer—*der landwirt*—near Cologne who posted for me the letter. But no one, after, could I find to post one."

After the war Willie headed back to Freiburg. But the city, which had been leveled by both Allied and German bombers, who mistook it for a French target, was hardly more than a spot on the map. The rubble, the bitterness, the shattered lives, were more than he could handle, and he sank into a despair he hadn't allowed himself to feel while he was running.

One day he ventured into the dense woodland where he and Lisle and their younger sister had played as children, hoping, perhaps, in some mystical way, to find some remnant of his family's presence, their spirit. He waited for a sign, a leaf grazing his cheek, perhaps, or a sudden shaft of light that might guide him toward the future, but he saw and felt nothing. He left Germany the next day.

"You went straight to Antwerp?" I asked.

"*Nein.* I have been traveling much. *Belgien. Frankreich. Die Niederlande.* No one has money, you see, but they has work. I work. They feed. Is *gut.*"

He told us how, after several months, he hitched a ride on a milk truck in Belgium, a *milch wagen,* that made stops along its route. One of the stops was Antwerp.

"How was it that you settled there?"

"Before the war, Antwerp was considered second only to Paris as a center for art and culture," David explained.

"Is good businesses there, a large Jewish quarter, *und* is Antwerp capital of the diamond world," Willie said. "*Und* is second largest port in Europe. Ships go from Antwerp *uber die ganze Welt.*" He raised his palm. "It is easy place to leave in a hurry. Even with bag of diamonds in pocket, you can go. *Verstehen?*"

"I understand." But did I? I was raised in a safe haven. My right to exist had never been challenged. Willie's life had been defined by fear and a profound need for legitimacy.

And David, who'd been shunted from home to home as a foster child, shared a similar itinerant background. I played with my food, wondering, not for the first time, whether my stability, or at least the perception of it, was part of what attracted David to me.

I looked at Willie. "You never married."

His expression turned wistful. "I meet woman in Antwerp. She is survivor *auch, aber* lost husband and baby in Dachau. We fall in love. She want me to move with her to Israel."

"Next to Antwerp, Tel Aviv is probably the largest center for diamonds in the world," David spoke up.

Willie sighed. "*Ja,* but I cannot go."

"Why not?"

He clasped his hands in front of him. "*War auch ein* fighter. She wanted to make *sicher* it does not happen again. She thought Israel was place to do that."

"You didn't agree?"

"I cannot *chance nehmen.* Take the chance." He flashed me a sad smile. "If God would not let the Jews survive in *Europa,* what are the chances in Israel, with *fiend*—enemies on all sides?"

I WAS BRUSHING my hair in David's bathroom, thinking about the similarities in Willie's and David's lives, when David's reflection appeared in the mirror. I smiled.

He didn't smile back.

"Is something wrong?" I turned around.

"No. Nothing."

"And my name is Grace Slick." I eyed him. "David, something's been bothering you ever since I got here."

He looked at me, then gave a little shrug. "It's just—it's just that you found out more about Willie in two hours than I did all week."

I put down the brush. "He was probably in the mood to talk. I just happened to be in the right place at the right time."

"I don't think so. I mean, he and Brigitte and I were together, and he—" He cut himself off.

"Who?"

An odd look came over him.

"Who is Brigitte?"

He padded into the bedroom. "Brigitte is the daughter of his late partner. The one who came into the business after her father died. They've been working together for years. But I don't think she knows as much about his life as you do."

I followed him in and stood on my tiptoes to kiss him. "I have a vested interest."

Finally, a smile.

We got into bed. "You know who would love to meet him?"

"Your father."

"Yes." I snuggled in close. "Willie is Lisle's brother. Your uncle. I'm sure Dad would give anything to be here."

My father had been in love with David's mother years ago when they were young. It hadn't worked out, and I sometimes felt Dad hoped David and I would make good on the promise he and Lisle hadn't. I reached for David's hand and ran it down my cheek.

He pulled away.

Five minutes later, his even, regular breathing said he was asleep. I lay without moving, trying to ignore the ache in my chest. He'd been through a lot. He was exhausted. That's all it was.

TWENTY-THREE

A LOW-SLUNG SUN flickered through the trees as I headed to a coffee shop the next morning. I'd thrown on my coat, hat, and gloves over a pair of David's sweats, but I opening the door, I realized I didn't need the insulation. Philadelphia winters have much less bite than Chicago's. I stuffed my hat and gloves into my pocket.

The Second Street Coffee Shop was, mercifully, not a Starbucks. Bigger and brasher, the décor consisted of brightly polished copper tubes, pipes, and curlicues that snaked up, down, and around, and even seemed to produce a cup of coffee. It had normal-sized tables, too, occupied by groups of two or more sipping their drinks, reading newspapers, and chatting. I selected half a dozen pastries that looked relatively healthy and ordered three lattes. As I waited for the order, I happily sniffed the aroma of fresh-brewed coffee and eavesdropped on two women sitting nearby.

"The problem is that the senior partners still think technology is just a word processor and spreadsheet," one of them said. "But they don't *have* to go to the law library.

They send associates like me." She speared a piece of cheese Danish.

"Did you see Jennifer yesterday?" The other woman looked off to the side. "She doesn't look so good."

"And IP, the one department you'd think would embrace it, isn't out front on the new system." The first woman looked off to the side, too, as if a third, unseen person were at the table. "You know what I think? Everyone's afraid to confront the Luddites. Nobody wants to upset the apple cart."

"She's lost weight, and she looked pale. I'm worried about her."

I turned back to the cash register, wondering if either woman would remember this moment a month, a year, a decade from now. What they were drinking, what they were wearing, what they said—or didn't say—to each other. Was that the way David and I had been communicating?

He was in the shower by the time I got back, so Willie and I set out breakfast in the dining room on a mahogany table. I took a blueberry muffin, cut it in half, and sat down opposite a large bay window with a view of the garden. Willie chose a raspberry scone and bit into it eagerly. It was Saturday, but he was wearing a crisp white shirt, tie, and dark pants. I pictured him in Antwerp on a weekend morning, strolling down the street, an umbrella in one hand, a bag of pastries in the other, eager to return home and devour his treat.

"How did you get started in diamonds?" I asked around a mouthful of muffin.

"You like them?"

"Who doesn't?"

"That's sure." He brushed crumbs of scone off his face. "A diamond is art. Better than Rubens. Even Van Gogh." He chuckled. "When I leave Freiburg, I take with me my mother's diamond necklace. Is small stone, barely one carat. But I keep with me."

"Your mother's necklace?" I imagined how the memory of his mother, embodied in that stone, kept him alive through the dark days of the war. How that necklace, and whom it belonged to, influenced his choice of career. How, even now, he cherished it, keeping it in a special place. "What happened to it?"

"I trade for a chicken in Belgium."

So much for my imagination.

"Nien." He held up a finger. "Do not *fuehl schlecht.* Feel bad. When I get to Jewish quarter in Antwerp, I meet diamond cutter. Marcel Berken. He needs help caring for equipment. I remember my mother's diamond. I think maybe it is way to *ehre mein mutter.* Honor her memory. So I work for him. No money. Just food. But I learn how to set bench. Clean tang and dop. Oil wheel with diamond dust."

"He's the one who taught you how to polish diamonds?"

"For six months, I just watch. Is important. With diamonds, one wrong cut, stone is—kaput." He made a brushing aside gesture with his fingers.

"Ruined."

"*Ja.* Ruined."

David came into the dining room, his hair still damp. When I passed him the plate of pastries, he flashed me a warm smile. My doubts melted away. I had been overreacting last night. He'd been stressed out. Tonight would be different.

"I learn slow," Willie went on. "The first diamond I cut, I make like my mother's *halskette*—necklace. Maybe she see it. I think she do." He paused. "After ten years, Marcel tell me is time to open my own shop. 'You are good, Willie,' he say. 'You see *diamanten.*' Diamonds."

"See the diamond?"

"You take yellow stone. Or brown. Maybe greasy. *Haesslich.* Ugly. Worse than quartz in sunlight. But you know inside is—how you say . . ."

"You see the possibilities?"

"*Ja.* Possibilities. It may be brilliant. Or princess. Maybe something else. But always it brings out inner *licht.* Light."

"I wouldn't know a rough diamond if I held one in my hand," I said. "What happened to the diamond you cut in honor of your mother?"

He patted his shirt pocket. "I have it still. I wait to give it to right person." He stole a look at David. A flush crept up David's neck. Willie finished his scone and pushed his plate away. "But enough from old man. *Was ist deine arbeit?* What work you do, Ellie?"

"I'm a filmmaker."

David translated. "*Direktor.* Film."

Recognition lit Willie's eyes. "Steven Spielberg, *yah*? *ET . . . Star Wars*?"

Star Wars was Lucas, but I didn't object. "Not exactly. I produce industrials. Corporate videos."

He canted his head.

"Let's say one of the diamond schools in Antwerp wants to make a video about diamond cutting. Or De Beers wanted to showcase some of their better quality stones. They might hire me to make that video."

Again David translated. "*Industriewerbung.*"

"I see. This is *gut*?"

"It's a living." Except when someone drops off a tape that shows a woman being murdered. "Oh." I turned to David. "I haven't had a chance to tell you. Officer Davis thinks they found the location where the tape of the woman was shot." I filled him in on the Russian dentists' murders, carefully avoiding any mention of Celestial Bodies.

"*Was ist das?*"

David explained. When he was finished, Willie said something in German. All I heard was *Russich.*

"What did he say? All I could make out was *Russian.*"

David waved a hand. "It's not important."

I remember my father's propensity to compare Russian and German Jews, usually to the detriment of the Russians. I'd always thought it was just an American practice.

David looked over, as if he knew what I was thinking. "It's not what you think. He was just saying he has to be careful with Russians. Especially now."

"Why is that?"

"That part of the world is in such chaos that people are desperate. They'll do anything to get by. He says you have to know who you're dealing with."

I pushed the half-eaten muffin away. Is that what had happened at home? The dentists were Russians—had they come into contact with other, more desperate Russians, who, for whatever reasons, caused their deaths? Were their murders the result of a robbery gone awry? Or, given what Davis said about the Russian mafia, an extortion or blackmail scheme that backfired?

Or were the dentists' deaths linked to the tape? Were they killed because they knew the dead woman? Or had something to do with the tape of her murder? And if that was the case, how long would it be before the killers discovered that I had something to do with the tape, too? I shifted uneasily. "I sense you don't think it's such a good idea for me to be involved with Russian dentists, cleaning ladies, and women with tattoos."

"You sense right," David said solemnly.

I was about to go on when Willie cut in. "*Was ist* 'tattoo'?" he asked. "I not understand."

I gestured toward David. "Tell him."

I caught the words *tätowierung* and *fackel*. Tattoo and torch. Willie's eyes widened. "*Tätowierung?* What look like, this *tätowierung*?"

"Here. I'll show you." I got up, took a piece of paper off the kitchen counter, and sketched out a rough version of the stars and torch. Willie took it, squinted, and put on his glasses. Then he looked up. "*Sage mir das noch einmal.* Tell me again."

David began repeating himself in a clumsy mixture of German and English. A moment later Willie held up his palm. "*Genug.*" Enough. David stopped. Willie looked over, his eyes bright. "I know this *tätowierung*. I see it before."

I stared at Willie, swallowing hard. "You've seen it before?"

He pushed himself back from the table, stood up, and went to the bay window. "Two, maybe three years ago, a young girl bring me rough stones. *Gelb. Braun.* Yellow, brown. Not bad. Probably from Africa. So I ask, where is *certifikat*?"

I cut in. "Certificate?"

David explained. "Any diamond that's bought or sold today requires a certificate that tracks their origin from the mine to the trading floor to the jewelry counter."

"Why?"

"There's always been illegal trafficking in diamonds, but it's become particularly fierce recently. Blood diamonds, they call them."

I frowned. "Isn't that where rebels smuggle diamonds out of Africa, sell them, and use the proceeds to buy weapons?"

David nodded. "It's not a large part of the market, but the word is these guys'll kill anyone who gets in their way. Women, children—if you're too close to the mines, or the couriers, or the rebels, or any other thing they don't happen to like."

"Why don't they ban the sale of diamonds from those countries?" I asked.

"They're indistinguishable from legally mined stones. And there are plenty of dealers who don't ask questions. So they get absorbed." David's expression was grim. "You can imagine that doesn't please De Beers or the other large dealers. So they pushed through a law that requires a certificate on every diamond that's traded."

"And this woman didn't have a certificate."

Willie explained. "I cannot sell for good price without *certifikat*. So I tell her *nein*."

"What did she do?"

"She try to convince me to buy. But I say to her something, too." His eyes twinkled. "I say young woman like her, to find different job. Too many danger. She listen, then put stones back in bag." Willie pointed to his wrist. "That's when I see. The same." He motioned to the sketch of the tattoo. "I ask her what is *das*? She say, it is nothing. Long time ago."

The nerves under my skin jangled. "Do you know anything about her? Her name? Where she was from?"

He shook his head. "It is long time ago. But she is *jeang*. Young. *Huebsch*. Pretty. Dark hair." He paused. "And we speak Russian."

TWENTY-FOUR

ARIN ARRIVED BACK in Yerevan during the summer of '93 with Tomas, one suitcase, and three boxes. She was surprised at how easy it was to pack up four years of her life. Had her stay in Georgia been that empty, devoid of significance?

She was dismayed to find that conditions in Armenia were just as harsh as Georgia—in some ways worse. In addition to a floundering economy, a blockade by Azerbaijan and Turkey had disrupted everything. The streets of Yerevan were filled with uncollected garbage; power and heat were in short supply. With no money to pay anyone, there were few jobs. Yet, perversely, store shelves bulged with luxury goods from the West. The problem was no one—at least, no one Arin knew—could afford to buy them.

She moved into her parents' apartment in a building that ticked and creaked and groaned. Her parents had been apparatchiks, her mother an office administrator, her father a minor party functionary. But her mother was now unemployed, and her father worked only two days a week, most of the time without pay. Her mother grumbled that things had been better under the Communists. Her father said it could be worse. Her mother agreed; the Turks could always invade again. Arin couldn't remember the last time she'd seen her mother smile.

Except with Tomas. When he giggled, full of delight at what life had to offer, Arin's mother would sweep him into her arms, nuzzling him and crooning nursery songs Arin vaguely remembered. And when he cooed, his entire body creased in smiles, her father's eyes twinkled for the first time in years.

Soon her mother began to take over Tomas's care. At first, Arin was reluctant: She knew Tomas better. As time went on, though, Arin realized Tomas was rekindling the joy in her parents' lives, bringing laughter and love back into their home. Her mother even started to hum again. Arin's only regret was that Sacha wasn't there to see it.

Once she was settled, she started to look for a job. Her first stop was the hospital where she had nursed Sacha. They needed plenty of help, her aunt said, but they couldn't pay. Maybe in a month or two. Next Arin tried the bank but met with the same response. Then the museums and the factories that had once thrived under the Soviets. Everywhere was the same: they needed workers, they couldn't pay.

When she couldn't find work at the outdoor market, Arin began to feel desperate. Rounding a corner back to Republic Square, she came across two women in too much makeup and not enough clothing, lazing against the side of a building. Their hostile stares warned her not to tarry. She was invading their territory. As she edged away from them, an image of Mika flashed into her mind. She pictured her friend in a squalid brothel, staring at the ceiling while men pawed over her.

She skirted the corner with a shiver, coming face-to-face with a couple who, seeing her shiver, crept away from her. They thought she wanted a handout, she realized. That's how bad it was: people afraid to walk past each other for fear of being prevailed upon. She backtracked to Abovian Street and the shopping district, where she strolled past silk dresses, Hermès bags, and electronic gadgets. Again she wondered who could afford these lavish goods.

A flock of pigeons flew down and alit behind her. Their heads bobbed as they foraged for food. They probably expected her to feed them, but she had nothing to give. She waved her arms, and the pigeons lifted off. She walked on.

At the end of the block she stopped at the window of a jewelry store, its wares seductively arranged on a layer of shiny white satin. In the center was a dazzling necklace firing sparks that seemed to come from within. Eight diamonds nested on an ornament that was strung on a thin gold chain. The stones were perfect round brilliants; fifty-eight facets apiece, each cut in a precise arrangement of bezels, stars, and pavilions. A catch released in her mind. Her grandfather had taught her that, she recalled with a start; years ago when she was young.

She stared at the necklace. She was a little girl, visiting his shop on the outskirts of Yerevan. A man with a sweeping white mustache and thick hair parted on the side, he would swoop her up in his arms when he saw her. She remembered long afternoons beside him on his bench, the faint aroma of pipe tobacco clinging to his clothes. Watching as he transformed ordinary-looking pebbles and rocks, the kind she would have thrown back in the creek, into jewels. It was magic, she thought then, watching a discolored yellow stone turn into a glittering diamond. Or a ruby, emerald, or amethyst. Like the fairy tale about the girl from the ashes who turned into a princess.

She would spend hours there, the shop quiet except for the hum of the revolving wheel, or the occasional car kicking up dust as it headed into town. Her favorite part was the polishing, the faceting that came after the cleaving and sawing and bruting. That's where the artistry lay, her grandfather claimed—the ability to see a stone and know, just by studying it, what design would enhance its color and clarity, would allow it to emit light, yet also hold it within.

Over the summers she learned how to recognize different types of facets, giggling when her grandfather tried unsuccessfully to trick her. She loved spending time with him. The jewels connected with something very basic and primitive within her. Something shiny, pure, and good.

The next day, she took the bus to the Yerevan Jewelry Plant in the center of the city. The Armenian diamond industry would never rival Antwerp's or Israel's or even New York's, but it was a vital, growing concern. The plant had gained prominence by taking in stones from Russia, cutting them into fine pieces, and then sending them back to the Russian market. Recently there was talk of joint ventures to expand markets beyond the East. Everyone loved jewels.

When the plant manager asked about her skills, she told him she'd been an apprentice years ago. And while she knew the equipment had advanced, she was confident she could learn quickly. What did she want to do, the manager asked. When she replied "Faceting," he laughed and gestured to the other cutters.

"You and all the other artists."

She looked him in the eye. The manager looked back. He admitted later that he knew she was lying, but there was something about her, he said. Her confident, almost hard expression. As if she dared him to challenge her. The courage it took to maintain such control in the face of deception intrigued him. So he hired her to take care of the equipment and clean the shop floor. It wouldn't pay much, only a few drams, but in her spare time, she could watch the cutters, assuming they didn't object.

Arin started the next day. Unlike her grandfather's shop, this was a huge factory. Every job was specialized; the person who cleaved wasn't the person who sawed or polished. No one took a stone from start to finish. Even the cutters were skilled at only one or two facets. But the volume of stones passing through the plant was enormous; Arin had never seen so many diamonds.

Her first task was to organize the supply room. The

room was chaos, supplies and materials flung everywhere. She sorted blades and dops and tangs according to size, labeled everything, and started to keep track of who used what when. Diamond dust was at a premium, industrial diamonds, too; she made sure the cutters had what they needed.

Once she inventoried the supplies, she took it upon herself to notify her manager when stocks needed replenishing and presented him with weekly reports. She also devised a new sign-in system for the workers, so management could keep track of their productivity. However, knowing that workers in the new political environment would not condone such scrutiny of their schedules, she suggested they be given a tiny cut of the plant's sales in exchange. The manager followed her advice; profits jumped the next quarter.

She still made time for cutting and spent hours with the polishers, particularly the ones who cut facets. She also studied the cleavers, who taught her their work was the most important part of the process. They were the ones who made the first cuts in a gem and determined its shape. But if they made even the tiniest mistake, the stone was ruined. Over time she learned to see a stone the way they did. She learned to guess—with surprising accuracy—how those cuts should be made.

Yet, it was clear Arin's managerial skills outpaced her technical, and when she was offered a promotion to assistant manager, she took it. Not only was it more money, but her boss said he would introduce her to suppliers and dealers. She would learn how rough diamonds were verified, and how the price was negotiated.

A YEAR PASSED, *and then two more. Her mother looked after Tomas, who, almost four, was a striking child with Arin's dark eyes, Sacha's blond hair, and nothing but mischief on his mind. Her father's job paid for the rent; Arin's covered their food, clothes, and extras. She bought Tomas a Game Boy, although they had to ration the batteries to run it. Her life took on a semblance of normalcy, even routine.*

But when her father had a massive stroke, her security threatened to implode. Her salary was not nearly enough to cover the hospital, his medicine, or their living expenses. Her mother, nervous and anxious, was no help. Every conversation began or ended with the fear that they would be forced out into the street. Arin grew tight-lipped and tense. Even Tomas, sensing the strain, was quieter than usual.

As the weeks passed, her father's health deteriorated. Arin grew bleak. For the first time, she wasn't sure she had the strength to shoulder her burdens. Her only solace was work; she felt safe among the diamonds and their clean, bright world, and she spent as much time at the plant as she could.

That spring, the roads rutted with mud, Arin borrowed a car and drove Tomas to visit his other grandfather. Despite her memories, she'd made it a point to maintain contact with the major general. Tomas should know his father's family. She was surprised her father-in-law still lived on the base. Sacha's mother had moved back to Russia years ago, but he had remained. He lived alone, grayer, stouter, and much less crisp. She wasn't sure how he made ends meet.

Over dinner Arin poured out her heart to him. Her father needed constant attention, intense therapy, and medicines they couldn't afford. Tomas would be starting school; he needed clothes and supplies. She wasn't sure she could pay next month's rent. And her mother was starting to look frail. Arin covered her face with her hands and sobbed.

Major General Dimitri Yudin nodded sympathetically and handed her a handkerchief. After she had pulled herself together, with abject apologies, he cleared his throat. "As it happens, I may be in a position to help."

Arin looked up. "How?"

"I have been exploring new ventures." He studied her with an intensity she'd never noticed before. "There might be a place for you. There are those who have need for your skills."

"What skills?" she asked slowly.

He lowered his voice. "Let's say, hypothetically, you could verify the legitimacy of diamonds. Uncut diamonds. Rough. If you were able to evaulate their worth, you could be talking about a significant stipend."

She'd heard about former soldiers who preyed on the army, destroying what little was left. Stealing weapons and arms that were sent to rebels in far-flung locations. Who paid for their booty with diamonds. She folded her arms. She wasn't shocked. She wasn't even surprised. But she was no longer the same girl she had been.

A few weeks later, she met Yudin at a hotel in Batumi, a Black Sea resort. When she arrived in his room, he passed her a pouch. She sat down at a desk and turned on the lamp. Opening the pouch, she casually tapped out the stones. Then she picked up her bag and fished out a jeweler's loupe, tweezers, a vial of heavy liquid, and a piece of equipment that resembled a pen attached to a box. Squinting through her loupe, she inspected the stones, examining their shapes and skins. She took out a soft cloth, polished the face on one stone, and looked through its window. She grunted, put down the loupe, and picked up the other piece of equipment.

"What is that?" Yudin asked.

She twisted around. She'd almost forgotten he was there. "A thermal diamond tester. They're used mostly for cut diamonds, but if you know what you're doing, they're equally effective with rough." She placed the sensor tip on a clear face of a stone.

Yudin watched over her shoulder. "Can you tell where they're from?"

"No one can." Still, she had a feeling they weren't from Russia. Or Belgium or Israel. These were yellows and browns, some of them muddy. She released the sensor and

smiled. "But they are real. They will make beautiful jewels."

Yudin let out a satisfied breath. As she slipped them into the pouch, he leaned back on the bed. "Tell me, Arin, do you have any thoughts where we might sell them?"

She looked at him. She knew what he was asking, but she couldn't do it. It was too risky. "They cannot come into Yerevan. Our supplies are strictly monitored." She would know; she had created the tracking system.

Yudin frowned.

"But there may be other solutions." She rose and started to pace. "I have contacts with dealers and clients now. Europe. India. The Middle East. One can always find people who do not ask questions."

His face smoothed out.

Over time a pattern emerged. She would meet Yudin every few months, usually in a neutral location. Once she authenticated the stones, she would arrange a legitimate business trip to Antwerp, Tel Aviv, even Bombay. After completing her plant business, she would see to her other affairs. She quickly learned which dealers were unconcerned about the provenance of stones and sought them out. Prices weren't as high as those for legitimate stones, but the stones were of good quality, and Arin drove a hard bargain. In return, she received a healthy cut of the proceeds.

There were always some dealers who refused. A dealer in Antwerp, a Jew, even tried to convince her to quit. It was a dangerous business, he claimed. A young woman like her should not put herself at risk. She thanked him, smiled, and went down the Hovenierstraat *to the next dealer.*

She made it a point never to ask Yudin about the origin of the stones, or how he paid for them. She knew someone had to be working with him, a silent partner, but she never asked who it was. At one point Yudin warned her the business was rough. Perhaps she should carry a gun. Nonsense, she scoffed. She was a professional from a legitimate factory in Yerevan. No one would harm her. She thanked him for his concern.

The money she brought in was put to good use. Her

father received medical help and made a significant improvement. Her mother took a vacation and bought a closet full of new clothes. Tomas was enrolled in the finest school in Yerevan. But the day Arin drove home a new Volga, confident she could afford the upkeep, was the day she felt she'd finally grown up. As the family congregated outside to admire it, she allowed herself the glimmer of a smile. Her family was safe, healthy, and comfortable.

As they traipsed indoors, Arin wished Mika could see her. She would be proud of her friend. But she hadn't heard from her in years. Arin hoped she was well. Mika deserved a better life, too.

Perhaps living well was the best revenge, Arin thought. She no longer believed in happy endings, but she'd managed to carve out one anyway. She'd crossed the line, but she was satisfied with the results. Grown up or sold out, it didn't matter. Life was good. There was no reason to question it. Or ask any questions at all. Except the size of her cut.

TWENTY-FIVE

AFTER BREAKFAST DAVID said he wanted to show Willie his office at Franklin National Bank. From there they would head over to the hospital. "I might not be back until tonight. What will you do?"

"Oh, don't worry," I said. "I'll hang around. Read. Maybe walk down to Penn's Landing." I kissed them both and wished them luck. Willie seemed to enjoy the fuss I was making.

Once they left, I called Rachel. Heavy snow was predicted for Chicago. She and Barry were getting ready for a serious weekend of video rentals and carry-out. After making sure Rachel knew where we kept the shovel, a flashlight, and extra batteries in case she got home before I did, I hung up.

I stacked the breakfast plates in the dishwater, wiped down the counters, made the beds. Then I checked the time and wondered what to do with myself for the next eight hours.

An hour later, I was on the couch in David's den, trying to read a novel. I couldn't concentrate. I kept thinking about the woman who tried to sell Willie diamonds in Antwerp. And the woman on the tape in Chicago. There could be hundreds of people with the same tattoo on their skin. Still, both of them had been young, dark-haired, and attractive. And Willie had spoken to her in Russian; the woman on the tape had shown up at the Russian dentists.

I thought about coincidence and Carl Jung's theories about synchronicity. I also thought about my promise to David not to court danger. But then I remembered something Fouad once said. We'd been weeding the lawn last summer during the dog days of August. The sun beat down on our backs. I was hot and tired and was ready to quit and let the weeds take over. Fouad kept at it, though, patiently pulling up chickweed, corn spurry, and plantain, despite the sweat that streamed down the back of his neck. "The Lord of Strength; so he attained completion," he murmured. Fouad likes to quote the Koran.

Sighing, I dug out my cell from my bag and called Davis. I might be overreacting. She might even be annoyed. But I felt a responsibility to see it through—at least to let her know what I'd discovered. She wasn't there, but whoever answered her phone said they would give her the message.

I disconnected. I was glad I'd made the effort, but I wondered what she could realistically accomplish. It wasn't as if she worked for the FBI or Interpol. Davis was a suburban cop with limited resources. How was she supposed to pin down the travels of a European woman who might or might not have been a diamond smuggler? How could anyone? It was like looking for a needle in a haystack. A three-year-old haystack; I wandered back to the sofa. She'd said an FBI guy was looking into the tattoo. Maybe he'd have an idea.

I went back to the book. This time I did get into it, and when the phone rang an hour later, I jumped. David and I have a tacit pact not to pick up each other's phones. Not that there's anything intrinsically wrong with it, but my home number is also my work phone, and it's important that messages get to me in a timely, accurate manner.

Which can be problematic when you live with a teenage girl whose idea of heaven is a phone in her ear and IM at her fingertips. It's taken a toll, but I've trained her—on pain of death—to let the machine pick up first. I try to do the same.

But as the rings followed, one after another, a twitchy feeling came over me. What if Davis was returning my call? No. She'd be calling my cell. Still, the damn thing should stop chirping. Finally David's machine clicked on.

"David, *liebchen,* it is Brigitte. I hope you do not mind. I could not wait another minute or hour. I take plane, and I am at Philadelphia *flughäfen*. Airport. Right now. I wait here for you here. At Liberty Pub in A terminal for one hour. Then I come in taxi to you. I have missed you so much, *Schatz*. It is not same without you. *Tschüs.*"

I frowned at the phone, uncomprehending. This wasn't a wrong number. The caller had addressed David by name. Something about the caller's name was familiar, too. Brigitte. I threw the book down. Brigitte was the daughter of Willie's late partner. David had been helping her figure out what to do with the shop. Whether to sell to De Beers. It was a business relationship. Except she'd just said something about missing him. Flying across the ocean just to be with him.

I got up, went to the answering machine, and replayed the message. David had only been gone ten days, and a woman was calling him *liebchen*. Declaring that it wasn't the same without him. I forced myself to recall what David had said about Brigitte. They'd been meeting with lawyers, he said. Discussing options, formulating proposals.

Apparently not just the business variety.

Maybe she had thrown herself at him. Yes. That had to be it. She'd come on to him—big time—and he hadn't worked up the nerve to tell her to take a hike. David was a sensitive man, and she was the daughter of his uncle's partner. He would never be harsh.

But then, why did she say it wasn't the same *without*

him? What had it been like *with* him? What had they been doing?

The blood drained from my head, and my hands grew clammy. Our relationship had been rocky lately, I couldn't deny that. A few months ago I'd even questioned whether we were right for each other. But David would never dump me for another woman. Especially without telling me, or preparing me in some way. Unless . . .

What circumstances would cause him to do that? I stared at his bookcase. An avid reader, he had filled his shelves with classics, recent novels, and nonfiction. He liked movies, too. But they were only pastimes. His true raison d'etre was the search for his family. He was consumed by it. Everything he did was in some way linked to it. I remember teasing him that the only reason he learned to surf the Net was to explore genealogy websites. I wasn't far off. Sometimes I thought he chose a career that required travel just so he could cull through dusty European archives.

Now, after decades of searching, he had found an uncle, his only blood relative. And a woman who'd worked side by side with him for years. A lump rose in my throat. David would consider her tantamount to family, perhaps in the same way he'd adopted us.

But what about *her*—this—this—I couldn't validate her with a name—woman? What was her stake in this? What sort of woman follows a man across the ocean after just meeting him? What did she want? I forced the lump in my throat back down and replayed the message again.

Her voice was honeyed and low. With that sultry Romy Schneider accent. She was probably tall, blond, and curvy. With big eyes. Big other things, too. A flash of anger tore through me. How dare she leave a message with all those sappy endearments? How déclassé. Distasteful. Women don't do things like that.

Unless they have a reason.

Unless they know how their message will be received.

Unless they've been intimate with the recipient.

I recalled David's behavior with me the past few days.

His impassivity. Lack of interest in making love. Maybe this affair wasn't all one-sided. Maybe David was an active player. Maybe he cared about this woman. I felt a tearing inside, as if my body were splitting apart, skin from bone. My vision blurred.

I consider myself a fairly assertive person. I don't avoid confrontations. But in matters of the heart, my confidence takes flight. Maybe it's the scars from my divorce. Or maybe it's something else. But it's hard for me to say what's on my mind. I usually try to paper over the problem. Pretend it doesn't exist. David isn't a great communicator, either, so we've limped along, hoping time and distance would smooth over our difficulties. They usually did. This time, though, there wasn't enough time, distance, or paper in the universe to smooth this over.

I stood up shakily and shuffled out of David's den. I went upstairs and stuffed my clothes into my suitcase. Then I took the steps down and let myself out. I felt like I'd aged twenty years.

By the time I hailed a cab, the sun had given way to dark clouds that looked pregnant with snow, but I wasn't registering much in the way of impressions. I felt as if I'd been suddenly dropped into alien territory, so far out of my element, I didn't want to absorb it. All I wanted was to get back to familiar surroundings.

The ticket clerk at the airport said there'd be no problem standing by on a flight to Chicago.

"Great," I said dully. "When does the next one leave?"

"Well . . ." she chirped. "That is the problem. It's snowing heavily in Chicago, and O'Hare is shut down." She flashed me an impossibly cheerful smile. "Come back in a couple of hours. Nothing's going to be moving before then."

I sighed, checked my suitcase, and headed for the nearest bar. It was before noon, but I'd just lost my boyfriend, I hate to fly, and I was stranded in a city I was beginning to despise. I trudged through the concourse, feeling heavy and lethargic. The airport wasn't crowded; it was Saturday and most travelers had already arrived at their destinations. I passed a couple, content to walk in each other's space, a bubble of love encasing them. A woman, walking fast, muttering to herself. Another man with a beatific smile, his hands clasped in front of him like some new age Buddha.

I climbed onto a stool at a small bar in the middle of the concourse. I was about to order a chardonnay when it hit me—Brigitte was at a bar in the same airport waiting for David. Liberty something. The international terminal. That would just upset me more than I already was. Especially if she was attractive.

On the other hand, I might never have another chance to see the woman who stole my boyfriend away. And knowledge *is* supposed to be power, though what power I could possibly muster in this situation escaped me. I thought about it, then slid off the barstool.

Liberty Pub turned out to be just a short walk outside the security perimeter to the next terminal—airport planners are probably required to make sure bars aren't too far apart so white-knucklers or bored travelers can get their fix easily. I expected lots of reds, whites, and blues, but it looked much like any other airport bar: small tables, plastic chairs, and windows with a view of gates.

I scanned the customers. Three men were at one table, couples at two others. Two women sat alone: an African American woman tapping into her laptop, and a brunette near the window talking into her cell phone.

I worked my way to a table next to the one on her cell and plunked down. I casually pulled out a book, all the while sneaking surreptitious glances at her. She was a striking woman: indeterminate age, thick chestnut hair, blue eyes, and from what I could see above the waist, a slim figure. Fashionable, too; she was wearing designer sweats that didn't look like sweats at all. Just the thing for a trans-Atlantic flight.

I leaned in, eavesdropping on her conversation. When I heard the same accent that was on David's machine, bile rose in my throat. This was Brigitte. I eyed her sideways, unsure whether I wanted to scratch her eyes out or put her on the next flight back to Antwerp.

"Oh, *liebchen,*" she was saying, "you know how I feel."

I slouched in my seat. Of course. How could I have been so stupid? David had a cell. When she failed to reach him at home, she would have tried his cell. She was probably talking to him right now. A wave of jealousy swept over me. I thought about leaving. Prolonging this ordeal, even under the guise of information gathering, was masochistic. But given my track record with men, masochist could be my middle name. I stayed.

"I come to you as soon as possible." She paused. "*Ja.* New York."

New York? I felt heat on my cheeks. Why were they going to New York? Was David taking her to see some Broadway shows? He'd never invited me to do that.

"Two, maybe three days. I bring papers with me. When they sign, I leave."

Papers? What papers?

"But he will sell. He is—*ich hab ihn in miner hand.*" Another pause. "*Nein.* His uncle, *der idiot,* will do what he says."

Suddenly comprehension washed over me. She wasn't talking to David. She was talking *about* him.

"And then, *chérie,* we start our life together. New York . . . *Europa . . . die Karibik . . .* We have much money." She turned away from the window, her eyes roving over the bar. "But I must go. He comes now. Any minute. *Ja.* I miss you, too. *Te amo.*"

I gasped. David? Coming here? Of course. He would have insisted on picking her up. He was that kind of person. But what if he spotted me when he got here? He'd know exactly what I was doing and why I was there. I couldn't let that happen. I had to get out.

Keeping my face averted, I rose from my seat and snuck out of the bar. I crept a few yards down the corridor and stopped at one of those faux Roman columns that are supposed to make a place look upscale. Planting myself behind the column, I tried to make sense of what I'd heard.

Brigitte was talking to someone in New York. A man she intended to meet once she made sure some "papers" were signed. Then she intended on traveling. But what papers was she talking about?

I sucked in a breath. The business. Willie's diamond business. It had to be. She'd wanted to sell to De Beers—David had mentioned that.

Now it made sense. She wanted the cash so she could take off with her New York boyfriend. Travel around the world. Which meant she was manipulating David—maybe Willie, too—to get it. I fumed. Who was this boyfriend? He spoke English, that much was clear. Which meant he might be an American. But where was his pride? His self-respect? Was he content to let Brigitte get what they needed by subterfuge? Or was he, in fact, directing her, telling her what to do, teaching her how to take advantage of two innocent men?

And what would happen to David? Once he signed the papers—and I didn't hold out much hope that he wouldn't—she would abandon him, leave him angry, bitter, and humiliated. It was the worst kind of exploitation. A spit of fury kicked through me.

I paced the corridor behind the column. David should know what Brigitte was doing. But how could I tell him? Given our history, he might not believe me. He might think I was fabricating it out of spite. He might even accuse me of trying to sabotage him.

If I did summon up the courage to tell him, I would have to stay calm. No theatrics. No histrionics. I could say I understood he wanted to end our relationship. And while I didn't want it to end, I would accede to his wishes. I could say I hoped he found the happiness he was seeking. In the meantime, though, there was something he needed to know about his new love.

It sounded adult. Responsible. Sad but loving. I went back to the column, keeping my eye on Brigitte.

It didn't take long. A few minutes later, David rushed in. His cheeks were flushed, making his snowy white hair even paler. He hurried over to her. She rose from her chair and pasted on a smile. They looked at each other for a long moment. She stepped forward. Then, the man with whom I thought I would spend the rest of my life, the man who had brought me happiness, the man who made me feel I had come home, drew Brigitte into his arms and kissed her on her lips.

Across the corridor was a ladies' room. I ran inside and threw up.

TWENTY-SIX

I HAVE TWO scars on my breasts from a time I'd prefer to forget, but when it's very wet or cold, they ache, reminding me of the delicate balance between life and death. They were throbbing now, but the pain slicing through my heart was worse. Seeing David with Brigitte was like watching a nightmare unspool in slow motion, knowing there was nothing I could do to stop it. No amount of crying or flailing could change its course. I felt like I was stuck in quicksand, each step a futile effort that would ultimately drag me under.

By the time I came out of the ladies' room, they were gone. I didn't see any reason to linger. There was nothing I could do, there was no way I'd go back to David's. I headed to the ticket counter.

It took over twelve hours to get back to Chicago. The storm dropped nine new inches of snow before tapering off, and a light snow was still falling when I landed. It was after one by the time I cabbed home from O'Hare. I paid the driver and lugged my suitcase to the front door. The fresh mantle of snow brightened the night, and the black limbs of the locust tree, etched against a gray velvet sky, leaped out at me. Snowplows whined and scraped at the other end of the block, but at my end was a soft, silent world that, in its stillness, seemed more contained and manageable than the one I'd escaped. I let myself in, grateful to be home.

THERE'S NOTHING LIKE a good depression to make you sleep. I woke to a bright winter sun throwing lemony shafts of light through the blinds. It was after eleven. I padded downstairs and brewed coffee, struggling to come to terms with the day. Fouad must have plowed the previous night, because my driveway was clear, with neat piles of snow catching sparkles from the sun. Fouad slips in and out of my life like an unseen spirit, smoothing out the kinks in my life without my being aware of it. I count myself lucky.

After showering and dressing, I contemplated doing a few loads of laundry but decided that would take entirely too much effort. The message light on my machine was blinking, but I couldn't bring myself to listen to it either. I sat at the table drinking coffee. I was halfway through my second cup when I heard keys jangling outside. A moment later Rachel burst through the door.

"Mommy! You're home!" She hurled herself into my arms.

Suddenly, my world felt better. I hugged her tighter than usual. I know the contours of Rachel's body almost as well as my own, but she felt different today. I tilted my head. "Did you grow over the weekend?"

She giggled and wiggled her foot. I looked down. Shiny new Steve Maddens with thick platform heels were welded to her feet.

"Pretty sharp."

"Daddy bought them for me."

"Lucky girl."

"I hope you don't mind." A male voice cut in.

I spun around. Barry was leaning against the doorjamb

of the kitchen. My ex-husband looks like Kevin Costner, but he's aged better. He has kept all his hair, has the sexiest blue eyes east of the Mississippi, and a body that, despite my best efforts to ignore, still quickens my breath. "Oh, hi."

He smiled.

I tried to ignore the ping that shot through me.

"When'd you get in?"

"Late last night." I motioned to the window. "Snow."

"We thought you weren't coming back till tonight."

"I didn't, either."

He tilted his head, then looked at Rachel, who was watching us curiously. "Honey, why don't you go upstairs and unpack?"

Rachel laid her hand on my arm. "It can wait."

I leaned over and tweaked her nose. She hates when I do that. "Do what your father says."

She scowled at both of us but hoisted her backpack over her shoulder and started upstairs. Barry moved to let her pass. "Mind if I have some coffee?" he asked.

I was surprised. Barry usually bolts as soon as Rachel climbs out of the car. I doubt he'd actually been inside the house more than twice since we separated, and once was to pack up his things. But then, he hadn't expected me to be here this morning. "Fine with me."

He stepped into the kitchen. I opened the fridge. He takes milk but no sugar. Funny how I remember. I took out milk and put it on the table along with a spoon.

He poured some in, stirred, then took a sip. "It's good." He raised his chin and looked at me over the rim of his mug. "So, how come you're home early?"

I frowned. "I—I had things to do."

"In the middle of a snowstorm?"

I shrugged and poured more coffee. I didn't care if he didn't believe me. It wasn't any of his business. I busied myself putting away the milk.

"Ellie, you look like you've just lost your best friend. You sure you don't want to talk about it?"

I closed the fridge door. I did want to talk—I wanted to

cry and scream and shout. Except Susan was away for the weekend, and Genna wasn't the kind of friend I confided my troubles in. But neither was my ex-husband. I shook my head.

"It's about David, isn't it?"

My eyes filled. I'd been holding it in for hours now, and I didn't have much left. I went to the table and sat down. Barry sat, too, and nodded sympathetically, which only made me more miserable. "It seems as if David has a new lady friend."

Barry arched his eyebrows.

I told him what happened. Usually when I discuss something with Barry, I feel pressured to condense or summarize my points. He's the fidgety type, and I recalled plenty of irritated looks when he thought I'd gone on too long. Now, though, he listened without saying a word.

When I finished, he ran a hand through his wavy brown hair, which was still remarkably free of gray. "I'm sorry, Ellie," he said softly. "That has to be hard."

Pain has a way of making the improbable seem natural, and his expression was so kind it kick-started a reaction in me. The ache in my chest flared up again, and tears rolled down my cheeks. I stood up and dragged my sleeve across my face. Barry stood up, too, and moved closer, brushing his hand down my cheek. Without really thinking about it, I clasped it. And before either of us could react, he slipped his other arm around me.

He pulled me close, and I buried my face in his shoulder. He stroked the back of my head. I looked up, and my stomach lurched. His eyes were soft, his lips parted, his expression eager. He wanted me. The strangest part was that I wanted him, too. He bent his head.

"What about Marlene?" I whispered. Marlene was his girlfriend.

"She's not you, Ellie," he said hoarsely.

I swallowed. He kissed me. As our lips met, something inside me swelled, and the old familiar rhythms surfaced, as if they'd been lurking in my body for years, just waiting to be summoned. Sex had never been a problem for us, even at the end. It would be easy to let those urges take over. To let my body melt into his.

But then awareness kicked in. Barry never put himself in a situation he couldn't exploit. It was his nature. He always had to seek the upper hand. And in my fragile state of mind, I was ripe for his machinations.

I pulled away. "You'd better go."

He released me reluctantly. "Are you sure?"

"I'm sure."

He paused for a beat, then gently tipped up my chin with his fist. His Bogie imitation, it had been a lovers' rite, our private ritual. He'd never had to say the words that went with it. We both knew them.

"You're really sure . . ."

I nodded. He dropped his fist, shrugged, and zipped up his coat.

An hour later nothing had changed, but I felt better. If nothing else, Barry's behavior was a reminder that relationships are never completely over. That the skeins that bind us remain entwined, impossible to unravel. And, in the final analysis, why would we want to? After the anger, the disappointment, the betrayal, those threads are the only things that link us together.

TWENTY-SEVEN

AFTER I DROPPED Rachel at school Monday morning, I called Susan. "This is an SOS—Serious Order of Shit."

When either of us declares one, the other knows to drop everything, no matter what time of day or night, and hook up immediately. The only detour permitted is for a pound of chocolate or bottle of wine. Or both.

"What's going on?"

"I'm so depressed, I could listen to Neil Young."

"That's bad." She paused. "Wine or chocolate?"

I thought for a minute. "Neither. But don't eat lunch. I'll pick you up at one."

"Can it wait that long?"

"It'll have to. I'm editing tape this morning."

Before I left for Mac's studio, I finally summoned the nerve to check my messages. Both were from David. Would I please call him, he asked in the first. He wanted to explain. He owed me an apology. By the way, Willie was doing fine and sent his regards. Please call, the second message said. "We really need to talk."

I punched "stop" on the machine. How dare he toss

around the ubiquitous word *talk,* as if relationships could be altered or transformed simply by pronouncing certain words. Did he expect me to ignore what I'd seen? To pretend it had never happened? I erased the messages.

Before going out, I checked the mailbox to see what had accumulated over the weekend. I don't check the mail every day; it's mostly bills and junk mail, so when I spotted an envelope with Fouad's name and address on it among the circulars and coupon books, I promptly opened it. Two pieces of paper fell out. One was a note scrawled in pencil by Fouad. He'd signed his name with a flourish.

I was shoveling the walk and found this under the stoop. I thought it might be important for you or Rachel.

I examined the other paper. It, too, was a note, more terse than Fouad's. Barely legible, the ink was smeared and faded. It looked like it had been lying in the snow for a while. I could just make out the words.

Please. You keep. Not safe for me to have. I come back.

I turned the paper over. No further message was on it. And no signature. I frowned. Was it a note from one of Rachel's friends? Had it dropped out of her trapper? I turned it over and looked at it again. The penmanship was full of curlicues, and the words leaned to the left. My heart thudded in my chest. I'd seen that handwriting before. On the envelope of the tape that was dropped off at the house.

I backtracked to the house, mentally blessing Fouad for his thoughtfulness, and called Davis. The note must have separated from the tape when it was delivered. Rachel brought the tape inside, but probably never saw the note.

When Davis's voice mail picked up, I called back and talked to a human. Dispatch said Davis wasn't due in until noon. I was on my way to Mac's now and would be meeting

Susan at one. Noon would work. I slipped both notes back into Fouad's envelope, dropped it into my bag, and headed out to the car.

I was backing down the driveway when Lillian Armstrong pulled up in her white Cadillac, blocking the end of the driveway. For someone who claimed to be a Florida snowbird, she sure was spending a lot of time in the nest. She lowered the passenger window and beckoned me over. Reluctantly, I climbed out of the Volvo.

"Just remember I told you so," she said when I was close enough to hear.

"Good morning to you, too, Lillian." Her eyes narrowed just enough. "What's going on?"

"Well." She paused theatrically. "Not only has my cleaning lady not shown up for the past week, but I can't get the damn service on the phone."

I bent my head toward her window. "What do you mean?"

"The number for DM Maids has been disconnected. And there's no forwarding information."

"Are you talking about the service owned by Halina Grigorev? In Mount Prospect?"

Lillian eyed me. "How did you know?"

I sidestepped the question. "When did this happen?"

"Sometime over the past week." She drummed freshly manicured fingertips on the wheel. "Did that policewoman come down on her? I told her I didn't know anything about her—their status. You don't think she's going to be coming after me again, do you?"

I knew the answer was no, but I just couldn't bring myself to tell her. "I wouldn't have any idea, Lillian."

"I told you how they are," she said tartly. "No work ethic. They don't care about doing a good job. Or treating people right. All they care about is—well, I wouldn't know, but you can bet it's not us." She snorted with contempt.

"I'm sorry this happened to you, Lillian, but I'm not sure there's anything I can do."

"I realize that." She glared. "I just wanted you to know.

I said you couldn't trust them. Not for a New York minute. Now I have to start all over again."

She didn't wait for my reply and pulled away, a puff of self-righteous exhaust trailing behind her.

I SPENT THE morning editing tape with Hank. A good editor is like a good musician: They both have to understand harmony, rhythm, and pace. Hank is both. He knows exactly when to cut and when to let a scene play. He also knows when to kick things up with an effect or musical bridge and when to tamp down for subtlety. And he plays bass on weekends.

We screened all the footage, tagged sound bites from Jordan Bennett's interview, and laid them in over shots of the apartment. I made notes of various pans and angles on the B-roll. We were going back to Cabrini tomorrow to shoot the kids moving in, and I wanted to make sure we replicated the same angles for a match dissolve.

After firming up tomorrow's shoot, I got back in the car. I still had twenty minutes before Davis was due in. I decided to swing by Sunset Foods for poached fish. Not only was their version—moist, tender, but firm—better than any restaurant's, but it would be an opportunity to see Stan the Fish Man. Stan has a killer smile, a great body, and recipes for everything from marinated shrimp to Chilean sea bass. Half the women on the North Shore are in love with him.

I was just passing the hardware store when I remembered we needed more salt for the driveway. I'd been meaning to get some for weeks. I turned in and ran inside. By the time I lugged a twenty-pound bag of salt to the car, annoyed there'd been only one cashier for seven customers, it was noon. The police station was a few blocks in the other direction. Flirting with Stan would have to wait.

The lobby of our police station looks like any other office building's, with recessed lighting, potted plants, and magazines fanned across a small table. As I waited for

Davis, I remembered sitting in this lobby last fall. The circumstances had been less sanguine.

"Hi, Ellie. What's up?"

I twisted around. I hadn't heard her come through the door. "Georgia. Did you get my message? I called you from Philadelphia."

She greeted me with a smile. "I took a few days off."

They must have agreed with her. The worry lines across her forehead were gone, and she looked relaxed. Was she with a boyfriend? Or family? I realized how little I knew about her personal life.

"I just got it," she said. "You called Saturday?"

"Yes, but since then, a couple of things have come up. First off, look at this." I rummaged in my bag and pulled out Fouad's envelope.

"What is this?" She asked.

"A note that came with the tape, I think. A friend who was shoveling my walk found it under the stoop. Check out the handwriting."

Davis squinted and studied the note. Then she nodded, more to herself than me, it seemed. "I'll keep this."

"That's why I brought it." "But that's not all," I went on. "I ran into Lillian Armstrong this morning. Apparently, the maid service she uses has dropped off the face of the earth."

She frowned. "Tell me."

I repeated what Lillian had said about DM Maids. She nodded again and looked down at the note. Then she glanced at the door that led back to the brass's offices. "You got a minute?"

"Sure."

She pushed through the door. At the end of a corridor was an open office. I followed her down into a square, featureless room with gray walls, a gray desk, and gray carpeting. Deputy Chief Olson sat behind the desk. His fringe of gray hair blended nicely with the surroundings. He rose and shook my hand. "Ms. Foreman. Nice to see you."

"Likewise."

His seat cushion made a plopping noise as he sat down. Davis and I sat across from him. Davis motioned to me. "Tell him what you just told me."

I repeated what Lillian had said. When I finished, Olson turned to Davis. "You'll check it out."

"Yes, sir." She held up the envelope. "There's something else. She just found this note outside her home and brought it in. It looks like the same handwriting that was on the envelope containing the tape."

Olson's expression grew curious. "Is there a name?"

Davis shook her head.

"It's been lying in the snow for a while," I said.

Olson opened a drawer in his desk and pulled out an evidence bag. He handed it to Davis. She put the note inside.

"I'd like to try and lift some prints."

"Give it a shot," Olson said. "But don't expect too much. It's been in weather."

"There's something else you should know," I said. "I was in Philadelphia over the weekend and I met someone who might have seen the woman on the tape." I told them about the diamond dealer who came into Willie's shop in Antwerp three years ago. "She had the same tattoo as the woman on the tape."

"Antwerp?" Olson's chair squeaked as he leaned back.

"Belgium," I said.

"That's a little out of our jurisdiction," he said dryly.

I shifted. "I realize that. I just wanted you to know."

He looked over at Davis. "Where are you on ID'ing the tattoo?"

"Haven't heard anything from the Bureau."

"Give them another push." He turned to me. "It's probably just a coincidence. It could be a common design. Maybe your friend saw something that looked similar, but wasn't exactly the same."

"There's no way to be sure?" I asked.

Olson shook his head. "Not without more information, time, and money. Which we don't have."

I changed the subject. "What about DM Maids? Is it possible there could be a connection between the woman on the tape and Halina Grigorev's disappearance?"

Neither officer replied. I shifted again. "Sorry. I know you don't want to talk about a case you're still working."

"No," Olson said. "That's not it." He considered me for a long moment, then nodded at Davis.

Davis cleared her throat. "We found out that Halina Grigorev is—or was—a cousin of the dentists."

"The owner of DM Maids was their cousin?" I felt a chill. "So they knew each other? How did you find out?"

Davis looked over at Olson. "We pieced it together from interviews with the dentists' neighbors."

I considered this piece of news. "If she and the dentists were cousins, and Petrovsky worked for her, is it possible she was the one who sent me the tape? And the note is from her?"

Olson leaned his elbows on the desk. "It's possible. Maids talk. One of the women who worked at your neighbor's might have heard something about you."

I laughed. "If it came from Lillian, I can imagine what it was."

Olson spread his hands. "Who knows? Maybe they heard you were a TV journalist and figured the tape would be safe with you . . . you know, confidentiality . . . a source . . . that kind of thing. The note, if it's real, would seem to imply that."

"But how would they have known Lillian?"

Davis shrugged.

Olson went on. "Or maybe they were counting on the fact that you'd hand it over to us."

"Why wouldn't they have done that themselves?"

"The dentists were operating without a license. For the second time in less than a year. Any brush with the law would have been big trouble for them."

I thought for a minute. "Do you think that's why they had a surveillance camera on the wall?"

"It's a good bet."

"They did anyway," I mused. "Ended up in trouble, I mean."

All three of us were quiet. I looked at Davis, then Olson. Why were they suddenly so talkative? They'd never been before. "Do you think they were the ones who—who disposed of the body?"

"Hard to say," Olson said. "But whether they did or didn't, they clearly didn't want to be fingered for the crime. They went to some length to avoid it."

"You seem pretty sure she was killed at their place."

"That's the good news," Davis cut in. "The lab says they got three different blood types from the samples."

"The sister, the brother, and the girl with the tattoo."

"Right."

"So what does it mean?"

"Nothing conclusive," Olson said. "It could be the dentists knew who killed the girl and didn't want them to get away with murder." He leaned back. "Or maybe Grigorev knew the real killers and talked her cousins into giving her the tape."

"Which she then got Petrovsky to drop off at my house."

Olson nodded.

"But it backfired."

He nodded again.

"Because someone—the real killers—figured out the dentists gave me the tape? And decided to make an example out of them?"

"Something like that."

"But who knew I had the tape? It's not like it's been on the news."

Olson hunched his shoulders. Davis refused to make eye contact.

Of course. Celestial Bodies. Someone at the strip joint told the killers we'd been asking questions. Showing photographs. Distributing business cards. That's how the word got back. Who was it, I wondered? Sofiya? One of the girls? The bouncer?

I studied the gray carpeting in Olson's office. Our visit might have triggered the death of the dentists—maybe Halina Grigorev's too. It also meant that someone at Celestial Bodies knew the killers. I almost asked Olson and Davis what they thought, but stopped just in time. I didn't know how much Davis had told Olson about that night. Or what she'd said in her report.

I stole a look at Davis, trying to tread cautiously. "Has anyone been back to Celestial Bodies?"

Olson nodded. "After the crime lab came up with zilch on the ballistics of that gun Davis found in the bathroom"—he flashed Davis an odd look—"Davis went back to nose around."

I cleared my throat.

"The girls had heard of the dentists." Davis took over. "Apparently, it's where you go when you're an immigrant and you don't have much money. But no one knew them personally. Or at least admitted to it."

"What about Petrovsky? Has anyone seen him?"

"We can't find him." She tossed her head. "If he's smart, he's on the run. Grigorev, too."

"Unless they're already dead," Olson said.

"One of the 'dancers' seems to have disappeared, too," Davis added.

"Which one?"

"The one that . . ." She snuck a look at Olson. "The blond. With the spiky hair. They said she didn't work there anymore."

The one whom I'd chased down the hall. Who had rifled through my bag. "You can't track her down?"

"It's not like she left a forwarding address."

I swallowed. It was clear Davis hadn't told Olson everything about our drop-in at the club. Still, two people were dead. And three more—Grigorev, Petrovsky, and the blond "dancer"—were missing. Were they dead? Was there a link between them and the tape?

I kept coming back to another question too. Why did Petrovsky drive from Mount Prospect to Celestial Bodies in the middle of a snowstorm in the first place? Clearly, he had some connection to the place, beyond that of "customer." He'd gone backstage as soon as he arrived, and he knew the layout well enough to make himself scarce when Davis questioned the girls. I wanted to ask Davis what she thought, but I didn't dare with Olson in the room. I might have to explain how Davis "found" the gun in the bathroom. And what happened after that.

Olson ran a hand over the top of his skull as if he expected to find a full head of hair. "Maybe the girl on the tape ticked off someone. She gets killed. Then the dentists tried to blow it wide open, and they get wasted, too. These people have nasty tempers. You don't want to piss them off."

"So I gather." I folded my arms. "At least the note's a step in the right direction. Maybe it will help you get to the bottom of this. Especially if you're able to get some prints."

The cops exchanged another look. Then Olson spoke. "The truth is, we may never get to the bottom of this. Even with the note."

"Why not?"

"Des Plaines is handling most of it now."

"What does that mean?"

Olson shifted uncomfortably. "The case file will stay open."

"I hear a *but*."

"We won't be actively pursuing it much longer."

"But you don't know who killed her. What about her family? Someone is probably going crazy wondering what happened to her."

Olson sighed. "Ellie, we don't have a body. Never did. Not that it makes a huge difference, although it might in court, if we ever got that far. But more important, we just don't have the evidence. No one's talking. To them, we're as much the enemy as the scumbags who killed the girl. Unless that note shows some type of dramatic evidence, which, frankly, I don't think it will, we just don't have the time and resources to keep going." He flipped up his palms. "I hope you understand."

DAVIS KEPT HER mouth shut as she walked me out until we got to the door of the police station. "I wish there was something more I could do."

"You've done more than anyone else would have."

She shook her head. "It wasn't enough."

"Stop getting down on yourself."

She shrugged and opened the door. "Listen, Ellie . . ."

"What?"

She shook her head again. "Nothing. You be careful, okay?"

TWENTY-EIGHT

I GOT IN the car and cracked the window. I understood why Olson was winding down. I also understood Davis's warning. It was obvious from the note I'd handed over.

Please. You keep. Not safe for me to have. I come back.

The person who sent me the tape knew it was dangerous to keep it, so they passed it to me. Which meant that if someone wanted to eliminate anyone or anything that linked them to the tape, Rachel and I were an easy and—now that the cops were winding up their investigation—unprotected target. Davis knew that, too. They—whoever "they" were—might well come back. And, the cops couldn't—or wouldn't—do much to help. I rolled up the window, suddenly chilled.

There had to be something more I could do. But what? I didn't know who or what I was looking for: Petrovsky or the two men on the tape? Or someone else?

I considered trying to trace the tattoo myself—a few

e-mails, phone calls, some Web surfing might get me somewhere. But then what? What if I uncovered an organized gang or cell of the Russian mafia? And they learned I'd been nosing around in their business? How could I defend myself against that?

I turned south on Waukegan Road, weaving between a minivan and a bus, both of which moved as if they owned the road. I'd been foolish to get involved in the first place. The woman on the tape, the killers, Petrovsky, they were all strangers—the kind of strangers, it was turning out, most safely viewed from a distance. The vague notion of responsibility I'd felt now seemed misplaced and naive. If something happened to Rachel . . . I chewed on a nail. The police were giving up. I should, too. I hoped it wasn't too late.

I HONKED WHEN I got to Susan's. She came out, looking perfect, as usual. She's the only woman I know who can wear a white turtleneck, flannel pants, and a Harris tweed jacket and not look like a Barrington horsewoman.

She settled herself in the front seat. "So, where are we going?"

"You'll see."

I cut over to the Edens and headed downtown. Susan smeared lip balm over her mouth. She always takes care of herself. We chatted about inconsequential things, knowing after ten years of friendship not to force issues. But when I merged onto the Kennedy, she pointed to one of the green road signs. "You passed Peterson."

"I know."

Susan used to live in Sauganash, and Lakeview before that, and she knows Chicago as well as I. She shrugged. But when I exited on Kimball and drove east on Belmont, she whooped. "Cinnamon rolls!"

I grinned.

"I figured it was either that or pizza. When you passed the exit for Malnati's, I knew."

Ann Sather's, a Swedish restaurant, is a popular place

for plain, wholesome food, especially breakfast, which they serve all day. But they're famous for their cinnamon rolls: dense, moist creations laced with cinnamon and topped with a dollop of icing. One of them has enough calories, cholesterol, and fat to kill you. But you'd die happy.

Although Sather's has five restaurants, they make the rolls at the Belmont location, and real connoisseurs won't go anywhere else. I parked around the corner, and we trudged down cracked sidewalks to the front door. The décor—clean, bright, and workmanlike—hasn't changed in thirty years. We grabbed a booth near the fireplace.

"Did you know at the turn of the twentieth century, Chicago had the second-largest Swedish population of any city in the world?" Susan said, sliding her napkin onto her lap.

"No."

"And did you know it was Swedes who built Wrigley Field? And founded Walgreen's?"

"Do you have some Swedish blood you never told me about?"

She laced her fingers together. "I used to date a guy whose parents were from Sweden. He taught me the only Swedish I know."

"What's that?" I imagined some endearment or romantic expression. Maybe something more graphic. You know the Swedes.

"For yag tala med Erik."

"And that means . . .?"

"It means 'May I please speak to Erik.' " A flush crept up her neck. "I wanted to impress his mother when I called."

A waitress, in dark slacks and a navy polo shirt with a green face imprinted on it, took our order. She seemed disappointed when we only ordered cinnamon rolls.

"You want to split an omelet?" I asked.

Susan shook her head. "The last one I had—not here"—she smiled up at the waitress—"looked like it had been run over on Willow Road. It kind of put me off eggs."

I flashed the waitress an apologetic look. She gave us her back.

"So, Ellie." Susan twiddled her thumbs. "Why are we here?"

"There's been a major disaster." I explained what happened in Philadelphia. She winced when I got to the part at the airport.

"I should have known," I grumbled.

"Known what?"

"He's a chip off the old block."

"How so?"

"Remember how his father and mother got together? David's apparently inherited those genes."

"What genes?"

"The 'I-can-do-anything,' opportunistic ones."

She frowned. "From what you're saying, this—this Brigitte is the opportunist. David sounds like the victim."

Tears suddenly stung my eyes. "I—I don't know, Susan. I'm confused. And angry. I can't think straight."

She laid her hand on my arm. "Don't worry, sweetie. We'll figure this thing out."

I went quiet, trying to gather myself together. Then, "You know what I don't understand? If he fell under her spell in Europe, why did he let me come to Philadelphia? And spend time with his uncle?"

"Maybe he wasn't sure. Maybe he needed to compare."

"So now I'm a piece of fruit in the supermarket?"

She shot me a look. "I know it's hard to believe, but he could be just as confused as you."

"If he is, then that's the least of his problems. This woman is deceiving him. Perpetrating a fraud. And he doesn't see it." I paused. "You know something? Maybe I should let her. I mean, she's obviously a master at manipulation. Maybe we could learn from her."

Susan ignored my comment. "Has he called?"

"Twice. I haven't called him back."

The cinnamon rolls arrived with two cups of coffee. I

speared a huge piece with my fork and stuffed it into my mouth. A sweet, melting sensation rolled over my tongue.

Susan cut a tiny sliver and chewed meticulously. "Talk about self-serving people. I know it's not the same thing, but I have to tell you what happened to Andy last week." Andy is Susan's son, a cheerful ten-year-old who loves baseball, soccer, and stamp collecting.

"What?"

"He hooked up with another boy to sell tickets to the Boy Scout pancake breakfast . . . you know, the one where the proceeds go to the Settlement House? They get points toward a badge, depending on how many they sell. So the boys decided to split the points down the middle. Fifty-fifty, no matter who sold what. Well, then Andy gets the flu, remember, and could only sell ten. The other kid sold twenty-two. And guess what. The kid reneges on the deal. Takes all the points for himself."

"What did you do?"

"What could I do?"

"Call the mother."

"Andy made the deal himself. I can't get in the middle. It's one of those hard-knock experiences I guess he'll learn from." She pushed her plate away. "But can you believe it? The whole thing was for charity to begin with. What's the point?"

"The badge," I said.

"Yeah, and this kid will get his. But the way he went about earning it was totally alien to the spirit of the thing."

"What else is new? There are always people who need to have an edge. Preferably at someone else's expense."

"Oh, Ellie, stop the psychobabble. It was greed. Pure and simple."

"Better Andy learns that now, don't you think?"

"Maybe." She sipped her coffee. "But it was a hard lesson."

A siren shrieked past on Belmont, its wail rising to a crescendo, then mournfully fading away. The waitress hovered nearby. I waved her off.

"You really do need to talk to David, you know," Susan volunteered.

I stiffened. "I can't. I don't know how he'll react. After believing for so long that he was alone, that he had no living relatives, finding his uncle has to have triggered a sea of feelings. And not just on a personal level."

"What do you mean?"

"There's got to be a sense of victory, too. You know, triumph that the Nazis didn't destroy everyone in his family."

"I guess. But what does that have to do with this—this Brigitte?"

"She's linked to his family. Indirectly, perhaps, but she's Jewish, and she's German. And she's been the person who's been closest to his only living relative." I stopped. "My God. I just got it."

"What?"

"Brigitte. Who does she remind you of?"

"Lisle," Susan said, not missing a beat. "His mother."

"Maybe that's the attraction."

"That she reminds him of his mother?"

I nodded.

"But this woman's a con artist. A charlatan."

"He can't see that. He might actually believe this woman is his destiny. Especially if she reminds him of Lisle."

"Ellie, that's irrational."

"Of course it is." I played with my spoon. "But let's be honest. David's quest—his obsession to find his family—has never been entirely rational to begin with."

Susan didn't answer. Then she cleared her throat. "About ten years ago," she said softly, "before you and I became friends, I was convinced Doug was having an affair."

I almost choked on my coffee. Susan's life was supposed to be perfect.

She ran a finger up the edge of her knife. "He was coming home late at night. He wouldn't tell me where he'd been. I was devastated. Ready to call it quits. File for divorce."

"Was he?"

She held up the knife. "I took the kids and went to my mother's. I know, how trite can you get? Anyway, she sat me down. It was probably the only real conversation we ever had. She made me realize that I wasn't pulling my weight in the relationship."

"What do you mean?"

"I mean, I was going to the grocery store, doing the cleaning, raising the kids. I thought that was what I was supposed to do. The problem was I wasn't thinking about Doug."

"How?"

"He was going through a hard time. The market was down. Things were tight financially. But I didn't know it. And he didn't tell me. It turned out he'd been moonlighting, trying to scrape together a few extra dollars."

"He never told you?"

She shook her head. "He was afraid to. He thought I'd think he was a failure and leave him."

"Which you almost did."

She smiled ruefully.

"What happened?"

"My mother told me to go home and talk to him."

"Did you?"

"I thought it over for a day or two. But then, yes, I went home." She put the knife down. "We talked all night."

"It obviously worked out."

"When we realized how much we cared about each other, the kids, and the marriage, we started to see options. Doug realized he didn't have to shoulder everything by himself. I realized I could help and went to work. It wasn't a lot of money—but it was there. He started to relax. I eased up on my expectations." Her eyes twinkled. "And now, well, things are pretty good." She looked up at the ceiling. "Thanks, Mom."

"If it doesn't kill you, it makes you stronger."

She shifted. "The point is you have to talk to David, if you think there's any chance to fix things."

I shook my head. "It's too risky."

"Ellie, since when have you run away from anything?"

But Susan didn't realize how profoundly inadequate I felt where relationships were concerned. I pushed my plate away. I felt like I was perched on a diving board, but I didn't know if the pool was full or empty.

THE NEIGHBORHOOD THAT Ann Sather's occupies is a work in progress. It used to be just the "North Side." Then it became "New Town." Now it's called "Lakeview," even though it's blocks from the lake, and there is no view.

After leaving the restaurant, we walked down the block, past several antique shops, a new hair emporium, and a Thai restaurant. The sex shop that used to be on the corner has gone, but the tattoo parlor across the street was still there.

I stopped, a tickle of awareness passing through me. A tattoo parlor! Could that be why I'd driven all the way down to Ann Sather's? I checked my watch. Just after two. We had an hour before we had to be back north. I started to thread my way through traffic, then stopped. I shouldn't be doing this.

As if reading my thoughts, Susan pointed to Krueger's Antiques a few doors away. "Why don't we check out some Bakelite?"

I looked at the antique store, then back at the tattoo parlor. On the other hand, all I'd be doing was asking a few questions. "In a minute."

Susan flared her nostrils and pointed her chin in the direction of the tattoo parlor. "Must you?"

I nodded.

She sighed and followed me across the street.

Chicago Tattoos and Piercing was so sterile and well lit it could have passed for the clinic I take my father to. We stepped into a large room—the studio, a sign said—filled with several dentist-type chairs and a phalanx of steel instruments. The sign said the shop prided itself on being the oldest—and cleanest—tattoo parlor in Chicago, and there wasn't a speck of dust, a piece of trash, or dirty needle to be seen. The place was so civilized there was even a waiting area, with a leather couch and soda machine. I looked around, half expecting to see a supply of surgical masks on hand.

The walls were covered with hundreds of designs from dainty butterflies and dragons to coiled snakes, and every conceivable animal, emblem, and logo in between. Large, small, conventional, obscene—I'd never seen so many tattoos in one place. Hundreds more were displayed in a thick binder on the counter.

Susan sat primly on the sofa, her purse on her lap. Besides us, the place was empty except for a man bent over a bucket of sudsy water, ringing out a mop. His gray hair was pulled back in a ponytail, and he sported a long gray beard. The skin on both arms was completely obscured by tattoos, and he wore an orange sarong. When he spotted us, be straightened up and gave us a beatific smile. I thought of one of those smiling Buddha statues you see in yoga studios.

"You've got to be kidding," Susan muttered under her breath.

The man put down the mop, folded his hands in front of his heart, and bowed his head. *"Namaste."* Greetings.

I did the same thing. The man in the sarong nodded approval. "Are you here for a tattoo?"

"Well, not exact—"

"You've come to the right place." He picked up the bucket and moved toward the counter. "We have some beautiful ancient designs. Asian, Buddhist, Thai, Indian."

"But—"

"First timers, huh?" He stepped behind the counter.

I tried to cut in. "Actually—"

He went on. "The ancients believed people took on the characteristics of the tattoos they chose. Different tattoos have different powers. For example, there's a tattoo called *sah riga lin torng* that brings adoration. On the other hand, *suk roop seua pen* is a tiger tattoo that causes its wearer to be feared. And the Thais thought tattoos could stop bullets."

He grinned. "It's part of a long tradition that sees pain as the way to tap into man's primal urge for meaning and belonging." Susan and I exchanged glances. "Women, too," he added hastily. "It's all very spiritual."

"We're not here for a tattoo," I said firmly.

He looked temporarily crestfallen. Then he brightened. "Maybe a piercing? I have some lovely navel rings and nose—"

"I was just wondering if you might be able to identify a tattoo."

"Oh." He looked disappointed. "Depends what it is."

"I can draw it for you."

He pulled out a paper and pencil.

I sketched out the torch and the stars. While he studied the design, Susan got up and picked her way into the studio.

He tipped his head to the side. "Where'd you see this?"

"A woman. She had one on her wrist."

"American?"

"I—I'm not sure. Why?"

"I've been in this business for a long time. Before I became a Buddhist, even. But I've never seen anything like that. Like I said, though, tattooing is a very old practice. Asians did it centuries before the Hell's Angels."

I watched Susan examine some of the designs on the wall. "Why'd you ask if she was an American?"

"Because if she wasn't, and you knew where she was from, it might trigger something. Like I said, I've been around these things practically all my life."

I hesitated. "What if she were Russian? Or from that part of the world?"

"Russian, huh?"

"Maybe."

"Well . . ." He fingered a tiny gold hoop in his ear. "In Russia, you got your prisons. And your gulags. You see a lot of tattoos there. Some are just general, but others could be specific to a particular prison. Even a ward."

"I wouldn't know whether she was ever in jail."

"Don't matter. The men—they like to brand their women." He grinned. "The women don't mind."

I pursed my lips.

"'Course, then you got your army folks, too," he said hurriedly.

"The Russian army?"

"Or navy."

Susan stopped at a row of tattoos on the wall.

I looked back at the sketch. "Do you think this could have been an army tattoo?"

"Hard to say." He stroked his beard. "But, you know, now that I think of it, I remember a guy who came in a while back. He had a torch with some kind of number on his shoulder. Wanted to add to it."

"A torch?"

"Yeah. It even looked a little like that there sketch. Dude said he was in the Russian airborne."

A buzz skimmed my nerves.

"Could be they're hung up about fire over there. I wouldn't be surprised. It's one of the most powerful symbols there is. For Buddhists, it's a medium of purification. Even more powerful than water."

"How so?"

He leaned his elbows on the counter. "A burning fire is the mind 'unawakened,' agitated, full of passions and delusions. The goal is to extinguish the fire so that the mind is released. Unbound. You're more aware. Closer to nirvana. It's in early Buddhist scriptures: 'The wise . . . they go out like this flame.'" He was starting to gear up again. "I can point you to a couple of books, if you're interested."

I hoisted my bag farther up my shoulder. "No, thanks. But you've been very helpful." I looked over at Susan. "Okay, Miss Susan. Let's go check your Bakelite now."

"Not so fast." She spun around and pointed to a tattoo that looked like a variation of a Celtic knot. "How much for this one?" she asked the tattoo artist. "And how long would it take?"

* * *

AFTER I DRAGGED Susan home and picked up Rachel, I stopped by Sunset, chatted with Stan, and walked out with twice as much fish as I needed. When dinner was over, I fortified myself with half a bottle of wine. Then I called David.

"Hello, Ellie."

His voice was measured. Cool. I heard a quiet commotion in the background. Was that Willie? Or Brigitte?

"You didn't call me back."

"I couldn't," I said. "I—I heard her message on your machine."

"I thought so."

"David?"

"Yes?"

"Tell me it's not true. This is just all some kind of horrible misunderstanding."

He didn't answer. An image of his hands stroking my skin swept over me. I pushed it away. "David?"

He cleared his throat. "I—I can't say that, Ellie."

Pressure built in my chest. The nightmare was back. "But—but what about us?"

He sighed. "Ellie, it's no secret you and I have been having problems. You couldn't call our relationship smooth."

"I—I was thinking we could work it out. I never—I didn't expect—this."

"I wasn't looking for it, either. It just happened."

"What happened? What was it about her? Tell me." Why was I doing this, torturing myself?

He was quiet. Then, "I don't know if I can explain it. I didn't realize it until I went to the airport. It was all—very fast. But when I saw her again, it was as if she was supposed to be there."

"Supposed to be there?"

"She understands me, Ellie. She knows what it's like to lose most of her family. To grow up on her own. And she doesn't want to charge off and save the world. She's content to stay home and take care of me."

"David, you've only known her two weeks. How do you know?"

"How did *we*?"

"Apparently, we didn't."

"She flew halfway around the world to be with me, Ellie."

"Oh, so distance is the mitigating factor? What if I had flown over and met you in Germany? Would that have made a difference?"

"You didn't."

I thought about it, I wanted to say. But I couldn't. I couldn't say anything. I felt drained. Nothing would make a difference, any way.

"What about Dad?" I said miserably. "And Rachel? What do I tell them?"

For the first time I heard uncertainty in his voice. "Tell— tell them . . . I'm so sorry."

Tears started to well up. "David, I can't pretend to understand any of this. I do think it has something to do with finding your uncle, and I understand that your perceptions might be skewed. That things might appear to be very different in a short period of time. But I—"

"Ellie, I've never seen things more clearly."

So much for talking it out. Susan was wrong. I blinked back tears. Then I remembered the airport and Brigitte's conversation on her cell. He might not believe me, but, in a way, I felt protective of him. And this might be the last chance I'd have. "David, be careful."

"Careful? Careful how?"

"I—I don't want you to get hurt."

"I appreciate your concern, Ellie, but don't worry. I'm fine. And I want you to know—"

"No, listen. I need to tell you something."

"Go ahead."

I let out a breath. "After I heard Brigitte's message on your machine, I went to the airport to go home. O'Hare was shut down because of the weather. So I went to the bar to check her out. She didn't know who I was. I sat at the next table. She was talking on her cell phone." I hesitated.

"David, she was talking to someone in New York. A man. She told him as soon as you signed the papers to sell the shop, she would come to him, and they would go away together. David . . . she told him she loved him."

There was silence.

"Did you hear me?"

"I heard you."

"You haven't signed the papers yet, have you?"

More silence.

"David?"

His voice was cool. "Ellie, I know I've hurt you deeply. I'm truly sorry. I should never have allowed you to come to Philadelphia and meet Willie. It wasn't fair. But I have to wonder whether you're telling me the truth now."

"David, do you think I would ever lie to you?"

"I didn't think so, but your timing is—well—it's suspect."

I knew I was grasping for straws. "David, she's not your family. She's not your uncle's family, either."

He was quiet for a moment. Then, "Neither are you."

THAT NIGHT THE demons invaded my soul. Not just the dybbuks who come after me for a tasteless comment or hurtful look. These were the darker ones, the ones who delight in pointing out my essential worthlessness. The ones who chortle gleefully that I will be unmasked, revealed to be the fraud I am. It was your fault you lost David, they sneered. If you hadn't been so cavalier, so driven, so insensitive, he would still be yours. I tried to argue it wasn't me. It was Brigitte. She stole him away. Not so, they scoffed. It's your fault. It always is.

TWENTY-NINE

IT WAS STILL dark when I met Mac and the crew at Cabrini Green. Jordan Bennett had given me the key to the apartment, and Mac started setting up lights. We would begin taping indoors, but when the moving van arrived, we'd take the camera off sticks and shoot handheld.

Jordan endeared himself to the crew by arriving just after dawn with coffee and donuts. When he passed me the box, I declined.

"You're the first woman I've met who turned down a free Krispy Kreme," he said.

"I'm boycotting them."

"They're the hottest things around."

"Any food that has its own fan site on the Web is no longer a fad—it's an obsession. A crass, unhealthy one at that."

Jordan cocked his head.

"How many fan sites for tomatoes do you see? Or string beans? It's exploitative. And commercial. I won't be a party to it."

"And you know it has its own fan site because . . ." He

looked puzzled, then smiled. "You wouldn't be surfing the Net for Krispy Kremes yourself, now, would you?"

I sniffed, trying to salvage the shreds of my dignity.

He offered the rest to the crew.

I bit my lip. "I'm sorry, Jordan. I'm in a lousy—I'm just not hungry."

"No problem."

The truck, donated by Feldman Development, showed up at nine. An enormous van of holding goods from two or three households, the meager possessions of six kids barely made a dent. We decided to shoot the furniture truck instead.

By the time it arrived, four of the boys had shown up. The other two kids had jobs and wouldn't be there until evening. The boys' eyes widened as they watched six beds, dressers, and desks being unloaded. It was just the basics, but for some of them, it was probably the first time they'd ever seen new furniture. Jordan had leased it for a year.

We followed the boys with the camera while they unpacked and started to set up. Three of them were African American. The fourth, in sleeveless denim shirt and multiple piercings, looked like a wannabe biker. I considered telling him what I'd learned about spiritual tattoos, but he didn't look like a Buddhist, and he didn't need the tattoos.

Although shy and withdrawn around us, the kids were easy and boisterous with Jordan, clinging to him as if he was a latter-day Fagin. Unlike Fagin, though, Jordan cared, and I made sure Mac got B-roll of him dispensing high fives to one, quiet words of counsel to another. After the kids put away their things, we shot short interviews with them.

We were just wrapping up when I heard the click of heels on the parquet floor. I turned to see Ricki Feldman trotting toward us. With a black sable coat thrown over some kind of designer pantsuit, she looked too upscale for the place, but I pretended not to notice. Jordan's look of surprise said he hadn't expected her to show up, either, but he gave her a warm welcome and took her on a tour of the apartment. She stuck close to him. Only once did I catch them smiling at each other in a way that went beyond professional. I pretended not to see that, too.

"How about I take you and Jordan to lunch?" she said when they'd finished the tour. "My treat."

I smiled politely. "Sorry. I have too much going on today."

"No problem." She waved dismissively, then turned to Jordan. "You'll come, won't you?"

"Just let me make sure the guys are settled." He headed back toward the bedrooms.

She followed him with her eyes, then looked at me. "So, how's it going?"

"We got some warm, beautiful footage of the kids and Jordan this morning."

"When do you shoot the congressman?"

"He'll be back in the district for Presidents' Day. We have an interview set up."

"Good. How about your friend David? Did you end up using him in the film?"

"No."

The look on my face must have brooked no argument, because she didn't pursue it.

Jordan came back out, cheerfully rubbing his hands. His manner was so open, so innocent, even, that my maternal, protective instincts snapped on. I hoped Jordan knew what he was doing. A relationship with Ricki Feldman was not for the fainthearted. But then, who was I to judge? I was no poster child for healthy relationships.

Ricki shrugged into her coat and started for the door. Jordan was two steps behind. Then she turned around. "Oh, Ellie, I almost forgot. I have a favor to ask you. You remember Max Gordon, don't you?"

I frowned.

"You met him in the restaurant with your friend David."

Why did she have to keep bringing him up? "Gold Coast Trust, isn't it?"

"Right. Well, he's breaking ground tomorrow on his new skyscraper. You know, the one just north of the Loop." When I didn't answer, she added, "Don't tell me you don't remember that, I told you about it at the restaurant."

I shook my head. Only Ricki Feldman would expect me to remember a conversation from weeks ago that lasted less than thirty seconds.

"He's developing the site near Wabash and Wacker," she said impatiently.

"Wabash and Wacker? Isn't that the site Donald Trump had his eye on?"

"That's the one."

Now it clicked. The proposal called for an eighty-story tower, the fifth-tallest in Chicago. It had generated the typical hue and cry: Some said it would destroy the skyline; others maintained it was critical for the city's survival. The mayor approved it, but for some reason, Trump bowed out. Happily, Max Gordon stepped in. I hadn't realized until now that was the skyscraper they were talking about.

"What's the favor?" I asked.

"Will you shoot the ground-breaking ceremony for me?"

I ran a hand through my hair. "Ricki, I'm not a news crew. I don't do that kind of work. Why don't I find you a freelance crew?"

"But I want you to shoot it."

"What time is the ceremony?"

"Noon."

I started to say okay—I could always use the extra money—but she didn't give me the chance. "This could lead to something big, you know. It's major construction, in the heart of downtown. I wouldn't be surprised if Max wants a video of the building going up. You'd definitely have a foot in the door."

"That's fine—"

"Ellie. This is big. It's on the same scale as Sears, the Hancock. Even the World Trade Center."

The remark hung in the air for a moment. Ricki actually winced. "Please," she said softly. "I'd like to give it to him as a present. He's been a real friend. And I know I can count on you to do a great job."

"Save the speech, Ricki. I was going to say yes."

"Oh." Her face relaxed. "Thanks."

The rich and their gifts.

"By the way. Since it's such short notice," she added, "if you have to charge time and a half, so be it."

THE CORNER OF Wabash and Wacker, a block north of the Loop, curls around a bridge that overlooks the Chicago River. South of the river, Wabash Avenue is noisy and gritty, with el trains clattering above, and older buildings crammed with tiny offices below. One-Eleven houses every medical specialist ever licensed, and if you can't find the right ring at Jewelers' Row, it probably doesn't exist.

The site of Max Gordon's tower, however, was north of the river, where property is more upscale. A huge lot on the east side of Wabash was surrounded by a chain-link fence. A man-made ditch, into which someone had thrown a load of gravel, had been dug in front. Inside, an area of hard-packed frozen ground stretched across the site, except for a small mound of earth that had been hacked up for the ground-breaking ceremony.

A podium stood a few feet away from the mound, and a gold banner with the words *Gordon Towers* in black letters hung behind it. Propped up against the podium was a shovel and two hard hats that had been painted gold. Of course. Gold Coast Trust.

A set of risers for the media had been set up about fifty feet from the podium. While Mac set up the camera, I snagged a program from a PR flunky who was trying to look important. The crowd was already gathering, and the news-people filtered in, camera crews and producers jockeying for position on the risers. I spotted an earnest female reporter whose first name rhymed with her last; she would regurgitate whatever she was spoon-fed. They all did. Made you long for the days of Phil Walters, Bill Kurtis, even Skippy.

A limo pulled up to the gate, and Max Gordon climbed out. Rounder and shorter than I remembered, he was wearing a camel's hair coat and muffler, but no hat. He was accompanied by a woman, his PR person, no doubt, and a linebacker-sized man who I assumed was a bodyguard. Why did he need protection? I wondered.

People usually mill around chatting before an event like this, but the temperature had plunged overnight, and the frigid air snatched clouds of vapor, siphoning them off like a powerful vacuum. People burrowed into their coats, stamped their feet, and looked longingly at two space heaters flanking the podium.

A second limo, with city of Chicago flags fluttering on both sides, pulled up, and the mayor emerged with a coterie of aides. I craned my neck, wondering if my old friend Dana Novak was with him. I didn't see her. The mayor greeted Gordon with a hail-fellow-well-met routine. Gordon's head barely reached the mayor's chest. A moment later, yet another limo drove up, and the governor appeared with his entourage. Max Gordon was clearly a player.

Ricki Feldman was there, too, looking stunning in her sable coat and matching hat. She kissed Gordon on the cheek and shook the mayor's hand, after which the mayor leaned over to an aide who whispered in his ear.

Mac started rolling when the speeches started. We'd discussed it on the way down. Speeches, cutaways, a little B-roll. Straight news style, nothing fancy. I scanned the program, searching for B-roll possibilities or, at least, familiar faces to shoot. A list of twenty names, the investors it turned out, was printed on the back. Gold Coast Trust was the lead, but I recognized several other banks and development companies. Feldman Development was number twelve.

After introductions, the mayor stepped up to the podium. "Good morning. Usually when a crowd gathers outside in this kind of weather, somebody is in trouble." The audience tittered. "Today is a happy exception: We're here to break ground on Gordon Towers, a welcome addition to the skyline of Chicago." He cleared his throat. "This facility will be much greater than the sum of its bricks and mortar, plumbing and wiring, windows and furniture. This is an important economic development project. Gordon Towers will bring hundreds of jobs to the area. It will attract retail businesses, too . . ."

He went on to list all the economic and social benefits that would accrue to the city because of the building. Then, "A diverse group of dedicated community leaders have contributed to the development of Gordon Towers, but none of this would have been possible without the leadership of the man standing to my right. Max Gordon was willing to step in at a crucial juncture. He staked not only his reputation, but the future of his bank. Why? Because he is committed to the city of Chicago. Lucky for all of us, he prevailed. Thus, today, as we slip spades into the soil, we celebrate not just the construction of an edifice, but the future of our great city. Thank you, Max Gordon."

Hearty applause followed. Then the governor rose and came to the podium, where he made some incomprehensible but, mercifully, brief remarks comparing Gordon to the state of Illinois. "Like Gordon," he said, "Illinois not only invests overseas, but tries to attract foreign investment to our shores so the state can provide decent jobs for our citizens."

I looked over at Gordon. His eyes were glazed with delight, and his smile was wide enough to sprout wings. When the governor was finished, he glided up to the podium. Before he stepped up, someone scurried behind it and bent down. Suddenly Gordon was six inches taller.

In his remarks, Gordon said this was the culmination of a lifelong dream. He thanked everyone from the mayor to his late father, an illiterate immigrant from central Russia, who, nonetheless, instilled a sense of ambition in his children. Then he and the mayor put on the golden hard hats. With the governor happily smiling behind them, Hizzoner picked up the shovel, dug into the soft mound of dirt, and scooped up a mound of earth. Cameras clicked, tape recorders whined. Milking the moment, the mayor flung the dirt, put down the shovel, and clapped Gordon on the back. The crowd cheered.

I glanced over at Mac. He nodded, signaling he had it on tape. I made a circle with my index finger, signaling back that he could get off sticks for cutaways. As he started into the crowd, the wind kicked up. Thick clouds were moving in from the west. The banner behind the podium flapped, and bits of trash blew across the ground. I pulled my hat low on my face and tightened my scarf. Others were putting on gloves.

A group of men in work clothes, heavy boots, and parkas—construction workers by the look of them—huddled near the fence. Gordon walked over and started to shake their hands. I motioned to Mac. Nodding, he made his way over to grab the shot. As Gordon worked his way through the group, one of the men moved out of the way to let his buddy greet "the boss." The man, tall and bulky, pulled out a ski mask and slipped it over his face. It was a navy blue mask, with red circles around the openings for eyes and mouth. As he backed up, I noticed he walked with a limp.

An uneasy feeling slid around in me. I pushed it away. The crowd started to disperse, and the news crews packed up, heading off to the next story. Mac came back to the risers, gave me a thumbs-up, and began breaking down the camera. I looked at the construction worker now making his way toward the exit. He was favoring his right leg.

Frowning, I turned around, but before I could say anything to Mac, Ricki planted herself in front of me. "Thank you for shooting this, Ellie. It means a lot to me."

I nodded, wishing she would go away. Instead, Ricki raised a gloved hand and waved at someone behind me. I twisted around. Max Gordon was wandering back across the construction site, the glow of celebrity, no doubt, keeping him warm. He acknowledged her wave with a dip of his head and started over. As he drew near, he slipped his hand inside his coat with a Napoleonic flourish.

Ricki introduced us, making sure to say that we'd met

in the restaurant several weeks before. Gordon gave me a blank stare.

"It was only a minute. There's no reason you should remember," I said, trying to be gracious.

He tipped his head to the side. Though the top of his head was bald, he had curly sideburns that refused to lie flat. "Yes. So you've been taking pictures?"

"We have."

"Are you with one of the news organizations?"

"No." I was about to explain why I was there when Ricki moved behind Gordon and mouthed: "It's a surprise!" She put her finger on her lips. I improvised. "I—I'm a freelance producer. We've been interviewing folks about the project for a possible show down the road."

"I see." His expression dimmed and he turned around as if to leave. Ricki held on to his arm.

I turned back to Mac. "Did you get any cutaways of the construction workers while he was doing the benevolent boss thing?"

"I did."

"You get a shot of the guy in the ski mask? The one with the limp?"

Mac looked over to where the men had been standing. "I think so. Why?"

I hesitated. I hadn't told Mac much about the situation up to now. "I don't know. I keep thinking I know him from somewhere."

"What are you talking about?"

"He seems familiar. Something about him." I shook my head. "Never mind. It's not—"

I stopped in mid-sentence. Mac had broken eye contact and was focusing on something behind me. I spun around.

Max Gordon was behind me. When our eyes met, he rocked back on his heels and gave me a thin smile.

I looked back at the construction worker. He was almost at the gate, still limping, the ski mask covering his face. Gordon followed my gaze. Then Ricki stepped between us. Flashing me an impatient look, she tugged on Gordon's arm. Gordon looked back at me. His smile had disappeared. He allowed her to lead him away.

I WAS ALMOST at Montrose on the Drive when the snow started. Heavy fat flakes slapped the windshield. Angry whitecabs roiled the lake. I wasn't sure what I'd witnessed, but I didn't like the feel of it. Max Gordon had been eavesdropping on my conversation with Mac; that was clear. His reaction to it, though, wasn't. For once, I was grateful to Ricki for hustling him away.

Mike Dolan, the forensic video guy, had said there were hundreds, if not thousands, of ski masks like the one worn by the construction worker. And what killer would knowingly wear the same clothing he'd had on when he was murdering a woman on videotape? No one could be that foolish—or arrogant. It couldn't have been the same mask. Or man.

Still, a veil of disquiet, as thick as the falling snow, settled over me. I cranked up the heat and turned on the radio. The weather people were predicting three more inches. I kept driving. It wasn't until I rounded the turn onto Hollywood that I realized I was wrong about something. There was no reason for the killer on the tape to have thrown away his ski mask. Or even be reluctant to wear it. He never knew he'd been recorded on tape.

THIRTY

Arin gazed at *the plane tickets in Yudin's hand. "Why?"*

"You deserve a vacation." He held them out. "You have earned it, my dear. These past few years have been most rewarding."

She knew that. Yudin had been bringing her stones on a regular basis; they were both making good money. She had moved her family to a small house and installed her parents on the first floor. She and Tomas lived above. They had ample food, clothes, and they went on vacation every year. Tomas, almost twelve now, loved soccer and hockey, and played both, thanks to the equipment she could afford.

Yudin still lived on the Vaziani base. Arin didn't see why. He rarely wore his uniform, and she never saw him involved in army matters. However, as an envoy of the new Russian government, he still traveled extensively, meeting with representatives from various industries and governments. It was after these "conferences" that he usually brought her a supply of stones.

Arin still traveled as well, mostly to European cities.

Sometimes when her business was completed, she would take a sightseeing tour on those large buses that clogged the streets. As the bus rumbled through unfamiliar neighborhoods, she'd watch people she didn't know and would never see again going about their lives. She'd wonder whether the woman with the baguette in her string sack was content, whether the man, his shoulders hunched against the chill, was happy. Afterward she would shop for trinkets for her family.

Still, tickets to the Caribbean? A hotel, as well? And all of it a gift? "I'm extremely grateful, Dimitri"—they'd stopped addressing each other by their family names long ago, except around Tomas—"but I cannot accept. I have my work at the factory. And Tomas. My mother should not be burdened with him. What would I do in any case?" Never one to idle, Arin could hardly get through a week at Lake Sevan every summer. What would she do in the Cayman Islands?

Yudin insisted. "You will find much to do. Sleep late. Eat well. Shop. Go diving. Please, Arin." He looked kindly at her. "We have come a long way together. I am indebted to you. This is just a small way to show my gratitude. Please do me the honor of accepting."

She studied him. Over the years, she'd developed a fondness for Yudin. It had taken time, but she'd come to realize that Sacha's death had destroyed his family, too. His wife, unable to recover from her grief, had left him; Sacha had been their only child. Arin and Tomas were his only relations. She and Yudin had come to a mutual acceptance, a kinship forged out of sorrow. And, of course, there was the business.

She considered the offer. Despite her travels, she'd never been west of London. She looked out at the gloomy, bitter day in Georgia, picturing white sand, clear water, tropical sun. Rich Germans and British flocked to places like this. She'd hear them in cafes and restaurants casually drop the fact they were flying in for a week or two. Why not her? The truth was that her mother could easily care for

Tomas. He was nearly old enough to fend for himself. Maybe Yudin was right. She deserved it.

SHE LANDED IN *Miami, and once through customs, transferred to a small plane for the flight to Grand Cayman. After collecting her bags, she climbed into the car that would take her to the hotel. Waves of heat shimmered up from the tarmac, and within five minutes, the back of her neck was damp. She rolled up her sleeves. She'd read up about the tropics. The natives referred to the sun as "the fire in the sky." Now she knew why.*

As they drove through Georgetown, she felt as if she had stepped into another realm. She'd never seen so many shades of green, nor such brightly colored blossoms. She smiled as she passed shops and buildings painted in such whimsical colors they might have come from a child's coloring book. She noted the British and American flags fluttering in the breeze.

Near the ocean the breeze dispersed the curtain of thick, steamy air, and when she arrived at her private villa, with a private swimming pool steps away and the beach just a few more, she sighed in delight. She unpacked and sampled a mango from a basket of fruit on the dresser. The card read in Russian, "Compliments of a friend." Yudin had attended to every detail.

At sunset she strolled along the water's edge, watching the sky turn pink, then coral, then purple. Tiny waves lapped at her feet. The smell of salt mixed with the tang of hot sand. Later that night she dined alone on the terrace of the hotel. She noted the appreciative looks from waiters and busboys. She hadn't thought about her appearance in years, but she must still look presentable. At one point, she thought someone on the beach might be watching her, but when she turned her head, she saw nothing except the fronds of a palm tree swaying in the sand.

It was on the evening of the second day, after a morning of shopping and an afternoon spent scuba diving with two

Germans and a Swiss businessman—she didn't speak the language, but it was charming what you could do with gestures and smiles—that Arin realized she'd never felt so relaxed. Even carefree. Yudin was right. She should have done this years ago. Perhaps tonight she'd try the restaurant the Germans had been so excited about—they'd written the name down for her. And tomorrow she'd take a Jeep ride around the island.

She had just finished bathing and dressing in her new Fendi sarong and tank, thinking how drab her winter clothes looked in comparison, when there was a knock on her door. She wondered if it might be the Swiss businessman. She'd seen his sly glances when he thought she wasn't watching. It wouldn't be unpleasant to spend an evening with him. The night, too, if it came to that. She opened the door.

She'd never seen the two men before. One was large and burly, the other small and thin. The large man, though well into middle age, apparently still clung to his vanity; his thinning hair was combed forward. The smaller man looked like his nose had been broken once or twice. They were wearing casual island clothes, but they looked uncomfortable in them, like little boys dressing up.

She felt a tickle at the back of her throat. "Da?"

The large man replied in Russian. "We are here to extend an invitation to you for the evening." He wasn't smiling. "We will take you."

Arin glanced warily at both men and shook her head. "Thank you, but I have other plans."

She started to close the door, but the small man blocked it with his foot and pushed his way in. The tall man followed.

"Your host will be most disappointed if you refuse," he said. "In fact, he insists that you come."

Arin glanced around. She'd had a near brush with danger once before when she was negotiating with a buyer. The man protested her prices were too high, and then suddenly pulled out a gun. Luckily, she'd been able to talk him down, but after that she made it a point to conduct business in daylight and only in well-populated areas. If she sensed trouble, she would simply walk away and melt into the crowd. Now, though, there was no daylight, no crowds.

But there was the phone. She spoke quietly, masking her fear. "If you do not leave this villa immediately, I will call security."

The two men exchanged amused looks and stationed themselves on either side of her.

She had no chance. Better to play along. For now. "Yes. All right. But who is this host you speak of?"

The large man answered, "You will see."

"And if I refuse to come?"

"You will not."

There was a window in the bathroom, Arin recalled. She'd opened it after her bath. "I will go. But please allow me to freshen up a bit." Grabbing her bag, she went in and started to close the door.

"The door will stay open." It was an order.

The men were brawnier and stronger than she was. She complied. As she applied a fresh coat of lipstick, she noticed her shaking hands. She forced herself to stay calm. Fearful people do not think well. She transferred a wad of money into her evening bag. She debated whether to take her passport, but decided to leave it in the room.

With night hugging the beach, the men led her out to a Range Rover that looked black in the light. As her eyes adjusted, she wondered if this was the act of a disgruntled customer. Mentally, she ran through her client list. The Israeli in Tel Aviv told her she drove a hard bargain, but he'd smiled when he said it. The Jews in Antwerp didn't care about price—they simply passed it on to their customers. The same with her clients in Geneva. It couldn't be a client, she concluded. No one except Yudin knew she was here. And Yudin didn't know her customers.

The car pulled away from the villa and started down Seven Mile Beach. She gazed out at the night. Tiny clouds, tinted gray in the moonlight, scudded across a navy sky. Hundreds of stars twinkled in the heavens. Was this a random kidnapping? She'd heard stories of young women who disappeared in the tropics. Hundreds of years ago, pirates took them captive. There was even an island named for them, somewhere in the U.S.

Twenty minutes later, they skirted Savannah on the southern coast and started east. The East End of Grand Cayman was more sparsely populated than Seven Mile Beach, and the coastline stretched into craggy rocks occasionally broken up by a villa. At Bodden Town, they turned inland into a thickly wooded area. The outlines of ferns, cacti, and palms loomed dark and menacing against the patchy moonlight. Finally the vehicle emerged from a thicket. In the center of a clearing was a brightly lit villa. The Range Rover swerved up to it, kicking up loose gravel.

Arin climbed out. The villa had been built in splendid isolation on a rocky ridge. Standing sentinel over the ocean, it was a two-story building with a pitched roof and glassed-in doors. Lush landscaping surrounded the front.

The men led her up a flagstone path to a glass door that spilled light across the sand. The small man slid it open and gestured for her to enter. They ushered her into a large, airy room with slate floors and stucco walls. A fan near the ceiling made slow, desultory circuits. A man was sprawled on the couch.

Arin gasped. He was older now, his face thicker, his dark hair silvered at the temples. But otherwise it was the same Vlad. The same crooked smile. Pale eyes that shone like fiery coals. Clothes that fit like a second skin.

"Hello, Arin."

A rush of fury broke over her, so powerful she was shocked. It had been over ten years since she'd seen him. She thought she'd flushed him out of her life, discarded him like a used rag.

"Hello, Vlad." She struggled to gain purchase over her emotions, and surprised herself with her calm. She looked around the opulent room. "You are doing well."

"As are you." He stood, his eyes tracking her up and down. "You are even more beautiful."

She nodded, forcing herself to think. The hotel. She'd thought someone was watching her last night. She'd had the same feeling while she was shopping. "You saw me in the restaurant."

"Among other places." He went to a bar built into the wall and poured a shot of Jack Daniels. He gulped it down, poured another, and offered it to her.

Among other places? Had he been following her? How many times had he seen her? She took the proffered glass. "What do you want?"

He padded back to the sofa and sank down. "There isn't much that I do not know about you, Arin." He patted the cushion beside him.

She snuck a glance at the men that had brought her here. The vain one hung back at the door. The smaller one had settled in a chair and was studying his nails. "I will stand."

A fleck of annoyance surfaced on Vlad's face, but he blinked it away. "Did you like the fruit basket?" He smiled. "I insisted they put in mangoes and bananas. You cannot get those fruits at home."

She didn't answer, but Vlad continued as if she'd thanked him properly. "Your business skills have developed quite nicely. Not that I had any doubt."

"My business skills?"

"The diamonds, Arin. You have a gift. Many gifts. But the diamonds—the way you have worked with Yudin. It has brought me much pleasure."

"How do you know about that?"

"I told you, there isn't much I do not know."

Suddenly another memory tumbled through her mind. Yudin and Vlad, meeting regularly in the major general's office. She had suppressed those memories when she left Georgia. She felt a sick twisting in her stomach. "You and Yudin. You have been working together."

He raised his glass in a mock toast. He reminded Arin

of a predator, seemingly lazing in the sun, but waiting to pounce on his prey in an unguarded moment.

She shifted. There was more. She had a feeling he was waiting for her to make another leap of logic. When she made it, the revulsion that swept through her was so fierce the glass slipped from her hand and shattered on the slate floor. "I've been working for you!" she cried. "All this time—Yudin . . . and I! We have been working for you!"

Vlad laced his fingers behind his head. "You must have known. You are not a stupid woman."

But she was stupid. She hadn't known. Or was it, she thought as the small man collected the broken glass, that she didn't want to know? She'd always suspected Yudin had a silent partner. For all his bluster and posturing and conference-going, Yudin wasn't smart enough to manage the business alone. Still, she'd never asked who it was.

Part of her must have known. The years she'd struggled to free herself from Vlad, to strip every vestige of his memory from her mind, had been a waste. She'd been caught in his web all along. She sank down on a chair, spasming between fear and loathing.

Vlad smiled, clearly enjoying her turmoil. "Come now, Arin. Did you think Yudin bought those tickets out of the goodness of his heart?" He snorted. "The fool does not have an unselfish bone in his body. But . . ." A mild frown spread across his face. "I was sure you knew. That your silence meant that you acquiesced."

She shook her head, not trusting herself to speak.

Vlad steepled his index fingers, tapped them against his chin. "I suppose it does not matter. In a way, it only reinforces what I have already decided." He swung his legs around and stood up. "I do hope you've enjoyed your little vacation, Arin, because it is about to come to an end. While I am certain you would prefer to while away the days and nights in this island paradise, and . . ." He paused. "I would like to while them away with you, that is not why you are here. I have a business proposition for you. An 'offer,' as they say in America."

Her mind was foggy, streaked with rage, but she forced herself to concentrate. To play along until she could figure out what to do. "What sort of offer?"

He kept his hands together as if he were praying. "There will be a time, quite soon, when Yudin will become . . . unnecessary."

Arin trembled.

"The market for blood diamonds has tightened. The politicians have listened to De Beers and have mandated those fucking certificates of origin. Which makes it difficult to market our stones. Prices are not what they used to be. I know you are seeing that."

He was right. Her prices had dropped—not significantly, but they were lower. "That is not Dimitri's fault." She was surprised to find herself defending Yudin, but it was clear—now—that Yudin was as much of a victim as Sacha. And Mika. And herself.

"Neither is it yours," Vlad said. "But Yudin has nothing more to trade. He was useful at first, particularly for the contacts he made at his conferences. But now there is just the arsenal on the base." He shrugged. "Most of the decent weaponry was 'procured' long ago. All that is left are the dregs—old Kalashnikovs that barely fire, grenades shipped back from Afghanistan. Nothing of interest to my current clients. Which makes him no longer necessary." He paused. "But you, on the other hand, are."

Arin tightened her lips.

"You see, while diamonds are only one part of my 'portfolio,' they are a significant segment, and I will be needing a new source."

She knew what was coming. Armenia's leading mineral exports were its precious and semiprecious stones. Cut diamonds, too. Every year Russia supplied Armenia with 30,000 carats of rough diamonds, plus a million carats of industrial diamonds for processing. In fact, over 25 percent of the world's diamonds now came from Russia, much of it through Armenia.

"You have a unique position at the Yerevan plant. You

see the best of the Russian stones. I was hoping that you—"

"You want me to steal them and sell them for you."

"Not sell. I have other venues for that." He went on, "I will pay handsomely. More than you ever received from Yudin. Your family and your son will live in luxury."

"If I steal for you."

He held up a hand. "No moral outrage, please—you have already been doing it for years. Now I have decided we should work together. You have a rare talent. A good eye. It would be a shame to waste it." He appraised her with a look that made her feel naked. "But you should know . . . the diamonds are just the beginning. Already I am bigger than Russia. There is no limit to where I can go."

Arin felt her face harden. "The U.S.?"

"The land of opportunity." He smiled. "I have contacts there. 'Associates.' "

"Through Yudin?"

"The bankers and businessmen he cultivated are falling all over each other to invest in Eastern Europe. Some choose not to look too deeply into those investments. They take our proceeds and invest them in legitimate American ventures. Businesses. Real estate. Even banks." He chortled. "And, of course, Mika is in Chicago plying her trade."

"She stared. "What do you mean, plying her trade?"

She already fucked everyone in Europe. Now she's doing the same in Chicago." He sneered. "I have kept track of her over the years, too." He ran his tongue over his lips. "But you . . . You are different. I have plans for you. I want you to be a part of my world."

She mustered all her self-control and reason. Pump him. Maybe she would discover something that would help her escape. "Your world? An outpost island everyone knows to harbor criminals? Why here, Vlad? Why do you not go back home?"

"Russia is no longer a place for an honorable man. The criminals in the Duma and the police have ruined the country. There is nothing to keep me there."

Arin stifled a laugh. Did he really consider himself honorable? He was a soldier. Trained for combat. And soldiers never retreat by choice. She had heard the stories coming out of Russia, how it was run by armies of street thugs and worse. If Vlad had left, he must have been squeezed out by more powerful thugs.

Except he wasn't behaving that way. He spread his arms wide, like a viceroy acknowledging his fiefdom. "I am happy here. Treated well. I pursue my own opportunities. All this . . . you could share."

"You want me to live here? With you?"

"In time, yes. Your son and your parents, too." He stood up. "You see, I am not the heartless animal you take me for."

No, she thought. He was worse. He had no heart. Or soul. All the people in her life, all the people who'd been important to her, he'd exploited for his own gain. "You had such energy, Vlad. Such passion. Men were devoted to you. But you squandered their loyalty. Ours, too—Sacha. Me. Mika. Yudin. How can you possibly think I would allow myself to be part of that?"

"I see." He folded his arms. "You are suddenly a woman of principle. It was acceptable to smuggle diamonds when it was just you and Yudin. But now that you know I am involved, it is a heinous crime? What has changed?"

"I have." Her rage had been mounting, building and sharpening until it coalesced into a palpable thing, a scythe that glistened and shimmered in her mind. "They say you can never know evil. That it will trick you. Change its face so you cannot recognize it. But they are wrong, Vlad. You killed my husband. Destroyed my best friend. Now I learn you have cheated my father-in-law. And me. I called you a monster once. You have not changed. You are evil." Her voice quavered. "But I will not allow you to inflict any more damage."

He waited, a half smile on face. She lunged toward him. She would claw his face, permanently erase that smirk. But he caught her wrists easily and yanked them up in the air.

A sharp pain sliced through her. His eyes grew cold. "Arin. You must know I will not allow you to ruin my empire."

He twisted her arms, forcing her to arch into him. As her body bent backward, he pressed into her and crushed his mouth on hers. She tried to pull away, but he had her arms pinned.

With his lips bearing down on her, Arin opened her mouth, hoping he would think she had surrendered. His tongue insinuated itself into her mouth. She bit down.

He jerked and fell back with a shout. Blood spurted from his tongue. He covered his mouth with his hand, a curtain of anger veiling his eyes. Arin staggered back, desperate to escape. But his men were too quick. One grabbed her by the waist, the other by the neck, and they wrestled her to the ground. They flipped her over, pinning her beneath the big one's meaty arms. Vlad crouched, his face looming above hers, and gazed at her with those pale, cold eyes. One of the bodyguards asked if they should take over. Vlad shook his head. For one fascinating but terrifying moment, Arin thought he might explode in rage.

But then something emerged from deep within him. Not a serenity, or even a quietude, but something silent and dark and icy. His expression smoothed out, and his features seemed to freeze in place. He didn't strike her. He didn't raise a hand. He took in a breath, his face only inches from hers.

"You see, my dear Arin, the secret is to remain in control. At all times." The crooked smile distorted his features. "You must work on that." He straightened up and nodded to the men. "Take her away. We will talk again when she has a different perspective."

As they pulled her to her feet, the cold metal of a gun barrel nuzzled her neck.

THIRTY-ONE

MAX GORDON WAS more than a "player," I learned when I Googled him that afternoon. Some considered him "The Little Engine That Could" of banking—albeit with the occasional emphasis on *little*. One of the articles I pulled up compared him to former Clinton official Robert Reich, but I didn't pick up the same affection they lavished on the diminutive Bostonian. More often it was the "small man cuts big swath through new markets" theme.

He'd grown up in the Flatbush section of Brooklyn, the son of Russian immigrants from Belarus named Grodzienski. After changing his name, he enrolled in Brooklyn College, the first member of his family to pursue higher education. He graduated with a degree in economics, then worked his way through NYU's business school and earned an MBA in finance. He was immediately hired at Chase, and after a flurry of internships, landed in their international banking department. His hiring was seen as an asset, especially since he spoke Russian fluently.

Even before Glasnost, he was well informed about the economies of Russia and Eastern Europe. In the seventies, he wrote a brilliant analysis of the U.S.-Soviet wheat deal in which he predicted a time when superpower politics would be less significant than commerce. Subsequent events seemed to bear him out. During the Arab oil embargo he recommended that the U.S. look into Russian oil as an alternative, and it was rumored that government officials did indeed hold private talks with the Soviets.

Gordon was involved in one of the first forays into Poland after Lech Walesa opened its markets in the late eighties, and after the Berlin wall fell, he helped organize the first economic development conferences focusing on East Germany and Czechoslovakia.

Another article said his interest in Eastern Europe was prompted by the fact that his family came from that part of the world. Gordon didn't disabuse anyone of the notion. "This is my way to give something back so others can realize their dreams, too," he was quoted as saying. But he added that no progress would be made on a large scale until all nations embraced free markets. I twirled a lock of hair. Not only an economic powerhouse, now he was Adam Smith? Others, though, took him more seriously, and he was sought out as an expert whenever the media focused on that part of the world.

Unfortunately, his personal life wasn't as successful. A stormy marriage to Karen Wise, also from Brooklyn, ended in a nasty divorce, and while the divorce proceedings were sealed, reports hinted at a stunning settlement. In the early nineties, he moved to the Midwest.

I found it curious that Gordon would leave the financial capital of the world for the Second City. But New York was crowded and competitive, he pronounced; new ventures were difficult to launch. That was probably true. If he'd already conceived the notion of starting a bank and building a skyscraper, Chicago *was* a more conducive climate, financially and politically. Even Trump had dipped his toe in the lake. Plus, Gordon's marriage was over, he had no children, and his parents had passed away. Why not make a fresh start?

Gold Coast Trust started small, but Gordon aggressively looked for opportunities and was credited with some ingenious investments. For example, he helped bring capital into Yugoslavia for the Yugo, the cheap car that was successfully exported to the West. And when the Soviet Union collapsed, he invested not only in basic industries like steel and oil, but less capital-intensive ventures as well, particularly software.

Money attracts money, he liked to say, and despite the risks of conducting business with politically unstable countries, Gold Coast Trust thrived, investing and building assets at the same time. When the economy turned sour here, moreover, the high interest rates he was collecting acted as a hedge against the slowdown and he continued to prosper, although publicly he downplayed his achievement.

He also kept up his networking, continuing to sponsor conferences in Eastern and Central Europe. That was critical, he maintained. Not only did these conferences provide a window for potential investors, but it was important that fledging businesses and industries study the successful methods used by Western captains of industry.

Of all the articles I skimmed, only one was less than praiseworthy. Written by a curmudgeonly Chicago financial analyst for his company's newsletter, it questioned the speed with which Gold Coast Trust had ramped up. A bank that went from rags to riches in ten short years, Donald Robinson claimed, was nothing short of a miracle, and miracles were in short supply in this economy. He advised readers to take a close look at this shooting star to make sure it didn't burn itself out.

I glanced at David's photo on the shelf above the computer. I'd taken it last summer when the three of us biked up to the botanic gardens. He knew Max Gordon and Gold Coast Trust; he could probably fill me in with more detail than a few articles. But calling him was out of the question. In fact, I should probably take his picture and throw it away. I sighed. I couldn't do that yet. But I did turn the frame around so that his picture faced the wall.

I printed out the articles and stashed them in a file folder. Then I went downstairs to brew a pot of coffee. While it was perking, I ran out to pick up Rachel from school. Her friend Katie climbed into the car with her. Back at the house, they grabbed a bag of cookies, two pops, and bounded up the stairs.

"Whoa, there, road runners. Where are you off to?"

Rachel stopped on the top step. "We need to get on IM. There's this really hot—"

"Sorry." On the way to pick Rachel up, I'd realized there was something else I wanted to check online. "I need the computer."

"Muhhthherrr . . ."

"Another half hour."

Katie looked crestfallen, but after a moment, Rachel recovered. "No prob. Let's jog over to the Forest Preserve. By the time we get back, we'll go online."

Katie shot Rachel one of those "are you crazy?" looks. She was apparently the type who thought clicking on a remote or a mouse was more than enough exercise.

"Tell you what," I said. "How about some cocoa to gird your loins?"

They both brightened. I made hot chocolate with marshmallows, which they sucked down like liquid candy. Then they put on their coats and headed outside.

Back in my office, I Googled "Tattoos and Russian army." Only one Web site popped up, revealing an obscure crest that was supposedly tattooed on White Army recruits during the Russian Revolution. Other links, however, and there seemed to be a slew of them, promised information about tattoos and Russian prisons. Recalling what the Buddhist tattoo artist said about tattoos and gulags and jails, I clicked on them.

Like most prison populations, tattoos were common in Russian jails. Of the 35 million people jailed in the Soviet Union between the mid-sixties and the late eighties, 85 percent were tattooed. Certain tattoos meant that a prisoner was a high-ranking criminal, a *pakhany,* or had some special status before he was imprisoned. Others meant they were one of the *razboyniki,* or mob. Some tattoos indicated a prisoner has done time in solitary confinement. Nazi imagery wasn't uncommon.

There was even a cadre of Russian street thugs known as the "Tattoos." Described as a cross between the Gambinos under John Gotti and Hell's Angels, the Tattoos were muscle men who ran the rackets and extorted payoffs. One of the Web sites claimed they had a virtual lock on almost every aspect of the Russian marketplace.

According to a Russian criminologist, tattoos were a passport, business card, and resumé all rolled in one. Criminals distinguished one another's rank in the underworld, their past incarcerations, even their area of "specialty" from their body art. But so did the police, who gradually learned to use tattoos to identify and apprehend criminals. As a result, the criminologist said, the application of tattoos might have peaked.

I took my empty coffee cup down to the kitchen and looked through the window. Rachel and Katie hadn't gone jogging. They were dragging some neighborhood kids around on a sled. I pressed my forehead against the windowpane. Icy tendrils of frost coated the glass. I ran my finger across it, letting the wavy wet line bisect them.

After all that research, I wasn't sure what I was looking for or what I'd found. Max Gordon seemed like a gifted businessman, and with the exception of the one article, above reproach. He had put his loyalty to his homeland to good use. Yet, a construction worker at his site wore a ski mask, the same mask worn by a murderer. Both men had a limp. The woman on the tape had been killed at a dental office. So were the Russian immigrants who owned it. The man who might have sent me the tape had connections to a Russian strip joint. And a tattoo that might have originated in the Russian army or prison was on the dead woman's wrist . . . the same tattoo that had shown up on a diamond courier in Antwerp.

I felt as if elements were whirling around me like

electrons around the nucleus of an atom. Everything required to restore order was there, but whizzing around so fast I couldn't identify them. Layered on top was an urgency, an edgy sense that I needed to piece everything together before . . . before what? I didn't know, but I had the distinct feeling I was running out of time.

I backed away from the window and went to the phone. I doubted it would make any difference, but I left a message for Davis telling her what I'd learned.

I CAME OUT of the bathroom that night to find Rachel curled up in my bed, engrossed in the end of civilization as we know it on her Game Boy. I threw back the covers, slid into bed beside her, and pulled the blankets up to my chin.

As she clicked on buttons and arrows, voices screamed, tones chimed, and colors flashed. I tried to determine some logic to the sequences, but the patterns were either beyond my ability to comprehend or totally random. After a particularly unearthly shriek, Rachel paused the game and everything went silent. Without looking at me, she asked, "How come you turned the picture around?"

"What picture?" I said, though I knew the one she meant.

"The one of David at the gardens."

I shrugged one shoulder, producing a slight lump in the quilt.

"There's a problem, isn't there?"

I took out my hand and smoothed out the covers. She put the Game Boy down and rolled onto her side. I sighed. I had to tell her sometime. "It seems as if David has a new girlfriend."

Her eyes grew round as plates. "What?"

I repeated myself.

"How could he?" Her voice turned suddenly suspicious. "What did you do?"

"As far as I know, nothing." This time.

"Then what happened?"

I explained as much as I felt she could understand.

"I don't believe this."

"I think it's pretty unbelievable, too." I bit my lip—it wouldn't be a good idea to fall apart in front of my fourteen-year-old daughter. "But there are times when things just don't work out." God, what a pitiful answer. "And we end up hurt." Just as inane.

"You know just what this sounds like?" She shot me a look. "It sounds like the junk you told me when you and Daddy got divorced."

Back then, I'd bought one of those "how to explain divorce to your kids" books. Its strict guidelines mandated that parents tell the child together in a neutral location. We should stress that it wasn't the child's fault. We followed the advice. It didn't work.

"I already went through it once." She bristled. "I don't want to do it again."

"I—I'm sorry, Rachel."

She rolled over, got out of bed, and stormed into her room.

The gas heater clicked on, and hot air pushed through the vents. I lay in bed wondering how life, which had seemed so normal a few weeks ago, had become so unsettled. David. The tape. Petrovsky. Max Gordon. I seemed to be the only person who cared about any of it. David didn't care about me; the police didn't care about the case; Ricki Feldman and Max Gordon cared only about their business.

But how do you learn not to care? To shrug off doubts and reclaim sleepless nights? Maybe I should take a few lessons. I switched off the light, for once welcoming the dark for its indifference.

THIRTY-TWO

FRIDAY NIGHT I dropped Rachel at Barry's for the weekend. His condo, on the third floor of a small, upscale apartment building, isn't far from the house—it was one of the more rational decisions he made when we broke up. Barry met us at the front door in the lobby, which, considering the frigid temperature, was surprising. Usually he lurks in his apartment, waiting for me to ring the bell and deliver Rachel as if she were a package from UPS.

He came out to the car and leaned his head in. "How 'bout you come to dinner with us? We're getting Thai."

"I—I'm already cooking for Dad."

"He can come, too."

Rachel told me how Barry's affair with Marlene, the aerobics queen, had cooled. Considering my run-in with her last fall, I wasn't unhappy. And despite their differences, Dad and Barry tried to get along. But I was feeling vulnerable, which was exactly what Barry was counting on.

"Thanks, but I don't think so."

Barry shrugged as if to say "I tried," and slipped his arm around Rachel.

"Bye, Mom. Tell *Opa* he owes me a game of chess."

THERE'S NOTHING LIKE the aroma of a good Shabbos brisket on a cold winter night. To some people, the smell is an aphrodisiac. I tend to think of it as foreplay—sniffing can be better than the main event. Tonight, though, Dad seemed impervious to its siren song. He'd been quiet on the ride up, but once inside, he proceeded to sit in three different chairs, like a wizened, male version of Goldilocks.

I lit candles, and Dad recited kiddush. After *Motzi* I served bowls of my homemade matzo ball soup. I dug in—I make good matzo balls, even if they come from a box—but Dad took one spoonful and pushed his away.

"Too much salt?" I looked over.

He reached for his cane, lumbered to his feet, and started to pace around the dining room table.

"What's with the *shpilches* tonight?"

He pressed his lips together. "I'm beginning to think that guy Kevorkian has the right idea."

I put my spoon down. "Excuse me?"

"At a certain point in your life, you get let out to pasture." I started to interrupt, but he overrode me. "No, it's true. Once you're over the hill, you're marginalized. No matter who you were before. And if you've got health problems on top of it, you're in even more trouble. People shove you into a corner, roll their eyes when they deal with you—"

He held up his palm when I tried to break in. "I've seen it happen. What I'm saying is if you get to the point where you can't even wipe yourself without help, maybe someone oughta give you a push into the Almighty's arms." He sniffed. "It happens a lot more than we think. It's just no one ever talks about it."

"You think that kind of thing should be sanctioned?"

He rounded the table. "Here's the thing, Ellie. Who decides when it's time to pull the plug? Let's say I draft a living will—you know, put in that no special resuscitation clause, if I think I'm gonna end up a vegetable. And say you're my executor. If I'm not in any shape to make decisions, how do I know you are? How do you know when it's time? Do you ask the doctors? Do you rely on your own common sense?"

"That's a lot of speculation."

"Exactly. Which is why it's all so crazy. What if you're just fed up—what do they call it now when you've had enough?"

"Burnout?"

"Right. What if you're burned out with taking care of me? How do we know—how does anyone know if the decision you made was in my interests . . . and not yours?"

I leaned my elbows on the table, remembering a conversation we'd had when I was younger and much more sure of myself. We'd been discussing medical miracles, and how they save lives, even though the cost of them might drive the patient into bankruptcy. I'd been arguing against the principle; it was creating a two-tiered health care system. Medicine for the rich and famous, I'd called it—middle-class need not apply.

"Who wants to live to be ninety-five, anyway?" I'd asked huffily.

Dad looked at me, then answered quietly, "The guy who's ninety-four."

I never forgot that. I repeated it now.

He sat down heavily. "But what if you don't know how old you are?"

I finally realized what was making him so morose. "Sylvia's worse, isn't she?"

He nodded slowly. "She needs more care than the place can give. But . . ." His eyes glittered. "Her daughter-in-law's ready to send her to one of those advanced care facilities. You know. The places you go when you're waiting to die. And everybody else wishes you would."

I winced.

"Her son isn't convinced she should go. He's got a good

nashoma, that boy. He wants her to move in with them. But his wife? Forget it. God forbid it interferes with her paddle tennis or their kid's soccer practice."

"Watch it," I said.

"Come on. You know what I'm saying. It's not the money. I'd understand it if they couldn't afford a decent nursing home, but they can. They can even afford in-home care. The wife just doesn't want to be put out."

"What about Sylvia? What does she think?"

"She just sits in her room." He sighed. "She stares at the clock all the time now. Keeping track, letting it wind down, I don't know. I visit her every afternoon, make her a cup of tea, and we talk. But, Ellie . . ." He turned an anguished face to me. "I can't do this again."

When my mother was dying of cancer, my father dropped everything to stay by her side. He nursed her, fed her, entertained her, comforted her. Watched as each day she became a little less of the person she'd been before. And when it was all over, he cried and packed up all her things for the Ark, a Chicago Jewish good-will agency. It was an experience no one should repeat.

I stood up and put my arms around him. "You don't have to."

He shaded his eyes with his hand. "She's got no one else."

I stroked the back of his head. "How much longer can she stay there, you think?"

"Hard to say. Maybe a month."

I was quiet. Then, "That month could be the best month of her life."

He looked up and gazed at me as if he was seeing me for the first time. "I suppose." After a moment, he hugged me. "Thanks, sweetheart." A glimmer of a smile played around his lips. "Okay. Time for some of that brisket that's been smelling up the house."

"HOW'S DAVID?" HE asked a few minutes later.

"Fine," I lied. One of us crying into our soup was enough.

Especially considering the time it took me to make it. I changed the subject and told him about the ground-breaking ceremony. He nodded when I mentioned Max Gordon.

"You know him?"

"I know who he is. Short bald Jewish guy. Sticks his hand in his jacket like Napoleon."

"That's him."

"Don't know a thing about him—except that he wants to be the Trump of Chicago. Why do you ask?"

I shrugged.

"I see right through you, sweetheart. You're your mother's daughter. She never could hide anything, either."

"You're right. I feel uneasy about the guy. But everybody else seems to think he's the best thing to hit town since Michael Jordan. I even did a search on him, and only one article was the slightest bit critical. And even that wasn't really critical. Just guarded."

"Why do you care about Max Gordon's reputation?"

"It's a long story."

Dad's eyebrows shot up as if I'd just pronounced a secret password. "I worry when you start out like that."

"I'm not in trouble this time. Promise." I tried my most reassuring smile. "But there are some strange—well, I don't even know if you could call them coincidences . . . more like confluences of events." I told him everything: the woman on the tape, the killer's ski mask, DM Maids, the van driver, Celestial Bodies, the dentists' office, the woman's tattoo, the note, Max Gordon's reaction to my comments about the construction worker.

His eyebrows went sky high. "How did you happen to meet the women at Celestial Bodies, if you don't mind my asking?"

"I—I was there. With the police."

He scowled.

I skipped the part about the gun at my head. "It was fine, Dad. Really." I passed him the meat. "So, what do you think?"

"I don't like you being involved."

"I'm not—not really."

He pointed to the gravy boat. "They don't know that."

I passed it over. "I know what you're saying, and I am trying to stay out of trouble. But I wonder if I should call the guy who wrote that newsletter article on Gordon. Maybe I'd learn something that would help."

"Dream on. What do you think the guy's gonna tell you? He has no idea what you're gonna do with the information."

"You're probably right." I sighed. "So what should I do?"

Dad took a bite of meat and chewed it thoroughly. "I don't know why I'm helping you—it's a sure sign of trouble. But I know someone who might be able to give you a heads-up on Max Gordon."

DAD'S BUDDY FRANK Mayer looks like a combination of Alfalfa and Albert Einstein. Tufts of frizzy white hair stick out at odd angles, framing his head like some ethereal halo. He was alone in the card room enveloped by a cloud of cigar smoke. A bright light hung directly over the table. A TV in the corner blared the news. His thick glasses almost obscured his eyes, but his face creased into a smile when he saw Dad.

"Jake. You're back early."

"Can't have you playing solitaire by yourself now, can I? How can you cheat?"

Yanking his thumb in Dad's direction, Frank looked over at me. "This from the guy who tells me that a thing worth having is a thing worth cheating for."

Dad positioned himself behind Frank. "Yeah. Me and W. C. Fields."

I smiled at their tough-guy banter. My father was as likely to cheat as the Cubs were to win the World Series.

"Slap the two of hearts on the ace," Dad said.

"Yeah, yeah," Frank grumbled. He looked down, moved the card, then looked at me. "And how's Queen Eleanor tonight? You look good, honey."

"Thanks." I touched his arm. "Frank, Dad says you used to work at Harrison Trust."

He grunted. "Thirty years. Still on the board of directors." He flipped over three cards, placed a queen on a king, then a two of clubs on the ace. "Why? You got a banking problem?"

"Not really." Dad and I exchanged looks. "I just wondered what you could tell me about Max Gordon."

Frank looked up from his game. "The little giant?"

I wasn't sure if he was being facetious. I nodded.

"Why?"

"I shot some video for him the other day, and I—I was curious."

"The ground breaking downtown?"

"That's right. I didn't realize he was such a big deal."

"Yeah, he's a big deal." He sounded unenthusiastic.

"He's not?"

"Oh, he's a big deal, all right."

"So, why—what is your take on him?"

Frank gathered up the cards and folded them together. Then he picked up a copy of the *Chicago Jewish News* on the next chair and patted the seat. "What do you want to know?"

I sat down. "Everything I read says he can't do anything wrong. Investing in Eastern Europe. Growing the bank's asset base at the same time. He's a hero."

"You believe everything you read?" I saw a reflection of the overhead light in Frank's glasses.

"I shouldn't?"

He paused. "Let's just say I wouldn't call him a *landsman*."

Landsman is one of those Yiddish expressions people use to refer to someone from the same town or region—a neighbor of sorts. My father uses it to refer to other German Jews, who can do no wrong, as opposed to Jews from other parts of the world. But I didn't think that's what Frank meant.

"You gotta wonder when a bank gets that big that fast," he went on.

"That's exactly what one of the articles said."

"Is that so?"

"Why, Frank? What's the deal?"

He shifted and picked up the cards. When he spoke, I got the feeling he was choosing his words carefully. "You hear things. On the street."

"What things?"

"About depositors, how the books are handled. Things like that."

"And?"

He shrugged. "He does a lot of business overseas. Always traveling. Deposits come in, deposits go out. Cash gets washed through. Suddenly he's got huge assets on his books. But some of the depositors don't exactly fit the profile of Fortune 500 companies."

My father cut in. "Are you accusing him of dummy investments? Or money laundering?"

"I would never make those kind of allegations." Frank smiled sweetly. "A man's reputation is at stake."

I tapped my foot. "Those lists are public, aren't they? His depositors, I mean. This isn't Switzerland"

Frank shook his head. "Banks don't have to disclose their customers, honey—unless there's some illegality involved. And then, if you have the right lawyer . . ." He grinned at my father.

"So he could be falsifying deposits?"

"Who knows? You can always find someone to do that kind of thing if the stakes are high enough. I could name you plenty of cases where a banker looked the other way or—God forbid—even took a kickback. Or parked the money in an offshore account for a while."

"But the auditors would find it, wouldn't they? There is a lot of federal interest in all that money because of terrorism isn't there?"

"That's where it gets interesting." Frank took off his glasses, pulled out a handkerchief, and started polishing them. "Maybe it was nothing, but a few years ago there were rumors about some audit issues at Gold Coast Trust."

He shoved the handkerchief back into his pocket. "Everyone was prepared for the worst. It was supposed to go all the way up. A really big deal. But somehow, it never did."

"How come?"

Frank put his glasses back on, pushing them over the bridge of his nose. "Who knows?"

I considered it. The governor and mayor had been at the ground-breaking ceremony. That didn't necessarily mean anything except that Gordon had contacts at the highest levels of government. He might be able to accomplish quite a bit behind closed doors. It didn't mean that he was using ill-gotten money to inflate his assets and bribing the necessary officials to look the other way. But even if he were, what did that have to do with the murder of the woman on the tape? It was a big jump from money laundering to murder.

I thanked Frank. Dad and I walked down to his apartment. He took out his key. "You get what you want?"

"I'm not sure."

"I don't like you looking into that *gonif*'s business."

"I know." I hugged him.

He opened the door. "You know, the Talmud makes a distinction between a *gonif* and a *gozel*."

"What's a *gozel*?"

He flipped up one palm. "A *gonif*'s a guy with a pen." He flipped up the other. "A *gozel* puts a gun to your head." He paused. "The thing is they both get your money, one way or the other."

I drove home wondering which type Max Gordon was.

THIRTY-THREE

I WOKE UP to gusts of wind bleating through the window. I lay in bed imagining a storm primed to let loose with punishing force. Then the phone trilled again. I rolled over to check the time. Four A.M.: a bleak, desolate time, between night and day, but beholden to neither. No one calls at that hour unless it's bad news. I reached for the phone, my pulse hammering.

"Ellie, it's Jordan Bennett." His voice sounded taut, like a rubber band stretched to its breaking point.

"Jordan." I couldn't avoid the gush of relief that flooded through me. It wasn't Dad, Rachel, or David. I switched on the light. "What's wrong?"

"Can—can you meet me down at Cabrini?"

"Right now? Why?"

He took a shuddering breath as if he was trying to pull himself together. "Ellie, just get here, okay?"

"Give me twenty minutes."

I threw on some sweats and raced down the expressway, trying not to think about what had gone wrong, but as the miles passed, I grew edgy. Just before I careened around the corner at Cabrini, I smelled the electrical burning odor, and as I turned onto the street where the apartments were, I saw the flashing lights, the fire trucks, and the police cars. The apartments were at the other end of the block, but a squad car blocked my path. I parked around the corner, then jogged back to a group of barricades that had been thrown up. A small crowd had gathered wearing bathrobes and pajamas with coats thrown over them.

On the other side of the police line I counted over a dozen men: firemen winding hoses and stowing equipment, uniformed policemen standing in tiny knots. Three fire trucks, one large engine, and four police cars jutted out into the street. Someone had aimed an arc light at the building, and the blue-white glare made for a dramatic—almost surreal—contrast between light and shadow. With the crackle from the radios and the occasional shout, I felt like I was on the set of an Ingmar Bergman film.

The odor of burning smoke settled into my nose and throat. I gazed at the building. The roof had partially collapsed, and two blackened, sooty walls were open to the sky. Plumes of gray smoke curled up. Looking around, I didn't see an ambulance. My stomach lurched. Had it already left for the hospital? Were any of the boys in it?

Near the barricades in a pocket of deep shadow, Jordan Bennett crouched on the curb, his shoulders hunched against the night.

"Jordan!" I called nervously. "What happened? Where are the boys?"

He lifted his head wearily, gazing at me with such a disoriented expression that I wasn't sure he knew who I was. I ducked under one of the barricades, but an officer blocked me, "Sorry, miss, you can't go through. There's an investigation in progress."

I eyed him, then pointed to Jordan. "That's my client."

"You a lawyer?"

"Ummm." I shot him an imperious glare. It wasn't a total lie. He *was* my client. For the video.

The officer studied me. I held my breath. He blinked. "Go ahead."

I dashed across the street and hunkered down beside Jordan. He was shivering through his coat. I gripped his arm. "Jordan, was anyone hurt?"

He shook his head. "They're okay. Everyone got out. DCFS has them for the night."

I blew out a breath, then retrieved a blanket from a fireman and draped it over Jordan. As he pulled it close, his shoulders heaved, and he started to shake. I put my arm around him. "It's okay," I whispered.

"No. It's not." He sobbed raggedly. "And it won't ever be."

I didn't say anything. After a few minutes, he wiped the back of his sleeve across his nose. "The smoke alarm is what saved them." He shook off the blanket and levered himself to his feet. "Damn thing was so loud, it woke them up. They bailed out in their skivvies."

"Thank God."

"Thank God?" He looked down. "How can you say that? They lost everything."

"They're alive. They're not hurt."

He was about to reply when the whine of engines punctured the silence. One by one, the fire trucks and police cars retreated down the street.

When I was a little girl, firemen would clang a bell when they left the scene of a fire; it was a signal that the fire was out and all was well. Not tonight. These vehicles slipped quietly back into the shadows of night. A red sedan and a patrol car remained at the scene.

Jordan watched the trucks disappear around the corner. "I'm going in."

"You can't. They won't let you."

A determined frown spread across his face. "They have to."

"Why?"

"I promised."

"Who?"

"You remember Steve, the guy with the earring?" The wannabe biker. "His father died when he was six, but before he went, he gave Steve his dog tags. From Nam. Kid kept 'em with him all the time. It was the only thing of his Dad's he had. I promised I'd try to find them." Jordan swallowed. "They were metal. Maybe . . ."

He intercepted a lanky man in fire regalia who'd just emerged from the building. As Jordan talked, the man pursed his lips, then shifted a clipboard from one arm to the other. He shook his head.

Jordan's shoulders collapsed.

I crossed the street.

"Look," the man was saying, "Even if I could let you in, you're not gonna find anything. I guarantee it. There's nothing left."

Jordan didn't answer. I started to take his arm, but he shook me off. He turned back. "You're wrong."

I dropped my arm.

"There is something left," he said.

The man raised his eyebrows.

"My word. I promised the kid I'd try. Please."

The man studied Jordan again. "Nam, huh?"

Jordan nodded.

"I was in Nam. Pleiku. Seventy-one." I could tell the guy was weighing, sifting, deciding. His expression softened. Then he spoke in a quiet voice. "This never happened, understand? I'm only allowing it because the fire is out, and we have a pretty good idea of how it started. But you never did a walk-through. Got it?"

Jordan's face cleared.

"Two minutes. And you follow me. No moonlighting."

"Thank you, Inspector . . ." I said.

"Connelly."

We followed him through the front door, now a charred mass of wood and peeling paint. Inside, the smoke had mostly dissipated, but the acrid odor was still strong, and there was a distinct chemical overlay to the smell. We walked into what had been the living room. The roof hadn't collapsed here, but the walls, or what was left of them, were swathed with random scorch patterns that looked like the product of some ghastly netherworld designer. Debris was strewn all over the floor, and our shoes left imprints in the sodden carpeting.

"The sprinkler system wasn't hooked up," the investigator said. "Would have made a big difference."

"I think they just finished construction," I offered.

Connelly grunted. "Feldman, right?"

"Yes." I was surprised.

Connelly headed into the larger bedroom. The bed coverings were burnt and shredded. Mounds of waterlogged debris covered the floor, the remains of the dressers and bureaus. The furniture had been new just a few days ago. I had video of them uncrating it.

"Any idea where he left the tags?" Connelly asked.

"He thought they were in the dresser nearest the wall," Jordan said.

Connelly shrugged his shoulders. The dresser was nothing more than a pile of rubble. I flashed back to what the Buddhist tattoo artist at Chicago Tattoo and Piercing said about the nature of fire. That when the fire is extinguished, old ideas and passions are released, thereby freeing the spirit.

Sure.

We followed Connelly back to the living room. My gaze moved to the pass-through to the kitchen. Two big pots and a frying pan sat on the stove. They were grimy and covered in soot, but they weren't scorched.

"It didn't start in the kitchen," I said.

Connelly shook his head. "The point of origin was over there. The outlet." He gestured to a V-shaped burn pattern snaking up one of the walls. I could just make out a blob of melted plastic at the nexus of the V eight inches from the floor. An adjacent window had blown out, and shards of glass framed an empty expanse of darkness. Remnants of scorched cloth hung from a metal curtain rod dangling from the window.

"The load was probably too much for the wires. Caused a flameout. Which set fire to the drapes. It spread fast after that," Connelly said matter-of-factly.

"How does that happen—that the load is too heavy for the wires? Were there too many electrical appliances?" Even as I said it, I couldn't see how. The boys didn't have a TV or PlayStation among them.

A frown deepened the lines on Connelly's forehead. He didn't answer.

"It wasn't arson, was it?"

"Oh, no," he replied quickly. "There's no evidence of that."

"But you said you have a pretty good idea what happened."

He hesitated. "I need to talk to the contractor. Verify what was used."

I started to get an uneasy feeling. "Why?"

Connelly shook his head.

"Look," I said gesturing to Jordan, "this man is my client. The building was part of a program he was running for foster kids. Kind of a halfway house for them, a chance to make it in the real world. It's totally destroyed now. He's gonna have to start over from scratch. Don't you think he has the right to know what destroyed it?"

Connelly studied both of us, then yanked a thumb. "Outside." We followed him back out to the street. "It looks like it was substandard wiring. Should have been a sixteen-gauge wire, maybe even fourteen, but it looks like it was twenty. The breakers didn't work right, either. Someone was trying to cut corners. Do it on the cheap."

I swallowed. "The contractor?"

"I've seen it before."

A muscle in Jordan's jaw tensed.

"That's it." Connelly waved a hand. "I've already told you too much. Get out of here."

I nodded and led the way back to the Volvo. Jordan slid into the passenger seat. I got in, turned over the engine, and cranked up the heat. Fortunately, the car warmed right away. Jordan stared straight ahead, his eyes glittering in a wash of light from a streetlamp.

"You okay?" I asked quietly.

He took his time answering. "All this time I've been trying to fight my way upstream, you know?" he finally said. "I've taken a lot of shit, but I figured if I could get something for my kids, it was worth it. And sometimes the system did work. For a while. But then something like this happens." He rubbed the back of his neck. "Tell me, Ellie, what am I doing it for?"

I had no answer.

"I really thought we had it nailed this time. Chicago's a great city, you know?" He looked through the windshield. "You get the sense that it's still a wide-open town. That it's not run by the old boys club. That if you have a good idea and you're willing to work for it, you can make it happen here. But then something like this happens . . ." He turned a haunted face to me. "And I can't even find a pair of godamned dog tags. Did I screw up? Or is it the system? I don't know."

RICKI FELDMAN FOUND us as the streetlights winked off and a perversely beautiful dawn shot rays of pink across the horizon. When she tapped on the window, Jordan, who'd been dozing, startled awake. He bolted upright, but stiffened when he recognized her. She looked pale, and her hair was tied back in a clip. Like me, she was wearing sweats, but I doubted hers came from Target.

Jordan opened the car door and climbed out. I got out too. Ricki threw her arms around Jordan. "Are you all right, honey?" She sounded worried.

When Jordan didn't return her embrace, she drew back. "I just talked to the fire inspector. He told me what happened."

"He told you?"

She canted her head, as if she wasn't quite sure why he was so cold. But Jordan either didn't notice or didn't care. "Why did you do it, Ricki?"

She looked uneasy. "Do what?"

His eyes narrowed. "Don't play coy. The wiring, damn it! The investigator told us the fire was caused by substandard wiring. Authorized by the contractor. Which was you."

She pressed her lips together.

"Was it so important to save a few bucks?" Jordan kept on. "I hope so, because you destroyed Transitions."

She drew herself up. Angry eyes spit fire at him. "I did it for you. You needed a place for your kids. Fast. I wanted you to have it. So I made it happen."

Jordan searched Ricki's face as if seeing her for the first time. I could tell he was surprised. And confused. Then his face dimmed. "If I ever thought I was putting my boys into any kind of jeopardy or risky situation on my watch, I would never have let them move in."

Ricki tensed. I could tell powerful emotions were roiling just beneath the surface. I thought about the road to hell. Part of me wanted to believe her. Give her the benefit of the doubt. But then I remembered her father's history, and I heard my father say, "The apple don't fall far from the tree."

"I thought you were different." Jordan's voice cracked. He faced me, and for an instant I thought he was he including me in the *you*. Then he whipped back around and grabbed Ricki's arm. "Come on, Ricki. I want you to see what you did."

Half dragging, half pushing, he started to move her across the street. But then a remarkable transformation occurred. Ricki pried herself free of his grasp and planted her feet on the sidewalk. Slinging her bag over her shoulder, she drew herself up. Her voice was like steel. "You need someone to blame, don't you? You can't accept this was an act of God. You have to hold someone accountable. Well, it's not going to be me."

My jaw went slack. She'd practically admitted to starting the fire a minute ago; now she was backpedaling. I felt as if a curtain had suddenly come down on her compassion, and a different Ricki Feldman had emerged. Arrogant.

Haughty. The daughter of Stuart. Don't let anyone challenge you. If they do, go on the offensive. Don't give away anything. Had she learned that at her father's knee?

I exploded. "An act of God? Christ, Ricki, the place was a ticking time bomb. You rushed through construction, paid off God knows who, and you have the nerve to call it an act of God? Don't try to weasel out of it. I won't let you."

"You won't let me?" She twisted around, her face a mask of fury. "Who are you to make demands, Ellie Foreman? Have you never made a mistake? Or are you so jealous that you'll say anything to get at me?"

My mouth fell open. "I'm not jealous. And the only mistake I made is letting you dangle money in front of me and taking it."

She glared. "That's right. I forgot who I was dealing with. The sanctimonious video producer who doesn't care about money but has a nice little shoplifting habit on the side."

I froze. Jordan stared at me.

"Do you think I'm stupid?" Her voice was cold. "I checked you out. I've known for years. So back off. And you," she cried scornfully to Jordan. "You're so naive you probably think things happen because you're a good guy. And your mission is so goddamn noble." She faced him. "You have no idea how many people it takes to do your dirty work just so you can look down from your idealistic perch and take credit for it." She shook her head. "I should have known better. No one knows how to be grateful anymore. No one says thank you. More the fool me for trying to do something good."

I cut her off. "This isn't about altruism, Ricki. This is about salvaging your reputation."

Jordan looked over at me, confused. "Reputation? What are you talking about?"

"Tell him, Ricki. Tell him what your father did and how you've been doing mitzvahs to atone for it."

She didn't say anything.

Jordan spoke up. "What the hell is going on?"

"Ricki's father built a housing development thirty years ago. Nice place. Near Joliet. Only one problem. He built it on top of a toxic waste dump. Which he knew about before he put up the houses." I told him about the children who'd contracted cancer. How three of them died, how the resulting litigation nearly ruined him. How Ricki took over afterward. "That's why she invested in Transitions, Jordan. She's been throwing money at charities trying to become respectable again."

"Ricki, is this true?" His voice was hard.

She wouldn't look at him.

Suddenly his face cracked, as if a sheet of glass had shattered. He turned around and started toward my car, his body sagging.

"Jordan. Stop," Ricki called after him. "We can work this out. I'll fix it." Her voice grew shrill. "Please . . . don't go."

He kept walking.

"What about us?" she pleaded. "You can't end it. Not like this."

He didn't answer.

She watched him get into my car. I followed him over.

"Ellie . . ."

I stopped. Our eyes locked. She looked at me without expression. Her anger seemed to dissipate, and she looked small and slight. Then, she squared her shoulders, as if deflecting the blow that had been aimed her way. I had the feeling she had made a decision. "There's something you should know," she said finally.

I couldn't imagine what she planned to throw at me now.

"Max Gordon called yesterday. Asking a lot of questions about you. I—I don't know why. He made me promise I wouldn't say anything to you." She hugged her elbows. "But . . . I thought you should know."

"What kind of questions?"

"Where you live. Who your friends are. That kind of thing."

I stood there for a moment, gave her a nod, and headed to the car. As we pulled away, the last image I saw was Ricki Feldman in front of the burnt-out shell of the building, gazing blankly at it, as if she still wasn't sure how or why it had all come down to this.

THIRTY-FOUR

I DROPPED JORDAN at his apartment, wishing there was some way to temper his bitterness and disappointment, but knowing there wasn't. I didn't ask what his plans were. After he found new homes for his boys, I guessed he would be heading back to California.

When I got home, I took a nap. I woke up heavy and fatigued. The sky had surrendered to dirty gray clouds. Though it was mid-afternoon, I made myself eggs, toast, and coffee. Comfort food. No one had died in the fire, no one was hurt, yet I felt as if I was mourning.

After eating, I decided to clean the house, an activity that usually centers me. Arming myself with sponge, bucket, and cleaner, I started in on the bathrooms. While I was scouring the tub, I stewed over Ricki's warning.

I didn't like the fact Max Gordon was asking questions about me, particularly after what I'd learned from Frank. It made me wonder—again—about the construction worker with the limp. Was he some kind of hit man? Did Max Gordon know him?

I sprinkled cleanser into the sink. Maybe Gordon had a

business relationship with the Russian dentists, a relationship that somehow went bad, and the woman on the tape was caught in the crossfire. But what business dealings would a banker of Max Gordon's stature have with an illegal dentists' office in the western suburbs? Even if he was laundering money from Russia, I couldn't see him filtering the money through them, and I couldn't imagine any reason he'd have to finance them. Why would he sanction the death of a woman in their office?

And what about Petrovsky, the man who delivered the tape to my house? Was he connected to Gordon, too? Maybe he and Gordon had a falling out, Petrovsky was out for revenge, and made sure the tape was exposed. Or maybe Petrovsky had been a construction worker before he started working for DM Maids. Maybe he harbored a grudge against the man with the limp.

I scrubbed down the counters in the kitchen. The Russians, the dentists, the idea of money laundering, even Max Gordon himself, were part of a parallel universe operating beneath the surface of my world. It was a strange, alien universe, of which I had no knowledge. I didn't even have enough information to formulate reasonable theories. Except that a construction worker on the site of Max Gordon's tower was possibly moonlighting as a hit man. And that Gordon was probing Ricki Feldman about me.

By the time I mopped the floor and cleaned the refrigerator, dusk was settling. Bilious clouds had moved in, bringing with them a brittle wind that made the morning's dawn seem like a cruel joke. I lowered the shades. We'd gotten to that bleak point in winter where the thought of more cold weather is intolerable, yet there's no hint of spring.

I sank down on the couch in the family room. If only there was a way to link or exonerate Max Gordon—or the construction worker—to the murder of the woman on the tape. I rubbed my eyes and stared at the silent TV, waiting for inspiration. But the screen just stared back at me, an empty black maw sneering at my predicament.

Of course.

I jumped up and ran into the kitchen. My bag hung over a chair. I rummaged through it and pulled out the tape we'd shot of the ground breaking ceremony—I'd picked up a window dub earlier that week. Back in the family room, I threw the tape into the VCR. If I could find a cutaway of the construction worker, I could take it to Mike Dolan. By comparing the two images, he might be able to determine if the man at the construction site and the man on the tape were the same.

I fast-forwarded through shots of the mayor and Max Gordon waddling up to the podium at warp speed, past shots of other Chicago VIPs frenetically talking, motioning, and stamping their feet. I was three-quarters of the way through the cassette when Mac panned across the knot of men near the back of the fence. As the camera moved from right to left, I slowed the tape to normal speed. Then I hit Pause. There, in the background, was the man in the ski mask.

"Yes!" I said triumphantly. Brightly lit, sharply focused, Mac's shot caught the man in the center of the frame. You couldn't see his face, but his shoulders and torso were well-defined, and his clothes were in focus. Plenty for Dolan to work with.

I grabbed the phone and called Davis. She might be sick of hearing from me, but she needed to know what was going on. She wasn't at the station—it was a Saturday night—but I left a message. I told her about Max Gordon, the video, and the construction worker.

"He was wearing a ski mask, Davis. Like one of the killers on the tape. I think Mike Dolan should take a look at it—first thing Monday—and compare the two shots. If you don't want to pay for it, I will." I didn't know how, but I'd worry about that later. "I'll call Dolan tonight. Oh—and I've discovered some things about Max Gordon. We need to talk."

I hung up. The house was quiet. Even the normal ticks and snaps and creaks were silent. I briefly considered going to Dad's. No. I couldn't run to my father's every time I was nervous. My thoughts strayed to the Colt 45 in the hall closet. I'd borrowed it from my father a year ago but never returned it. I had protection.

I left a message for Dolan—he was out, too—and started watching an HBO movie. Either it was pretty lousy, or I was still tired, because the next thing I knew, a sweep of headlights spilling across the window jarred me awake. I watched the play of light on the blind. When a car passes the house, the lights slide from left to right and then fade away. But this time, the lights snapped off in the middle of their arc.

A car door slammed. I raised myself from the couch. The clock on the VCR said it was after eleven. Rachel was with Barry tonight. I went to the window.

A black Buick was parked at the curb. A chill ran up my spine. Petrovsky! What did he want? Did Max Gordon send him? I hurried to the hall closet and pulled out the Colt. I stood by the door, estimating the time it took to walk from the curb to the house. When enough time had elapsed, I aimed the gun at the door and tried to remember what Dad had taught me about using the gun. Something about pulling back the slide, chambering a round, assuming a shooter's stance. I prayed I would remember how to do it. I prayed even harder I wouldn't have to.

I was clutching the gun in both hands when the doorbell rang. A disconnect sliced through my brain. People who want to harm others generally don't ring doorbells. Still, better to be sure. I released the safety, peered through the peephole, and sucked in a breath.

Standing on my doorstep was the blond from Celestial Bodies. The one with crossed eyes who'd been lurking at the dressing room door. Who pawed through my wallet. She stamped her feet and gazed through the peephole. She was dressed in cowboy boots, jeans, and a thin leather jacket. With her wastefully thin body, she could have passed for a boy. Why was she here? I kept the latch hooked, but opened the door a crack.

She greeted me with a self-assured nod, as if dropping by my house was a routine event. I peered out at the Buick. I didn't see anyone inside. She followed my gaze. "Is okay. I am alone." Her voice was low and throaty.

"Is that your car?"

"It is friend's. I borrow." She motioned impatiently. "We go now and talk. I have not much time."

I was still taking in her last comment. "Petrovsky is *your* friend?"

She looked like she wanted to forcibly pull me out of the house. "My friend. Yes." She spotted the gun that was still in my hand. Her expression turned quizzical, as if she was surprised, even amused, that I felt the need to brandish a weapon. I lowered the gun.

"You come with me."

"Go with you? Why should I go anywhere with you?"

"We must. Go talk. Have coffee."

"I'll make coffee here."

She cast a furtive glance around the front yard. "No. Is not safe."

"What do you mean?"

She looked at me. "Please. Is important. We talk."

"Why should I believe you?"

"Because I know the woman on the tape." She motioned to the door knob. "Please. Open door."

I didn't know what to do. The last time I'd had contact with this woman, I'd nearly lost my life. Tonight, though, she looked purposeful. Intense. Even a little sad. And if she knew the woman on the tape . . . I hesitated, then took the latch off the door.

She pushed through, peeled off her jacket, and headed into the family room. I hung back, slightly awed by her brazenness. She looked over her shoulder to see if I was following.

I laid the gun on the hall table. "Who are you?"

"My name is Mika." She spun around. "The woman on video—she is—was—my friend. Her name is Arin."

My pulse quickened. Still, I forced myself to be cautious.

This woman hadn't done me any favors at Celestial Bodies. I stood at the edge of the family room. "You ran away from me at Celestial Bodies. You rifled through my bag. How do I know you're not setting me up now?"

"You bring police. Yuri there. I cannot talk."

"Yuri?"

"Manager of club."

The bouncer. I considered it. She could be telling the truth. She was a woman—defenseless, alone—she had to go along with the program. Still, I hesitated. Mika shot me a look, then crossed her arms at her waist and started to strip off her T-shirt.

"Hold on. What do you think—"

"I am showing you something." She proceeded to pull the shirt over her head and tossed it onto the chair. She wasn't wearing a bra. "Look." She touched her left breast.

"I'm sorry. This is . . . I'm—"

"Look!" she insisted.

I glanced over. Tattooed on her left breast was a small torch. With two stars rising out of the flames. I swallowed.

She flashed me a small smile, retrieved her shirt, and put it back on. "You see now."

I nodded dumbly.

She tucked the shirt in her jeans. "I am thinking Arin dead because of me," she said softly.

"You? How?"

"I am sending her to dentist." Her bottom lip quivered. "But we not talk here." She zipped up her jacket. "I see Starbucks close by. You meet me there."

"Wait a minute. Am I in some kind of danger?"

She answered indirectly. "Your street have many places to hide. We go where there is people." She backtracked to the door and out to the Buick.

I peered out the window. If someone was hiding in a shadowy corner or driveway and we left the house, they could follow us. But Mika was right. Staying here—isolated and alone—probably wasn't a good idea. I grabbed my coat and followed her out. Before I left, I stowed the gun in the hall closet.

I followed Mika to the coffee shop at the corner of Willow and Central. Inside, Mika ordered a latte. She waited for me to pay for it. I ordered one, too, and paid for both. It was nearly closing time, and aside from the young man at the counter, there were only two people in the place. So much for trying to blend in with the crowd.

I sat at one of the small tables near the window. "*You* were the one who sent me the tape."

She nodded. "I tell you I come back, no?"

"Yes, but I didn't get the note until—well, it doesn't matter now."

She sat down and pried the lid off her drink.

"How did you get the tape?" I asked. "And why did you send it to me?"

She took a sip of her coffee and promptly screwed up her face. She set the cup down. "When I first come to U.S., I am working as maid. For your neighbor."

"You worked for Lillian Armstrong?"

She nodded again. "I see you one day with camera. Lights. All in big truck. I know you are TV person."

Mac's van. He must have been picking me up for a shoot. I started to shake my head. "But I'm not—"

She flicked her hand. "When Arin dead, I get video and tell Petrovsky bring it you."

"Petrovsky?"

"He—he is looking out for me. Even after they make me go to club. He like, how you say?" She searched for the word.

"Like a brother?"

"*Da.* Like brother."

"Is that why he came to Celestial Bodies?"

She frowned, as if she was having trouble following me.

"The night of the snowstorm. When I showed up. We followed him over."

"Ahh." She nodded. "*Da.* He is bringing me dinner sometimes. And vodka."

"Is that what he was doing the night of the storm?"

"He is coming to make sure I am okay. I am having flu before."

"Is that why didn't you deliver the tape yourself?"

"No. I cannot bring tape because I cannot leave club. They bring us. They take home. I am like prisoner. So I write note. But now, you see, I am gone." She shrugged.

"What did you think I would do with it?"

"I want you to give to TV. Or police. After we talk."

"Why?"

"So that—this will all stop."

"What? What must stop?"

She lifted her chin and looked around, as if checking for potential pursuers. "I want to talk to you at club. But I afraid. No more."

"Who were you afraid of?"

She was silent. Then, "Vlad."

"Who is Vlad?"

She paused. "He was my husband."

I sat very still.

"He was officer. In Russian army. Lieutenant." A wistful look passed over her face. "But when Soviet Union fall, he—he is getting into pies."

"Pies?"

She curled and uncurled her fingers. I shook my head. What was she trying to say?

She leveled me with an impatient look. "He get in things. Bad things."

A flash of understanding passed through me. "He had his fingers in many pies."

"*Da.* He is starting with drugs. Cars, vodka, girls. Then weapons, even diamonds."

"And you went along?"

"What choice I have? I—we have nothing. No money. No food. Not even house. Vlad say we not bad ones. Real criminals in Duma and police, he say. And Kremlin."

"But he's still in Russia, and both you and Arin were—are here. How is he connected to Arin?"

"Arin's father-in-law is Major General Yudin of the Vaziani base." At my puzzled look, she added, "In Georgia. Where we is living. He and Vlad together do business."

"Arin lived on the base, too?"

"Her husband is lieutenant like Vlad."

"And her father-in-law was involved in criminal activities?"

"Sure." She shrugged. "They start before government fall."

I frowned at the casual, almost offhand reference to such endemic corruption.

"Is Arin's husband involved, too?"

"Arin's husband dead." She averted her eyes. "She has son, you know. Tomas."

"I didn't know."

We were quiet for a moment. "Vlad and I apart long time now, but he leaving Russia three years ago. Rival groups too much—how you say—fighting in."

"Infighting?"

"Yes. He go to Grand Cayman."

I remembered what Frank said about parking money in offshore accounts. Grand Cayman was the mother of all havens. "Grand Cayman? Why there?"

"They have new partner. He and Yudin. An American. Very high up."

"An American? Are you sure?"

She nodded. "When we still in Georgia, Vlad and Yudin is meeting with him. He—the American—get them into U.S. with good money."

"Good money?"

"How you saying when you turn bad money into good?"

"Money laundering?"

She took another sip of her coffee and nodded vigorously. *"Da."*

I drew in a breath. The pieces were falling together. "Do you know this man's name, this American?"

"Nyet."

"Mika," I said, "have you ever heard the name Max Gordon?"

"No. Who is this man?"

"An American businessman . . . with ties to Russia and Eastern Europe."

"I not know this man." She leaned forward. "But I know Vlad. He is never giving up. And he never forget. He say he will rule world someday." She paused. "He will kill me, you know."

"Why?"

"Because I tell you these things."

I frowned. "So why are you?"

Her eyes clouded. "He make bad my life. Kill my friend. Is enough."

"He killed her?"

"She is coming to me from Cayman. She see Vlad. He want her. She tell him no. His men beat her. But she get away. Then find me at club."

"But Grand Cayman is a thousand miles from here. He couldn't—"

She snorted. "Vlad is powerful. He have friends everywhere. Even Chicago. He say kill, they kill. Like that." She snapped her fingers. "I tell her to go to dentist, then go away. Far." She looked down. "But is not enough time. They find her."

I rubbed my eyes. An image of Arin on the tape came back to me, rising to greet her killers, her face hopeful, expectant. "If he's that powerful, how come he hasn't come after you?"

She gave me a long look. "He is."

"He is?"

"After dentists killed, I go away. I know they come for me."

I remembered Davis saying how she'd disappeared when she went back to Celestial Bodies. "You ran away after we showed up?"

She nodded. "Petrovsky help."

"You're both on the run?"

"Da."

"But how do you know they're coming after you?"

She put her cup down again. "Sofiya say," she hissed. "She see Arin when she come to club."

Sofiya. The head dancer. The madame. Sofiya and the Angels. "Sofiya knows Vlad's men?"

"Everyone is knowing Vlad's men."

"Okay." I let out a slow breath. "So how did you get the tape in the first place?"

She shifted slightly, almost imperceptibly. "The dentist . . . Russian who is killed . . . he is being my customer."

"He was your—oh."

She shot me a look that defied me to stand in judgment of her. "When Arin come, her tooth gone. She need help. I am sending her there." She looked down. "I am not knowing they find her. Afterward, he and his sister is needing to go away. He very scared."

"The dentist?"

"Da."

"He had reason to be," I said sadly. "Did he—was he the one who . . . disposed of Arin's body?"

She nodded. "He must. But he doesn't like. Last time he visit me, I tell him to bring me tape. He give it me. I give you."

"I get it." I sipped my latte. "But there's something . . . well . . . Vlad is—was your husband. Why do you think he would kill you?"

She gave me a sad smile. "He kill anyone who stand in his way."

"Why didn't he kill you before this?"

"He is having no reason to kill whore." She shrugged. "Until now."

THIRTY-FIVE

SHE COULDN'T MOVE *afterward. The pain was so total, so overwhelming, she wanted to surrender to it, let it swoop down and take her away. At times it did. She wasn't sure if she'd fallen unconscious or slept. When she finally came to a sustained awareness, it was dark. For a moment she panicked, thinking she had gone blind. Gradually, though, objects materialized out of the dark, and she was able to discern shapes that were blacker than others.*

She was in a room. On a bed. A bare mattress. No sheets or blanket. It was night, but a weak blue light filtered through the room. Coming from somewhere behind her. She tried to go toward it, but waves of dizziness rolled over her when she moved. She had to force herself to breathe.

She didn't know how much time went by while she lay still and motionless. When the wooziness subsided, she mentally checked her body parts. Her limbs seemed to be intact, but a sharp, excruciating pain tore through her jaw. She wondered if it was broken.

Gingerly she felt around the bone. A large bulge that radiated fire protruded from what had been smooth contours of flesh. Her face must look like one of those topographical maps Tomas studied in school. But she couldn't dwell on him now; she might fall apart. She pulled herself to a sitting position. More dizziness.

She concentrated on her breath. Hold it in. Let it out. Again. In time, the room stopped spinning, and she leaned toward the light.

A window. And it was open! She lifted her head. A languid, tranquil breeze wafted over her. The sky had cleared, and a pale wash of moonlight illuminated the room. Hundreds of stars pixillated in the heavens. They seemed much closer here than they did at home.

Slowly she got up and shuffled to the window. Why was it open? And why hadn't they tied her down? She was clearly their prisoner. Had Vlad ordered them not to? No, Vlad was cruel. A man without compassion. There had to be some other reason.

She discovered it when she leaned her head out. Below her was a two-story drop to a large slab of bare cement. There was no landscaping around it, no furniture to act as a cushion. Her body would shatter on impact if she was foolish enough to jump. They knew that.

Past the deck was the beach. The property sat on the rim of a cove that was protected by a sandbar. Beyond it, the waves were treacherous and fierce, but they diminished to gentle swells by the time they came ashore. In the opposite direction was the forest she'd been driven through. For some reason it seemed thicker than it had a few hours ago. As if the vegetation was slowly proliferating, encroaching, turning the island into jungle.

She leaned her head out the window, trying to gauge how many meters it was to the forest. She couldn't tell. She was about to stretch farther when the beam of a flashlight bobbed below. She ducked back inside just in time to see a large man rounding the side of the house. A weapon was holstered at his side. Of course. There would be regular patrols. She wondered how frequently he made rounds.

She threw herself back on the mattress. Nothing in her

life had prepared her for this. She had grown up loved and secure. Met her husband in her first flush of womanhood. Moved with him to Georgia, certain they would lead a charmed life. Now, thirteen years later, Sacha was dead, and she was the prisoner of his best friend. Was that the sum total of her life? Did fate intend her to spend the rest of her life on this island?

No. That unacceptable. She sat up. She wondered when dawn would break. The hour seemed late. Perhaps, if they were sleeping . . . She got off the bed and jiggled the doorknob. Locked. Her shoulders sagged. She lay back on the bed and stared at the wall, trying not to feel suffocated. She couldn't give up.

She was still staring at the wall when she saw it. The faint outline of a door. Cut into the wall, it blended in so well she'd missed it before. She jumped up. The shape of the door was barely visible. More like a hairline crack. She inserted her finger in the crack and tried to pry it open. Nothing moved. Her finger throbbed with pain. She took a breath and tried her fingernails instead. Nothing. She bent down. The crack seemed to be wider near the floor. She lay down, slid the tips of her finger underneath the sliver of space, and pulled. After an excruciating moment during which she feared her fingers might be ripped from her hand, the door opened.

A closet. Filled with women's clothing. Arin scrambled to her feet, frowning. Whom did these belong to? Did Vlad have a woman? She hadn't seen a trace of one: no smudged lipstick on cigarette butts, no cosmetics or perfume lying around.

She slid the hangers along the rod. Nearly twenty dresses, skirts, and tops, most of them scanty affairs with no backs or sleeves. Why were they here, locked away in a closet with no handle? As she browsed, she noticed a white tag on one of the skirts. She moved to the next outfit and noticed another. Another on the next. The clothes had never been worn.

Why did Vlad have a closet full of new women's clothes?

Unless . . . She lifted off one of the hangers and held a blue-and-green sundress against her body. Without trying it on, she knew it would fit her perfectly. He had bought them for her.

She shivered uneasily and put the dress back. Had he planned to make her his prisoner all along? The proposal about siphoning stones through the Yerevan plant must be a sham. He was going to keep her here. As his harlot. His plaything. A harsh sound escaped her lips. When did he intend to show them to her? Did he believe a closet full of clothes would compensate for her loss of freedom? That she'd allow herself to be dressed in his clothes like a doll?

And what happened when he tired of her, as he surely would? For Vlad, the pursuit was the game. Once he had triumphed, his interest would wane, as it had with Mika. And Sacha. And Yudin. Then what? Would he turn Arin into a common whore, too? Or a thief? She gazed at the clothes. She had a sudden impulse to set them on fire. Exorcize the evil. Watch the flames engulf them, swallow them whole, leaving nothing but a mound of clean, smoldering ash.

She was imagining a glorious conflagration when the idea came to her. She moved back to the window and looked down. It might work. She went to the closet, ripped the clothes off their hangers, and flung them on the bed. Then she started to tie them together, knotting them as tightly as she could. Blouses, skirts, dresses, pants, even halter tops. She remembered Tomas practicing knots in HASK, the National Scout Movement in Armenia. She couldn't remember which knot was the strongest. She should have paid more attention. Then again, it probably didn't matter. The rope was only as strong as its weakest link.

Gradually, she knotted together ten, twelve, fifteen pieces of clothing into a rope about ten meters long. She pulled on the knots to test them. They seemed to be holding, but she wouldn't know for certain until she tried it. At which point it might be too late. But she had no choice.

She crept back to the window. It was dark and quiet

below. No flashlights. No guards. Nothing but the thud of surf gently buffeting the beach. If she made it, she would sprint toward the thicket and make for the highway. Someone would pick her up. Back at the hotel, she would grab her passport. Then she would leave this evil place. She knew where she would go. But first, she had to escape.

Looping the clothes rope around the leg of the bed, she knotted it firmly, stretched it across the floor, and dropped it out the window. But as she raised the window, the glass squeaked against the frame. She stopped, her heart hammering in her chest. A minute passed. Nothing happened. She allowed herself a small victory breath. Then, grabbing the end of the rope, she crawled through the window. For the first time in her life, she prayed to God, asking him to keep the rope in one piece just long enough.

THIRTY-SIX

Mika threw her coffee cup into a trash bin and exited the coffee shop. I followed her out, wondering how to get her and Davis together. I knew she wouldn't go to the police, but if I could get her to come back to the house, maybe Davis would meet us. But Mika refused to come back, and she wouldn't tell me where she was staying. The best I could do was extract a promise from her to call me the next morning. I wasn't at all sure she would follow through.

I said good-bye and headed for the parking lot in back. I was anxious to finish screening the dub of the ground breaking ceremony and get time codes for Dolan. The lot was separated from the building by a narrow alley, puny by Chicago standards. It seemed darker than usual as I crossed it, and I noticed the halogen spotlight attached to the rear wall of the coffee shop was out. That was strange. Halogen lights were supposed to last forever.

As I got within ten feet of the Volvo, two men leaped out of the shadows and surrounded me. One was big and burly, and I knew instantly that he'd walk with a limp, just as the one sneaking around my back would be smaller with lank, greasy hair. I tried to run, but the small man grabbed me and pinned my arms. Pain arced from my wrists to my shoulders. I smelled his unwashed hair.

I struggled, but he clamped tighter. I cried out. The big one growled. The staccato sounds reminded me what a guttural language Russian was. I heard a snarl in response, and the pressure on my arms tightened so much my knees buckled. I tried to sink to the ground, hoping to somehow slip out of his grasp, but the pressure of his grip was so strong, it kept me upright.

A pair of headlights flickered past on Central. "Stop!" I screamed. "Please. Help men!" The headlights kept going.

"Shut up." The burly man planted himself in front of me and raised his hand as if he might strike me. Even in the dim light, I saw that his pupils covered the entire surface of his eyes, giving him a dark and empty expression. A sick feeling spread through me.

"Where's Mika?" I cried. "What have you done with her?"

He barked something to his partner, whose response was to tighten his grip even more.

"Help!" I winced and screamed again. I was desperate. "Someone! Call the police!"

A powerful blow caught me on the side of my head. I went down, my face slamming against the ground. Everything melted into dots. The dots started to spin. Then everything went black.

I THOUGHT I felt ice on my back as I came to. The feeling spread to my arms and legs. I opened my eyes gradually. I was lying on an expanse of hard-packed, frozen ground. I tried to wiggle my hands and feet, but they were bound, and even the slightest movement caused pain to radiate from the back of my head. I closed my eyes and started repeating the mantra I was taught in TM thirty years ago—it still helps me to relax. When most of the throbbing had eased, I cracked my eyes.

The moon, drifting in and out of stray clouds, cast wavering shafts of light over everything. As my eyes adjusted, a collection of dark, hulking shapes emerged out of the gloom. Immense, bulky machines. Bigger than cars. Some had hydraulic arms extending from their bodies. Others looked like huge shovels with giant teeth attached. One had a huge roller mechanism in front. The long arm of a crane snaked up from another. Scattered around the machines were different-sized pipes and tubes, some iron, some concrete. All the steel made it seem colder than it was.

The night was peppered with arctic wind gusts, but a murmur of voices cut through the air. I rolled in their direction. A group of men was gathered near a trailer about thirty yards away. In addition to the two goons who'd attacked me were two other men. One was tall and slim; even in a heavy jacket, he moved with grace. The other, wearing an overcoat far too big for him, was small and chunky.

Max Gordon.

He was engaged in an intense conversation with the burly construction worker. I couldn't understand what they were saying—they were speaking in Russian—but the man's shoulders slumped. Gordon must have been reaming him out.

I called out, but something covered my mouth, and the noise came out as a groan. The men looked over. The tall, slim man started to gesture, but Gordon waved him off and came toward me. From my angle on the ground, his head loomed unnaturally large, giving him a queer, dwarflike appearance. The tall man followed him over.

"Good evening, Ms. Foreman," Gordon said pleasantly.

I didn't answer.

"I apologize for the surroundings. I would have preferred to be indoors, as, I'm sure, you would as well. Unfortunately, we had no choice." He glanced over at the tall man, who had halved the distance between us. "My colleague here is going to take the tape off your mouth so we can conduct business. He assures me, however, that if you scream again or cry out in any way, he will kill you. Do you understand?"

I made no reply.

"Do you understand?" Gordon repeated.

I nodded.

The tall man bent down and ripped the tape off my lips. I gasped in pain. Gordon winced, but the tall man's eyes were empty. He straightened up and barked something in Russian. Gordon hunched into his overcoat, and when he replied, I heard the tension in his voice. For some reason I remembered Dad trading in his double-breasted for a down parka last fall. I was in my sweats now. With no coat. They must have stripped it off when they brought me here. I shivered.

"It *is* cold. So let's make this quick, shall we?" Gordon hooked his thumbs in his pockets.

I tried to lift my head to answer, but the pain forced it back down. The tall Russian pulled out a gun.

"Please, Ms. Foreman, don't make my friend nervous," Gordon said.

The man aimed the gun at my head. I ran my tongue around my lips. "What do you want?"

"The video of the ground-breaking ceremony. It's the only piece of evidence connecting me to that dirty little business in the suburbs. It would be prudent for me to have it."

Prudent indeed. "What dirty little business are you referring to?"

"Don't prevaricate. You're wasting time. It's unlikely that my—my associates will be able to find the tape without your help. They have no idea where to look. You must tell me where it is and how to identify it."

"And if I refuse?"

Gordon slid his eyes to the man with the gun. "It will not be pleasant."

My mind worked feverishly. A VHS copy of the ground-breaking ceremony was in my VCR at home. But the original was locked up in Mac's studio. Even if they did get hold of my copy, the original would be available for the police.

But they didn't necessarily know that. In fact, many people don't differentiate between originals and dubs. They don't realize that, like CDs and computer files and diskettes, we always make copies to edit from. If Gordon had been asking for a computer file, I wouldn't have a prayer. They'd know to demand the original. But this was video. It was worth a try. I started to tell them where to find the copy when I heard a muffled groan.

I turned toward the sound. A few yards away was a lump I'd thought was a mound of steel pipes and tubing, but now it was moving, rolling over. In the dim light, I saw it was Mika! Like me, her hands and feet were bound, and someone had stuffed a gag in her mouth.

The man with the empty eyes backed away from me and trained his gun on her instead. With his free hand he removed the gag. I couldn't see her face, but her body language was oddly relaxed. Not at all tense.

"*Halloa,* Vlad."

"*Halloa,* Mika." He pulled the slide back on his automatic.

Vlad! I remembered what she said about him killing her. "Don't . . . don't hurt her," I begged.

Vlad's eyebrows lifted, and he spoke sharply to Gordon. When Gordon replied, Mika stiffened.

"We won't hurt her if you tell us where the tape is," Gordon translated.

Was he lying? Mika's words earlier seemed to suggest he was. Still, I didn't have many choices.

"Where is it?" Gordon pressed.

"At my house. In my VCR. I was looking at it when—earlier." I didn't need to tell them about Mika's visit; they probably knew anyway.

Another conference in Russian. Vlad motioned to the small man with the greasy hair. They conferred, after which the small man trotted toward the gate.

They were going for it! The greaser had almost made it to the street when Vlad called out. The man stopped abruptly. I held my breath. Vlad must have realized there had to be copies. I steeled myself. Vlad said something in Russian.

"Da." The burly man rummaged in his coat and threw the other man a cell phone. The smaller man pocketed it and headed out to the street.

I let out my breath slowly. It was okay. For the moment. I tried to calculate how long it would take to retrieve the tape. At this hour with no traffic, about thirty minutes each way. I had an hour to figure out how to save my life. And Mika's.

While we waited, Gordon stationed himself away from Vlad and started to pace. As he reversed direction and started back, a worried expression swept across his face. It deepened as he completed another pass. I got the feeling he wasn't quite sure how he'd ended up at a construction site in the middle of the night alongside criminals and murderers.

A glimmer of an idea came to me. The only evidence connecting Gordon to the murder of the woman at the dentists' was the shot of the construction worker on the groundbreaking video. And that was thin at best. The police might use it as a pretext to investigate further, but the tape itself wasn't incriminating. All it did was illustrate a sleazy, but not necessarily criminal, association between Gordon and the killer. Gordon was a shrewd man. He had to know that. According to Dad's friend Frank, he'd figured how to elude criminal prosecution in the past. With good legal advice, there was no reason to think he couldn't do it again.

But that wouldn't free him from Vlad. Gordon needed capital; Vlad needed legitimacy. Their lives had become inextricably linked over the years. They had become a two-headed hydra, and, like the mythological monster, the destruction of one would guarantee the demise of the other. Watching Gordon now, though, I doubted if he was prepared to go down with Vlad. He might even be hanging onto a vague hope that he would be spared, released from the web Vlad had spun.

I tried to ignore the pain and numbness spreading through my body and took a quiet breath. "You look as surprised as I am, Max."

Gordon stopped pacing and rocked back on his heels. My stomach knotted. Had I said the wrong thing? The burly killer squinted at me, as if he was trying to figure out what I was doing and whether he should do something about it.

Then Gordon took his hands out of his pockets. "It wasn't supposed to come to this."

"I know that, Max." Use his name. Make it personal.

"I'm first generation, you know."

"Tell me." I kept my voice low.

"My parents had nothing. My father dropped dead of a heart attack in the boiler room of a hospital. My mother was a seamstress. She never had a day off. I wanted to prove that coming here wasn't a mistake."

"You did." Praise him. Keep him talking.

"When I started at Chase, it was a dream come true. And then, when I started working with Gorbachev's right-hand man . . . the major general . . . I knew I'd made it. He rocked back on his heels again. "I just don't know how it came to this." He cut himself off, almost on the verge of tears.

"Oh, I bet you do," I said softly.

The man with the limp edged closer.

"You know when it started to go bad." I tried to keep my voice sympathetic.

He sighed. "After the collapse. It was the chaos. Everyone pushing, struggling. Scuffling. Whatever it took to make a few rubles. I looked the other way at first. And then . . ." He shook his head. "When I started to pay attention, it was too late."

"It's never too late, Max." I groped for the right words. "You—you still have so much to offer. Don't let Vlad put that in jeopardy."

The burly man scowled. He was trying to decide whether to tell Vlad I was talking. I didn't have much time.

"You never intended to get involved in the seamy side of this—this business, did you? Vlad forced you into it. And once you realized how deep in you were, you got scared. Isn't that right?"

Gordon hunched into his coat again and snuck a glance at Vlad.

"You can end this, Max. No matter how dark it seems right now. All you have to do—"

The man with the limp shouted to Vlad. I froze in mid-sentence. Vlad smiled faintly, whispered something to Mika. Her reply was to spit in his face. His smile disappeared. He rose to his knees, still keeping the gun trained on her.

Suddenly, the tones of a cell phone, ironically sweet and benign, chimed. Gordon pulled it out of his pocket and flipped it on. A moment, he snapped it closed. "He's got it. He's coming back downtown."

That was the cue. The Russian lunged toward me, bent down, and picked me up. I struggled against him, but with my hands and feet tied, it was useless. As he started to drag me off, I tried to twist back toward Gordon, but Mika's voice rang out, loud and clear. "Go. Now. He will kill you."

Vlad leaned back over Mika and tenderly cradled her neck. At first I thought he was ministering to her, pillowing her head with his arm. Then he looked into her face, pointed the gun at her temple, and pulled the trigger. Her body slumped.

Vlad scrambled up and shouted to the goon who had seized me. The man deposited me on the ground and hurried over to join Vlad. Together they dragged Mika's body across the site to a spot where a dozen large holes, about five feet in diameter, had been drilled into the ground. Some of the holes were filled with concrete pillars. Concrete chutes lay nearby. A sick feeling spread through me. They were going to bury her in one of the holes! I don't know anything about construction, but from the size of the chutes, the holes had to be thirty or forty feet deep.

No one would ever find her! The two men spoke. Then Vlad looked over at me and nodded.

After she'd been disposed of, they would come for me.

I watched, horrified, as the two men rolled Mika's body over to one of the holes. I heard the sound of over scraping, then a thud. Then a gaping silence. Vlad spoke again, and the man with the limp came over to me. He scooped me up and headed back to the holes. I made one last effort to extricate myself from his hold by stiffening into a plank.

It didn't work.

My heart hammered in my chest. I was desperate. I decided to appeal to Gordon one more time. But when I craned my neck to see him, he wasn't there. I squirmed and wriggled and finally caught a glimpse of him retreating into the shadows of the equipment.

He was running away!

Vlad must have seen Gordon, too, because he yelled something sharp to my captor. The man with the limp stopped, and practically dropped me on the ground. A faint fishy smell drifted over me. We must have been just above the river. Vlad pulled out his gun, and the two Russians closed in on the equipment from both sides.

My chest went tight. They were going after Max. Then they would come for me. I started at the dark mass of equipment, a deep well of hopelessness engulfing me.

It was over. I should accept it. Suddenly, a roar split the night. Followed by the scrape of grating gears. A huge piece of equipment started moving out of the shadows.

Something that looked like a bulldozer or an army tank advanced slowly on thick tires. A long arm protruded in front, and attached to it was an object that resembled the jaw of a huge, mechanical monster. As the machine rolled forward, the jaws opened, revealing enormous serrated teeth. They looked like they could pulverize or crush any prey they snared. Max Gordon was at the controls, grinning maniacally, and steering it in my direction.

I rolled from side to side, trying to wriggle out of its

path. But for every inch I moved, Gordon adjusted his direction, and the jaws crept closer. I kept slithering until I felt cold metal at my back. I was up against the barbed wire fence. There was nowhere else to go.

THIRTY-SEVEN

THE CRUSHER WAS inches away when sirens blasted through the air. A phalanx of Chicago police cars screeched to a stop on Wabash. Panic shot across Gordon's face. The crusher stopped, and he tore out of the seat. The motor was still running. He bolted across the construction site, coattails flapping behind him. He was almost out of sight when a female voice shouted through a megaphone.

"It's over, Gordon. Give it up!"

Davis!

"We've got you surrounded," a male voice added. "It isn't worth it."

Gordon slowed and turned around. Light slashed across his face, making deep runnels and shadows. His eyes seemed to bug out in astonishment, as if he couldn't quite believe he, a respected businessman, the creator of Gordon Towers, was facing off with a team of Chicago cops. Raising his arms, he slowly advanced toward me and came to a stop a few feet away. He opened his mouth to say something. A shot rang out.

He stumbled forward his lips twitching. For a moment,

he remained upright. Then he keeled over on top of me. As I struggled to breathe, I thought I felt his chest expand and contract, but I wasn't sure. When I heard him wheeze, though, I shouted.

"He's alive! Help him!"

Everything happened at once. More shots. Shouts. The roar of the crusher. The splash of something breaking the surface of the river. Between the noise, the struggle to breathe, and the pounding in my head, I started to drift off. My last conscious thought before the police lifted Gordon's body off me was a sense of surprise that I wasn't cold anymore. His body heat had warmed me.

THE PARAMEDICS PUT a temporary bandage on the back of my head but said I had to go to the ER. I told them I would after I talked to Davis. Meanwhile, the cops called for more officers, and evidence technicians showed up to process the scene. Davis hovered in the background while a Chicago detective questioned me. After I'd gone through the chronology of events at least three times, he told me I could go.

Davis came over to the ambulance where I was on a gurney. "How are you?"

I felt weak and exhausted, and I wasn't sure I ever wanted to go through another Chicago winter. "I'll live."

She stuck her hands into her pockets. "You had me worried."

"That makes two of us." I touched the back of my head. Pain stung my skull. I dropped my hand. "How did you do it, Davis?"

"I got your message a few hours ago. I was gonna wait until Monday to follow up, but there was something in your voice—I don't know. I decided I ought to call you back."

I nodded.

"When you didn't pick up, I went to your house. I figured the worst it could be was a false alarm. When you didn't answer the door, I called for backup. Once we went in and saw the videotape, I put it together." She mimicked pressing a button with her finger. "It was still paused on the shot of the guy in the ski mask," she said. "Then the other asshole showed up."

"With the greasy hair."

Davis nodded.

"They made him come back for the tape."

"We took him down outside your house. Got him to tell us what was going on. Then we called the Eighteenth District and headed down here. We didn't let him call until we were a few minutes away." She shrugged. "You know the rest."

"I'm glad it's over." I paused. It's too bad about Gordon."

"Too bad?"

"He didn't have a gun. They didn't have to shoot him."

"They?"

I yanked a thumb at the patrol cars parked at the curb.

"It wasn't us, Ellie."

"What are you saying?"

"The cops didn't shoot him."

"You didn't?"

"One of the Russians did."

"Vlad!"

"In the back. But he'll live. The medic thinks the bullet didn't hit any vital organs."

"Where—what about Vlad?"

Davis looked down.

I repeated myself.

She waited a fraction too long. "He got away, Ellie."

"No!"

"We weren't fast enough. He jumped into the river."

I dimly remembered thinking I'd heard a splash just before I went out. "The water's got to be close to freezing. Did he make it?"

"Don't know yet. CPD's sending divers. We got the other two, though."

"He got away, didn't he?"

"We don't know that. But even if he did, we got our quota of bad guys tonight."

I started to shake my head, but a rush of pain made me stop. I let my eyes close. A moment later, I snapped them open. "Now I get it!"

"Get what?"

"I didn't realize it until just now!"

"Realize what?" Davis prodded me.

"Mika. What she said. Just before Vlad shot her."

"What are you talking about?"

"Before Vlad killed her, she cried out, 'Go. Now. He will kill you.' I thought she was trying to warn *me,* but it couldn't have been me. She knew I was bound and gagged." I looked at Davis. "It wasn't me she was trying to warn, Davis. It was Gordon."

Davis frowned.

"She knew he was next. That Vlad would kill him. And she was afraid for him." I paused. "She was about to die, but she was trying to help someone she didn't even know."

Davis didn't answer for a moment. Then she put a hand on my shoulder. "If you hadn't tried to help her, you wouldn't have ended up there yourself."

"Maybe."

"Right." Davis smiled. "Maybe."

One of the paramedics came over and told me it was time to go to the ER. I looked past the site, down the length of the river. Over the lake the eastern sky was lightening. The wind had subsided to a gentle breeze. Dawn would be breaking soon.

THIRTY-EIGHT

A WEIGHTLESS BAND of flurries dusted the ground as Davis pulled up to the curb the next afternoon. I opened the door, feeling the urge to catch snowflakes on my tongue.

"You okay?" Her face was pinched with worry.

I patted the bandage on the back of my head. "They shaved the back of my head and made a few stitches. Nothing that won't heal."

She closed the door. "Good. Listen, Ellie. I want to apologize. If I'd called you back when I should have—"

I raised my palm. "Stop. You saved my life."

"But if I'd talked to you earlier, come over to the house—"

"You might have been ambushed, too. I'm just thankful you put it together as fast as you did."

"It was hard not to, once we had the greaser. You'd been raising questions about Gordon, and then, when we saw the tape in the VCR, well, that clinched it." She smiled. "Nice work."

"More like dumb luck." I started into the kitchen. "You want a beer?"

She hesitated.

"Sorry. You're still on duty?"

A strange expression passed across her face. "As a matter of fact, I'm not. Sure. I'll have a beer."

I got two bottles of Heineken out of the fridge, opened one, and handed it to her. "So, what happens now?"

"You know the drill. Gordon will recover and hire a fancy lawyer."

"He won't walk, will he?"

"Probably not. But guys like him usually find a way to weasel out of major time."

I leaned against the counter. "Charles Colson."

"Huh?"

"One of the guys who was convicted in Watergate. He found Jesus while he was in jail. I'm sure it helped when it was parole time. Can't you just see Max Gordon as a rabbi? Or a Talmud scholar?"

"Hey, if it means one less bad guy out there, who are we to carp?"

"I guess." I opened my beer and took a swig. "Did the divers find anything in the river?"

Davis shook her head.

"So the worst of the bad guys is still out there."

"Parasites sometimes survive, even though they destroy their host. The good news is we've smashed his operations in a big way. Any dreams he had about creating a beachhead in the States are up in smoke."

"But he's still alive. How do we know he won't be coming back for me, or—God forbid—Rachel? Or Dad?"

"There's no guarantee, Ellie, but remember he's lost most of his clout. With Gordon out of the way, and Celestial Bodies gone—"

"What do you mean, Celestial Bodies gone?"

"Des Plaines is taking it down. Enforced prostitution. White slavery. It's over for them."

"Sofiya, too?"

"They're gonna hit her up for pandering and pimping."

"And the girls?"

"Not sure. They'll check their immigration status, probably try to send a few into rehab, but for the most part, they're on their own."

"But couldn't they end up—back on their backs, so to speak?"

"I guess they could. But at least Vlad won't be controlling them. He's out. He lost face. His 'associates' will be moving on."

"Still doesn't make me feel real secure."

"Look, Ellie. Even if we found him and brought him to justice, he could get off. You know how it goes. Witnesses don't show up. Evidence suddenly gets lost. In a way, you're probably safer with him on the run. He's probably back in the Caymans by now, anyway. Or Russia." She swigged down more beer. "Our pals at the Bureau say they'll be on the lookout for him. Who knows? Maybe they'll even find him."

My wound started to throb. I put my beer down and slid my fingers lightly over the bandage. "Tell me something."

"What's that?"

"If Vlad was powerful enough to do everything he did—and get away with it—then what the hell did we accomplish?"

She didn't answer for a minute. Then, "We got Gordon. We shut down a sex prison. It's a start."

"A start."

"It was a huge network. Two continents, five countries, God knows how many people."

"Greed knows no borders." I picked up my beer. We were quiet. Then, "Why did she do it?" I asked.

"Why did who do what?"

"Mika. Why did she blow it all wide open? That took tremendous courage."

"When you don't have much, you're not afraid of it being taken away."

I took a sip of beer. David's expression told me not to follow up. There was another spate of silence.

"So, what do you think'll happen to Gordon Towers? Think it'll get built?"

Davis shrugged. "They always do."

"I guess you're right. A consortium of developers will probably jump in." I laughed. "I bet Ricki Feldman will be one of them."

Davis started. "Who?"

"Ricki Feldman. The woman who hired me to shoot the ground-breaking video. And tipped me about Gordon."

"Stuart Feldman's daughter?"

I frowned. "You know her?"

She didn't answer but the color drained from her face. Then she said, "I—I was on the force when her father got into trouble."

"Well, then, maybe you knew she's been trying to rebuild her reputation. Except that the woman has never done anything uncalculated in her life. Which makes me wonder why she told me Gordon was asking questions. Was it a mitzvah—a good deed—or a self-serving act? You never know with people like her."

Davis kept her mouth shut. Her eyes were pools of blue reflecting glass. I sensed there was more to it, but whatever history she and Ricki Feldman shared was going to stay off the record. I changed the subject. "So, Davis, what did Olson say? Do I start calling you Detective Davis now?"

"I wouldn't count on it."

"What do you mean? You did a great job."

She tossed back her beer and looked for a place to pitch the bottle. I opened the cabinet under the sink. After she threw it in the trash, she turned to me with a wry expression. "When we were doing a postmortem, I told Olson what happened at Celestial Bodies. With the gun."

"The gun you 'found' in the bathroom?" She nodded. "Why?"

"The lying." She shrugged. "It was bothering me. Olson gave me a pat on the back. Told me what a good job I'd done. How proud of me he was. Then he suspended me."

"He what?"

"I falsified a report."

"But you solved the case."

"Doesn't matter. It's a major violation."

"But you did it to protect me. The bouncer would have killed me—maybe you, too—if you'd given him back the gun."

She shrugged again. "We don't know that."

"Come on, Davis. You know what would have happened. Look. Olson wasn't there. What if I called and—"

"Ellie, forget it. There was also the fact that I used my own car to stake out DM Maids instead of an unmarked. And that I had you with me in the first place. None of that's in the cop handbook."

I heard the finality in her voice. "So, wh—what are you going to do?"

"Take some time off. Travel. Maybe go down to Georgia." Another shrug. "Maybe I'll find something I like doing better than this."

That was a lie. Davis was a cop. A good cop. She'd be back.

I threw my beer bottle into the trash. "Well, good luck."

"Thanks." She started for the door, then stopped. "You know, I didn't think I'd like you when this started. But I do. Take care of yourself."

"I like you, too."

She smiled.

"One last thing," I said.

"What's that?"

"Who tells the family? Arin's, I mean? Mika said she's got a son."

"Officially, I'm not sure. One of the guys on the force speaks Russian. I thought I'd track them down and give them a call."

I thought about Arin's son, whoever he might be. Jordan's foster kids. David. Even Davis herself. "And one more child grows up without a mother," I said quietly.

THIRTY-NINE

Rays of bright sun glinted off the windshield, hinting at the long summer days to come. I opened the door of Susan's car and slid out.

"Thanks for lunch."

"It's the least I could do." She motioned to my head.

"Thank God for Davis." I curled my fingers on the door handle. "I can't believe they suspended her. She was doing what she thought was right."

"No, she wasn't, Ellie. She lied. Compromised her colleagues' trust."

"She saved my life."

"She's young. She'll survive it. Maybe even learn from it."

I took my hands off the window. "It's strange, you know. The ones who were already rich—Gordon, Vlad, Ricki Feldman . . . hell, even Brigitte . . . they were the greedy ones. But the ones who had nothing—Mika, Petrovsky, Arin . . . they looked out for each other. They cared. Somehow, it doesn't seem fair."

Susan didn't reply.

"And then there's Jordan Bennett."

"What about him?"

"I wonder what will happen to him now."

"Jordan sounds like a man with resources. He'll probably run for president."

I laughed. "He's too good for that."

Susan smiled. "Speaking of the witch, what have you heard from David?"

"Not a word." My smile faded.

So did Susan's.

"Don't. Don't you dare feel sorry for me."

"Okay. So what's Barry up to?"

"He reverted to type. Has a new girlfriend, Rachel says. Some blond bombshell with young kids. Julia something."

"Not Julia Hauldren are you nots?"

"I think so. That's her name."

"God, Ellie. She lives around the corner from you."

"No!"

"Yes. Right off Happ Road. Her kids are in school with Rachel."

"What?"

"They're younger, of course. First and second grade."

"Oh, great. Just what I need! Can't wait to run into them at the next concert. Or bake sale."

Susan pulled down the cuffs of her silk blouse. "Life is full of burdens, but you will bear them."

"You sound like Fouad." I spotted a crocus, its little purple stalk cheerfully struggling against the snow. He would be back soon. I smiled.

I WAS PUTTERING around the kitchen, getting ready to pick up Dad for dinner, when the phone rang.

"Hello, Ellie."

My stomach flipped. "Hello, David."

"How—how are you?"

"I'm good. What about you?"

"This—this is the hardest call I've ever made."

I steeled myself. "Why?"

"I made a huge mistake, Ellie, and I wonder—"

I wasn't sure I'd heard him right. "A mistake?"

"You were right. Brigitte took off right after we signed the papers."

"Oh," I said softly.

"We could void the sale. Keep the shop. But Willie doesn't want to. He—he's going to stay over here and get treatment. The doctors are confident they can help him."

"That's good news. But are you sure about the shop? She took you for—"

"It's obvious she wanted—or needed it more than we do. And . . ." He paused. "It's only money."

Only money. I know about "only money."

"Ellie, I have a lot to do. Getting Willie settled. Coming to terms with myself. Working things through. But I want to ask you something."

"What's that?"

"Will you—well, do you think you could ever forgive me?"

I started to walk with the phone. "Forgive you?"

"I know I hurt you. Terribly. And not just you. Your father, Rachel, I let them down, too. I let myself down. I don't know how it happened. It was as if I—"

"Was under a spell?"

"Something like that." He cleared his throat.

I walked to the window and stopped. Assuming I could forgive him, even put it behind me at some point, David and I were fundamentally different people, with different ways of thinking and behaving. We hadn't done such a good job accommodating—or communicating with—each other in the past. Indeed, if I were honest, that was one of the reasons he'd ended up in Brigitte's arms.

But maybe we weren't trying hard enough. Or maybe we were making too much of those differences. Maybe they were just separate sides of the same issue. I thought about the way I felt in after making love. The way he laughed at all my jokes. The way his eyes sparkled when we were together. Didn't we deserve the chance to try together—just one more time? I felt my heart tugging to be with him even now.

Then I remembered how I felt at the airport in Philadelphia when I saw him with Brigitte. I couldn't go through another betrayal. Not again.

"I—I don't know, David. I'm going to need to think about it."

He was silent. Then he made a quiet noise in the back of his throat. "Well, at least it's not a definite no."

"No. But it's not a yes, either."

"I understand."

More silence.

"I'll call you in a few days, okay?"

"Okay."

I hung up. A lot could happen in a few days. I gazed out the window. Out on Happ Road, a truck thundered by, its clatter arcing and then fading away. A dog barked. The sun was just sneaking down past the tops of the bare trees. Almost six, and it was still light. I grabbed my coat and went outside to look for signs of spring.

ABOUT THE AUTHOR

A transplant from Washington, D.C., Libby has lived in the Chicago area twenty-five years. When not writing fiction, she writes and produces corporate videos. She has also worked in television news and public relations, and can occasionally be spotted in those venues. She holds a BA from the University of Pennsylvania, and an MFA in film production from New York University. She lives with her family, and a beagle, shamelessly named Shiloh.